THE GOOD AMERICAN

THE
GOOD
AMERICAN

TED FLICKER

SHALAKO PRESS   SANTA FE   NEW MEXICO

This book is dedicated to

Barbara Joyce Perkins
Flicker

Who for thirty years has
Taught me the meaning of
Love, fidelity, honor and friendship.
Without her I would not be.
With her I am all that I could be.

T.F.

www.good-american.com
Registered Internic Domain Name

Copyright © 1997 by Ted Flicker
First Internet Edition. All rights reserved.

Cover art "The Standard Bearer" by Patrick McFarlin
Back Cover photo by Barbara VanCleve
Cover design by Jean Lamunière

SHALAKO PRESS

Shalako Press
Post Office Box 8470
Santa Fe, New Mexico 87504, USA
electronic mail address: novel@shalako.com

International Standard Book Number: 0-9654089-0-6
Library of Congress Catalog Card Number: 96-070253

Printed in the United States of America

This is a novel. It's characters and scenes are purely the creation of the author. The Jew Laws of Bavaria and various German states did exist. The physical details of *The North Sea* are accurate though, to the author's knowledge, there was no ship of that name making scheduled transatlantic crossings for the North German Line at the time.

Particulars of life in New York City in the mid 1850s are accurate. Five Points was probably more squalid and more violent then described. There was a gang called the Dead Rabbits. Men fitting Brannagan's description existed, but he is a fabrication. German-Jewish-American society in New York was as described, but the Loebs of this story are fictional.

Historical characters presented, with the exception of their names and their presence in some of the places where they have actually been placed in history, are also the invention of the author. There was no First American Hussars. While the Civil War battles, such as Gettysburg, have been based on records of battles fought, details of the engagements of the characters have been fabricated for this tale.

BOOK ONE

THE HORSEMAN

"He who would distinguish the true from the false must have an adequate idea of what is true and what is false."

— Baruch Spinoza

§1

THE CELEBRATED HORSEMAN, FRANZ JOSEPH VON RITTER BARON von Breitenstein, was born neither celebrated nor titled. The great event took place in a wooden farmhouse, in the year numbered by the Christians 1840 and, more appropriately, by the Hebrew calendar 5601. His parents' home was located in the shadow of Castle Falkenbrecht, eight miles from the small Bavarian town of Dittelheim. Jakob Gershomsohn, Joseph's father, thought by many to be the finest horse trainer in all of Bavaria, held the still-bloody infant aloft and announced, "He will be the greatest horseman in the world."

Jakob Gershomsohn had jet black hair, deep-set eyes and a prominent nose under which hung a huge cavalry-style mustache. Jakob was of average height and slight of frame, but on that frame were stretched the most powerful muscles in the district. He some—times seemed a giant.

The first son in thirty-two generations of Gershomsohns to choose not to become a rabbi, Jakob, while not officially banished from the Jewish community that huddled in the Dittelheim ghetto called the *Judengasse*, or Jewstreet, lived apart from it by choice. He made no secret of his dedication to the works of the ex-communicated Jewish philosopher Baruch Spinoza. Like him, Jakob outraged the Jewish community by his rejection of ceremonial Judaism, revelation, redemption, prophecy, miracles, and God's authorship of the written and oral Torahs. Yet Torah, Talmud, Zohar and the writings of the great sages were his constant study. Jakob embraced the idea that it was only with true knowledge—seeing things as they precisely were—that happiness could be achieved. He passionately believed that as a man reached an exact understanding of his life he achieved freedom. With that freedom he could then determine the course of his life and live by his own will.

As a disciple of the Enlightenment and a child of the Age of Reason, Jakob set about instructing his infant son with the same gentle but firm training he gave his fine horses. By the time he was four Joseph was fluent in German, Hebrew and Yiddish. (Although Jakob considered Yiddish a slave language, he knew it was essential for a modern Jew.) But young Joseph's real genius was with horses. The boy was the riding prodigy of the province. Count von Falkenbrecht, who owned that part of Bavaria, called Joseph "the Mozart of horsemanship," and on a number of occasions had the child perform classic equitation for his exalted guests. Had the boy not been Jewish, the count would have sent him to the great Spanish Riding School in Vienna.

Jakob was determined that his son make his way in the world better equipped than he had been. To that end, in addition to Joseph's rigorous study of horses, father and son pondered the Talmud and the Torah, scrutinizing the holy books through the lens of Spinoza.

When Joseph reached his sixth birthday Rebecca, his mother, insisted that he have proper Jewish playmates. If he grew up only with the *goyishe* peasant children, how would he ever find a wife? Jakob, although skeptical, agreed to let her take Joseph to Dittelheim's Judengasse to the beginning classes of the *cheder*, the school for the Jewish children. The elders of the Jewish community, with more than a little trepidation, accepted the son of the heretic for two reasons: as an honor to the boy's grandfather the great Rabbi Menachem of blessed memory, and to receive the blessing of saving a lost Jew.

Although Joseph wanted to ride his little red roan, Strawberry, into Dittelheim for his first day in school, Rebecca drove him to town in the two wheeled basket-weave buggy that his father had said was fit for a princess. As they approached Dittelheim, Joseph heard his heart pound. What if the school was a bad place? What if it was dark and like a dungeon? Didn't his father once say the *shul* was mostly underground? Weren't dungeons underground? What if they did bad things to children? What if they punished children for mistakes by tying them to slimy walls? And the rabbi? Hadn't Joseph once heard his father say the rabbi was a *schmuck*? And when he asked his mother what a schmuck was, didn't she say schmuck was a bad word and he shouldn't ever say it again?

On the few occasions his father had brought him to the Jew-street, Joseph had seen the synagogue from the outside. It didn't seem to be such a bad place. It wasn't nearly as huge and scary as the church. Next to the synagogue was a little building that his mother said was the cheder: it was gray with a brown door and two windows. A few children were walking into the school and a few more standing around. As Joseph and his mother drove to the entrance, Joseph saw the students stop talking and stare. He studied them carefully, looking for the face of a new friend. But he saw nothing that comforted him.

He had little experience with other children, but he did know about horses. You never ran to strange horses; you stayed back and let the horses get used to you. Then you advanced toward them carefully, letting them know you were nice. Joseph begged his mother not to dismount but to let him go into the school by himself. He didn't move toward the school until she had left. Then he turned and walked slowly toward the boys standing by the school's entrance. The boys were all bigger than he, older and wise in the ways he had to learn, so he was careful. As he drew close, he smiled and said, "Is this the cheder?"

"No," answered the fat one. "It is the *mikvah*."

Although he had never seen one, Joseph knew the mikvah was the ritual bath. His face grew warm. "Oh," he said politely. "I'm sorry. Could you tell me where the cheder is?"

At that the other boys punched each other in glee and ran into the school. Joseph stood uncertainly still. Rabbi Solomon, a man with a shiny bald head, fierce eyes, and a black beard, appeared in the doorway. "You. *Shaygets*. In here. Now!"

Joseph, mortified, ran into the school. When he entered the small room, the boys, sitting two to a table, turned to stare at him. Joseph saw no friendly faces. The room was overheated and sour smelling. The rabbi took Joseph by his shoulder and sat him alone at a table with space for two.

Throughout his first day, Joseph spoke aloud only when reciting with the other children. Once, when the rabbi called on him to read, he was so slow in starting that the rabbi mocked him. The children laughed, and for the rest of the day Joseph tried to become invisible.

When school ended he waited quietly on the opposite side of the street for his mother. The laughter at the start of the day, the rabbi's unfriendliness, the sense of isolation, all made Joseph shy. Then a noise brought his eyes up from the cobblestones. Led by the fat boy, the children were slowly walking toward him. Soon they had gathered in a circle around Joseph. He tried looking at his shoes. A few of the bigger boys laughed. They talked to each other about him as if he were not there. Joseph's face burned with shame. He couldn't understand why they were being mean. Perhaps it was his fault. He looked up and smiled through his shame. The fat boy, the one who had said mikvah, and who smelled of stale goose grease, said, "Look, he smiles like the village idiot. Now we have a school idiot."

When tears appeared in Joseph's eyes the boys chanted, "Cry baby! Cry baby!"

That evening, when Jakob heard about Joseph's day at the cheder, he hugged his son. Then he held him at arm's length and, looking directly into his eyes, said: "You are Joseph Gershomsohn. In you flows the blood of the priests of the Jews. We have been rabbis for six hundred years in Germany, and before that for five hundred years in Spain, and before that advisers to the Caliphs of Arabia, and before that your blood goes back in a direct line to King David. You will accept insult from no man." His hands gripped Joseph's shoulders, "Listen to me, my son. What you must do tomorrow you must do. It's a very hard thing. When you get to the cheder tomorrow morning..."

Joseph interrupted, "Please, Poppa. I don't wish to go back there. Please don't make me. Please."

Jakob's voice grew gentler but no less firm. "You must return. But I promise you it shall be for a few days only. You must go back, just as when you fall off a horse, you must immediately remount. For two reasons: first, to show that you can go back if you choose; second, to show that no one may insult you without paying a price."

Joseph was frightened. "What Poppa? What must I do?"

"Without a second's hesitation, you must strike the first child who insults you. Punch him in the face."

"Must I?" Joseph was horrified. He had never hit anyone.

Jakob nodded. "Make a fist," he said.

Joseph made a tiny, six-year-old fist.

"With all your strength, hit my hand." His father held up his palm. Joseph smacked his fist into it.

"You closed your eyes," Jakob said. "And you made a wild swing. The trick is to look exactly where you want to hit. And then drive your fist straight forward from the shoulder. See?" He demonstrated. "Now do it again."

Joseph did. This time his fist struck the center of his father's raised hand.

"Good. Now, to add power you step with your right foot and at the same time throw your shoulder into the blow. Like this..." Again he demonstrated and again Joseph imitated his father perfectly. They worked for the rest of the day.

That night, Joseph lay awake thinking about the fight he was going to have in the morning. He thought about how big the fat boy was, and when he finally slept he dreamt he was on a large rocky promontory engulfed in impenetrable blackness. In the distance a benign little cloud, at first puffy white, began to grow and move toward him. As it grew, it mutated into an ominous billowing of grays. The closer it came, the larger and darker and more violent it grew. Joseph became afraid. The enormous cloud was taking up all the space. And when the gigantic cloud filled the universe and Joseph found himself unable to breathe, at the moment of his own death, the cloud exploded and became hundreds of tiny little white clouds that immediately began to grow and roil into the awful grays. And as each cloud grew it seemed that it would occupy all the space there ever was. The clouds, filling the whole universe, surrounded Joseph and his breathing stopped for an even longer period, until he thought he, like the clouds, would burst into a hundred little Josephs. Again the clouds burst and again hundreds and hundreds of small clouds started to grow. He woke just as the first light seeped into the sky.

That morning, over his mother's objection but with his father's silent approval, Joseph rode Strawberry to the cheder alone. His gloomy thoughts were interrupted when, on the road to school, he approached a squadron of Royal Wittelsbach Hussars, glittering in smart black and silver uniforms. From the moment of his first demonstration of his horsemanship to Count von Falkenbrecht, who commanded these hussars, Joseph had been allowed to spend time around the regiment barns. His riding skill amazed the hussars and led to his becoming something of an unofficial mascot. Now as they drew near, Joseph imperceptibly gathered his horse between his hands and his seat and, by both driving the horse forward into an energetic canter and rhythmically restraining him, he converted his forward energy into an upward movement so that the horse, while still cantering, slowed to a walking speed and at the same time rose higher with each step, making it seem as if he were floating in the air. The fierce warriors laughed. The lieutenant ordered a salute, which Joseph proudly returned as he floated by.

His euphoria lasted until he arrived at school. Although he was early, the other children were already waiting by the closed door. Joseph could see they were impressed with his horse and his riding. He hoped that would make them like him. Smiling, he approached the school from the opposite side of the street and executed a classic half-pass: as the horse continued to move forward, it changed gait to a sideward motion, traversing from one side of the street to the other without a turn. Joseph completed the show by bringing Strawberry into a piaffe, gently trotting his pet in place, and dismounted with a flourish, expecting applause. But instead he was met with silence. His smile faded and his face turned red. Taking a breath, he walked around the horse and joined the other Jewish children. Some shied away. But the biggest blocked his passage and said, "My father says your father says Hashem did not write the Torah." His tone was belligerent.

Joseph answered. "Priests wrote it. A lot of them. Eight hundred years after Sinai." The children fell silent. They had never heard heresy before.

The fat boy came up to him and put his face next to Joseph's nose. "My father said your father is from the devil."

Joseph punched the face. Blood ran from the fat nose. Then the other big boys fell on Joseph and pinned him to the ground. "From the devil," they shouted. "From the devil!" The fat boy with the bloody nose spit in Joseph's face.

"Spit on the devil," he shouted.

One by one, the school children danced up to Joseph and spit into his face. When he tried to turn his head the fat boy grabbed his ears and held Joseph's face up to the spit.

Joseph, insane with rage and humiliation, knew the street was filled with adults. Why didn't they stop it? At one point he jerked his head to the right and, behind the window of the cheder, he saw a face watching. It was the rabbi. Only after the cry went up from the fat boy, "Kick the devil!" and the smallest children began to do so, did the rabbi run out into the cobblestone street and drive the boys away. When he lifted Joseph to his feet, Joseph broke away, ran to his horse, and galloped out of the Judengasse.

That night, in the moments before he fell asleep, Joseph decided that he would kill the fat boy.

The following morning they were waiting for him again. Joseph rode his horse up very close and the children fell back. From his saddle Joseph said, "Cowards. You are all cowards. You are brave when it is twelve against one, but you are too coward to fight me one at a time."

"Oh yeah? You are a *goy,* and Hashem hates you, and if you get off that goy horse I will beat you into soup."

"Yeah?" retorted Joseph. "Sure you will, Goose Grease. You with your fat belly and all your friends. You are too coward to try to fight me all alone."

Some of the other children laughed and yelled, "Goose Grease! Goose Grease!" The fat boy's face colored. He turned angrily to Joseph.

"*Shaygets,*" he shouted. "You get off that horse and I will kill you all by myself. You hear? All by myself."

"Fair fight?" Joseph looked at the three other big boys. "Just me and Goose Grease. You stay out?"

They were all grinning. Now they had a good fight to watch and a new nickname for Pauli.

Pauli attacked as Joseph dismounted, taking him by surprise, and knocking him to the ground. In size and weight Joseph was no match for the larger boy, and Pauli punched him repeatedly in the face. The fists were like the exploding clouds, and they would have engulfed Joseph. But he rebelled. "No," he screamed. "No!" His rage grew until he knew he was going to kill this fat smelly thing. And in the moment Joseph knew it, the fat boy knew it too. He froze in a sudden panic, just long enough to allow Joseph to free one hand with which he struck a round-house blow, again making the fat boy's nose bleed. The fat boy raised his hands in dread, his voice rising to a wail, and Joseph squiggled out from under him, rolled him over, and climbed on top of him. The crying fat boy, terrified beyond wit, resigned from the struggle. Joseph took him by the ears and banged his shrieking head against the cobblestones. In that instant the other children knew that Joseph meant to kill Pauli too. They ran screaming into the school.

By the time the rabbi pulled Joseph away, Pauli was screaming incoherently. Blood ran from his nose, tears from his eyes, and feces from his pants. "*Malach Hamoves!* Devil!" the rabbi bellowed as he struck Joseph.

The following day Joseph's father appeared with Sergeant-Major Stumpf of the Royal Wittelsbach Hussars. "Joseph," he said. "Your mother and I have made a mistake. You're not ready for cheder. You will stay home and go to a school that is equally important for a Jew. As we have always done, I'll continue your education, and Sergeant-Major Stumpf will teach you how to properly fight."

Sergeant-Major Hans Stumpf had been bred for the cavalry. Every Stumpf in the recorded history of his family had ridden into battle astride a horse. His physique seemed to be the result of natural selection: legs so bowed they fit every horse, light weight coupled with powerful shoulders, and arms with wrists as thick as their elbows. And because none of the Stumpfs had ever risen to the ranks of officer, the line had perfected the instincts of instant obedience to their superiors and fierce command of their inferiors. All of Hans Stumpf's progenitors had been sergeants-major, because they were all smart enough to do the job and never so smart as to appear impertinent. Without the Stumpfs there would have been no Wittelsbachs, and both knew it.

Joseph had a natural gift for learning, so he was eventually able to fool his father about studies such as Spinoza and the Torah, which bored him. Spinoza was not horses and Torah not cavalry. He paid only enough attention to those subjects to win his father's approval. His real reading was about horses and war. He devoured every horse book borrowed by Stumpf from the von Falkenbrecht library—from the ancient Greeks through the Baroque *haute école* to the writers of his own time. The study of God simply could not compete with horses.

On a hot summer day when Joseph was seven, he lay on his back in a field of clover and watched the billowing white clouds above. He listened to the distant buzz of a bee gathering pollen. He smelled the yeasty loam of the earth beneath him and the green sweetness of the grass. When he spread his arms and his legs he felt attached to the planet and thought he sensed it turning. As the clouds slowly rolled and reshaped themselves in the stratospheric winds, questions came to Joseph. Who made the clouds? The earth? The grass? The horses? Him? In that moment all that he could remember of Spinoza's ideas about God seemed false. God was there, and nature was here. If he could see nature and not see God, that was proof that they were separate—God there, and Nature here—not only from each other but from him. He was not, as his father had taught him, one with God. God was separate. God was there in the clouds. God was huge and everywhere above him, and lying on the ground, Joseph was thrilled in awe of this stupendous God.

Another day, when he was ten and he and Stumpf had just completed a vigorous hour of saber-work from horseback, his mother gave them each a large bowl of buttermilk. As they sat in the shade of the barn sipping the milk, Joseph said, "When I join the Royal Wittelsbach Hussars, I will work hard to become a sergeant-major like you." He was so filled with fantasy that Joseph missed the momentary dark look on Stumpf's face.

Joseph continued, "Then when we are in a war I shall cut off so many Turkish heads that the general will have to make me an officer. Then one day I shall win such a victory that the king will make me a general. And then, when I am a general, I will make you my *aide de camp* and we shall win so many victories that the king will make us both noblemen."

"You cannot ever join the Hussars," Stumpf said. "Not the Royal Wittelsbach. Not any kind. I thought you knew that."

Joseph was thunderstruck. "But why?"

"Because you are a Jew. Jews can't be in the military. Not any kind of military. Not even the infantry. Jews can't fight. It's the law."

"But didn't you say I was as good as any of your troopers? Didn't you say that when I was full grown I would be better than any of them? Didn't you?"

"That has nothing to do with it. You are a Jew and Jews can't fight. It's the law and it's plain and simple. Jews can't fight."

Joseph was so devastated it took him days to question his father. Jakob was as astonished by Joseph's ignorance as Joseph had been by Stumpf's words. He blamed himself for his failure to educate his son to the realities of being a Jew, and he sought to make up for this error by teaching him the social history of his people from the Babylonian conquest of Judah to the present. But at ten Joseph was already a proud warrior and these lessons in Jewish history only ignited his rage. In the days that followed, his training with Stumpf became more intense; they shifted from childish fun to preparation for war. It was his mother who first noticed the change. One night she said to Jakob, "He is only ten, but he is no longer a boy." She wept silently in his arms.

In Joseph's fifteenth year, when Jakob felt he was properly prepared to deal with the traditional Jews of the Jewstreet, he astonished them by asking—more in the form of a command—that his son be prepared in the traditional way for his bar mitzvah. For that preparation he allowed the rabbi only six months.

On his first day at the cheder Joseph was met by a committee of the elders of the community who told him that to protect the other children from any heresy he might have learned from his father, he would be the only child in his class. Joseph thanked them politely and said that he already knew how to be a Jew and had enough of their smelly little school the first time around. He informed them that they could take their cheder and put it in the place where the sun never shines. He then executed a smart military about-face and left.

At home his father, although amused, sternly explained that even when one had no respect for authority, it was wiser when one required something from that authority to show it at least some esteem. Joseph would have to apologize to those he had insulted and return to his studies.

"But I know the Torah, Poppa. Why do I have to study it with them?"

"Because you are a Jew and you don't know the Torah the way Jews know it. Because you are a member of the nation of Israel. You should know what now passes for what Israel thinks. It isn't enough to know what I have taught you. You must know what they, the mice, think. Who knows? You may decide they are right and Spinoza is wrong."

§2

"**W**AS THERE FOG?"

"What?"

"Was the sun shining?"

"What sun shining?"

"Was he on a hill or in a valley?"

"What are you talking?"

"Here in the Torah it says, 'God said to Abram, "Raise up your eyes and from the place where you are now standing look to the north, to the south, to the east, and to the west. For all the land that you see, I will give to you and to your offspring forever." ' So where was Abram standing? On a hill? Maybe he was near-sighted, maybe..." The rabbi cuffed Joseph on the side of his head, and threw him out of the cheder.

Joseph didn't understand why the rabbi always became so angry when he asked such logical questions. Wasn't he there to learn? Didn't learning require investigation? The grubby little school seemed a complete waste of time to him, but he had promised his father that no matter how many times he was thrown out he would continue to his bar mitzvah. His face still reflected the confusion he felt every time this happened.

It would have seemed more natural if that odd, sensitive face had been pale, but Joseph's skin was burnt brown by an outdoor life. Even so, the bronze skin didn't camouflage the poetic black eyes ablaze with innocent passion. Every emotion, no matter how ephemeral, rippled across his face like a zephyr on an alpine lake.

Thunder was waiting for Joseph in the narrow street below. Coal black, glistening in the afternoon late summer light, he was the object of the ghetto children's frightened and enthralled stares, and darker looks from their parents. A four-year-old stallion sixteen hands tall, Thunder was a prince of the house of Trakehner, a breed founded by King Fredrich Wilhelm I of Prussia and developed by his son Fredrich the Great as the premier cavalry horse in the world. The Trakehner was noted for his balance, his natural suppleness, and most of all, for his extraordinary athletic ability. In all of these traits Thunder excelled, and also in loyalty. He stood quietly where Joseph had left him.

Thunder, who through narrowed lids had been eyeing the street urchins with suspicion, released the tension in his neck and back when he saw his master in the doorway. He opened his eyes wide, pointed both ears forward, licked his lips, and made a few chewing gestures to welcome him.

Joseph returned the salute with a pat on the neck. He put away his anger at the rabbi for the horse, and allowed his body to completely relax. Thunder followed suit, matched his breathing to his master's, swished his tail, and quietly nickered.

Aware of the people crowding the narrow lane, Joseph in one liquid movement stepped from the ground to Thunder's back, setting him in motion down the street as if they had never been separated and never at rest. There was barely room in the street for the horse and the pedestrians, yet the boy and his horse moved forward as if they were alone.

As they walked on, Joseph pretended to ignore the pedestrians and listened to the clip-clop of Thunder's hooves on the cobblestones of the Judengasse. He heard them echo off the jumble of houses crowding the narrow lane: shadowy houses too tall for their tiny plots of land, ramshackle houses with rooms piled one on top of another to avoid or conform to the ever-changing Jew taxes. The clutter and unnatural darkness incensed Joseph.

Why, he asked himself, did the Jews live like that? This was one of the questions he had started thinking about at the age of six. He could find no satisfactory answer to this or any of the others that passed through his mind every day he rode the serpentine of the crowded Judengasse. The gauntlet of eyes always left him with a deep sense of oppression. It also produced an almost-unbearable loneliness. These were his people, and yet not his people. He heard, but pretended not to, the muttered insults, "Shaygets" and "Malach Hamoves." Why did they all hate him so? Joseph rode as if on parade before the king, shoulders back, head high. After all, he was the son of Jakob Gershomsohn.

Three miles from town, Joseph saw Schloss Falkenbrecht rising from the highest hill in the district. The restoration of the castle, which had stood on that spot since the Romans were driven away, had begun a hundred years before and had been completed only the previous summer.

The current prince of the palace was Brigadier General Count Rupprecht Franz Leopold, and three other titles and four more names, von Falkenbrecht. Although Joseph had never been inside the palace, he had spent much time in its stables and had met the count on many occasions. Joseph modeled his behavior and carriage after the count who was, he felt, the most dazzling human on the planet.

Just below the rocky promontory on which Schloss Falkenbrecht sat was the present count's reason for existence—the home of the Royal Wittelsbach Hussars. Nearly a mile in length and half as wide, the parade ground rolled up to the line of the seven buildings of the hussars. At their center the headquarters building rose one full floor above the others and was topped by an oversized cupola.

As Joseph and Thunder rode past the parade ground the evening call to colors was taking place, an event that only coincided with Joseph's ride home on those occasions when he was thrown out of the cheder in the first half hour of his lesson. Six hundred mounted men in black and shimmering silver, drawn up in five ranks of 120 each, faced the road along which Joseph rode. He could feel their eyes following his progress: admiring eyes for Thunder, envious eyes for him. Thunder's knees rose to a new rhythm; his back seemed to lower three inches and stretch six. With his neck arched and his eyes on the road ahead, he trotted to a waltz audible only in Joseph's head.

From Thunder's gait others heard their own waltzes. General Count von Falkenbrecht, mounted on his chestnut Trakehner, Hektar, gazed at the stallion and the boy astride him and hummed the melody of the Maria Theresa Waltz. Sergeant-Major Hans Stumpf chose as he always did the Drunkard's Waltz, which was the only one he knew. And as always, he sighed. Joseph was magic with horses.

Second Lieutenant Otto von Exing, only two years older than Joseph and recently posted to the Royal Wittelsbach Hussars, had no waltz in his head. A Junker whose family dated its titles back to Charlemagne, von Exing was graciously permitting the Royal Wittelsbachs the honor of completing the cavalry training he had begun as a cadet in Berlin. Von Exing glared at the magnificent horse he had been unable to purchase and wondered why the Bavarians, who had sensible Jew laws, neglected to make one forbidding Jews to own such fine horses.

Jakob Gershomsohn was working with the big gray gelding he was preparing as a parade horse for von Falkenbrecht when he caught a distant movement on the road. He sighed and shook his head. Joseph was home early again. Whatever the reason, Jakob promised himself he wouldn't laugh. The boy had to learn respect for authority, even if authority had the misfortune to have as its representative a fool who hadn't any idea how to teach.

As Joseph rode up he saw his father, eyes blazing, huge mustache drawn down in a ferocious scowl, booted legs apart, lunge whip behind him flexed between his hands. Jakob never beat his son. However, he did believe that a carefully measured cuff here and there, nothing more than a shock to get his attention, was good for the boy.

"So, what this time?" Jakob asked.

Suddenly Joseph's body and mind, straining so hard to reach into manhood, collapsed. He looked like a child. Thunder, feeling the change in balance and sensing the boy's mood, shifted uneasily on his feet. Joseph dismounted. As quickly as he could he told his father about Abram.

In spite of his vow Jakob laughed. What a piece of work his son was! In his own way, a way completely separate from his intellectual acceptance of Spinoza, Jakob lived with the anthropomorphic God of the Jews. And in the traditional Jewish way, he had an ongoing and often-contentious personal relationship with the deity. But often, as in this moment of laughter, he silently thanked God for the miracle of his son. With such a son a man didn't need a big family. Jakob's eyes filled with pride. Joseph saw this and made the mistake of grinning. Jakob now had to administer a cuff. Respect for authority was necessary.

Later as the alpen-glow faded from the distant mountains, they sat on a bench in front of the wooden house. Inside, Rebecca was preparing supper. Jakob puffed on his long pipe and studied his son who was braiding new leather reins for Thunder.

"So," Jakob started. "You want the same conversation again?" Joseph looked up. Jakob raised his hand to stop any interruption and went on, "I know this conversation. I have memorized it. You'll say, 'If I'm going to make my life as a trainer of horses for the cavalry, and if I'll always live here, not in the Judengasse with the other Jews who hate us anyhow because we are not Jews like they are Jews, and the rabbi hates me and calls me Shaygets every time I walk into his smelly little cheder, and if a bar mitzvah is just ceremonial Judaism and all I have to know is horses, so why do I have to be a bar mitzvah?' And I'll say to you it's not enough to know Spinoza. It's not enough to know the Torah and the Talmud as well as you do. Because you are a Jew you also have to know what the other Jews know. You have to know Jewish tradition the way they know it. To be Jewish is to know the Torah the way *they* know it even if *they* are wrong. So let's not have the conversation."

Without looking up from his leather work Joseph said, "I have a new question. You want to hear it?"

"I can hardly wait. Ask."

"Why do we have to be Jewish at all?"

Jakob nodded. "Interesting. What do you mean?"

Joseph put down the braiding and looked at his father. "We do nothing Jewish. We don't live in the Judengasse. We don't keep Kosher. We don't go to *shul*, even on the High Holy Days. Yes, we keep the Sabbath and we celebrate Passover. But that is not enough to be Jewish. We are probably the only Jews in all Bavaria who own land outside the ghettos, and it's a horse farm. Who ever heard of Jews training horses? Buying horses? Yes. Selling horses? Yes. But breeding and training horses? Who ever heard of it? All we get for being Jewish is that I have no friends. The Jewish kids are forbidden to be my friends, and the gentiles won't do it. They won't let me be a cavalry officer because I'm Jewish."

"A blessing."

"What's the point?"

"The point, Herr Philosopher, is that you are Jewish because you are Jewish. Your mother is Jewish, so you are Jewish. Thirty-five hundred years of Gershomsohns have been Jewish, so you, the last to bear the name, are also Jewish. In a few years when you get married, your wife will be Jewish...."

"How do you know?"

"Because I know. Your children, may they give you as much trouble as you give me, will also be Jewish."

"Poppa, seriously. Why do I have to go on with this...," he struggled to find the right word, "...misery of a bar mitzvah?"

Jakob sighed the last puff of smoke from his lungs. "Seriously? Because the whole world isn't horses. I know. I know. Right now your whole world is. But there is more, and when you grow older you will discover it. You are born a Jew. You can't help that. And because you're a Jew the world will be hard on you. So if you're going to suffer for your birthright, at least you should know what it is for your people. At least if you know, you can decide. You'll make your decisions from some knowledge. You think I care about the bar mitzvah? I don't. I care about the studying for the bar mitzvah—what you learn of the other Jews. You must know them and their traditions, because these mice are the Jews of Europe. Rabbi Solomon? A schmuck. Instead of throwing you out this afternoon he should have praised you for thinking enough to ask about Abram's eyes. He should have seen what a wonderful mind you have and he should have engaged it. But the schmuck is the only rabbi we got, so you will treat the schmuck with respect. And no matter how many times you get thrown out, you'll go back the next day, and I expect you will continue to use your head and ask the questions that you want to ask. That's all I ask. Ask."

"But if he won't answer?"

"Sometimes it's enough to ask."

And ask he did. He asked, "Rabbi, what about the fish?"

And the rabbi, recognizing the tone, looked sharply over his glasses. "Fish? What fish?"

"Here in Noah, God says, 'I myself am bringing the flood.... All that is on land shall die.' And then He tells Noah to bring all the animals and birds onto the Ark but never mentions fish, and since fish can live in water, does that mean that fish don't count or that God loves fish best?"

Again, Joseph went home early enough to show off Thunder before the hussars.

But on other days Joseph stayed. And he learned, in addition to how to perform his bar mitzvah service, that either the God of the Jews was an impotent braggart or there was no God at all. And as the weeks went by, in spite of the clouds and the grass and the horses and Spinoza, he tended toward the latter conclusion. He became angrier than ever. If there was no God, there was no reason for them to be Jews. If there was no God, the suffering of the Jews was a great crime. But what if there was a God? That was the more troubling of the two possibilities. If there was a God, He clearly preferred the Christians to the Jews. The Christians had everything, the Jews nothing. Why was that? As far as Joseph could see, with the exception of him and his father and mother, all the Jews he knew were keeping their side of the covenant. They prayed all the time, went to shul all the time, and kept the commandments. Joseph became obsessed by these thoughts.

Three months before his bar mitzvah, Joseph decided two things. He would complete his bar mitzvah for his parents' sake. Then he would stop being a Jew.

General Count Rupprecht von Falkenbrecht was born the previous century, in the year that Benjamin Franklin died. Fifteen years later, as a cadet, he distinguished himself in the battle of Austerlitz, and the following year was presented to Napoleon during the occupation of Berlin. At six feet three inches, he was tall for a hussar, but nevertheless he became the best of them—the finest horseman and the fiercest fighter. During the next forty-five years he distinguished himself in every major European military engagement and fought innumerable duels.

Count von Falkenbrecht sat by his fire in his trophy room, sipping a fine old sherry and thinking about Joseph Gershomsohn and his horse. They had waltzed by the regiment again that afternoon. There never had been a horse like Thunder. Thunder, he mused, was a perfect name for a boy to give his black stallion. He thought of riding that horse during the week of the king's birthday hunt and the sensation the animal would cause.

After a polite knock his valet entered, bowed and said, "I am sorry to disturb you, Herr Count, but the boy from the horses, the Gershomsohn boy, insists on seeing you."

Von Falkenbrecht was too wise a soldier not to believe in serendipity. "Show him in."

Joseph wasn't prepared for the room's grandiosity. He stood in the entrance trying to comprehend it. His first impression was of its enormous height. His eyes followed a series of white vaulted arches up to a coffered ceiling and rested for a moment on the banners, pennons, standards, and battle flags suspended from spear-tipped shafts just below. Colorful, faded, and occasionally tattered flags circled the room. Instinctively, Joseph knew these had been captured by von Falkenbrechts since the beginning of history. Below the flags his eyes rested on a series of shields, alternating between the coats of arms of the Falkenbrechts and their cousins, the ruling Wittelsbachs. Between the shields and at a level ten feet above his head, the walls were covered with what looked like enough game trophies to repopulate all the forests of Bavaria. Below the antlers and stuffed heads, the plasterers and painters had created a ledge of rocky outcroppings, tree trunks and fallen trees, behind which was a painted backdrop representing various natural habitats and from which a parade of stuffed beasts menaced the occupants of the room below. Joseph saw his first lion, tiger and leopard. A grizzly bear, fifteen feet high, roared at the sky next to a charging rhinoceros. He wondered if the ugly one-horned monster was a unicorn but rejected the thought, for he knew the unicorn was a white horse with a long silver mane like an Andalusian.

Below the diorama the white walls ended in dark wood paneling against which suits of armor filled the spaces between huge gold-framed paintings. These were the first paintings Joseph had ever seen. He felt dizzy and had to concentrate on his breathing. The paintings were large—eight by ten feet—but to Joseph they filled the whole universe: plunging horses, roaring cannon, sabers flashing in the sun. It was all wonderful. He wasn't sure how long he had stood staring at the wars on the walls when he slowly became aware of the silence around him, then the crackling of a fire. He looked toward the huge stone fireplace.

The count was seated on a chair so magnificent Joseph thought it might have been a throne. He wondered if all counts had thrones in their castles. Did they have them in every room? When they traveled, did they take their thrones with them? He blushed for his stupidity. But since that was what had brought him there, he gathered his wits and straightened up. The spirit of the paintings was in him. He could conquer all. But then he faced his first obstacle. Between him and the count there was an expanse of carpet so beautiful that Joseph was unsure if it was meant to be walked on. He stood no longer a conqueror but a confused boy looking for a path around the sea of color.

Instantly understanding the boy's discomfort, for he was neither an insensitive man nor an unobservant one, von Falkenbrecht rose and crossed the carpet to Joseph. "Come in, my boy." He took Joseph's arm and led him to the two chairs by the fireplace. It was then Joseph saw the other chair looked like a throne too, and felt a double fool for his earlier thoughts.

Joseph stood uneasily by the second throne while von Falkenbrecht resumed his seat in the first. Joseph cleared his throat and lightly stamped a foot. Von Falkenbrecht watched the boy's discomfort and rather enjoyed it.

"So. You have come to see me."

Joseph nodded, unsure how to begin. The words he had rehearsed vanished from his head. "Herr General, sir," he said. "Would you like to have Thunder?"

Von Falkenbrecht was startled. "But I understood the horse wasn't for sale at any price."

"He's not. I would never sell Thunder. But I will give him."

"You would give him to me?"

"Well...trade. I would trade him."

Curious, thought von Falkenbrecht. "For what would you make such a trade?"

Joseph's confidence left him again. He began shifting his feet like a nervous horse. "Well..."

"Sit down, boy."

Joseph dropped onto the second gold chair. Von Falkenbrecht leaned across the small table and patted the boy's knee and in the gentlest of voices said, "This is a momentous decision. Think for a moment. Take your time and tell me why you would contemplate giving up your pet."

"Because I don't want to be a Jew. I want to be like everybody else. I'm going to run away and join a cavalry in another country. And I want to be a general one day. And to do that I need to be a gentleman—not a Jew. A man with a 'von' in front of his name."

Von Falkenbrecht suppressed a smile. "And what does that have to do with the horse and me?"

"I go to Hebrew school to learn to be a Jew. Why can't I come to you and learn to be a gentleman?"

Now von Falkenbrecht could no longer restrain his laughter. He threw his head back and roared like a cavalryman. Joseph turned beet red, jumped to his feet and started across the oriental rug. But von Falkenbrecht flapped his hand. "No, don't go. I'm not laughing at you. On my honor, I'm not laughing at you."

Joseph looked at the general in some confusion.

"I'm laughing," von Falkenbrecht said, "at the idea of presenting you at court as my nephew von—of course, von Ritter—the knight. You are part horse, aren't you? Ritter is an ideal name for your new self. What a joke on the king! He has always maintained he could sense the presence of a Jew."

Joseph stood and watched the count.

Von Falkenbrecht's laughter wound down. "My boy, what a quick temper you have. You must learn to control it; that I warn you. With that temper and a 'von' before your name, there is no doubt you'll fight your share of duels. I find this amusing. Well, well, come back and sit down. We have much to discuss."

Joseph remained where he was. "Why were you really laughing?" Now von Falkenbrecht's face turned glacial, and when he spoke his voice was cold.

"Why were you really laughing, Your Excellency? When you address me you will call me Your Excellency, or Excellency, or you will start your sentences with 'Excuse me, Herr Count,' or 'Pardon me, My General.' But you will never again assume such ill-mannered familiarity with me or any of your superiors again. Do you understand that?"

Joseph nodded.

"You will never again nod at me. You will say, 'Yes, Excellency, I understand.' Say it."

"Yes, Excellency, I understand."

"Good." Von Falkenbrecht sat back in his chair and Joseph started to return to the other. "Stop. You will stand where you are till I tell you otherwise." Joseph stood still.

Von Falkenbrecht stared at him for a moment, thinking: "The boy is like a fine colt. He needs to be handled with a firm but loving hand." He astonished himself by making a comparison with his idiot nephew. Joseph, despite his low origins, was everything he would have wanted in a son: bold, intelligent, gifted, imaginative, beautiful. Whereas Egon, his nephew, was an effete coward with the intelligence of a puppy. What, he allowed himself to wonder, could this boy become to me? Whatever it was he needed to take a firm hand right from the start. The formal tone was the correct choice. Cadets, even those of royal blood, had to begin with discipline. "Has Sergeant-Major Stumpf taught you to stand at attention?"

"Yes, My General."

"Then do so."

Joseph braced himself, feet together, thumbs along the sides of his legs, chin and shoulders pulled back, chest out, eyes staring straight ahead at nothing.

"Good. What else have you learned?"

"Excellency, Sergeant-Major Stumpf has trained me in all cavalry drill and maneuvers. I can charge a melon on a stick and make two slices from the top third as I pass."

"What else?"

"I can do the same thing when he is waving the stick with the melon."

"What else?"

"I can discharge a pistol from a charging horse and most of the time I can hit somewhere on a man-size target."

"Astonishing. I have never seen anyone except by accident hit anything with a firearm from a moving horse. What else?"

"My General, we practice stationary shooting with the pistol and the musket."

"And how good are you at that?"

"Herr Count, I always hit the bulls-eye."

"Naturally. And what, may I ask, does Sergeant-Major Stumpf get in return for all this instruction?"

"My General, I show him how to feel the horses."

"Which means?"

"Excellency, when a horse misbehaves, shies, or won't learn, people think it is crazy or bad. But if you know how to feel it, you can tell where it hurts."

"And what does hurting have to do with it?"

"Most horses misbehave because they hurt some places you wouldn't think of looking, and because they hurt, they begin to forget those parts of their body and so they move badly or shy, or other bad things."

Von Falkenbrecht allowed the lapse of "My General" because he knew he was in the presence of genius. "Explain that."

"Take Thunder. When he was a two-year-old, my father was going to destroy him because they thought he was crazy. They thought there was something wrong with his right eye because he always shied right to left and you could never tell when he would do it, like he was only blind sometimes, or crazy. But I knew what it was."

"What?"

"There was a bone on his neck, what they call a 'vertebra,' about eight inches back from his poll. It was out of place, like it had been hurt when he was young, and grew crooked. It must have happened to him when they halter-broke him. It happens to lots of horses during halter-breaking. Most of them get head shy, which is why my father, since I showed him about Thunder, doesn't do it the way everybody else does any more. He uses a way I thought up. It takes less time, and the horse is never afraid of a halter and never head shy."

"I'll hear about that later. Tell me about this *feeling.*"

"First, you very lightly touch the horse everywhere. That's how you can tell if everything is all right."

"How do you know?"

"You just do." Joseph smiled apologetically, and shifted his weight uneasily. "I'm sorry, My General, but it's hard for me to say how. But I can show you on Thunder. I showed Sergeant-Major Stumpf. He is slow but he is learning."

Von Falkenbrecht nodded. "Continue. When you find the place that hurts, then what do you do?"

"First, you must know that when a horse hurts, he tries to forget that part of his body, and other parts of his body as well if they connect to the part that hurts. And after a while those parts become sort of numb. He can use them but he doesn't really feel them anymore. It's like part of his body is blind, not his eyes, and that makes him spooky. So you have to remind him that those parts exist and that he can use them."

"Massage?"

"No, sir. Massage is good for some things. But for this you have to begin to touch those parts of his body in a certain way."

Von Falkenbrecht sighed. "I know, you can't explain. You have to show me."

"Yes, sir."

"You are showing this to Stumpf?"

"Yes, sir."

"So. It is enough that Stumpf knows. I have other questions. Are you truly serious about this proposition? Will your father allow it? I warn you I will not get on his bad side. The man is the best breeder and the finest trainer in Germany."

"Sir. My father is a gentleman. When I'm gone he will honor my obligations. He will not be pleased, but he'll accept it."

"Everyone knows that Thunder will let no one ride him but you. Even if we go forward with this charade, how will I ride him?"

"My General, I can show you what to do and in minutes he will be as loyal to you as to me."

"Truly? In minutes?"

Joseph's face flushed red again. "If the Herr Count doubts my word then we have no further business." He had already spun on his heel before von Falkenbrecht, again amused, stopped him.

"My apologies, Herr von Ritter. I sincerely apologize. Please don't go."

Joseph turned, his scowl back in place.

Von Falkenbrecht began to pace. "It is, of course, mad, completely mad, what you propose. Perhaps that is why I accept."

"So," he continued, "this is what you will do. You will report to this room every day at precisely 1700 hours. We shall work for two hours. The first thing you have to learn is to hide that temper of yours." He quickly slapped Joseph on the face. Joseph backed off glowing scarlet, tossing his head and flaring his nostrils. Von Falkenbrecht laughed.

"See? You glow like a beacon and behave like a stallion. Oh, we shall have so much work to do. But you'll learn. Gentlemen don't unintentionally show their feelings. And that shall be our first work. That we shall do every day. Next in importance is speech. Your accent and your German are atrocious. Each day I shall require you to listen to how I speak, and then to mimic me. Your posture is already excellent. That, of course, is from riding. And the rest: fencing, not saber but foil and épée; clothing, wine, table manners—oh yes, table manners. We shall dine together, frequently. You will learn what to eat and how to eat it, and other pleasures."

Von Falkenbrecht walked over to a sideboard and refilled his sherry glass. He was astonished at how young he felt. What a prank! He thought of his idiot nephew, and of another idea that doubled his pleasure.

"It occurs to me that one of my estates, Breitenstein, in Austria, has a transferable title of baron. I was thinking of giving it to a fool relative. With a real title, you'll only be a partial fraud. It makes everything far more interesting." He strode around the room. "A name. You'll have to have a proper aristocratic name. You might retain Joseph, perhaps with a Franz in front of it, and we shall think of a suitable addition of old family middle names, but for now Franz Joseph von Ritter has a nice weight to it. Then we add Baron von Breitenstein and I can hear the ring of the chamberlain's voice in the Royal Palace announcing 'Franz Joseph von Ritter Baron von Breitenstein.' "

"Lovely! I shall enjoy this, creating new aristocrats. God knows I've killed enough of them. Perhaps if we proceed correctly, with what you can do with horses, you might not have to go abroad at all. If you are a good student the king might take to you. His majesty, like me, is besotted with horses. Enough. That's quite enough for today. A little heady, isn't it? Go home. Take very good care of Thunder for soon he will be mine. And you? You'll be Franz Joseph von Ritter Baron von Breitenstein."

§3

Having made his decision, Joseph no longer cared about the rabbi. He planned to do his Torah studies with the man and not ask any questions. The rabbi was twice a fool: once for believing that the God of the Jews was the One God, and again for thinking that the jealous, forgetful, fumbling, mean-spirited God was all-powerful. Thus, in the light cast by the wisdom of his new and perfectly formed understanding of Rabbi Solomon, Joseph controlled himself in the same way he did when he had a nervous horse. Each time, just before he entered the cheder, Joseph slowed his breathing and allowed his body to relax. In the presence of the rabbi, he linked his breathing to that of the old man, then imperceptibly slowed it so that the rabbi, without realizing, followed suit. Both of them felt calm. Only the rabbi was unaware of the mechanism that had provided his peace.

At first the rabbi was suspicious. And why, he thought, shouldn't he be? In the passing of twenty-four hours, Shaygets Joseph, the emissary of the Devil, had metamorphosed into a Jewish angel: studious and polite, the glow of rebellion vanished from dangerous eyes. Was it a miracle or a trick of the Devil? That the change in Joseph was nearly too much for the old rabbi came as no surprise to Joseph. Horses reacted similarly. Sometimes it took weeks of quiet handling to gain their confidence. Biding his time, Joseph never varied from his gentle training routine. The old man's confusion grew. At last he consulted his mystic manuals to ascertain if the boy was possessed by a demon, but, because he never understood the more arcane portions of the Cabbalah, he surrendered to the new Joseph.

One night, at the conclusion of the evening prayers, the ten men constituting the leadership of the Jews of Dittelheim remained behind to discuss Joseph. They put away their prayer books and gathered at the benches at the front of the *bimah,* the dais from which the service was conducted.

The facade of the synagogue of Dittelheim gave no hint of its interior. Plain, square and no taller than the buildings around it, it was built in 1376 and reconstructed in 1733. The law forbade any Jewish religious structure to challenge the spires of the Christian churches, but the traditions of the Jews also imposed architectural requirements, such as one that demanded that synagogues be higher than the surrounding buildings. The synagogue of Dittelheim was the result of complex interpretation. The floor was placed deep below the ground level, thus the Dittelheim synagogue was taller on the inside than the Dittelheim houses were on the outside.

The congregants entered through an unprepossessing door into a humble vestibule. Here they encountered two plain plank doors. The one on the left led to a short flight of stairs that dropped three steps to the women's balcony—the strict separation of the sexes was mandatory for religious observance. The door to the right opened on a magnificent stone staircase that descended in stages to the sanctuary. At the center of the room, small by big city standards but large for Dittelheim, stood the bimah: a pentagonal stone platform rising four feet from the floor, adorned with lacy carved stone rails, an ancient carved wooden lectern and five thin pink marble columns, each surmounted with a gilded Corinthian capital, and all supporting a tall, open-work wrought-iron crown. On the wall facing Jerusalem stood the holy ark, framed with the same pink marble used for the columns of the bimah and hung with a scarlet velvet curtain on which the lions of Judah, embroidered in heavy gold and silver threads, guarded the tablets of the commandments.

Stored in the holy ark were the most prized possessions of the Jews of Dittelheim: the four Torahs. All four scrolls contained the same words—the five books referred to by the Christians as the first five books of the Old Testament, and by the Jews as the Torah. Each of these scrolls had been calligraphed by holy scribes in Jerusalem: the oldest scroll six hundred years before; the newest a hundred and fifty years after that. Each was enrobed in a different colored silk velvet cover that was also richly embroidered in gold and silver. On the largest sat a gold and silver crown. It was hung with a silver breastplate suspended from a silver chain. The remaining Torahs were decorated with delicately worked silver finials over the staves and smaller silver breastplates. Hanging just in front and above the ark was the bronze eternal lamp, crafted in Alexandria in the fourth century and brought to Dittelheim from Spain after the expulsion of the Jews at the end of the fifteenth century.

The ceiling of the Dittelheim synagogue was a frescoed barrel vault, the curve of which ended at a flat arch just above the ark. There colored vines and flowers flowed around a centerpiece of the Lions of Judah, tan against a blue background, this time blowing red trumpets. With their left paws raised, holding the trumpets to their mouths, they used their right paws to support a large floral wreath whose center was white with black Hebrew letters. The Hebrew was the first verse of Psalm 130:

> Out of the depths I call to you, O Lord,
> O Lord, listen to my cry;
> Let Your ears be attentive
> To my plea for mercy.

The men immediately noticed that the rabbi had put on his prayer shawl. This happened only when the most solemn events were taking place: the announcement of new and more repressive Jew laws, or an outbreak of plague. Even Rubenstein, the butcher, fell silent. The rabbi raised his hand.

"Perhaps a miracle," he said, his voice strange. The men looked at each other. The rabbi continued. "A sacred blessing has been granted to the Jews of Dittelheim. I have come to report to this community that the Prodigal has returned. The boy, Joseph Gershomsohn, has become the finest student I have ever seen. It is as if...as if...Hashem, blessed be He for he is One, inspires the boy." He went on to detail to them the change in Joseph, and the depth of Joseph's scholarship. He concluded: "We, the Jews of Dittelheim, have here a holy blessing. Maybe it is the will of God that in this boy we shall have one day a great rabbi, a sage, an immortal teacher, a Maggid—the Maggid of Dittelheim!"

The discussion of this possibility continued for most of the night. And in the same evening, as the elders of the synagogue rejoiced in vigorous debate, in the cellars of Schloss Falkenbrecht there was another kind of rejoicing.

"Wine is a feast for all the senses: sight, hearing, smell, taste, noblesse. First, eyes. Admire the goblet in which the wine is to be poured. Look at it. See it. The noblest of wines is served only in the finest of crystal. Never in ordinary glass. Better to not drink at all. Tap the vessel with the edge of your monocle. Listen to the ring."

Von Falkenbrecht touched the crystal with his own monocle and held the wine glass to Joseph's ear as if it were a tuning fork. Joseph smiled and in his new accent said, "So pure a tone. You think the angels sing like that?"

Von Falkenbrecht laughed. "Say that to the archbishop and you will have a patron for life. Next we fill the glass. Notice, not more than a third full. That leaves room for the nose. Not yours, the wine's. But before the smell there is more yet of the feast for the eyes. Hold the glass to the candle thus, and then savor the fine deep ruby color of the wine. Only the Lafite, and only the '36 Lafite properly decanted, has this particular dark crimson." Mesmerized, Joseph allowed his eyes to draw him into the color.

"Is this how rubies look?"

"No. Gems are another study. Gems are hard and cruel. They exact a price for their beauty. But the noble wines are soft and giving. They gratify every sense. Now the smell. Swirl it gently and with delicacy, not a sword thrust, but a gentle insertion, like first entering a virgin...."

Joseph couldn't keep the blush from his face. He knew nothing of sex, although he was addicted to a certain pleasurable practice which he thought he had invented. Von Falkenbrecht recognized the blush.

"Aha," he said. "You blush at the word virgin because you are a simple country lad, a virgin by God! It presents another and wonderful part of our little university. There is a place, what is called a 'House of Pleasure,' in Vienna. In due time we shall go there and further your education. That will indeed be amusing."

Joseph was both aroused and embarrassed, and his face reddened.

"This will cease at once," von Falkenbrecht said, speaking quietly but with cold command. "You will not dare to allow your face to color in my presence. Not ever again. Stop this instant."

Joseph closed his eyes and thought about how he had been forced to bridle his own feelings in order to control Thunder as a colt. He concentrated on his breathing and found that peaceful place at his center where he was always safe.

Von Falkenbrecht nodded. "But now we are discussing wine. We are speaking about what is called, 'the nose.' You insert your nose into the glass. Sniff gently. No snorting. Gently inhale. So? What do you smell?"

Joseph gave himself over to the scent in the glass. He closed his eyes and drifted. "I can't describe it. It's sweet. No, not sweet but rich, like fresh black earth. And berries. And something else but I don't know what. Wood? New-cut oak? Is that correct?"

"It is not just correct. It is perfect. And I see I have again under-estimated you. You have yet another natural gift. So interesting in a Jew. Why, I wonder, has your God given you so many gifts? Perhaps of the Chosen People, you are the Chosen One.

"Forgive my laughter. It is not at you. The idea of the Messiah becoming a wine snob appeals to me. The king will be amused. Now I suppose I'll have to suffer the rhapsodies that will pour forth once you taste the damned stuff. Sip. Swirl it around in your mouth without gargling, if you can. Slowly swallow, and astonish me with your poetic erudition."

Joseph took a sip, made a face and then spit the contents of his mouth onto the earthen floor, followed instantly by the contents of his stomach.

Each dawn, as the rabbi unwrapped his *tefillin*, he thought again of the boy. A miracle. Hashem, blessed be his name, ruler of the universe, had moved his little finger and the wild boy, previously possessed by the devil, was now an angel. And who would have believed it? The boy had the potential to be a great cantor too.

Joseph had his own dreams, but not always while asleep. For one, he sat astride a prancing charger. Sometimes he wore the scarlet, blue and gold uniform of a marshal of France, leading Napoleon's armies to victory at Austerlitz. On other occasions, thousands of horsemen followed him as he swept across the desert to drive the Muslim hoards out of Eretz Yisroel and reestablished the Kingdom of David with himself proclaimed the true heir. On more modest excursions into fantasy he fought duels: sometimes on horseback, saber to saber; other times on foot, standing on elegant green lawns by cool blue lakes with swans and weeping willow trees. Always before driving the point of his épée through his opponent's heart, or placing one shot precisely in the center of his nemesis' forehead, Joseph permitted himself to say something profound. It was something he had read in his father's books. It was so profound that upon reading it for the first time, Joseph knew that he had come home. He had discovered the path he would always follow. When he asked his father, the wisest man he knew, about it he found his interpretation had been correct.

What amazed Joseph most about this one simple sentence was not that it was absolute truth, but that the idea contained in it wasn't new to him. It put into exact and glorious words what he had always understood but couldn't form in his mind. Soon Joseph quoted it in full during his fantasies. Using his most aristocratic accent, he repeated, " 'He who would distinguish the true from the false must have an adequate idea of what is true and false.' Spinoza. Baruch Spinoza, the Dutch-Jewish philosopher." But as his fantasies became more complex he found this long quotation something of a clumsy impediment to the drama of the moment, and so shortened it to a private code word, "Spinoza," shouted just before he pulled the imaginary trigger or thrust home his sword.

But between Joseph and the God of the Jews, it was real war. And, in a world where he was an outsider among people who were themselves outcasts, Joseph created his own bill of indictment against the God of the Jews. It was not he, Joseph Gershomsohn, who was rejecting the Jewish God, but the God of the Jews who had failed. He needed to know more about that God, and he devoted himself to secret Torah studies as diligently as he did the other things in his life that mattered most to him. On the surface of the Torah he found exactly what the rabbi wanted him to find, and he dutifully presented himself as the Saved Jew. But late at night, on his own, he dove into the Torah, searching every page, every verse, every sentence, and every word for the evidence to build his case against the God of the Jews. What he searched for he found—proofs of God's vanity, mendacity, impotence and failure. It wasn't a Bible. It was a confession to high crimes against Man.

One night he became a polytheist.

In God's own words Joseph found proof that the God of the Jews was only that. Not of the Egyptians, not of the Canaanites, not of the Hittites, not of the Muslims, not of the Christians—only the Jews. One little God among many. A minor God of a ruined people.

The discovery had begun innocently enough. Back when Joseph was still asking the rabbi dangerous and impertinent questions, he had asked one he thought quite harmless.

"Rabbi, here where God says, 'Let us make man with our image and our likeness,' what does the 'us' mean?"

The rabbi was pleased at the question. "Ah," he sighed, "that is of the most profound meaning. It is very interesting that you should notice such a thing." The rabbi clasped his hands together and *davened* over them as he spoke. "The great sage, Rabbi Moses Ben Nahmen, known as Nahmanides, who was also called Ramban, in his great commentaries on the Torah says on this subject that in saying the word 'us' God is speaking to all the forces of creation so they would participate in the creation of his crowning glory, Man."

The tradition of Torah study required dialogue. For thousands of years Jews had been studying in the form of question, answer, and argument. It was the only method available to Joseph. Thus, to himself he asked: if God needed help in creating Man, and the rabbi and even the great sages agreed that this was so, what could that mean? And to himself he answered: It can only mean God was not all-powerful.

He was astonished by the answer and asked himself, If this was the case, did that mean there were other Gods? It had to be.

The sages were calling them forces of creation, but if Eden was only one small place in the world—and there was proof of that because Cain and Abel were the only two children of Adam and Eve—where did all the people come from that were going to see God's mark on Cain's head? And if Eden was one small garden created by a minor God, that would explain why, when God was angry with the world, He didn't destroy it and start over again. Why He had to save Noah and his family and two of each species as breeding stock. God *couldn't* do it over again. Not by Himself. That was why there were still snakes in the world. God hated snakes. Why didn't they perish in the flood? He surely wouldn't let the hated snake on the Ark.

There are snakes because there were snakes in all the other parts of the world that were not flooded. As there were all the unclean animals. Would God let unclean animals on the Ark?

Not likely.

So there had to be some other place—a place not flooded.

In the words tumbling through his mind he shouted to himself: "And when God expelled Adam and Eve from the garden, He said, 'Man has now become like one of us in knowing good and evil.' "

"Us?" That was another proof that God was not alone in Heaven. Did God mean by that "us" that man was now like the Gods? And then to prevent man from becoming a God by living forever by eating of the Tree of Life, God banished Adam and Eve from His Garden.

What did God fear? Would it have been so bad if Adam and Eve, who were now as smart as God because they had eaten from the Tree of Knowledge, also lived as long as God? At last Joseph saw it clearly. God denied man immortality out of fear, and if God was afraid—and how could a God be afraid?—then God was not all-powerful. One look at the condition of the Jews and you could see that all the other Gods were more powerful.

With each night's secret studies Joseph's anger burned hotter, until on the day of his bar mitzvah he realized that there might not be any God at all. It came to him as a revelation as the Ark was opened to reveal the holy scrolls of the Torah. There was no God. The Torahs before him, swathed in silk and bedecked with silver and gold and wearing jeweled crowns, were all made by men. All of these people behind him bowing to the luxurious objects in the Ark were savages dancing around wooden idols. It was idolatry, and if there were a God, He would have never permitted it.

On that bar mitzvah Saturday, all of the Jews of the Judengasse were crowded into the little synagogue to share in the blessing of the Prodigal's return, and perhaps to assess the new economic prosperity that would result from a sage of their very own.

That morning, as they drove the team of American trotters to town, his father had said, "I have seen your light at night. I see how tired you are. Not enough sleep. You study with the schmuck at the cheder. You study all night. You study with von Falkenbrecht."

Joseph was astonished but, to his own amazement, unafraid. He remained silent, waiting for his father to continue. Jakob didn't take his eyes from the horses and the road. "How do I know about von Falkenbrecht and his goy lessons? I know because to von Falkenbrecht you are only important for one horse, a wonderful horse, but one horse. I, on the other hand, am important for years to come for the best horses he ever had. To von Falkenbrecht you are an amusement and I am business, and in his business, the cavalry business, he knows he cannot do without me. So I know everything."

"And?" Joseph asked.

"And? So you want to be a goy. I understand why. It's not so good to be a Jew. But can a horse become a duck? A duck is a duck. A horse is a horse. Even if the horse thinks he's a duck, he is a horse."

"You won't try to stop me?"

"Stop you? Today, my son, the Jews of the Jewstreet say that you are a man. I have known since you were five years old that you are more a man than all of them. How can I stop a man from making a mistake? A man must make his own mistakes. What I can do for you, I have done. So you want to be a goy. An aristocrat. Go try. But remember. Remember that as long as we live, your mother and I, you have a home here."

Hot tears poured down Joseph's cheeks.

"Cry," his father continued. "Men should cry. Me and your mother, you have not yet given us reason to cry. We are proud that in spite of what you and I both feel about it, you did this bar mitzvah. We are even proud that you have the courage to try this thing with von Falkenbrecht. But we don't like it. We are deeply sad that you will go away for who knows how long. But you make us proud." Jakob turned to look at his son.

"And one day when you are a marshal of France riding in front of the whole army, and I am a little old man—a rich little old man because you will give me the contracts for all the French horses—standing next to the king of France, I will turn and say, 'See that marshal in his gold uniform? That's my son. He's a Jew.'"

The rabbi believed he had never witnessed a more perfect bar mitzvah. Surely Hashem, blessed be He who ruled over them with love and joy, had seen it too.

On the Sunday night after his bar mitzvah, when Joseph knew there would be nobody in the synagogue, he left Thunder home and took an ordinary bay mare into town. He quartered her at a livery stable behind the Hotel Post, and then walked to the Judengasse where, under the cover of darkness, he made his way to the synagogue. Joseph paused in the dark shadow between the rabbi's little house and the synagogue and waited until his heart calmed. This was the most dangerous part. When he was sure he was unseen, Joseph proceeded silently along the wall to the front door of the synagogue. There, using a bent horseshoe nail, he picked the big padlock and let himself in.

The vestibule was unlit. Joseph leaned against the closed door. There is still time to go home, he thought. I don't have to do this. He remembered his talisman: "He who would distinguish the true from the false must have an adequate idea of what is true and false." He whispered the word, "Spinoza!" and set about his task. He knew the door to the sanctuary was on the right and, arms extended before him, made contact. Before opening the door he paused again, letting his eyes adjust to the darkness.

The smell nearly overwhelmed him. He felt assaulted by the pungent aromas of old leather books mixed with the ever-present rotting damp from the stone walls against the earth. The stink of a decayed people, he thought. This is not a house of God. It's a crypt. It's where the goyim buried the Jews.

Drawing up his chest and squaring his shoulders, Joseph studied the huge darkness. The subdued glow from the eternal light's minuscule flame emitted enough illumination for Joseph to navigate through the room. He moved toward the steps leading down into the cavernous sanctuary and stopped.

The small flame of the eternal light played a more important part than Joseph had realized. Now he could make out some of the painted vines on the ceiling, and at the far end of the sanctuary he could see the two painted lions with their trumpets and the medallion they guarded. Joseph couldn't quite read the Hebrew letters in the medallion, but he knew what they spelled. He had long ago memorized the detested verse:

> Out of the depths I call to you, O Lord,
> O Lord, listen to my cry;
> Let Your ears be attentive
> To my plea for mercy.

Why? he wondered. Why are Jews always crying from the depths? Why always begging for mercy? And from whom? A God who let them get in the depths. Aloud he whispered, "Spinoza!" and charged down the steps into the gloomy sanctuary.

Joseph carefully made his way through the benches to the bimah, which was larger than he had remembered. He mounted the platform and approached the carved lectern. There, feeling his way with his fingers he found the drawer in which the *shofar*, the ram's horn, was kept. He opened the drawer and as he reached out for the sacred object, he felt as though his hands stopped of their own volition. "Spinoza!" he whispered, and he snatched the shofar from the velvet cover.

The light from the eternal flame seemed to grow brighter as Joseph approached the holy ark. Flames danced off the gilded lions on the velvet covering of the sacred container. Joseph paused. The drape had never been pulled back without sacred prayers. He knew the prayers and was tempted to say them. Then he laughed and, lunging at the curtain, pulled it aside. No lightning struck him down.

Now only two polished wooden doors stood between him and the most holy of holies. To open the ark without the proper prayers and blessings was even more sacrilegious than drawing the curtain. He was convinced his not wearing a hat or a prayer shawl compounded his sin. He wished he didn't care. Joseph swallowed, closed his eyes for a moment, and thought of all the reasons that had brought him to this place. He opened the doors.

Joseph was unsure if the richly robed Torahs were glowing on their own or magnifying the light from the one little flame above them. He stared at the sacred scrolls, the Torahs, the words of God, God's laws, and he waited.

Nothing happened.

God did not strike him blind or dead.

Ignoring his fear, he reached into the ark and removed the crown and breastplate from the largest of the Torahs and put them on the shelf. He lifted the Torah to his shoulder in the traditional manner and, feeling the smooth fabric caressing his cheek, he waited.

God did not smite him.

Joseph turned his back to the holy ark and lowered God's laws to the shadowed floor. Next to actually desecrating the scroll, this was the greatest sacrilege of all.

Nothing happened.

God did not send plague or earthquake.

God did nothing.

Joseph stared heavenward. When God did not appear, or do anything to protect or avenge his holy scroll, Joseph put the shofar to his lips and blew it to attract God's attention. Deeee-yit! Deeee-yit! Deeee-yit! Dit Dit Dit Dit Dit Deeeeee-yit! The ancient sound reverberated off the curved ceiling, ricocheting from the walls, splintered by the brass chandeliers and the ironwork of the bimah. Joseph looked up at the ceiling.

"Look at me, God! Look what I have done. If you are there, do something. Do it or I will know you are not there. Do it!"

A shriek filled the air and a sharp blow hurled him to the floor.

§4

"**D**EMON!"

Joseph was thrashing on the floor, gasping for air. He saw the Torah snatched from the floor. As the first sucks of air began to fill his lungs the same foot struck him again.

"Devil! Blasphemer!"

A glancing blow jolted his head. Flashes of white exploded in the blackness that engulfed him. A searing pain drew him to his knees. His ear was being yanked from his head. Disoriented, reeling, Joseph was hauled to his feet and propelled toward the steps. Even though he knew the rabbi was right next to him, tearing at his ear, it seemed as if he heard the old man's voice screeching at him from a great distance.

"Devil! Your father...blasphemer! The thousandth generation!"

Joseph stumbled and clutched at the bimah rail. As he did, he saw something in a dark corner. It was a woman. A stranger. How could he see such a woman so clearly in that dark place? The woman laughed.

The rabbi dragged Joseph up the stairs and pushed him through the front door into the street. There the shock of the chill night air restored Joseph's balance. In a convulsive motion he pushed the old man away and was about to smash him to the ground when a voice stopped him.

"Who would have believed such a sight? Jews fighting! Rabbits fighting! It is more singular than an honest Jew. Unbelievable."

Joseph turned. Had the full moon not risen to its zenith, the Judengasse, which had no street lamps, would not have been so brightly lit. Had the moon not been haloed and slightly veiled by an icy wisp of clouds, the sight might not have been so fearsome. The horsemen wore the black and silver uniforms of the Royal Wittelsbach Hussars. And with their tall, black fur hats they looked more specter than human; huge black shadows glinting with metallic menace. But even in the subdued light Joseph recognized the horses. Two had been trained and sold by his father. Another one, Pepper, had only recently been sold to a new officer of the regiment. The fourth was Siegfried, the huge, clumsy gray Holsteiner that Otto von Exing had brought with him from Munich.

Joseph looked from the horse to the rider. Second Lieutenant Baron von Exing stared down at him and the rabbi as though they were filth. At the age of seventeen, von Exing was already a powerful brute. Six feet two inches tall, muscled like a circus strongman, he was obsessed with the power of his body and the power of his name. Von Exing and the three hussars were drunk.

For a moment no one moved. Joseph concentrated on the horses. They were uneasy, excited, ready to attack or flee. He felt their muscles quivering, and could see white showing around their dark eyes. Behind him the rabbi was standing quietly, waiting for the inevitable. Behind the rabbi, the Judengasse was empty. The windows were dark, but Joseph knew there were eyes peering at them from the black behind the glass. Mice! he thought.

At a sign from von Exing, two of the hussars walked their horses around Joseph and the rabbi, blocking any possibility of escape. Then von Exing eased his horse closer, backing Joseph and the rabbi toward the wall of the synagogue.

"Ah," he said. "I see we have the little Jew who is too proud to sell his horse to a gentile. Proud, as if you have a right to pride? Perhaps you are a revolutionist? Perhaps, like the French rabble, you think you have rights? Your problem, Jew, is that you don't know your place. Perhaps, like a horse, you need to be trained. Do you think you need to be trained?"

Joseph's rage gathered, and then focused on the arrogant man astride his equally dim-witted horse. Joseph moved toward him. "Von Exing," he said. "Come down off your stupid horse. We shall see who will train who."

The hussar next to von Exing laughed. "The boy is right. Your horse is stupid. The boy knows his horseflesh. Siegfried is stupid even for a horse."

Von Exing's face flushed. "It's against the law for a Jew to challenge a gentleman," he told Joseph. "So in addition to the crime of brawling in the public street, you violate the law by insulting your betters. I can see we will have to teach you manners. But you are only the second order of business. First we must tend to our own education. We came here to be educated." Turning to the rabbi, "You are the Jewpriest, are you not?"

Rabbi Solomon, aware that God had created this moment for him, joined Joseph in the middle of the street. He stared into the Prussian's eyes. "I am not a priest. I am a rabbi. A teacher."

"Good." Von Exing smiled at his companions. "Why else would we have risked the health of our valuable animals in coming to this filthy Jewstreet, but to seek enlightenment? Jewteacher, we wish to know the answer to this question. Why did you kill Christ our Lord?"

"The Romans killed Christ."

"But it was the Jews who condemned him. Pilate begged the Jews not to do that. The good Roman soldiers were only doing what the Jews demanded. Isn't that so? The Jews killed our Lord. Isn't that so?"

"He was a false Messiah."

"What? What?" Von Exing turned to the other officers. "We were right to come here for our educational purposes. But it also seems that where we came to learn, we must teach." To the rabbi, von Exing said, "Jewteacher, I shall say a sentence. When I am done you will say it back to me, exactly as I said it. Say, 'Our Lord Jesus Christ is the only true Messiah.' " The rabbi turned his back on von Exing and started to walk away.

"Jewteacher!" Von Exing shouted. "You will say, 'Our Lord Jesus Christ is the only true Messiah,' or I will split your head open like a rotten melon!"

The rabbi stopped and spoke without turning. "There is no reason to continue to talk with you. Nothing will change. You have come here to kill Jews. So if the Lord Our God, blessed be He for He is One, wishes my death, I am ready." With that the old man bowed to the east, closed his eyes, and began saying the Shema and the seven repetitions of Adonai Hu Ha Elohim.

Von Exing rode his horse into the rabbi and knocked him to the ground. Joseph started forward but, as he did, he felt a saber point in his back. A wine-dulled voice behind him said, "Not yet Jewboy. You get your turn after him."

The rabbi scuttled about on his hands and knees, trying to avoid von Exing's horse's hooves. Every time he rose, von Exing skillfully maneuvered his horse to knock the old man back to the ground. The others laughed.

"Are you sorry, Jewteacher, for what you did to our Lord? Be careful, Jewteacher. My horse almost stepped on your head. If your head were to hurt his hooves, I should have to be most severe with you."

The sword point against Joseph's back gave and jiggled as the hussar holding it focused on the activity in the street. Turning swiftly, Joseph used one arm to knock the blade aside and, with the other, he reached to the horse's head, just below the ear and behind the eye, and pressed. The horse reared and the rider, already off balance, somersaulted backward out of the saddle. Joseph snatched the saber out of the air as it flew from the hussar's grasp. With a leap he replaced the man in the saddle. The animal knew there was no longer any need to fear. Joseph asked the horse to jump to its side, bringing its bulk into violent contact with the horse of the second hussar. With both the other animal and its drunken rider off-balance, Joseph easily smashed his saber hilt into the man's face, drawing blood and tumbling him to the ground. The hussar crawled toward the shadows.

Joseph turned his horse and faced von Exing and the other officer whom Joseph now recognized as someone who had always treated him decently. The man backed his horse away, laughing, and shouted, "Look, von Exing, a Jewboy on a horse. That should be more sport for you than an old man on his knees! Teach him his place."

Recovering from his momentary astonishment and drawing his saber, von Exing charged at Joseph.

Joseph waited quietly. Then, as von Exing came closer, Joseph asked the horse beneath him to pirouette and the animal spun on its haunches. In the same moment Joseph parried von Exing's thrust and, as the Prussian hurtled by, Joseph slammed the flat of his own saber against von Exing's shoulders, almost knocking the large Prussian from the saddle.

The remaining mounted hussar hooted. "Baron von Exing, where are you going?" he shouted. "Turn around and teach this impudent Jewboy a lesson!"

Von Exing savagely wheeled his horse and again charged Joseph. But again Joseph and his horse, moving as one body, stepped aside, allowing Joseph to slash von Exing from the bridge of his nose across his cheek to his jaw. Blind with fright and howling with pain, von Exing dropped his saber and gave his horse a series of frantic and confused commands. The beast, absorbing its master's panic, reared, throwing its head just as von Exing in his own hysteria leaned forward, causing the back of the horse's head to smash against von Exing's face. Von Exing, his nose crushed, clattered to the cobblestones.

Joseph eased his mount toward the fallen Prussian, his sword arm extended toward him.

"That is enough, Herr Gershomsohn."

Joseph turned. Behind him the remaining mounted hussar, his saber still in its scabbard, his previous amusement gone, sat stiffly in his saddle. "You have beaten him in fair combat."

Joseph prepared himself to fight this hussar as well. But something in the man's voice made him realize the hussar was offering no contest. The fight was over. Joseph calmed himself and surveyed the scene. The first two hussars remained on the ground, both staring at Joseph. Above them the cloud had drifted from the moon, unveiling a merciless gray light. In it Joseph looked at the trembling black and silver mound sprawled on the cobblestones. Von Exing's saber glinted in the hard light a few yards away. From the mound came the sound of sobbing. Then the clatter of receding hooves overwhelmed the whimpering as von Exing's Holsteiner fled down the Judengasse.

Joseph now turned to check on the rabbi, who stood flattened and quiet against the synagogue door. The man was unhurt. And as Joseph turned back he saw, by the moonlight, pale whispers of faces in the dark windows of the Judengasse.

Joseph moved toward von Exing who staggered to his feet. The mounted hussar spoke softly, "Let him go. You have won. His honor is ruined. Let him go."

"His honor?" Joseph raged. "What does trampling a defenseless old man have to do with honor? This Prussian scum came here to piss on our honor. Oh yes. Believe it. We Jews have honor. Did you think, you gentlemen of the Royal Wittelsbach Hussars, that only you have honor? Look at that old man. Look how weak and frightened he is. Yet for his honor, he was willing to die rather than defame his people, his God. For his honor he was going to allow himself to be trampled to death. Will this piss-Prussian die here in this dirty little Jewstreet for his God? Will you?"

He advanced his horse a step toward the hussar. The officer backed his horse away. Joseph turned his horse to von Exing and, leaning down, placed the point of his saber against the Prussian's throat. Von Exing stood transfixed.

Joseph said, "Say, 'Jesus Christ is not the Messiah.' "

Von Exing said nothing.

Joseph spoke louder. "Say it, Christianboy, or I will kill you this instant. Say, 'Jesus Christ is not the Messiah.' "

Von Exing mumbled.

"What? Say it louder so your comrades in honor will hear you. Louder."

"Jesus Christ is not the Messiah," von Exing whispered.

"One more chance, Prussian pig. Shout it so everybody in Jewstreet can hear. It's the last time I will tell you."

Von Exing's shout came forth as a scream. "Jesus Christ is not the Messiah!"

§5

"**A**USTRIA," JOSEPH'S MOTHER SAID. "LET HIM GO HIDE IN AUSTRIA. There at least they speak German. It's not so far. We could see him...." She was unable to finish.

Jakob put an arm over her shoulder. "No. All he knows is horses. He will have to earn his way with horses. He is too good and too young to hide it. The world of good horsemen is too small. Sooner or later the von Exings will hear of him. Besides, my son will not hide. We will not ask him to live in hiding."

They were sitting in the kitchen, where all family conferences took place. A plain brass oil lamp, hanging over the scrubbed wood kitchen table, illuminated the low ceiling of clear varnished pine planks and beams, as well as the three anxious faces. Untouched bowls of potato soup and unbroken black bread lay before them. A kettle simmered at the back of the white tile and iron stove. On one side of the stove stood the wood-box on which Joseph had carved an edelweiss when he was six. Joseph studied the room, and every detail became precious.

"Listen!" Joseph was on his feet and moving toward the window. "Horses! Two of them."

Jakob reached for a set of loaded pistols he had placed on the sideboard when his son had returned home. Then he blew out the lamp. The three waited in the dark. The horses came fast and reined up outside the front door. A heavy fist hammered on their door.

"Herr Gershomsohn!"

"Stumpf!" Jakob said. He quickly relit the lamp and carried it through the sitting room to open the front door. Sergeant-Major Stumpf, carrying a leather valise and a dispatch case, stood aside to allow Count von Falkenbrecht to enter. As he did, Jakob closed the door.

Von Falkenbrecht studied Joseph. "It would have been better for you, the regiment, and that fool von Exing had you killed him. You did no one a favor by taking his honor and leaving him his life." He turned to Jakob. "No doubt you have been making plans for your son's departure?"

Jakob nodded. "We know he can go nowhere in the German-speaking world. Just before we heard you coming, I was about to suggest France."

Von Falkenbrecht shook his head. "Not France. Not any of the Italys. Not the Lowlands, England, or Russia. My friends, he can go nowhere in Europe with safety. The von Exings are related to all the highest nobility. Technically, Joseph has violated a number of laws. He will be hunted as a criminal." He turned to Joseph. "Von Exing has already tendered his resignation from the hussars. It is a resignation in disgrace. By now he should have shot himself. That he will not is further proof of his cowardice. The von Exings will send him to live in exile, but you they want destroyed. If the police can't accomplish that, they will arrange for your assassination."

To Jakob, he said, "It would have been difficult for Joseph to have made more powerful enemies. Of course, he can hide in Europe if you choose." He turned back to Joseph. "But you will have to give up horses, and you will always be in hiding."

Then Joseph heard a voice, clear and yet distant. It was a woman's voice. It said, "I am God. I have remembered my covenant. I will bring you to the land regarding which I raised my hand."

"America," Joseph whispered to the others, and then wondered why he had so spoken.

"So far," his mother sobbed.

Jakob, his face bleak, nodded. "America is good. They have fine horses there. Many Germans are going there. Many German Jews go there. A man can have a future there."

But the voice, Joseph wondered. Was it a trick? Was it from the excitement of the fight? It was so clear. And why America? He had never thought about America. He didn't even know what kind of hussars the Americans had.

Von Falkenbrecht said softly, "There are no American hussars. They have no tradition of cavalry. Can you give up that dream?"

No cavalry? Joseph was shocked. He tried to think of another country. But to his astonishment he couldn't even think of the names of those European nations surrounding Bavaria. How was that possible? The harder he concentrated the less he was able to think. He closed his eyes and calmed himself. Then he thought of a country. America. But it wasn't his voice! It was that other voice, the one that said, "I have remembered my covenant." But that was impossible. There was no God! And if there were? Would God speak to him? Would God speak with the voice of a woman? God would have already struck him dead. No. The voice was the result of his strain. If it had said America, it must have meant America.

"I am going to America," he said.

"And the cavalry?" his father asked.

"If they have no cavalry, then perhaps they need me to show them how to make one." Joseph tried to say it as a joke.

Von Falkenbrecht found it easier to talk cavalry than to face the loss of the boy. "They have mounted troops, dragoons really, but they call them cavalry." He turned to the sergeant-major. "Stumpf!" Stumpf passed him a dispatch case, which the count opened. He handed some papers to Joseph.

"You'll have to travel safely. You'll also need a start in the world. This paper legally transfers to you the title Baron von Breitenstein."

Jakob put an arm over his son's shoulder and tightened the one around his wife's back. They stood still, the three of them, clinging to each other, believing and disbelieving. Von Falkenbrecht continued as if he were issuing the day's orders. "This paper commissions you lieutenant of the Royal Wittelsbach Hussars under the name Franz Joseph von Ritter Baron von Breitenstein." He handed the document to Stumpf, who gave it to Joseph's trembling hands.

The count handed the next paper to Stumpf for transfer to Joseph. "This document informs all to whom it may concern that you are on leave to make certain studies of foreign cavalry." Von Falkenbrecht looked directly into Joseph's eyes. His voice remained in military control, but his eyes were moist. "In addition, in the event you require further *bona fides,* I give you permission to refer to me as your uncle."

The count turned to Stumpf.

"Stumpf!" he ordered.

This time Stumpf opened the large leather valise and pulled out a uniform of the Royal Wittelsbach Hussars which von Falkenbrecht handed to Joseph. "This uniform was recently made for one of the young officers who assaulted you and the rabbi," he said. "He sends it along with his profound apology for the incident and wishes to assure you he will never again take part in such activities. It should fit. He appears to be about your size. If not, I am sure your mother can make the necessary changes. I suggest you stay in uniform until you are safely out of Europe. The police and the agents of the von Exings will not think to question an officer of the Royal Wittelsbach. Do it honor by behaving in the most reserved and scrupulous manner."

Joseph's homesickness was replaced by exaltation. He was a baron! A baron and a hussar! Joseph was desperate to wear the uniform and ride Thunder all the way to America. Thunder! The excitement induced by the title and uniform subsided. The price for all this was Thunder. Joseph's arms fell limply to his sides.

"When must he leave?" Jakob asked, but he already knew the answer.

"Immediately," replied von Falkenbrecht. "I suggest you ride to Poppenlaur. From there a steamboat goes to Bremen. I'm told the steamboat arrives every morning at five and leaves again at six. The trip takes twenty-two hours. By eleven tomorrow morning, when I shall enter my office to find an official and, I am sure, grossly distorted report of the events in the Judengasse, you should be many miles from here. Once I have this official report, I shall be obliged to send to Dittelheim and request that the magistrate come see me. When he does, after keeping him waiting a suitable few hours, I shall order him to find you and arrest you for your unprovoked assault on one of my officers. Stumpf!"

Sergeant-Major Stumpf stepped forward.

Von Falkenbrecht continued, "Sergeant-Major Stumpf has something he wishes to say to you as well."

Stumpf, unable to stand at ease in the presence of his command-ing officer, nearly shouted: "I will miss you, Herr Baron. You are the best man I have ever trained. Wherever you go, remember what you have learned from me. I will never forget what I have learned from you." He then unfastened his saber and presented it to Joseph.

"It is not grand," he said. "My father carried it against the Turks, and before him, his father against the French. It would bring honor to my family for you to wear it."

Joseph accepted the saber. "I shall miss you too." Then he turned to von Falkenbrecht. "Pardon me, Herr Count." He spoke slowly and carefully. "If Your Excellency would come with me to the barn, there is the horse."

Thunder was waiting anxiously in his stall. This was the first day that he and his master hadn't worked together. Something was wrong. He stamped one foot nervously and twitched his tail. Then he heard his master coming. But not alone. Stranger steps were with him. It was dark. Why was his master coming in the dark? What were the other steps?

"Thunder," Joseph called softly.

The horse put his nose close to his master's, but didn't touch it until he received permission.

Joseph gently placed one finger just above his eyes. Thunder lowered his head and rested his nose against his master's chest.

"This is Count von Falkenbrecht," Joseph said. "He is your new master. I will go away. Your new master will take care of you. You must love your new master as you loved me. He will take care of you, and you will have a wonderful life with him."

To von Falkenbrecht, Joseph said, "With your finger, sir. Here, like this." He demonstrated it. "Lightly make a small circle on his head. Here, and here too. A little harder. That is correct. Here too. Here and here."

As von Falkenbrecht touched the horse in the way that Joseph showed him, Thunder dropped his head lower and lower, until Joseph had to reach down to caress his ears. "Now, sir, pull his ears the way the coachmen do—like this." Joseph willed his tears not to come and showed von Falkenbrecht how to make certain movements at varying degrees of pressure on the horse's neck, back, belly and rump. By the time they had finished, Stumpf had brought the two horses on which they had arrived. He transferred von Falkenbrecht's saddle and bridle to Thunder.

Joseph forced himself not to look away. "There is just one more thing Herr Count," he said.

"Yes?"

"Before you mount, you must talk to him."

"Talk to him?"

"Yes, sir. Tell him who you are and that you will take care of him."

Von Falkenbrecht paused. "Stumpf!"

Sergeant-Major Stumpf snapped to attention.

"Yes, My General."

"Walk away. Over there by the paddock."

Von Falkenbrecht watched until the sergeant-major was out of earshot. He turned to the horse. "Thunder," he commanded.

Joseph interrupted. "Softly, Excellency. Like to a child."

Von Falkenbrecht started again, this time in a gentle voice. He felt a complete fool. "Thunder," he said, "I am your new master. I will see to it that you will be well looked after. If you are as good to me as you were to Joseph, then we shall be great friends and no horse in all Christendom shall have a better life." He looked at Joseph. "Is that correct?"

"Yes, sir. But you must do it every day."

"Talk to him every day? Is that really necessary?"

"Yes, sir. It's the way to make him only your horse."

"What do I say to him?"

"Anything. I always tell him how I am feeling and what we are going to do that day."

"I see."

"And, sir, the way I just showed you how to touch him?"

"Yes."

"You must do that every day too."

"My groom..."

"Excellency, it must be you. If the groom does it, he will become the groom's horse, not yours. The groom can curry and brush him...."

"That's a relief."

"But you must do the touch part before he is saddled."

"Every time I ride him?"

"In the beginning. Later on when you are sure he is your friend, you can do it three times a week."

Von Falkenbrecht laughed. Then he reached out and hugged Joseph. "Good-bye, Franz Joseph von Ritter Baron von Breitenstein. God be with you. If I'd had a son, I'd have been happy to have him be you." Then, turning, he vaulted into the saddle and trotted Thunder out of the barn. Stumpf followed, leading the other horse. They rode away.

§6

"So BEAUTIFUL," JOSEPH'S MOTHER SAID, TEARS FILLING HER EYES.
"So beautiful, my baby." She threw her arms around Joseph and
held him. He was already wearing his new uniform, the black and
silver of the Royal Wittelsbach Hussars.

Joseph hugged and kissed her, but he was desperate to gallop
through the night air, to stride into the Poppenlaur stable and say
to the livery men in his new accent, "Baron von Breitenstein," and
to accept their awe, deference and respect.

"Enough, Rebecca," Jakob said. "Let the boy go. It is time."

Rebecca kissed Joseph on his cheeks, his mouth and his forehead, and then stood away from him, gazing at his uniform. "I know
you are a man. A grown man. But still, always, you are my baby."
She wiped her eyes with the backs of her hands and smiled. "You
must write to us, Joseph," she said. "Every week. Your father will
read me the letters. And promise, Joseph, you will not go away for
always. Promise me that."

"I promise you, Momma. I will write to you and Poppa, and
when you see me again, I will be a general!"

He kissed her and turned to his father. "Good-bye, Poppa." They
embraced briefly, with great strength. Then, separating from his
father, Joseph took up his valise and started for the door.

"Aren't you forgetting something?"

Joseph turned to his father, who attempted to mask his feelings.
"Just like that? You pack a bag and go out the door to America? It's
across the road? Maybe just beyond Dittelheim? A little journey. A
journey that requires nothing except the use of a horse for a few
hours. Maybe it is a long journey. So tell me, my son, how will you
pay for this long journey? The Herr Baron thinks that because he's
an officer and an aristocrat, the world will feed and clothe him?
How does von Ritter propose to pay for his steamboat ticket to
Bremen? Or the passage to America? Or, if you will excuse me, such
mundane things as food and lodging?"

Joseph felt himself blushing. "Poppa, I forgot."

"We noticed." Jakob held up a canvas belt. "Joseph. You aren't
a baron. You aren't a hussar. A horse is a horse. You are a young

man with no real experience of life starting out into a real world. You must never, you understand me, never forget money again.

"We waited, your Momma and I, for you to mention this subject. And we are frightened that you did not. Listen to me, Joseph. Now that you will be on your own, you must think about money. Money gives you freedom to decide what to do with your life. With money you choose. Without it others choose."

Jakob lifted a heavy canvas money belt. "There's a hundred gold guilders in here. That's a very large sum of money—all that your mother and I have saved. If you throw it away, we can give you no more. If you use it wisely, it will take you to America and keep you for a very long time. There's enough to keep you and to set you up in a horse business.

"Joseph, I ask you to think about money all the time, until you know it without having to think about it, like breathing. Both are necessary for life. It's my last advice to you. Think about the money."

But Joseph was thinking how the money belt spoiled the line of his elegant uniform. As soon as he had ridden out of sight he dismounted, removed the cumbersome belt, put a few coins in his sabretache, and tossed the belt into his bag. He was free! On his own! The world was waiting, and he would take it by storm.

Joseph was riding Peter, a giant thoroughbred gelding, one of the fastest horses in his father's barn. He asked Peter for the hardest, swiftest ride in the horse's life. And yet, when the sky began to lighten—a warning that he might be too late for the steamboat—Joseph eased the big horse into a slower gait and then walked him for the last half-hour of the journey. Even if it meant he would miss the boat, Joseph would not deliver a hot, wet horse to a strange livery stable. One could never be sure they would take proper care in cooling down a horse once the owner went about his business.

The side-wheel steamboat *Woglinde* floated ghostly white in the morning mist. Launched the previous year, she was a modern wonder, the finest expression of German industrial craftsmanship. Two hundred and fifteen feet long, thirty-two feet wide and only drawing six feet nine inches of water, she was propelled up and down the rivers by twin paddle wheels each measuring twenty-nine feet in circumference.

At five fifty-four in the morning, the first class passengers were snugly asleep in their mahogany-paneled cabins, while the lesser beings of the lower deck huddled in blankets, shivering in their sleep wherever they found space. First Officer Heinrich Kurtz, his voice modulated to whispers so as not to disturb the important personages in the cabins above, supervised the loading and stowing of the last of the cargo bound from Poppenlaur. Above him the captain paced, shooting impatient glances at the ship's clock. When he could bear it no longer, he whispered a warning to Kurtz to hurry the loading. Ready or not, the boat was leaving at exactly six o'clock. The captain was not a man to miss by even one second a scheduled departure. Did Kurtz think schedules were made to be broken?

His father was right. The livery stable was on Dreihoofeisen-gasse. Joseph clattered through the door of the large barn and leaped from his saddle. The place looked reasonably clean and the water in the troughs fresh. It would do. Playing the role for which he had trained so hard, he used the toe of his boot to waken the boy asleep in the first stall.

"You there!" His accent was perfect. "Boy! Get up this instant!"

The stable boy, eyes wide, jumped to his feet.

"Unsaddle this horse." Joseph commanded. "Walk him for exactly forty-five minutes. Wash him and rub him down. Give him a double measure of oats. At midday he is to have grass hay and again at sundown. The hay is to be fresh, dry, and green. Do you understand me, boy?"

The boy nodded dully.

Joseph continued. "This horse's name is Peter. Say it. 'Peter.' "

The boy repeated, "Peter."

"Good. Peter is the property of Count von Falkenbrecht. You will look after it with complete and perfect attention. Do you understand me?"

The boy, terrified, nodded.

"Good. Tomorrow Herr Gershomsohn, Count von Falkenbrecht's master-of-horse, will arrive to fetch Peter. As he is the greatest horse trainer in Germany, he will know instantly by seeing the animal if you have disobeyed my instructions. If you have, you shall answer to the magistrate. Do you understand?"

The boy bobbed his head.

"Good." Joseph flipped the boy one of his gold guilders. "That should take care of everything."

The boy stood in mute stupefaction, staring at the coin in his hand. It was equal to nine months' salary. Joseph unstrapped his bag and saber and walked toward the river.

The *Woglinde* was easing away from the dock as Joseph approached. He ran with all his strength, leaped across five feet of open water and landed easily on the low deck. Kurtz hurried toward him.

"Mein Herr?"

Joseph carefully placed his monocle in his eye and stared at the man for a moment. As instructed by his mentor, he waited until the officer's shoulders drooped and eyes darted down. When the man was sufficiently cowed, Joseph spoke the words he had rehearsed in his head all the way from Dittelheim.

"I am Lieutenant Franz Joseph von Ritter Baron von Breitenstein on special assignment from the Royal Wittelsbach Hussars. I require...," here Joseph was unsure of the exact word. Journey? Transport? Neither sounded aristocratic enough. He paused for a moment as he ran over his choices and selected the one that felt best. "...Voyage to Bremen."

"But Herr Baron, we have no available cabins. Besides sir, this is most irregular. Passengers must first acquire tickets for passage from the offices of the Great German Rivers Steam Navigation Company."

Passage! Joseph said to himself, and vowed not to make the mistake again. He wondered if the sailor could see his blush in the early morning light.

"And sir, with no cabins available, the regulations specifically state that we may not take any new passengers. I shall have to signal the captain to stop—Herr Gott, he will be angry—and let you off. Forgive me, I beg the Herr Baron."

"Let me off?" Joseph roared. "Let me off and the king shall hear of it!" He enjoyed seeing the man flinch. Now, having applied the whip, Joseph offered the carrot. He smiled. "My dear ship's officer—officer?"

"First Officer Kurtz, Excellency."

Excellency! Joseph thought. This is wonderful! Aloud he imitated von Falkenbrecht in his most soothing diplomatic tones. "My dear First Officer Kurtz. I am on a special mission. For the state. You understand?"

The man, who didn't understand at all, nodded his head.

"Good. I am sure that if you tried, you might find a..." Did the man say cabin? Shouldn't he have said room? Bedroom? Was that where one slept on a ship? In a cabin? No, cabin sounded too small, too ordinary. "...Bed-chamber where I might sleep. You understand, a bed-chamber?" Joseph handed another of his gold guilden to the man.

First Officer Kurtz nodded his head vigorously. "Oh yes, sir. Please sir, may I offer my own little cabin? It is very small, but it is private."

First Officer Kurtz, never letting the gold coin out of his caressing fingers, closed the door behind him, leaving Joseph alone. He looked around him and thought it the most romantic, magical place in the world. The uniform, the title, the fantastic ride though the night, the encounter with the stable-boy, the mad dash for the boat, the easy control of First Officer Kurtz. Magic!

Once in his new bed, Joseph listened to the rhythmical pulse of the engines below him, the soft splashing cadence of the side wheels churning near his head. It was all very pleasant. What an adventure!

§7

JOSEPH'S FIRST IMPRESSION OF BREMEN WAS OF PANDEMONIUM. But as he paused in the doorway of the steamboat's covered dock, staring into the vast number of horses, the confusion of vehicles and people, the shouting, the running, the wagons and the carts, it became immediately apparent to him he was wrong. It wasn't chaos. It was order. The glorious and clamorous order of the city. Joseph was so struck by the city's electrifying presence that he could barely move away from the dock shed. His eyes next went to the horses. So many different kinds, he thought. Heavy draft horses—Schleswig and Rhineland. Foreign horses—the dappled gray Boulonnaise from France, and the gigantic Shires from England. Most of the horses seemed well cared for, others he was pained to see were hungry or suffering from fatigue. Then there were the vehicles—long, short, tall, some loaded with lumber, one with the largest load of hay he had ever seen, others heaped and stacked with all sizes of barrels and bales. Coaches, carriages, landaus, phaetons, buggies both two and four-wheel, char-a-bancs, horse-cars and red omnibuses on tracks laid in the cobblestone street, filled with people and drawn by teams of bored draught horses. Yes, he thought, boring work. Poor fellows. But it must be the only boring thing in this city. My God, the city!

The stream of pedestrian traffic flowing by Joseph suddenly cast out a bit of flotsam, a small man carrying a large bundle, who dashed against Joseph and nearly knocked him to the cobblestones. The porter who had carried Joseph's valise from the river steamer held him to keep him from falling over.

"Be careful, young sir. Here in the city you have to keep your eyes about you." Joseph estimated the porter was between forty and fifty. He wore a soft blue cap and smock of the same blue, with a brass badge showing the number seven on it. His rheumy eyes darted constantly about as if he expected to be attacked from any quarter, and the few teeth left in his mouth explained his sunken cheeks. The porter had put a leather strap around Joseph's valise and carried it on his back as if it weighed three times as much.

"Which ship you be on, sir?"

Joseph drew himself up and looked down at the man. "Baron," he said. "I am the Baron von Breitenstein. You may address me as Excellency or Herr Baron."

The man bobbed his head. "Which ship, Excellency, you be on?" There was a hint of mockery in his attitude.

"I haven't decided yet on a ship." Joseph looked around. The harbor was filled with vessels. To his right and left were a variety of docks, some covered by sheds, others with imposing buildings. Flags and signs appeared at every level: Bremen-Hamburg Line, Amsterdam Line, Southern Freight Line, London Direct, Africa Line, Scandinavian Freight Lines, Bremen Steamship Company, and in the distance he saw a tall building of gray stone, with a cupola, and below the cupola were the words for which he was searching: North German America Line. And a little farther off he saw a low brown building with the large sign: New World Shipping.

"There," Joseph pointed. "We are going there."

But getting there wasn't as easy as he thought. For one, the boots supplied him by the remorseful hussar were too small. Then there was the problem of the saber and the sabretache, both dangling from his left side at knee and calf height. They were appropriate accoutrements for the horseman, but not the pedestrian. Experienced hussars forced to proceed on foot acquired techniques to keep these implements from entangling themselves with each other and with the wearer's legs. Joseph, unfortunately, was ignorant of these skills.

First he tried walking on the outside of his feet, then on his toes, then on his heels; then he experimented with the pidgin toe walk and the splay foot, while at the same time tending to his errant sword and gyrating purse. All of this he did while attempting to retain the upright rigid dignity of an officer of the Royal Wittelsbach Hussars. The combined effort produced an astonishing display of lurching, rolling and stumbling. Adding to his intense discomfort was the day's unseasonable warmth. With his fur busby, his black wool uniform and fur-lined pelisse, Joseph's face dripped with sweat. His monocle kept slipping from his eye, and each time it did he just barely managed to catch and reinsert it. He could also feel his wool jacket dampen and chafe at the armpits. To his gratification people scurried out of his way, creating a constant path before him. In spite of his afflictions he exalted for a moment. As usual, von Falkenbrecht was right: behave like an aristocrat and people will defer. But it was when he turned to ask the porter a question about the proper steamship line that he saw the difference between the scene before him and of that behind him. Ahead of him, the street was normal: people going about their daily activities and paying proper respect to their betters. Behind him, those who had passed him with what he had assumed was proper deference had stopped to comment to each other on his progress. And they were laughing! People were laughing at him!

He was mortified. For a wild moment he wanted to draw his saber and charge them. If only he had Thunder. No, his new identity was all he had. Ignoring the pain in his feet, placing his left hand on his sword hilt, he turned and continued on his way as if he were on parade. By controlling the sword, he stopped some of the confusion around his legs with the sabretache. By ignoring the pain in his feet, he walked as von Falkenbrecht had taught him. People no longer cleared a path as before, but he also could hear no laughter behind him.

At the offices of the North German America Line, a middle-aged man in a black suit hurried across an oriental carpet and greeted him with a small bow. "Good morning, Herr Lieutenant. How may I assist you?"

"Von Ritter," Joseph snapped. "Baron von Breitenstein. I require...," he searched for the correct word. What was it First Officer Kurtz had said? "...Passage to America."

"If you will come this way, Herr Baron." The man led Joseph across the carpet to his desk which, like the wainscoting of the room, was made of fine dark oak. Joseph took comfort in the quiet, soft interior of the room. He had never been in an office before and was pleased to find the place a proper setting for a gentleman. The clerk extracted a printed form from a drawer and looked expectantly at Joseph.

"And when does the Herr Baron choose to sail?"

"Oh, today."

The clerk repressed his small surprise. "Ah yes, Herr Baron, that would be convenient. However, our next sailing of the *North Sea* will depart for New York City in America on the twenty-seventh of this month. That is three days from now."

Joseph was disappointed and confused. What would he do now? Where would he go for three days? Where would he sleep? "I need to go today," he said. "Today. I must go today. I am on urgent business."

"I am so sorry, Herr Baron," said the clerk. "Our deepest apologies. The *North Sea* departs in three days, and even then it is with profound regret that I must inform you she is completely engaged. There isn't even a second-class berth available."

"You mean you have no room?"

"Please forgive us, Herr Baron, but there isn't a single accommodation remaining on the *North Sea*. The ship has a full complement of passengers."

"Don't you have more ships?"

"Oh yes, sir. There is the *South Sea*, and the line is building a third ship to be launched next year. The *South Sea* is at this very moment on her way to Brazil. In thirty days the *North Sea* will return from New York and shall go again to New York ten days after arrival. Sir, ours are the swiftest and most luxurious ships in the transatlantic service. Passage to New York is frequently accomplished in ten days. The company would be pleased to reserve passage for you on the next sailing of the *North Sea*. There are still a few of the finer staterooms available."

"But I have to go today."

"Forgive me, Herr Baron, but might I suggest you inquire at some of the other companies. Of course, none are as swift or as luxurious as our steamships, but there are continual sailings to America. I believe that New World Lines has a ship that sails this very evening, sir. However, if the Herr Baron will allow me to point out, that ship is completely unsuitable."

"Thank you. Where is this New World Lines?"

"If the Herr Baron will turn left when he exits these premises, he will see their dock. It has a rather large signboard."

"Oh yes. I saw it. I remember. Thank you. Good-bye." Joseph rose, and the clerk bowed as he walked out of the office.

The porter scrambled to his feet as Joseph appeared. "Shall I take the bag inside, Herr Baron?" A dirty little grin twitched about his mouth.

"No. I have decided to sail with the New World Line."

The man looked at Joseph with unconcealed glee, "New World is it? Is the Herr Baron sure he wants New World?"

"Of course I am. Pick up the valise and come along."

The old man hauled the bag to his back and trotted along behind Joseph. "Does the Herr Baron know New World is just sail ships?"

Joseph didn't, nor could he imagine what difference it made. "Of course I do."

The old man emitted a wheezing laugh. Joseph turned, ready to knock him to the ground.

"Are you laughing at me?"

"Oh no, sir. I always laugh. My wife, Frau Genz, says I am the most cheerful man she ever met. No sir, I would never laugh at an officer and a baron. Never in this life, sir." Joseph knew the man was lying, but he didn't know how to react.

As he turned and started toward the shipping company, he saw an exquisite English thoroughbred being unloaded from a steamship on the pier next to him. A knot of hussars in yellow uniforms supervised the unloading of the horse. Yellow uniforms? Joseph searched his memory. He had studied all of von Falkenbrecht's military books. The only all-yellow uniforms were the Neapolitan Hussar Guards. But they were in Italy. Then he became afraid. What if they saw him? What if they questioned him? Several looked in his direction. He pretended not to have noticed and hurried on.

New World Lines was located in a low, brown building with a rickety arched wooden facade. Behind the building an open pier reached out alongside a nearly foul, three-masted semi-clipper ship. She had been converted from a general cargo ship when the immigrant trade blossomed in the 1840s. The ship carried 244 passengers on a voyage that took from six to nine weeks, depending on the wind and sea conditions. In return for forty dollars, each of the passengers was entitled to a bare wooden bunk and one meal a day. Every voyage was sold out.

The porter cleared a path through a crowd of peasants and foreigners blocking the door to the shipping office. Joseph instantly picked out the Jews with their hats and beards. "Fools!" he thought.

Inside was a huge, gloomy, crowded hall. The dim light filtered through filthy windows so that the somber-clad crowd merged with the shadowed brown interior. They all seemed to be speaking at once. The porter shouted, "Make way for the officer!" and with that he opened a path through the murky mass. As Joseph approached the counter the room fell silent. They were afraid of him. Good, he thought. Fear is respect.

The older of the two clerks behind the counter, a man with sparse blond hair, spectacles, and a gray coat, respectfully nodded his head to Joseph. "Yes, Herr Officer. Can we be of service?"

Joseph cleared his throat. "I require passage to New York, in America."

A murmur rose in the hall and died down when the clerk spoke. He couldn't hide the look of astonishment on his face. "Does the Herr Officer…"

Joseph interrupted him. There was something about the man's face that annoyed him. "Herr Baron."

"Forgive me, Herr Baron. Does the baron know what kind of shipping line this is?"

"You take passengers to America?"

"Yes, Excellency."

In a move he had often rehearsed in his mind, Joseph snapped a gold coin on the counter. "I require the best bedroom on the ship."

"Excellency, we have no bedrooms."

"Well, whatever you have. Give me the best." Someone in the crowd sniggered. Joseph turned in a fury. The room fell silent. He returned to the clerk. "What do you have for me?"

"Only what we have for them." The clerk nodded at the crowd. "Which I am sure is not correct for the Herr Baron. Perhaps the Herr Baron meant to go to the North German America Line."

Joseph knew he had done something wrong but he couldn't imagine what. He blushed. "You have room on this passage tonight?"

"Yes, Excellency, we are selling the last few spaces now. But..."

Joseph roared at him. "I'll take whatever you have!"

The clerk sighed, took the gold coin, gave him a few silver coins in change, and handed him a piece of paper with a number and a letter on it.

"What is this?" Joseph asked.

"A ticket, sir. The letter is the deck. This is the letter C, for C Deck, which is at the very bottom of the ship. The number 225 is for your bunk."

"Bunk?" Joseph was feeling sweaty again. "What is a bunk?"

The old clerk glanced at his compatriot and sighed more deeply. "A bunk, Herr Baron, is a wooden bed."

"You are selling me a bed? Not a bed in a room?"

"That is correct, sir. We have no private cabins on this ship. We only have beds. They are wood. Like wooden shelves. You must supply your own bedding. All the beds are together in a large room."

"No rooms?"

Joseph's attempted shout emerged as a squeak. The hall exploded in riotous laughter. There was an authoritative shout from the front entrance. "Silence! Silence, you scum!"

Joseph looked up to see a splash of bright yellow and shimmering silver against the gloomy mass. Three of the yellow hussars glowered at the crowd. The one in front showed the silver sleeve braid of a major. He had a ferocious mustache and wore his brown hair in the five braids of the old Napoleonic hussar style. The yellow major shouted again. "You dare to laugh at an officer of the Royal Wittelsbach Hussars?"

The room fell silent.

The three officers strode to Joseph, who automatically saluted. The major saluted back and nodded toward the porter. "That your kit, lieutenant?"

"Yes, sir." Joseph replied.

The major back-handed the porter, knocking him to the floor. "You. Get up and bring the lieutenant's luggage." He turned to Joseph. "Come with me, lieutenant."

Joseph followed the officers, a black spot at the center of a martial sunburst. Ignoring the pain in his feet, he matched the rapid gait set by the yellow hussars and mimicked how they managed their sabers and sabretaches. When they reached the other three yellow hussars, who were attending the beautiful chestnut thoroughbred and six other horses, they halted. The major ordered the porter to put Joseph's bag on the dock and leave. The old man asked for his pay.

"Pay?" the major shouted. "You laugh at an officer of the Royal Wittelsbach Hussars and you expect pay? Here's your pay!" He kicked the porter. "Swine! Pigdog! Out!"

The old man scurried to a safe distance and then turned to look directly at Joseph. "Jew!" he shouted. The porter turned and ran away.

How had the porter known? A horse is a horse. Would the yellow hussars know? Would they beat him before taking him to the authorities? Joseph resolved they would have to kill him first. He moved his right hand to his saber.

The yellow hussars broke into raucous laughter and the major slapped Joseph on the shoulder. "It isn't necessary to kill him, lieutenant. We don't kill them so quickly any more. Not after '48. Besides, if we killed every wharf rat who cursed us we'd be knee-deep in blood. And if we spent all our time disciplining them, when would we have time for fun?" Then he became serious. "Now, boy, what were you doing in that ridiculous place?"

The danger past, Joseph spoke as von Ritter. "I must get to America. The one over there," he pointed to the *North Sea* at her dock three docks away, "is all full."

"And why is an officer of the Royal Wittelsbach in such a rush to get to America?"

"I am Franz Joseph von Ritter Baron von Breitenstein," Joseph said. "My uncle, General Count von Falkenbrecht, has sent me on a mission of the highest importance." He studied the major for a brief moment. The man appeared to be his father's age, and he seemed as much a hussar as von Falkenbrecht. Joseph chose his course and proceeded. "It is a question of the honor of the Royal Wittelsbach."

"A question of honor?" The major was impressed. "You are so good with a saber?"

Trembling, Joseph nodded.

The major studied him for a moment. Then clicking his heels, he saluted. "Von Wolfheim," he said. "Major, Neapolitan Hussar Guards. Personal Equerry to His Majesty Ferdinand II of the two Sicilies. These are Lieutenants Prince Salina and Count Nanerini." Both officers clicked their heels and saluted. They each said something to Joseph in Italian, which he didn't understand.

Joseph returned the salutes and said, "An honor," to each.

"Now what is this horseshit that you can't get on the *North Sea?*" von Wolfheim asked.

"They told me they're full."

"Horseshit! Come with me." He strode off, followed by the two yellow-clad lieutenants. Joseph hurried to keep up. As they burst into the offices of the North German America Line, the clerk shot to his feet and raced to greet them.

"Von Wolfheim. Equerry to His Majesty King Ferdinand II," von Wolfheim said. He indicated Joseph. "Baron von Ritter is on a personal mission for His Majesty King Maxmilian II of Bavaria. It is imperative that he sail on the *North Sea.* You will arrange it immediately."

The clerk quickly excused himself and disappeared through a door Joseph hadn't noticed earlier. A moment later he reemerged, followed by a portly gentleman in a long black coat and impeccably white shirt with a gray striped cravat and pince-nez glasses. He bowed to the company.

"Gentlemen," he said. "I am Ingo von Biersdorf, director of this line. Herr Schmitt has informed me of your requirements. It is the custom of this line to reserve one suite of staterooms until the last moment before sailing in the event that an illustrious personage should require it. We shall be happy to place it at your disposal. Would you please come into my office?"

Joseph and von Wolfheim followed the man to the next room. The two Neapolitan lieutenants remained behind.

The most prominent feature of the room was a large window overlooking the busy harbor. Von Biersdorf walked to a huge oak sideboard near the window and lifted a cut crystal decanter. "Schnapps?"

Von Wolfheim nodded, and von Biersdorf filled two glasses which he brought to the two officers.

"Thank you, but I do not drink," Joseph said.

Von Wolfheim was astounded. "Don't drink? Royal Wittelsbach, and don't drink?" He reached out and took the glass intended for Joseph and knocked it back as quickly as he had the first.

Von Biersdorf sat at his desk and produced a printed form. He looked up. "If the baron would be so kind as to give me his full name."

Joseph did so.

Von Wolfheim added, "The baron is the nephew of Count von Falkenbrecht, which makes him a cousin to the king of Bavaria."

Von Biersdorf said, "We are honored, Excellency," and put his pen to the paper. "You shall occupy the suite second in size to the royal suite, which has been taken by the prince of Meklenburg and his family. Your suite consists of a sitting room and a bedroom, done in the latest fashion." He sighed with pride. "The cost for these accommodation is twelve hundred and fifty marks. How would Your Excellency care to pay?"

"I have gold," Joseph said. "Guilden."

Von Biersdorf made a quick calculation. "That would be twenty-five guilden, Herr Baron."

"They are in my bag, which I am afraid is back with your corporals," Joseph said to von Wolfheim, as if this were insignificant. Von Wolfheim walked to the door and murmured something to one of the lieutenants, who left. While he was gone, von Wolfheim regaled them with his recent adventures in England, including how he lost a horse race he was sure he would win. Unfortunately, on his advice, his king had purchased the losing horse before the race and he was now taking the beast back to Italy.

The lieutenant soon returned with one of the corporals carrying Joseph's valise. Joseph carefully opened it, trying not reveal his peasant wardrobe, and extracted his money belt. He then counted out the twenty-five coins for von Biersdorf and threw an uncounted handful into his sabretache. Von Wolfheim's eyes followed the shiny metal as it went from belt to sabretache and rested on the innocent boy who possessed it.

When their business was done they walked outside. "Three days," von Wolfheim said. "You have a place to stay?"

"No, sir."

"Good. You stay with us."

"Thank you, sir, but…"

"Horseshit! You are my guest. It is the least an officer can do for a comrade of his old regiment."

Joseph's uneasiness intensified. "You were with the Royal Wittelsbach, sir?"

"Fritz. You must call me Fritz. Yes. We are comrades, although I expect my departure was taken before you were born. Von Falkenbrecht and I campaigned together. I had a brilliant future until an unfortunate incident with a young lady resulted in my taking up residence in Italy. And you? How long have you been a hussar?"

"One year," Joseph lied quickly. Von Wolfheim translated their conversation for the two Italian lieutenants.

At the dock, where the corporals were waiting with their horses, Joseph walked over to the thoroughbred and examined him. While he was doing so he became aware that the others had stopped talking and were watching him. When Joseph was through, the animal had forgotten its terror of the voyage.

"This is the horse that lost the race in England?"

Von Wolfheim nodded.

"A wonderful horse must have beaten this one."

"Not such a good horse. I was sure we would win."

"This is an exceptional animal."

Von Wolfheim was studying him again. "Really?" he asked. "Interesting. Good. First we take the horse to Castle Wehdel. You work him. You tell me how fast you think he is, and we will win a fortune from Wehdel." He turned to the others and spoke in Italian. One of the corporals tied Joseph's suitcase to a saddle and von Wolfheim tapped it, saying something in Italian. Laughter followed, and the six hussars mounted their horses. Von Wolfheim smiled to Joseph. "You may ride the English horse," he said. "I am sorry we have no extra saddle but we didn't anticipate a guest."

Joseph smiled back, grasped the mane of the thoroughbred, and with a bound was on his back. And on horseback, be it Bremen or the North Pole, Joseph knew he was home. They rode through the doors and through the crowds in the vast station and Joseph immediately knew, as they were the only people inside the huge room on horseback, that this was not the common practice. Von Wolfheim rode as if the place were empty, and people scurried out of his way. A uniformed guard opened a barrier and they walked the horses onto an empty platform next to which was a wondrous conveyance. Joseph stared at the engine, tender, parlor and stable cars, and guessed this vehicle was meant only for them. The whole train was painted pale blue with pink decorative floral motifs in the paneling on the sides of the cars. All bore shields with the owner's coat of arms.

When they dismounted, the corporals led the horses up a ramp into the stable car. Joseph followed quietly. He was astonished to find carpet in the aisles in front of the twelve immaculate stalls. It smelled sweet and clean. One day, he silently vowed, I shall have such a train.

When Joseph walked into the parlor car, von Wolfheim was seated at an inlaid card table, a deck in his hands. He looked up at Joseph. "Piquet? You do play cards?"

§8

"**B**EGINNER'S LUCK," SAID PRINCE SALINA TO COUNT NANERINI. "Yes, luck," replied the count. "Look at him. He draws the best cards. Mother of mine! Another trick. How much has he won?"

"Thousands. Everything Fritz has, and then some."

The train, after an hour and a half journey, came to a halt at the village of Wehdel. Joseph was both proud and embarrassed: proud of his newly discovered prowess with cards, embarrassed he had won so much from his new friend.

They stepped down from the train and von Wolfheim led Joseph to the shade of an oak tree while the men unloaded the horses. "Now," he said to Joseph. "I know about you and cards—deceptive innocence, lethal technique. Tell me about you and horses."

"What do you want to know?"

"Are you as good as I suspect you are?"

"I'm very good."

A trace of amusement flickered over von Wolfheim's face. "That we shall see," he said. He signaled and a corporal ran up. "Corporal Shultz, we are going to have a mounted saber drill. Go to the village. Get melons, and poles." Von Wolfheim pointed to a recently mown field. "Set up a course there. Then go to the inn. Beer and sausage for the villagers. Lieutenant von Ritter is buying." He turned to Joseph. "Come. We shall see how good you are. You don't mind buying the village a drink or two do you?" Von Wolfheim turned and strode toward the horses.

Joseph trotted along beside him. "No. Not at all."

"I propose a contest. We'll run the traditional course. One melon each for the cutting blow, one for the slash, and one for the thrust and carry off. The first to miss loses. If neither of us misses, the first one across the finish wins. Fair enough?"

"Yes, but..."

"But? Have you not told me you are very good?"

"I am. I wish to propose something to make it more fun. Can we agree to take two cuts at the slash melon, making the second cut before the melon hits the ground?"

"Really? Why not two cuts to produce a clean slice from the center of the melon? Say not more than two inches thick?"

"You mean, we must cut a slice from the center before the melon falls from the pole?"

"Exactly."

"That will be fun."

"To make it interesting, I suggest we wager on it."

Joseph's face fell. "But I don't want you to lose any more money to me."

Von Wolfheim's humor tightened slightly. "How much did I lose to you?"

Joseph shook his head. "I'm not sure. A lot. I can count it." He started to reach for his sabretache.

"Not necessary. Somewhere around four thousand. I suggest we double it. Winner take all."

Joseph's face darkened. "But then you would owe me eight thousand...."

"Will you stop that!" Von Wolfheim spoke sharply. "My God, how were you brought up? Didn't anyone teach you about modesty? Humility? The appearance of humility? You think you are so good? Good! Let's find out. You ride the English horse."

"But Fritz. That wouldn't be fair. He is by far the best horse."

"How can you tell?"

"Look at him. The balance between that long neck and the power in the rump. The depth of his girth. What huge lungs and heart he must have. And those sloping shoulders! He is all power and balance and grace. His legs—so slender with so much bone. And his muscles, like liquid. Look how they flow under the skin.

Someone has carefully exercised that horse. Just look at that clean muscle development! Did you ever see such perfect hooves? Even on that little walk through the city I could feel the flex of each joint. And I can tell he has the will to win. Of the seven horses, he's the fastest. That's a horse with which you can do anything. He may even be as good as Thunder."

"Thunder?"

"My horse."

"Ah. And you think this English horse is the best horse, do you?"

"He is."

Von Wolfheim unexpectedly found himself tangled in a web of feelings. He wanted his money back, but he also felt a need to protect the boy. "Let me tell you about that horse," he said. "He is a racehorse. He has been bred and trained to do only one thing— to steeplechase. He knows nothing about cavalry. No saber has ever been swung over his head or past his eye. He has never experienced a charge. I tell you this to offer you an opportunity to choose another of the horses."

"Thank you. That's good to know. But I'll ride him. What do they call him? Anaximenes?"

Von Wolfheim sighed. "Yes, Anaximenes."

"What does it mean?"

"My God, boy, didn't you have any education? Anaximenes was the pupil to Anaximander. Do we have a wager?"

"We do." Joseph smiled at his friend. How wonderful all this was! He was really a hussar about to engage in a contest with a seasoned veteran. And with a wager for more money than he had ever heard of! In the distance he saw the corporals setting up the two rows of staves and placing melons on them, while the villagers were lining the edge of the field.

As they strode to their mounts Joseph asked, "Fritz, who owns that train?"

"Didn't you see the Bourbon crest? It belongs to my king. Ferdinand of the two Sicilies. Why?"

"Can anyone own such a thing, or is it only for kings?"

Von Wolfheim stopped and glanced at Joseph in amused astonishment. "You want a private train?"

Joseph was embarrassed. "Of course not, I was just asking."

"Good. Get on your horse." The impudence of this boy! His own train! Did he think he was Napoleon?

While they were walking their horses to the field, Joseph absorbed the mood of his mount. He could feel the soft ground beneath his horse's hooves. He signaled the animal that all was well and would continue to be so. Joseph then drew his saber and showed it to the horse, first to one eye then the other. Then in answer to a slight shift in Joseph's posture and an almost invisible movement of his fingers on the reins, Anaximenes changed the rhythm and spring of his walk. To the hussars observing this, the horse suddenly seemed taller, more fluid, as if its hooves hardly touched the ground.

The horsemen came to a halt thirty yards from the two lines of posts topped with melons the size of a human head. Von Wolfheim turned to Joseph, "When Salina drops his glove we go. Remember, full gallop. First across the line. One miss and it's a forfeit. Ready?"

Joseph turned and smiled. "Ready," he said. But turning to von Wolfheim was a mistake, for in that instant the glove was dropped and von Wolfheim shot away. An instant later Joseph's horse, too, was in a full gallop. And an instant after that he raced by von Wolfheim.

The first melon was the cut; Joseph's saber split it in equal halves. In the next bound of his horse he approached the second melon. A forward slash took its top away and as it started to topple from the pole, a backward slash cut a two-inch slice from the remaining section. The final melon was easy, merely a thrust with the tip of his saber. He speared it, allowing the point of his saber to penetrate only to its center, and carried it aloft as he brought the big horse into a trot and made a circuit of the field. It was only then that he heard the cheering from the villagers and the hussars. Joseph thought it the greatest moment of his life.

Von Wolfheim trotted over. On the tip of his saber he held the dripping slice of melon that Joseph had carved. "I have never seen this done before."

Joseph was perplexed. "But...but it was you who suggested it. You said a two-inch slice."

"I wanted to see if you were as good as you seemed."

"But you lost another four thousand."

"If you can do it again, I will get it back. Can you do it again?"

"Yes."

"And if I say a one-inch slice?"

"I think so."

The Good American

"Show me."

For the next hour, Joseph demonstrated h
inch slices and then, when requested, three-i
melon into quarters before it hit the groun
while jumping the thoroughbred over barr
over one side of his horse so as not to be se
also spent nearly a thousand of his winnings on beer and
for the villagers.

Count Wehdel stood at the window of his card room and watched the hussars canter up the long poplar-lined drive to his Gothic castle, a giant crenelated structure with octagonal towers at all four corners.

A sporting gentleman, the count was wearing the latest English fashion of mismatched jacket and trousers. Heavily anointed with macassar oil, his yellow hair was parted in the middle and fell on either side precisely to the tips of his earlobes. The count affected a gold rimmed monocle which he felt enhanced the ordinary blue of his small, greedy eyes.

A servant in bottle-green velvet livery met the hussars at the door and handed their busbies, pelisses, and swords to two servants dressed in duller green broad cloth. This castle, Joseph quickly realized, was not the home of a soldier: no game trophies, no battle flags, no armor or weapons graced the pink and white marble walls. The four hussars were led from the great entrance hall and its sand-colored marble staircase into the game room decorated with paintings of horses. All were thoroughbreds, and all were either posing in stiff positions with equally stiff personages holding their reins, or frozen in actual races.

Von Wolfheim introduced Joseph to Count Wehdel. But when the count said, "Dear Baron von Breitenstein, welcome," Joseph almost laughed. The count's voice was as high as a woman's and squeaked and then changed to sing-song as he greeted Lieutenants Salina and Nanerini in Italian. Joseph wondered how it was that everybody spoke Italian.

A servant, carrying a heavy silver tray holding stemmed glasses edged with gold and filled with gently bubbling champagne, entered the room.

"Gentlemen, a welcoming libation," the count said.

...eph smiled politely and raised a hand, "Thank you so much, I do not drink spirituous liquors."

The count removed his monocle and stared openly at the young hussar. Then he turned to von Wolfheim, "He doesn't drink?"

"Sad but true."

"Unbelievable!"

Von Wolfheim looked gravely at the count and said in English, "Very young. Not yet a man of the world. Perhaps it has fallen to us to aid in his education." He repeated this in Italian for Salina and Nanerini.

The count smiled in anticipation. He turned to Joseph and asked, "My dear baron, do you speak Italian?"

Joseph smiled and shook his head. "Only German, I am sorry to say."

"What, not even French?" the count asked.

Again Joseph shook his head. "Just German."

"No Latin or Greek?"

Joseph, embarrassed, wanted to mention his fluency in Hebrew and Yiddish, but decided against it. He smiled and shrugged. "Just German."

"Wherever was this boy educated?"

"We have him fresh from his country estate," von Wolfheim said. "He's the nephew of von Falkenbrecht."

"Really? How charming!" The count smiled at Joseph, who noticed for the first time that the man's teeth were all separated by small spaces, like a baby's. "I have had the honor of the great soldier's presence in this house. And he is well?"

"Quite well."

"Excellent!" With a quick, meaningful glance at von Wolfheim, the count indicated the as-yet-untouched glasses on the tray. "My dear Baron von Breitenstein. It appears we have a dilemma of the most delicate nature. For five centuries it has been the tradition at Schloss Wehdel that all guests upon arrival and departure must drink a toast to the angel Salbabiel, guardian of love and potency for the Wehdels. Should any guest refuse, the countesses of Wehdel will become barren and the house of Wehdel shall disappear. If your vow of temperance is religious or philosophic, my family is doomed, but if it is for any other reason, please enlighten us so that we may plead that you save us from extinction."

Were they mocking him? He looked at von Wolfheim, hoping his new friend would rescue him. But it was not to be.

"Forgive me," Joseph said, "but wine makes me ill. I fear that should I imbibe, I shall become instantly…" Should he say sick? Sick seemed such a low word for such elegant company. "…Ill." Joseph felt a moment of reprieve and waited to be excused. But the count, his face unreadable beyond his curiosity, persisted.

"How ill? What symptoms do you show?"

"I am terribly afraid that with the first sip I shall instantly vomit."

Von Wolfheim turned his face away so as not to allow Joseph to see his grin and made a quick, quiet translation for the two Italian officers, who saw no reason to mask their amusement.

Count Wehdel pretended to be shocked. "And for that inconvenience you would doom me to no heir? Come, come sir. Surely you would not deny me children?" He turned to the servant standing by the door. "Bring a large champagne bucket. No ice. Empty." The servant hurried away.

Joseph was racked with uncertainty. How awful to vomit in front of all these fine people. But what else could he do? It would be wrong to violate a five hundred-year-old custom. But if he drank he would vomit. How could he vomit in so fine a room? "Perhaps if I might enjoy my champagne," his voice cracked, "outside?"

"Alas, dear baron, the tradition is that the toast must be made inside the house. In the very room where one is first greeted."

The servant returned with a large silver champagne bucket; two more servants promptly followed, one with a silver basin filled with water, and the other holding a white towel with an embroidered crest. The count then took a glass of champagne from the tray, and the others followed, all displaying the most solemn of expressions. Joseph stared at the one remaining glass and attempted to summon his courage with a silent invocation of Spinoza. But Spinoza failed him. Joseph was unable to distinguish what was true in this situation and what was false. He took the glass.

Count Wehdel raised his glass. "Salbabiel!" he said, and drained the liquid. The others followed suit. Joseph looked at them and, without further thought, emptied his as well. Nausea seized him immediately, and the wine returned almost as fast as it had gone down his throat. Joseph availed himself of the empty silver bucket and washed his face from the silver basin, then turned to the others.

The Italians were grinning. Von Wolfheim also smiled and, clicking his heels, saluted with his refilled glass.

"The tradition is that one drinks a toast for each person present in the room," the count said gently. Joseph threw up after each of the next three glasses, but managed to keep the fourth down. When he opened his eyes he saw Prince Salina hand a sum of money to Count Nanerini, and heard Wehdel say to von Wolfheim, "By George sir, that's a hundred I owe you."

They had been betting on him! Joseph turned to von Wolfheim, his face cold more from anger than the chill perspiration from his recent exertions.

"Thank you for your kindness. I am immediately returning to Bremen."

"Oh dear, you are angry," the count said. "We've offended you. Accept my deepest apologies if we have given offense and permit me to explain."

Joseph nodded, trying not to look confused.

"You see, dear baron, in this house it is also the custom to bet on anything involving chance. When we saw your unfortunate state it occurred to me that you could be cured of your illness if only you were given the opportunity to practice self-control. And look what happened! I was correct. It is a memorable occasion. You no longer have to exist in this sad world without the comfort of the nectar of the Gods. I am honored that whenever in the future you raise a glass, you will remember poor old Count Wehdel and his Perrier-Jouët with some affection."

"You were betting on my vomit!" Joseph said.

The count shrugged and smiled. "In this house the wager is king. I hope you have no similar aversion to gaming?"

"Aversion?" said von Wolfheim. "The boy has taken eight thousand from me just on the journey here.

The count raised his pale eyebrows in appreciation. "Eight thousand? In what games?"

"Piquet on the train—beware of the boy and cards. And then an equestrian contest. A form of gaming which you have never witnessed and which you would do well to forgo while von Ritter is here. Unless, of course, you wish to risk everything."

"And what is this equestrian risk?"

"It's too late in the day to show you. I suggest we spend the evening at cards and in the morning you'll pit your finest horseman against von Ritter, and I promise you the boy will empty your treasury."

The count studied Joseph for only a brief moment before turning to the card table. "Well then, dear baron, since we shall have to wait till the morning to test your horsemanship, let us see if you stand up to your reputation at cards. Piquet, did you say?"

Von Wolfheim nodded. "Piquet. Whatever stakes you choose. I propose a side wager on each hand."

"You are very sure of yourself, aren't you?"

Von Wolfheim smiled mirthlessly. "You play against the boy for whatever amounts the two of you choose. But against me, after you look at your hand, you decide yes or no. A thousand a hand. Agreed?"

"Agreed. I hope you have the key to your king's treasury." He sat and indicated the chair opposite him to Joseph.

Joseph felt no fear. Had he not just played piquet for the first time in his life and won every hand? Did he not have the same natural gift for gambling as he did for horses? A God-given talent? He laughed at himself. There was no God. That he also found funny. All those fools who believed in God and there wasn't any. He found he was feeling quite comfortable in this room with these grand *goyim,* his new people.

As Joseph sat down a servant placed a fresh glass of champagne at his side. He took it and drained it without a breath. The servant with the empty bucket started toward him, but Joseph waved him off. Then, like the others, Joseph waited a moment to see what his stomach would decide. When it did not rebel he giggled and held out his empty glass for a refill. The others laughed with him. To Joseph's amazement, the count was right. He could now drink without vomiting.

He drained the glass and again held it out.

"May I have another?"

§9

WATER. IF HE COULD JUST GET SOME WATER HE MIGHT NOT DIE. His tongue, hard and thick, filled all the space in his mouth and stuck to its roof. But even greater than his thirst was his need to breathe; only a small bit of air could pass his swollen tongue. When he moved his head, a sharp pain seared the space behind his eyes and dropped into the back of his jaw. When he moved his limbs, his muscles hurt and his joints ached.

Joseph knew he was dying. A disease had overtaken him in the night and now he would never be a marshal of America. He would never again know the joy of riding great horses. He would never see his parents again. The door of the room crashed open.

"What!" von Wolfheim shouted. "Still in bed?"

Joseph squeezed his eyes closed.

"I am dying," he said, his voice raspy and hoarse.

"No, you are not dying," von Wolfheim said. "It isn't that easy. My congratulations, von Ritter. You are suffering your first hangover." He crossed to a nightstand, poured a large glass of water and brought it to Joseph.

Joseph carefully maneuvered his legs over the side of the bed and sat up. Von Wolfheim put the glass in Joseph's quivering hands. "Can you hold this?"

"Yes," Joseph whispered. He locked both hands over the glass and slowly brought it to his parched lips. Von Wolfheim returned to the nightstand and soaked a towel in water.

Joseph sipped. His tongue slowly resumed its former shape, size and texture, and with each trickle of water a measurable degree of life returned. When Joseph drained the glass, von Wolfheim handed him the wet towel.

"Put your face in that for a moment."

Joseph obeyed and the cool of the wet cloth transferred to his forehead and cheeks.

"Good. Now on your feet. We have a busy day. You must win back all our money." He moved to the wall and pulled on a tasseled silk ribbon. After knocking softly a servant entered, carrying Joseph's sponged and pressed uniform.

Not since Joseph was a baby had anyone ever dressed him. He blushed and fumbled, but at last submitted.

"Your foot, Herr Baron," the servant murmured.

Joseph extended a naked foot to be encased in a stocking. While submitting to the dressing he examined the room. Larger than any of those in his own home, it was small by comparison with the rest of the castle. The big four-poster bed hung with dark brocade dominated the room, and the walls were covered with equally dark tapestries—browns, tans and wine reds, all faded into a dusty monochrome. It depressed him.

"Your right arm please, Herr Baron."

"Raw," Count Wehdel said as a servant cracked open an egg and dropped its contents into a silver goblet. "Add two large spoons of cayenne pepper. Stir four times," continued the count. "Now, just a pinch of gunpowder." The servant's white-gloved hand reached into a jeweled box and, with blackened index finger and thumb, withdrew a pinch of powder. "Let it float on top like that." He touched it with a burning taper, and it burst into a small puff of flame and smoke. "Excellent." He turned to Joseph, "Now, dear baron, you must drain the goblet all at once and your indisposition shall immediately disappear."

Joseph took the goblet with apprehension. Could people drink gunpowder? What was cayenne pepper? Was it as spicy as regular pepper? Nothing could be worse than the pounding in his head. If this concoction would cure it—and why would they all lie to him?—then down his throat it would go. And it did. And they were almost right.

Next, von Wolfheim had Joseph drink a cup of steaming coffee and then the count insisted he eat a proper breakfast: two English kippers, six scrambled eggs, four fat country sausages with strawberry preserves, and two thick slices of crusty black bread with sour cream and honey. Joseph ate everything heaped on his plate and discovered that, while he was not cured of his aches and dizziness, he had added serious gastric discomfort to his misery.

The conversation over breakfast took place in German, English and Italian, leaping about in language and subject matter so swiftly that Joseph could comprehend only the bits and pieces pertaining to horses.

Count Wehdel turned to him. "Really? Von Wolfheim says you think Anaximenes is an unbeatable horse?"

It made Joseph feel slightly better to think of horses. "He is one of the best horses I have ever ridden."

"Unbeatable?"

"I cannot imagine a faster horse."

"What if I told you that the horse that beat him at Ascot is right here in my stables?"

"That's a horse I would like to see."

"And so you shall. This instant." The count left the table and started for the door. "Come, come," he said.

Joseph rose a bit too fast for his head, and clutched the chair for support.

Von Wolfheim, looking worried, held his arm. "Get a hold of yourself boy," he said quietly. "You have to win our money back this morning."

"What money?"

Von Wolfheim sighed. "You don't remember?"

"What?"

"The card game."

"I remember."

"What?"

"The card game. Some of it. We started to play but..."

"You don't remember do you?"

"No. Did I lose?"

"We all did."

"A lot?"

"Fifty thousand for you. Twice that for me."

Joseph almost fell. Von Wolfheim quickly took hold of him. The count popped back through the doorway. "Everything all right?"

Von Wolfheim rolled his eyes and nodded toward Joseph. "Go ahead," he said. "We'll join you in a moment." He watched as the others continued on their way. To Joseph he said, "Fifty thousand is a lot of money. Can you cover it?"

A catastrophe, Joseph thought.

"Can you cover it?" von Wolfheim repeated.

If he couldn't, Joseph was sure he would spend the rest of his life in a dungeon. "Yes," he lied.

"Listen to me, boy. I am going to double it on a race between you on Anaximenes and the count's horse. Steeplechase. Are you too sick? Tell me now and we'll take our present losses. Can you ride?"

Joseph wasn't sure he could even walk the rest of the way to the stable. "Yes," he said.

"Well enough to win?"

"Yes."

Von Wolfheim grinned. "Good." He punched Joseph on the shoulder. "After that we'll really clean up with the saber and melons. We're going to have a glorious day!"

Joseph's spirits rose only slightly when he saw the stables. The first horse barn with stalls for fifty horses smelled as sweet and clean as the private stable-car on the train. A groom in green and tan livery led a black thoroughbred out to Joseph, who examined it. He then turned to the others. "This is the horse that beat Anaximenes at Ascot?"

"He is," answered the count, with pride. "And I purchased him on the spot. A king's ransom. I could have had either horse, but I chose the winner."

Perhaps it was the buzzing in his head that distracted him, but Joseph replied, "You chose the wrong horse."

The count's face clouded. Von Wolfheim translated for the two Italians, who laughed.

"You think so?" asked the count.

"Oh yes he does," said von Wolfheim. "And what the dear baron thinks is what I also think, about horses, of course."

"A match race, then?" the count asked. "Your king's Anaximenes against my Othello?"

"Yes. And the course?"

"My new cross-country course. Thirty jumps, each more difficult than the last. But I warn you, I have the advantage. My Othello has already raced over it two times and has established the record."

"In that case, shall we discuss odds?"

"Dear Major von Wolfheim, I leave that entirely to you."

"Well, then..."

The count politely interrupted, "Forgive me," he said. "When you figure the odds I do believe that you must consider the condition of your rider."

"Thank you, Count Wehdel. That's most generous of you. Shall we say two to one, our favor?"

"But you are too generous. I claim the host's privilege of suggesting four to one. Ah," said the count, "allow me to introduce my rider."

Joseph looked up to see a small man with a leathery face.

"This is Mr. Alfred Dobbs. Until he saw the wisdom of coming here to look after my establishment he rode for the prince of Wales." To Dobbs he said in English, "May I present Major von Wolfheim."

Von Wolfheim nodded, displeased. It was obvious that the little Englishman was experienced well beyond the boy.

"Prince Salina and Count Nanerini."

They each also formally nodded.

"And this," the count indicated Joseph, "is your competition, von Ritter—which means 'knight' in English. The Baron von Breitenstein." In German he said to Joseph, "May I present Mr. Alfred Dobbs, your competitor?"

The two horsemen studied each other. Joseph saw an older man with an ideal horseman's body. Something in the man's hard black eyes made Joseph uneasy. Dobbs in turn saw only a young sick boy. He quickly asked the count to place a considerable bet for him.

"You are that confident?" the count asked.

"Too confident," von Wolfheim said in English.

"Well, sir," Dobbs answered. "Confident enough so that if the major is interested in a side bet, I'll go another hundred that the lad doesn't even finish the race."

"Bravo!" said the count.

Von Wolfheim thought it wise not to interpret for Joseph. But Dobbs turned to Joseph and said in crudely accented German, "I just bet you wouldn't finish the race."

Joseph's face turned bright red. He started to say something but von Wolfheim, who saw Dobbs' remark for what it was, a ploy to erode Joseph's confidence, put a restraining hand on his shoulder.

"Von Ritter," von Wolfheim said, "in past cross-country races what was your most difficult jump?"

"I have never ridden a formal cross-country course."

Dobbs guffawed.

What an interesting morning it was going to be, von Wolfheim thought.

They set off on their tour.

Count Wehdel's cross-country course covered six miles. As he viewed it Joseph's heart sank. It was the most difficult course he had ever seen. The track was serpentine, crossing a stream in four different places, filled with abrupt hills both forested and open and slopes that appeared to be sheer cliff faces. A miscalculation here would result in injury or worse to both rider and animal.

The first jump was the only easy one: a double fence over a ditch, the rails four feet apart. The second was over a stone wall into a fake farm yard with two bounds needed to jump a high hedge to escape. The third was a wagon loaded with sacks and placed between a stone out-building and a tree. Joseph saw a choice there: either jump the wagon, which would be quick but dangerous; or permit a fleeting touch down at the center of the load and pushing off with the hind legs. By the eleventh obstacle the jumps seemed nearly impossible. One at the bottom of a steep slope through thick woods hardly gave enough distance for the horse to gain adequate speed to jump over the angled logs jutting over a water-filled ditch, and almost assuredly not enough distance to clear the ditch once over the logs. Even Thunder couldn't have made this jump.

Joseph tried to focus on what little he knew about Anaximenes. He tried to picture the horse's conformation and reviewed each of the animal's muscles. Could the horse be pushed beyond his limits? Did he lose the race at Ascot because of his lack of confidence? Did he spook at the unknown? Could Anaximenes be paced or would he exhaust himself going flat-out all the time? Joseph's thoughts were only of the horse. It didn't occur to him to fear for his own safety.

Jump twenty-six seemed lethal. It was a pole fence placed on the crest of a short rise at the end of a steep downhill grade, a grade just long enough so that if a horse gained too much speed before it jumped it would touch down too far on the precipitous slope on the fence's other side and then be unable to rise quickly enough to keep from crashing into the opposite embankment.

"This is the one. He'll fall here," said Dobbs.

Joseph turned a calm face to the older man. "If you are so confident," he said, "why not bet me? Can you cover five hundred pounds?" Joseph wondered what a pound was. Pounds of coins? Of silver bars?

It was so easy for the rich to bully the poor, Dobbs thought. He couldn't cover the bet, but he was sure of winning. It wouldn't be the first time he had bet with nonexistent money. Besides, he knew just exactly what he would do on this jump to ensure that the boy baron would lose. "Agreed, Herr Baron," he said. "We are on for five hundred pounds you don't survive this jump."

Why was the devil Englishman so confident about this jump in particular? Joseph wondered. With the others watching, Joseph walked his horse around it several times. He couldn't imagine why the jockey was so willing to bet so much. Where was the trick? Was it something Dobbs knew about Anaximenes? Did Anaximenes not have true stamina? Is that why he lost at Ascot?

Jump thirty consisted of two high stone walls joined at right angles in a deep marsh. Here if a horse were in top shape it could succeed only with the greatest difficulty. But to ask a horse at the end of a brutal race to make these jumps was asking the impossible. Yet Joseph had been told that the Englishman had set a record over this course.

Back at the stable Joseph requested an hour alone with Anaximenes. Dobbs laughed out loud at the request, but the ever-solicitous count made the arrangements and Joseph was taken to an indoor arena with Anaximenes. After the groom closed the door behind him, Joseph began with a minute examination of the horse's body. His aching head forced him to repeat many of his actions. As he worked he knew that he was missing something, but how could he not know something about horses? Panic numbed the edges of his consciousness. Why was Dobbs so sure he would fall at jump twenty-six?

To prevent his disquiet from spreading to Anaximenes, Joseph turned his back to the horse and tried to calm himself with deep breathing. He failed. Tendrils of terror reached down his arms to his fingers, and a chill film of moisture formed over his face. He was doomed.

Then a weight rested on his shoulder and he felt warm, moist breath on the side of his face. Anaximenes had placed his chin on Joseph's shoulder. Automatically, Joseph's hand came up and gently stroked the soft skin around the horse's nostrils, and as he did he felt his own breathing link to that of the animal. Anaximenes had not caught his panic. The opposite had happened. The horse had come to his rescue. "Good boy!" Joseph said softly. He turned and stroked Anaximenes, first on the face, then his neck, and then over his body, and soon the two were breathing in perfect unison.

Joseph harnessed Anaximenes to a lunge line and studied the horse as it walked, trotted and cantered in circles to the right and to the left. Next, Joseph performed a series of leg exercises, stretching Anaximenes' legs slowly, forward and back, up and down, giving the horse such deep relaxation that its penis dropped from its sheath. All the while Joseph worked with the horse, he spoke to him. He told Anaximenes about the race they were going to win, what each jump looked like, and how they would attack it. Joseph next mounted Anaximenes bare-back and walked him across the arena to the stadium jumps. "No big effort here, Anaximenes. We're just going to find out about each other."

At the end of the hour Joseph and Anaximenes joined the crowd. Von Wolfheim was pleased to see that the greenish tint had disappeared from Joseph's face.

Joseph turned to von Wolfheim. "That race at Ascot," he asked, "how did Anaximenes run?"

"He led the field from the start."

"And faded in the last quarter?"

"Precisely."

"And Othello? Dobbs was riding him?"

"Yes."

"Where did he run in the pack?"

"Third from the start, then at the halfway pole, second. Constantly moving up and falling back. Every time he came close to Anaximenes, Anaximenes put on an extra burst of speed to stay ahead. It was magnificent. But he paid the price in the last quarter."

It was as simple as that. Joseph put his arms around Anaximenes' neck and pressed his face to the horse. "Listen," he whispered to Anaximenes, "you must let me be the one who decides when we go full out. If you go too fast too soon you won't have the strength to win. Dobbs knows this. That's why he comes up behind you and falls back. He's trying to make you tired. Please, Anaximenes. Let me decide when to go."

Dobbs swung up on Othello, moving with a grace that made Joseph ache with longing. If only one day he could sit a horse that well. Not von Falkenbrecht, not even his father displayed such easy mastery. In that moment Joseph understood why Anaximenes, superior in every way to Othello, had lost to the black horse at Ascot. It was because Dobbs had been riding Othello.

Once astride Anaximenes, Joseph had to control his fear for the horse's sake. But the horse knew. Anaximenes smelled the excite—ment of the others. Then he was afraid. Something bad was about to happen. He looked around. Where could he run away from the danger? He stretched his neck, testing the bit. Could he pull the reins from his rider's hands? The rider's hands were gentle and they gave when he pulled, but there was a point where they stopped. The hands made a place where if he stayed, he felt safer. Now his ears rotated, searching for the bad thing. He monitored his rider, checking the feeling of safety. The rider was not afraid. But he didn't give up the plan for flight. When his rider brought him up beside Othello, Anaximenes discovered what was bad. It was the man on Othello. He saw his rider look at the bad man. The bad man showed his teeth to his rider and Anaximenes felt something. He felt it on his back and on his sides and in his mouth. His rider was afraid.

As before, Prince Salina elegantly raised a yellow glove and dropped it. Anaximenes saw the yellow thing flutter to the ground and bolted.

"Easy. Easy, Anaximenes." Joseph's voice was calm. He shifted his weight back slightly and eased the horse from his wild flight into a controlled gallop.

"Good boy." Joseph was no longer afraid. He could hear Dobbs riding close behind him. The little Englishman was just another rider on a beatable horse. Anaximenes felt this confidence in his rider and allowed himself to feel it too. When his rider asked him to slow he slowed. It was fun to lope at this easy pace. If he needed to go faster he could. Whenever he wanted to, or whenever his rider asked him to. He could run away from any danger. But then there was that sound that made his blood run cold, the sound of the bad man.

Joseph heard it too. In a low, harsh voice Dobbs was calling to Anaximenes. "Dogmeat," he was saying. "Dogmeat."

Joseph felt his horse panic beneath him. Taking his reins in one hand, Joseph used the other to caress Anaximenes' neck. "Good boy." He spoke in a low, reassuring voice, "Good boy. I'll take care of you."

Anaximenes found comfort in the sounds and slowed his pace. He felt better.

Othello shot by them. Dobbs cursed Anaximenes. Why had the fool horse fallen behind? The boy was smarter than he thought. No matter. The boy would fall at jump twenty-six.

Joseph was surprised at Dobbs' pace. Was Othello so strong that Dobbs could go so fast so soon? What was the Englishman trying to do? Joseph took Anaximenes over the first three jumps easily, and as he did he observed how Othello jumped ahead of him—a certain fault of rhythm appeared in Othello's gait as he approached the jumps, took off, and landed. Combined with the furious pace Dobbs was setting, that fault would cause Othello to tire long before the thirty jumps were completed. But Joseph also saw the mastery with which the Englishman rode Othello. Dobbs perfectly compensated for the odd rhythm. Seeing this, Joseph had to wonder. If Dobbs was so good, why was he setting such a dangerously furious pace?

By the eleventh obstacle, the first of the most difficult jumps, Joseph saw Othello was tiring. Too early, he thought. Or was it a trick? Then at the approach to jump thirteen, which Joseph expected would appear as he emerged from the thick woods, he momentarily lost sight of Dobbs and then came bounding around a turn to find Dobbs blocking the narrow path with Othello at a walk. Joseph had to veer Anaximenes into the trees to avoid a collision. Anaximenes exploded into a full panic, and it took all of Joseph's skill to maneuver the horse back on the now-empty path.

Joseph walked Anaximenes for a moment to restore calm in both of them. When they reemerged from the trees Joseph knew what Dobbs had done. Jump thirteen was the one with the short approach from which he needed to get tremendous speed to clear the stream. The Englishman had slowed him to deprive him of the necessary momentum. If he rode back to regain the distance for the speed he would fall too far behind.

"Go!" Joseph shouted, and set Anaximenes into a run that both knew wouldn't be fast enough to clear the water on the other side of the logs. But at the moment when the horse's feet were set right, Joseph asked and Anaximenes jumped. As they sailed over the top of the logs, Joseph lightly touched the horse with his spurs and Anaximenes kicked with his hind legs. His hooves bit into the top log and pushed off with enormous power. They were across the stream.

Anaximenes had been frightened, but he had trusted his rider and they landed safely. Now Anaximenes knew that with this rider he could do anything.

Joseph allowed Anaximenes to increase his speed until they were just behind Dobbs. Then he slowed the animal enough so that

Othello, sensing them behind, increased his pace. He heard Dobbs laugh as he let his horse run.

At obstacle twenty-one, a double jump over a twelve-foot-wide ditch and a hedge, Othello failed to clear the hedge. To Joseph's astonishment, Dobbs fell off his horse. Joseph was elated and eased Anaximenes into a quieter stride. The next four obstacles seemed almost easy. But Joseph was mentally preparing himself for jump twenty-six, where the Englishman had said he would lose. He reviewed his plan. The trick was to take this jump, at the bottom of a long downhill slope, at a moderate speed—just fast enough to keep the horse going but not so fast as to land too far down the steep grade, otherwise the horse wouldn't have enough room to clear the short bank abruptly rising on the other side.

Perhaps it was his hangover, or perhaps his inexperience in serious competition, but Joseph didn't hear Dobbs approach. Suddenly there was a rush of hooves, a whistle and slap as Dobbs' crop came slashing down on Anaximenes' flanks. Anaximenes erupted, racing toward certain destruction.

Joseph leaned forward. "Trust me," he whispered, and he gently gathered Anaximenes between his seat and his hands. He listened to the horse behind him; he could tell it was moving at the correct speed to make the jump. At the last possible second, he wheeled Anaximenes to the right, urged him to a fury of speed, circled back and came up behind Dobbs and within the same movement used his own crop on Othello.

Terrified, Othello leaped forward. Joseph brought Anaximenes to a halt and watched. As Dobbs and Othello cleared the barrier, Joseph heard Dobbs scream, "German cunt!" A moment later Othello appeared on the other side of the jump—riderless.

Joseph walked Anaximenes back the appropriate distance and then, at the proper gait, ran to the jump and cleared the two barriers. As he did, Joseph saw Dobbs writhing on the ground, his right leg lying at an odd angle.

At the finish line the count looked up in amazement.

"By George!" he said. He strode over and shook Joseph's hand. "Good Heavens! Dobbs can't be that far behind. Did he fall?"

"Obstacle twenty-six," Joseph said. "Perhaps you might send someone."

"And Othello?" The count wasn't concerned for the servant who had ridden his horse.

"Here he is," Joseph replied just as Othello trotted over to them. A groom ran forward and took the horse. The count ordered several men to fetch Dobbs. It was the last thought given to the Englishman, except for the moment it was discovered he could not afford his bets. The count covered for him and dismissed him.

That midnight, after a supper during which Joseph was taught to hold down the finest French red wines, the Neapolitan Hussars carried him aboard their king's private train and escorted him to Bremen. A card game lasted the duration of the ride and, as on the previous train trip, Joseph was unable to lose. Of all of these events Joseph had only hazy fragments of memory, except one. He clearly remembered von Wolfheim handing him a valise filled with his winnings. The shiny alligator bag was stuffed with bank notes and gold coins—many more gold coins than he had started with. He was fabulously rich.

Joseph fell asleep thinking about the castle he would buy in America and the beautiful stable he would build for his wonderful horses.

How easy it is to become rich, he thought.

§10

To the eye accustomed to the aesthetic grace of sailing ships the steamer *North Sea* might appear ugly, but to enthusiasts of the burgeoning Industrial Revolution she was the embodiment of the new beauty: hard evidence of man's power to control nature. These windless days were perfect proof. Graceful wind ships would have wallowed slack-sailed, but the *North Sea*, her great twin paddle-wheels driving her at 15.908 knots, proudly thrashed her way across the gentle swells. What did it matter that an unadorned straight stem, and not a graceful clipper bow lifting a proud bowsprit to the heavens, split the ocean? The *North Sea*, in fair weather or foul, crisscrossed the Atlantic on man's schedule.

The ship's rocking motion made Joseph think of his mother, and he put his arms around his pillow. How pleasant, he thought. Then he had a nice dream. He and Thunder were riding over an un-dulating field of sweet green clover. But the dream faded and he could feel the linen threads of the pillow pressing against his cheek, and he could smell the strange air. It was moist and fresh, but without the loam-smell of earth or the scent of animals, and his bed was moving up and down. He opened his eyes. It wasn't the bed that was moving. It was the room. Through an open round window Joseph saw the horizon gently seesawing. He laughed. He was on the ship and it was sailing on the sea! The bed was surrounded by blue velvet curtains pulled back on the sides, with a cherrywood rail a foot high at his shoulders and feet, and dipped in the middle. The room was just long enough for two beds attached to the wall, and two chairs upholstered in the same blue velvet sat on a yellow carpet. Against the opposite wall was a dressing table, a mirror and two lamps. To the left of the dressing table was a closed door, and to the left of that an armoire with a mirrored door and a chest of drawers attached to the wall. The room was paneled in polished cherrywood with a painted frieze of flowers and sea nymphs.

Joseph was puzzled to find he was wearing an unfamiliar night-shirt. He got out of bed and almost fell. Then letting his knees and ankles take the motion of the floor, he centered his weight and found his balance. Like a horse, he thought. Very nice.

Opening the armoire he discovered his uniform, sponged and pressed. Next to it hung, to his horror, his peasant clothes. Some-one had seen his peasant clothing! What would he say? The alligator bag containing his winnings was on the floor next to his busby, but he didn't see his boots. His saber leaned against the back wall of the closet. He took the alligator bag and carried it to the unused bed where, after opening it, he grinned. Then he upended the bag and, when the last note fluttered out, began making order of his wealth.

Tidy stacks of gold coins, neat bundles of currency, seventy-five gold Maria Theresas, a hundred gold guilders, and seventy-five gold English sovereigns. The bank notes were marks in various denom-inations. And there were two drafts on the Rothschild Bank of Bremen to pay to the bearer in the amount of a hundred thousand marks each. His fortune added up to four hundred thousand marks. He dreamed of the great horse farm he would make in America and of the gratitude the Americans would feel when he taught them about good German horses.

He heard a light tap at the door.

"Come in," he said in his best aristocratic accent. The door opened and a small, balding valet wearing the livery of the North German America Line entered. In his hand were Joseph's polished boots.

"Excuse me, Herr Baron," he said, his eyes glancing at the fortune spread out on the bed. "I am Wissenkopf, your valet, Excellency. Breakfast is being served in the dining saloon. If the Herr Baron is prepared to rise, I shall assist him to dress."

"Yes," Joseph said. "I am hungry. Let's by all means dress."

Wissenkopf put the boots on the deck and looked uncertainly at the armoire. "Excuse me, Herr Baron," he said. "Has something happened to the Herr Baron's luggage?"

"My luggage?"

"There was only the one suitcase...."

"Ah yes," Joseph said. He was pleased his mind worked so quickly. "And four large trunks. Black. With my crest on them."

Wissenkopf looked as though he might cry. "Begging the Herr Baron's pardon, but they were not put on board. I have checked everywhere. The officers who accompanied the Herr Baron onto the ship last night left only the one suitcase and the alligator bag." He stole another glance at the money piled on the bed.

Joseph frowned. "But all my clothes. Everything for the passage. In the suitcase I have only my rough clothing for when I work with the horses." He paused as if just realizing the size of the calamity facing him. "My trunks didn't arrive? God in heaven! What will I wear?"

Wissenkopf's basset-like eyes filled with compassion. "Calm yourself, dear baron. It may not be as impossible as it appears to Your Excellency. You have your uniform. The other officers onboard always wear their uniforms. I shall clean and press it every evening before dinner, and I will find some suitable linen so that Your Excellency will have fresh undergarments." The valet smiled hopefully. "And I've taken the liberty of borrowing a few items for the Herr Baron from the ship's slop-chest. The night shirt and a dressing gown..."

"This?" Joseph held out the hem of his night shirt.

Wissenkopf nodded modestly. "Certain items are always carried on board for unforeseen events." He glanced at Joseph's mangled feet. "And I have taken the liberty of stretching the Herr Baron's boots. They will be more comfortable now."

Joseph felt a tendril of trust for the man. "Thank you, Wissen-kopf. That was good of you." He decided to take a risk. "I confess to you this is the first time I've traveled. I want to reward you for your kindness, but I'm not sure what the proper amount of, I mean, the correct sum... What I mean is, I don't wish to insult you by giving you too little. So I want you to take the correct amount. No! Take more than what's normal. You must take an extra amount."

Wissenkopf blushed slightly. "Forgive me, Excellency," he said. "That would not be correct." He peeked again at the fortune on the bed. "If the Herr Baron would allow me to advise him?"

"Please."

"The usual gratuity, Excellency, is always extended at the end of the voyage and is five marks. If the servant has been especially attentive you might add a mark or two, but under no circumstances should the gratuity ever exceed ten marks." His gravity was funereal.

Joseph crossed to the bed and took a hundred-mark note. "Here," he said. "Please accept this."

Wissenkopf backed away in astonishment. "Oh no, sir. That is far too much."

"But it's for more than being a valet." Joseph took Wissenkopf's hand and forced the money into it. "It's for teaching me. I'm a rude country boy. I have no experience in travel. I need a guide. If you don't help me I shall make a fool of myself before the other passengers."

Wissenkopf nodded. "With the baron's permission?"

"Yes. Please. Speak."

"You have already done certain damage to your reputation among the other passengers."

Joseph was astonished. "But how?"

"Your arrival, sir. You were carried on board by a boisterous group of Italian officers. You all sang songs in Italian. Our chef who speaks Italian told us. Somewhat bawdy songs, he said."

"I sang in Italian?"

"It seems you sang the loudest, sir."

"In Italian?"

"Yes, sir."

"But I don't speak Italian."

"You did last night, sir."

"You are sure? Me? Italian?"

"I heard you myself, sir. The chef said it was excellent Italian."

"Me?"

Wissenkopf nodded.

"Italian?"

Wissenkopf nodded again.

And then Joseph remembered mimicking the Neapolitans and how liquid the Italian words felt in his mouth. He laughed aloud. "Come, Wissenkopf," he said. "We shall dress. Then you'll show me all about the ship. For the hundred marks you shall teach me about traveling."

Wissenkopf tilted his head from side to side and shrugged his narrow shoulders. "As Your Excellency wishes." He tucked the hundred marks in a pocket of his striped vest.

On his tour Joseph learned that all the passenger staterooms opened into the great saloon, a seventy-foot-long sitting room lushly carpeted and richly appointed with silk sofas and chairs. The walls, paneled in rose, satin and olive woods, were inlaid with the coats-of-arms of the various German states and numerous gold-framed mirrors reflected the light shimmering down from skylights set in the ceiling. Above the great saloon, the grand dining room and passenger cabins, the deck ran in a straight line from bow to stern. On it were three clusters of deck houses. The most forward was built around the two funnels and between the paddle wheel boxes. In these were the quarters for the captain and the officers of the ship. Aft was another deck house containing the kitchen, a pastry baking room, and a barber shop with an innovative chair that Wissenkopf told Joseph was invented in America. It swiveled in a complete circle and, when the back tilted, produced a footrest.

At the ship's stern the deckhouse was devoted to a smoking room for the convenience of the gentlemen, and an interior staircase permitted communication with the great saloon below to protect the men in rough weather. Just aft of this was a cubicle for the helmsman whose only view of the world was the interior of the smoking room. He steered the ship by a series of commands issued by bells.

Then Wissenkopf took Joseph back to the dining saloon and turned him over to the *maître d' hotel,* who led Joseph through the tables of white linen, glittering silver and sparkling crystal. Although the room was filled with soberly dressed men and women, it was the eyes that fascinated Joseph: curious eyes, amused eyes, and some disdainful ones. An officer in a red and blue uniform, French, Joseph correctly guessed, saluted him with a slight nod. Then he realized why he was being singled out: because of his noisy boarding with the Italians and von Wolfheim. It made him smile.

"It is good to see such a happy face so early in the morning." A thin man with an extravagantly curled chestnut beard rose from his place at a small table.

What was this? Was it customary to be seated with a stranger? Joseph made a slight bow and clicked his heels. "Von Ritter," he said. The other man also bowed. But it was a larger bow, a parody of the custom.

The maître d' introduced them. "Herr Baron, permit me to present the famous artist, Herr Karl Albert. Herr Albert, may I introduce to you Herr von Ritter Baron von Breitenstein."

Joseph once again made a slight bow and clicked his heels. This time the stranger laughed. With a wave of his hand he dismissed the maître d' and continued the gesture to indicate the chair opposite him. "Please, von Ritter. Do join me."

Joseph tried to size up Karl Albert without appearing to stare. What he saw was a tall man with friendly hazel eyes, curly chestnut beard and mustache, and a face thin enough to suggest emaciation. But Joseph was most struck by Karl's wardrobe. A large yellow silk bow cascaded from the folds of his tan shirt's soft collar and nearly fell to his waist. His dark brown velvet jacket flashed with small glimmers of honey light as it moved.

"Welcome to the leper colony, von Ritter."

Joseph's confusion was evident.

"I am seated alone because I am an artist, which is socially unacceptable. Though they," he airily indicated the room, "compete with each other to purchase my paintings, my manner of living offends them. In short, since it is well known that artists inhale opium, drink absinthe, and espouse free love, I am an outcast. You are here at the lepers' table because of your disgraceful arrival. You might have escaped with merely some shocked amusement, but you were seen by *him*." Karl pointed at a silver-haired gentleman seated with his wife and daughter in the center of the room. "The proper Prince Meklenburg. It is said that every year he visits his cousin Queen Victoria to instruct her in manners."

Joseph's eyes slipped past the prince to fix on his lovely blond and pink daughter. How could such beauty have human substance?

"Ah," said Karl. "I see you have noticed the Princess Elizabeth. Aphrodite, goddess of love, come once again to make men careless of their mortality. And though only ten paces away, as distant and as unreachable as if she were breakfasting on Mount Olympus. Look how she is guarded by her jealous father, the great god Zeus, hurler of thunderbolts, protector of propriety. And beside him his consort in respectability, the mother Medusa."

Joseph turned to him, "The great god Zeus?"

Karl nodded solemnly. "In this incarnation Zeus is Prince Meklenburg, and his gorgon wife the mother of Aphrodite. I have it on good authority that you have been exiled from their Elysium and imprisoned on my little island of lost souls by personal order of His Zeusness."

"You said the great god Zeus. Is Zeus another name for," he almost said Hashem, "for God?"

Karl wasn't surprised at the ignorance but that the young nobleman would admit it. "Yes," he said. "Zeus was the principal Greek god."

A chief mess-steward appeared at their table with a waiter by his side. "But before this lofty conversation," Karl said, "perhaps you had better order your breakfast."

Joseph turned to the steward. "Coffee," he said. "Coffee and two kippers, six scrambled eggs, four country sausages with blackberry preserves and black bread with sour cream and honey. And did I say coffee?"

"Yes, Herr Baron." The steward was pleased. The young baron might have been rowdy last night but he ate like a proper gentleman.

"You always eat like that?" Karl asked.

Had he made an error? He had ordered exactly what he had for breakfast at Schloss Wehdel. "Yes. My mother always insisted on a proper breakfast." What had he done wrong? "Oh! Wine! Champagne! I didn't order champagne. I'm peculiar that way. I don't drink champagne with my breakfast. But please tell me about this god Zeus."

"But what about Aphrodite?"

"Who?"

"The goddess over there in the pink dress."

Joseph glanced at the girl. "She is very beautiful," he said. "The most beautiful woman I have ever seen. But please, who is the god Zeus?"

Karl paused to be sure the hussar wasn't making fun of him. "Zeus," he said, "was the most important of the ancient Greek gods."

"Then they do not worship Zeus now?"

"Not for two thousand years."

"If you say he was the most important of the gods, that means there were other gods. Yes?"

"Yes. Many other gods. You studied no mythology?"

"No. Just horses."

"Do you know about centaurs?"

"Oh yes. The half-man, half-horses. But they are from a fairy tale."

"No, they are part of the time of Zeus. The classic Greek period. They were demigods."

"Are you saying that some gods were half-human?"

"The Greeks believed it, and they gave us Plato and Aristotle. You have heard of Plato and Aristotle?"

Joseph shook his head.

"Ah," he sighed, an empty canvas. "They were philosophers. The greatest philosophers the world has ever known. All that we think now, they thought before us. So, if they believed there were centaurs, there may have been centaurs. People nowadays, even important people, like kings and philosophers, believe there are angels. Have you ever seen an angel?"

"No."

"Neither have any of them. But they believe they are there. So why not centaurs? Why not Zeus? Zeus is dead now of course."

"But gods are immortal." Joseph was excited. "If Zeus was a god, how could he die?"

"There were no more Greeks left who believed in him," Karl said. "When the ancient Greeks were defeated and their culture was overwhelmed, they stopped worshipping their gods. Worship is to a god as water is to a mortal. A god cannot live without it. There must have been a great dry despair on Olympus. Gods everywhere, singing their songs of death, dropping parched to their marble floors."

Electrified, Joseph spoke too loud: "I knew it! God can die!" Several heads turned to him, and a small man in a mouse-colored suit repeated the words into Prince Meklenburg's ear.

"Correct," Karl continued as if lecturing at a university, not unaware of the shock waves his theories were sending across the saloon. "When mighty Rome ascended, so did Rome's new gods rise. Jove and Juno and the legions of others. And when the Visigoths sacked Rome, they murdered Rome's people and thus her gods. I see the very same thing happening now in America. The spirit gods of the native Indians are being massacred by the barbarian Christians." Warming to his subject, Karl raced on.

"Is there more than one god? My dear baron, there may be as many gods as there are people. We each may have a god of our own. The animals probably have their own gods as well. And the plants and the rocks. Gods? Ye Gods! There may be as many gods as there are the uncountable stars in the firmament!"

"Do you really believe that?" Joseph asked.

"How could I be an artist and believe otherwise? The purpose of art is to see truth. And what is truth but a momentary glimpse of what may be the unknowable? I believe God or gods are to be searched for everywhere. My gods I have found in many places. I find gods in the gorges and rivers of the Rocky Mountains. Some sing to me from the highest peaks, or whisper through the gold and purple rays of sunsets of such beauty that even after experiencing them I still cannot imagine they exist."

Joseph leaned toward the artist, "Do you think the God of the Christians is the same God who made the covenant with Abraham?"

The artist shook his head. "Not likely. But for the tenacity of the Jews their old God would have gone the way of Zeus. I expect old Yahweh is around, but not much fight's left in him. An old God living on the dole from a poor people. You aren't eating your kippers. How does a Bavarian officer come to fancy English kippers?"

"Oh. From my friend Count Wehdel. He likes English things. Would you like some?" Without waiting for an answer, Joseph placed one on a plate and handed it to Karl. "And so the Christian god is the strong one now?"

"Your friend Count Wehdel is right. This fish is excellent. Your question depends on which Christian gods you speak of: the Catholic, the Protestant, the Eastern Orthodox. But enough of this god talk. It's our first day at sea, man! And there is the question of the Princess Elizabeth. I saw how taken you were with her."

"She is the most beautiful woman I've ever seen." Joseph stopped eating and sighed, "But it is foolish for me to think of her. She is a princess."

"You're a baron. Is your title old?"

"Yes."

"You're well-connected?"

"My uncle, Count von Falkenbrecht, is a cousin to the king of Bavaria."

"You're wealthy?"

"I have a fortune."

"Good. Then all we have to do is overcome her father's distaste for you and you may have a delightful shipboard romance. Have you ever been on a ship before?"

"Never."

"I guessed as much. First time away from home?"

"Yes."

"Thought so."

"Do you really think I can meet the Princess Elizabeth?"

"A ship is a small world. It will be difficult not to meet the lady. The problem is to do so with the smiling approval of her parents."

"Her father thinks I am a rowdy. He has sent me to eat with an artist." He smiled at his new friend. "In a leper colony."

"That's no problem. After breakfast the passengers all take their morning walks around the deck. Since you are who you are, you have the right to approach the Prince. Bow low, introduce yourself and mention your uncle, the cousin to your king, and say that you wish to apologize for your disgraceful arrival, and that you would understand if he chose not to speak to you for the rest of the voyage. Say to him that you are so humiliated that, if it is his wish, you shall place yourself under arrest and stay in your quarters for the duration of the voyage. He will be suitably impressed."

"But what if he says to do that?"

"He won't. But if he does we shall find a way out of it. My God! What a voyage this is turning out to be! God and romantic intrigue on the very first morning."

He rose and stood at attention. "Herr Baron, since we are destined to become the greatest of friends, may I have the honor to call you by your first name?"

Joseph rose to his feet. "You may call me Joseph."

"And you, sir, may call me Karl."

The deck was filling with passengers taking their morning constitutionals. For the most part the men wore blacks and grays, with stovepipe hats to protect them from the Atlantic sun. The women appeared in muted colors especially prepared for outings, with a daring new design: separate blouses tucked into the waistbands of skirts that belled out to the bottom of the boot. The more modern ladies held their wide skirt shape with a patented tilter—a graduated series of resilient, steel wire rings held together with tapes. It weighed a mere half a pound and required only one crinolined petticoat to cover it. The less modern were burdened with eight layers of padded, quilted and whaleboned petticoats. They took shorter walks on deck.

Joseph and Karl joined the outer ring of the promenade as it followed the hands of the clock from bow to stern, stern to bow. The inner ring of strollers walked in a counterclockwise motion which allowed them to greet each other with metronomic regularity. Mixed in with the gentlemens' black and grays and the ladies' plum and avocados was the occasional bright plumage of the half-dozen military men. With each revolution of the deck they saluted each other, giving their right arm and hand nearly as much of a constitutional as their legs. The French officer in the blue coat and red trousers of the Imperial French Cavalry always added a slight nod to his salute to Joseph.

At the conclusion of the constitutionals, the ladies withdrew to their staterooms for a costume change while the gentlemen remained on deck for cigars and pipes.

Prince Meklenburg smoked his cigar at the bow with the captain and Prince Nikoli, nephew to the Russian tsar, with whom Meklenburg was traveling to America to meet with Commodore Vanderbilt for a discussion of a new railroad from Berlin across Russia to the Pacific Ocean.

Joseph stood in the shade of one of the huge funnels rehearsing his apology with Karl who, when he decided his pupil was ready, sent him forward. Joseph calmed his fears with thoughts of how well he had been accepted by von Wolfheim and Count Wehdel and the Italians. His feet no longer hurt, thanks to Wissenkopf, and his uniform was comfortable in the cool sea breeze.

When he reached the three men at the bow, Joseph brought himself to attention and saluted. The captain returned his salute. The other two turned to look at him and Joseph saluted them as well.

Meklenburg was a fat man with short silver hair, a long mustache and a perpetually red face. He suffered from high blood pressure. No one, not even his mother, ever called him kind or generous. When he saw who was saluting him, he found himself affronted by the audacity of the Bavarian pup.

"I am Joseph von Ritter Baron von Breitenstein," Joseph said. "I have come to Your Excellency to offer you my most profound apology for my outrageous conduct on boarding this ship last night. I offer no excuse, only contrition. My behavior, though never intended as such, was insulting to you and your family. I have disgraced my uncle, Count von Falkenbrecht, and my regiment, the Royal Wittelsbach Hussars. If it is your pleasure, I shall place myself under arrest and for the remainder of the passage keep myself locked in my stateroom."

The three men were astonished. The silence that followed was at last broken by Meklenburg. "Lock yourself in your cabin?" he said. "You can go to the devil for all I care. Your disgusting behavior was nothing more or less than I would have expected from a relative of the sodomite von Falkenbrecht. Or, for that matter, from the Wittelsbach rabble he commands."

Joseph ripped off his glove and slapped the prince.

§11

THE SLAP PRODUCED A MEDLEY OF REACTIONS. MEKLENBURG, because of his princely position, had never been challenged in his life and was instantly paralyzed with fear. Prince Nikoli, his cousin, was pleased to see his fatuous cousin so discomfited. The French officer of the Imperial Cavalry who had observed the exchange came forward and, saluting, offered Joseph his services as a second. Karl hurried to stand at Joseph's side to support him. The captain, quickly assessing the consequences to the North German America Line of the death of either passenger, profusely apologized to both parties and placed himself between them. In the name of maritime law, he forbade the duel.

Meklenburg, finally mastering his voice, shouted, "Turn this ship around and put this insolent dog ashore!"

The captain replied that this could not be done.

"Then put him in irons!" Meklenburg commanded.

Prince Nikoli touched Meklenburg's arm. "Dear cousin," he said quietly to the German prince but still loud enough for the interested parties to hear. "Such an act might be regarded in the highest circles as dishonorable. At this young officer's age I myself dispatched

Pretrovsky under a similar provocation. The young baron may be impetuous, but he is well within his right. Although I'm sure it wasn't your intent, you did offer egregious insult to his family, his regiment and his honor. I believe you excluded only his mother and his horse. May I ask, are you familiar with the weapons of the duel?"

Meklenburg started at him in shock. "I know nothing of weapons. Why are you asking this?"

"Pardon me, dear cousin. Allow me to act for you." The Russian prince moved to Joseph and his entourage. To the French colonel he asked, in French, "I beg your pardon, sir, but are you an old friend of this gentleman?"

"I am not, sir," the Frenchman replied. "But I am prepared to offer my services."

"Thank you." Prince Nikoli turned to Karl and spoke in German. "And you, sir? Are you acquainted with this young officer?"

"I am," Karl lied. "I have had the honor to know him since he was a child."

Joseph was too focused on the object of his rage to pay attention to the conversation around him.

"Excellent." Prince Nikoli turned to the others. "If you would excuse us for a moment." He led Karl to a place near the rail and out of earshot of the others. "As one gentleman to another, can you tell me, is the boy accomplished with weapons?"

Karl nodded. "He is a duelist. There is no weapon in which the baron is not an expert. At fourteen he fought his first duel, killing the lover of his father's mistress. In this circumstance my duty to the baron requires me to violate a confidence. The baron is traveling to America as a result of a recent unfortunate event in which a certain personage had the bad judgment to impugn the honor of a lady dear to the baron. The personage is now deceased. His Majesty, having grown weary of the baron's duels and fearful of depleting his nobles, has suggested a few years of travel until the youthful temper has been cooled by maturity."

"I thank you for your kindness."

"Not at all. But sir, I feel there is something you should understand."

"And that is?"

"As I say, I know the baron very well. He will not rest until his honor is satisfied. Once on dry land, he will pursue the matter. It will become a *cause célèbre*. He will pursue it over the face of the globe until either the duel takes place or Meklenburg's honor lies in tatters and no decent family will receive him."

Prince Nikoli smiled. "I suspected as much. I was like that when I was a boy. Thank you." He returned to Meklenburg. "My dear cousin," he said. "The matter is grave. I suggest an immediate apology."

"Are you mad?"

"I assure you, dear cousin, the matter must be satisfactorily concluded here on this deck or when this voyage ends you will either have to fight the duel or face dishonor. The tsar will never receive a dishonored man. If you don't apologize now, we will never build our railroad."

Joseph hadn't moved from the spot where he had issued the challenge. He thought of nothing but the insult. He was not sure of the meaning of "sodomite," but he knew it was derogatory. No matter what the captain said, one of them had to die.

The prince stopped just beyond arm's length and, his face purple, made a slight bow. "Herr Baron," he said. "I was wrong. It is a well-known fact that Count von Falkenbrecht is a great German hero and the Royal Wittelsbach Hussars are among the most gallant in the world." His voice was so constricted with rage that it descended to a whisper. "I spoke intemperately. I beg your pardon."

A great wave of warmth spread through Joseph. "I thank you, Your Excellency," he said. "I hope Your Excellency will now accept my apology for my behavior last night. I am sure my offense was so grave as to cause Your Excellency to be justifiably angry."

The prince wanted someone to choke the life out of the boy. "Yes, Herr Baron. Your behavior was disgraceful but I accept your apology." He started to move away.

"Your Excellency?"

The prince paused and half faced him again.

"May I have the honor to call upon your daughter, the Princess Elizabeth?"

"*Formidable!*" Colonel Soulé exclaimed. The officer gazed at Joseph in admiration.

"In life, as in art," Karl said, "there is something called 'timing.' Some people have it naturally. Others must learn it." Karl shook his head in wonder. "You're lucky the Russian was there. Otherwise I think Meklenburg would have leaped on you."

"I made a fool of myself, didn't I?" Joseph asked. The three of them were seated on deck chairs near the stern of the ship. The other passengers remained at a discreet distance.

"*Mais non!*" Colonel Soulé said. "Not at all! What you did was in the first instance only honorable. And in the last, to ask to see the girl, and to ask it at that precise moment—that was *romantique. Poétique. Formidable!*"

"I'll never meet the princess now," Joseph lamented.

Karl smiled. "Let's say that rather than never, you should consider that it's not likely. But life holds many mysteries. The Arabs have a word for it. *Kismet.* If it is meant to be, then it is meant to be."

Colonel Soulé added, "But even on this small ship, even with the dragon eyes of the mother and the father standing guard, there will be a way. *Pour l'amour* there is always a way. Remember always Romeo and Juliet."

"But they died," Karl interjected.

"For Shakespeare, but not for all time. I have myself recently seen a production of this play where the poison that Romeo takes is a false brew and he wakes in time to prevent Juliet from taking her own life. The greatest romance demands the greatest obstacles. I assure you, my friends, for Joseph to ask the father in that moment was an act of romantic genius."

Karl slapped the arm of his chair. "By God, colonel, you are right. The timing was perfect. Joseph, you must consider retiring from the hussars and devoting yourself to the muses."

Colonel Soulé raised an objecting hand. "And give up the military? This one is a natural soldier." He turned to Joseph. "You are good with the épée? The foil? The saber?"

Joseph shrugged. "I'm not sure," he said. "The man who trained me said that I was very good mostly with the saber. I studied some épée but not very much foil. I'm excellent with the pistol and the musket."

"Then you have never fought a duel? Sword or gun?"

"No. Yes. Once. Sabers on horseback."

"*Formidable!*" Colonel Soulé was impressed. "That I have never done, and I have been fencing master at Saint Cyr."

"I thought cavalry was your specialty," Karl said.

"Yes. It is my profession. But the fencing is my art. I travel now to teach cavalry tactics at the American military academy, West

Point. I only hope some of them will also choose to learn the blade. And you, young Baron Joseph, will you show me what you know?"

"Yes," Joseph answered. The Frenchman taught cavalry tactics, he worried. He wished he had his horse on board, for Thunder would impress the colonel. "But I have only my cavalry saber and no fencing costume," Joseph said.

"I have everything. Will you show me now?"

Joseph agreed, and soon Colonel Soulé had him outfitted with a mask, gauntlets, costume and slippers. They then returned to the afterdeck where the colonel laid out a proper fencing court. Curious passengers crowded around to watch.

Colonel Soulé suggested that they start with épée, the most difficult. Next they worked with fencing sabers.

"Not bad," the colonel said. "Not bad at all. You have a gift for the blade, but not yet enough technique. Since I must fence every day, and since you have much to learn, perhaps we might spend a profitable hour each morning at this sport. By the time we land you will be good enough to engage champions!"

An elegant young man in an excellently cut dove-gray suit stepped forward. "Forgive the interruption please, gentlemen," he said. "I am Ambrose Fitzhugh-Reid of Terrarouge, Georgia. I have enjoyed your exhibition of swordsmanship and wonder, if it is not an intrusion, if I may join you? I have had some experience at foil and épée."

Joseph's first look at an American pleased him. Fitzhugh-Reid had an open, friendly face, with sandy hair, guileless blue eyes, and a soft blond mustache above an amiable mouth. It seemed to Joseph as if there were no secrets behind that face.

"How do you say in American?" Joseph asked Karl. "I should be pleased if you would join us?" Karl told him and Joseph then turned to Fitzhugh-Reid and, in a perfect mimicry of Karl's rough German-English accent, repeated the phrase.

The two young men were not evenly matched. Joseph had the greater talent and was able to make many more hits. After their bouts Colonel Soulé suggested that, weather and sea conditions permitting, the three of them meet each morning and in return for the exercise he would teach them how to become expert fencers.

Fitzhugh-Reid invited them to join him for a morning brandy in the saloon. There the valet, Wissenkopf, told Joseph that because of the unpleasantness with Prince Meklenburg, the captain had suggested that they choose different sittings for their meals. The prince had already taken the first seating for all meals which, if the baron didn't object, would have him dining at the second seating.

"Much better," said Karl. "It's always the most interesting people at the later sittings. After all, that's where we met."

"That's acceptable." Joseph told Wissenkopf. To the others, Joseph lamented, "But now how will I ever see the princess again?"

Colonel Soulé was elated, "Ah, but now it is the best possible romance. Now there will be *les petits billets,* servants to bribe, secret meetings in the ship. It will be marvelous."

With gentle amusement Karl explained the problem to Fitzhugh-Reid. "If I may presume on our so recent acquaintance," the Southerner said in his soft, Georgia-accented French which Karl translated, "Since we dine at the same sitting, let us dine together. This delicate problem then can be presented to my wife Amalee who, being a proper Georgia belle, has been reared in the gentle art of romantic intrigue."

At the same gathering it was decided that Joseph should learn English: Fitzhugh-Reid was to be his teacher. After their first hour of language class the conversation eventually drifted to America. Karl spoke first. "America is the hope of the world," he said. "It's the place where any man can choose his life. It's a place of such gigantic beauty that it redefines the relationship between man and the gods. I paint the landscapes of the West. Along with the beauty I see the tragedy. I see the coming destruction of the red natives. I paint them as fast as I can. I paint their faces, their villages, their ceremonies, their way of life—all soon to be swept aside by the white tide. And of the white world, men rise from poverty to vast wealth, and others are degraded and destroyed by a system that demands men give the most they have or be consumed. And yet with all its brutality, I see a new race on this earth—Americans, the first truly free-born people of the world."

Joseph was pleased by these images. If a man could rise from poverty to be a prince, what could he not do with his fortune? He might become a king!

"I have not seen the West," Fitzhugh-Reid said, "but I've had the privilege of viewing Mr. Albert's paintings. Were I an adventurous man I would travel to see such magnificence. But I know that nothing I could see there would match the beauty of the canvases that Karl has painted."

Karl made a graceful bow from his seat.

Fitzhugh-Reid continued. "The America I know is much of what Karl has articulated. A place where a man may make of his life what he will. My great-grandfather came to Virginia as an indentured servant. He earned his freedom and went south to farm a small homestead. His son, my grandfather, increased that holding, and after the Revolution sold the land and moved to an empty part of Georgia where he began with only a few hundred acres. The plantation he started, Terrarouge, now has twenty-five hundred acres under cultivation. I'm afraid it is really the only America I know." He smiled at Joseph. "I can promise you, sir, should you visit us at Terrarouge, you will see America at its most gentle and beautiful. And you will be pleased to find the finest horses in America."

Joseph's eyes lit. "But what breed are these, the finest horses in America?"

"That, sir, depends on whom you happen to make the inquiry of," Fitzhugh-Reid said. "I raise the finest Hunters in the state, bred from American Thoroughbred and Irish Draught. My neighbor, Mr. Blount of Magnolia Hall, is of the opinion that his English Hunters are superior. We spend a fair part of the year testing each other on that score. Most plantations also have American Saddle Horses or Tennessee Walking Horses for the go-a-calling days. If you haven't ridden one of our gaited horses, it might be a new pleasure for you."

"I have heard of these American gaited horses. I'm most anxious to learn about them," Joseph said. "I am going to America to buy land where I will raise the finest horses in the world."

"What kind of horses do you plan to breed?"

"You're familiar with German horses in America?"

"I'm afraid I don't know anyone who has them."

"Sadly, I must concur with our young friend," Colonel Soulé said. "Although we French have several great breeds for the cavalry, I myself prefer the Trakehner."

Joseph was too young to appreciate the compliment and rushed on. "I will bring over from Germany a great Trakehner stud. Colonel Soulé is quite correct. The Trakehner is the greatest cavalry horse in the world. Do you think where your castle is..."

"I am sorry to disappoint you, Joseph," Fitzhugh-Reid said, "but we don't have castles. We have modest wooden houses. We call our estates plantations."

"Thank you. Do you think the country where your plantation is would be a good place for me to make a horse plantation?"

"That question is debated among my friends. I believe that it's a mite too warm in the summers for only breeding horses. If I were going to start a horse farm I expect I would look to one of the good grass states, such as Virginia or Kentucky. If I am not being too inquisitive, how large a place are you planning to buy?"

Thinking of von Falkenbrecht's holdings and of Schloss Wehdel, Joseph replied, "About twenty or thirty thousand acres."

At that a man at a nearby table, who had been listening to this conversation while writing letters, put down his pen.

"Excuse me, gentlemen," he said in a New York accent. "I couldn't help but overhear your conversation. Perhaps I might be of some assistance to the baron." The man had a powerful build, carefully brushed dark brown hair, and no mustache or beard. He produced a calling card from his vest pocket.

"My card," he said. "I'm Aaron Augustus Bussey. I have the honor to be the president of the Great Western Steam Navigation, Rail & Land Company." He turned to Joseph. "Baron, may I congratulate you on your courage this morning. I must say in your place I don't know I would have acted with such restraint. But I suppose that's just one of the many differences between European gentility and us rough colonials."

Karl translated for Joseph, who smiled politely. The man made him uneasy. Aaron Augustus Bussey stood too close and spoke too loud.

"Thank you," Joseph replied in his new English.

"I couldn't help overhear you talk about the size acreage you need," Bussey said. "Don't think, gentlemen, that I've risen to sell you land. I buy land. I don't sell it. Leastways I don't sell it till I run a railroad over it and build some towns. Then I sell it. But as we are all voyaging together, I thought perhaps I could offer this brave young man some hard-earned advice. And that advice is, Mr. Baron, go west. On just the other side of the Mississippi River the opportunity of land acquisition is gigantic. Why, you could have a hundred thousand acres for the same price you might buy a tenth of that in more developed parts of the country. Mind if I sit down?" He did so without waiting for an answer. "Sorry gents, I don't believe I got your names."

Out of courtesy they each stood and gave their names.

"The West is where the future lays," Bussey continued. "My railroads and steamboats will make every corner of it accessible. When you land in New York, Mr. Baron, you come see me at the St. Nicholas Hotel on Broadway. I'll put you in touch with any number of syndicates reaching out to the great West."

At that moment the second seating was announced.

With Amalee Fitzhugh-Reid presiding at dinner that afternoon, Joseph, Karl, Colonel Soulé and the Fitzhugh-Reids became close shipboard friends, a temporary family which evoked envy in the outsiders. Amalee, seventeen years old and married for seventeen weeks, considered herself wise in the ways of the world as she had grown up in the finest mansion in Savannah. Amalee wasn't quite pretty. The first impression of her face was of character over beauty: a long, strong jaw line and deep, dark eyes arrayed below straight raven brows and peering over prominent cheekbones.

"Fiddle!" she exclaimed. "I just bet that princess already has her eye on you. A handsome soldier in that dramatic uniform? Why, if I wasn't already spoken for, I'd set my cap for you myself."

Fitzhugh-Reid beamed at his bride. "Didn't I tell you, gentlemen? My Amalee is an authority on the subject."

"Sweet peas and molasses!" Amalee returned the beam to her husband. "It is only what every proper young Savannah lady is taught: French, needlepoint, and the fine art of romance. My aunt, Miss Duville, who never married but is rumored to have had the most scandalous past, said I was the best pupil she ever had. The proof, of course, is that I married the greatest catch in Georgia." And then she blushed.

Joseph thought Amalee a most wonderful woman—so wise, so charming, so filled with life. Perhaps blond hair and pink skin weren't the only things that mattered. Were she not taken he would have surrendered his heart to her in that moment. But just as he was about to stand and swear his eternal fealty, a movement to his right caught his eye. Joseph looked up and saw shimmering red hair, violet eyes, a moist, bruised-looking mouth and a voluptuous figure. Then he heard an ugly sound. It was Bussey and it was directed at the lady. "Make no mistake, you're a pretty woman," Bussey growled, "an ornament like my watch fob, but a very stupid woman. You will never again presume to have such a thought. You hear me?"

Joseph, who saw a tear emerge from one of the violet eyes, restrained his anger. The woman must be Bussey's wife. He couldn't interfere. But there was something dark about Aaron Augustus Bussey.

The days began to slip by, measured by the journey of the sun from horizon to horizon and by the steady rhythm of the two great paddle wheels. The crowd of passengers watching the fencing lessons on the afterdeck increased daily. The ship divided into two camps. The younger passengers admired Joseph, and the older, more respectable ones coalesced around the Meklenburgs.

But even a large ship is a small place and it was inevitable that, in spite of the separate dinner times, the two factions would meet. Joseph always respectfully saluted the prince, and the prince always nodded in correct acknowledgment. Joseph always smiled directly at Princess Elizabeth, and she always demurely cast her eyes down.

Occasionally Joseph and the other men of his group had closer encounters with Aaron Augustus Bussey. These usually took place during that time when the men gathered for smoking and various liquors. Although Bussey hinted he would like to join in their poker games, he was politely ignored, yet he remained affable. On several occasions Joseph observed the man behave cruelly to his wife. Once he saw Bussey raise his hand to tip his hat and Mrs. Bussey flinched like a terrified horse.

On the fifth morning at breakfast, Amalee announced the momentous meeting between Princess Elizabeth and Joseph would take place that night. Joseph was so elated he ordered champagne.

"She is just the most cunning little thing!" Amalee said. "Speaks perfectly lovely French. Yesterday, when I was showing her my daguerreotypes of Terrarouge, we just naturally fell to speaking of men. I told her all about how the men of Georgia go a-courting, and she just out and asked me if the baron—that is you, my dear Joseph—was the monster everybody said he was. And I told her that you were the gentlest and most romantic of men." She laughed. "And I found out that she thinks any man who could frighten her father like you did must be someone she just has to meet."

"But when?" Joseph asked. "Where? How?"

"Why, at midnight, at the back of the ship where you all fence. There are only two ways to get there, around either side of the smoking room. Ambrose and I shall mount guard. He on the right, I on the left. The princess shares a room with her chaperone who has come to a complete understanding on the matter with me. She will sleep through the princess's little outing. It is, I assure you, all arranged. And did I tell you that when the Meklenburgs return to Germany they will announce the Princess Elizabeth's marriage to the king of Carpathia, a man nearly three times her age? With a purple nose and perpetual catarrh? The chaperone considers this an outrage against her beloved child." Amalee looked at Joseph. "And it was also helpful that she heard the servants gossip about the millions you have in the captain's safe."

Joseph was pleased but puzzled. "How do they know that?"

Fitzhugh-Reid answered. "Your valet. They say he saw a fortune on your bed and begged you to put it in the safe."

"There are very few secrets on a ship," Karl said.

"But the meeting with the princess?" Joseph asked.

"That's different," Amalee said. "Some secrets can be kept. At least long enough. This will be just among us. And the chaperone will be discreet too. She believes the fates have brought you along just at the right time, or that beautiful girl could go to her grave with never a romantic moment in her poor little life. And did you notice the moon is full? It's witching time."

At ten o'clock Joseph dismissed Wissenkopf and pretended to retire. But as soon as the valet left, Joseph jumped out of bed. Lighting a lamp, he pulled off his nightshirt and stood by the open porthole, allowing the chill sea air to wash over his body. Then he put on his dressing gown and went into the parlor of his small suite. There he lit another lamp and paced, rehearsing the appropriate words to romance a princess in the moonlight. With each passing minute his confidence faded. He looked at a clock. It was eleven-thirty. He should dress. He was just turning to go back into the bedroom when he thought he heard a knock at his door. Perhaps it was just the creaking of the ship? Then the door opened and in stepped Mrs. Bussey, who quickly closed the door behind her.

She held a torn remnant of an amethyst dressing gown against her naked breasts.

"Please," she whispered. "Please help me."

§12

THE SOFT LIGHT IN MRS. BUSSEY'S VIOLET EYES DIMMED, HER PALE hands fell away from her breast and she slipped silently to the carpet. Joseph knelt down. He took one of her wrists in both his hands and started rubbing it.

"Frau Bussey," he whispered. "Frau Bussey. Please. You must wake up." To his intense embarrassment he was staring at her naked breasts. He quickly reached for her torn gown and covered her. As he did his fingers brushed across her flesh and he burned with shame. He concentrated his gaze on her face. "Frau Bussey. Please." She didn't stir.

Gently Joseph slipped his arms under Mrs. Bussey's shoulders and knees and lifted. When he straightened up, the dressing gown once again slipped, revealing her nakedness. Joseph forced himself to look away as he carried her to his bed in the next room. There he covered her with a blanket. He walked to his nightstand and moistened a wash cloth with which he quickly bathed his own face. He moistened it again and, carrying it dripping to the bed, placed it on Mrs. Bussey's forehead.

Her eyes opened. "This time," she whispered, "I thought he would kill me."

"Mr. Bussey?" Joseph asked, also whispering. "He beats you?"

She let the blanket fall and turned to reveal her back. Joseph recoiled in shock. Her creamy white skin was a thicket of ugly welts. "He ties my wrists to the bed and beats me with a belt."

"My God!" Joseph said.

She whispered on. "Augustus was drunk. I worked my hands free, and when he turned I pushed him. He fell and I ran. I ran to you because you were so brave with that horrible Meklenburg. I knew you would protect me."

"Madame, I shall." Joseph took his saber from his closet, unsheathed it and stood facing her. "If he comes here I shall keep him from you."

"Your door?" she asked. "Is it locked?"

Joseph moved to the door. There he heard drunken footsteps approach, pause, and move on. Joseph then locked the door and returned to his bedroom. Mrs. Bussey's torn gown was crumpled on the carpet. She was lying in his bed, the covers drawn up to her neck.

"Would you hold me?"

At five minutes past midnight a hurried conference took place on deck. "You must go to his stateroom at once," Amalee whispered urgently to Fitzhugh-Reid.

He glanced at the hooded figure of the princess waiting at the afterrail and rushed down to Joseph's stateroom. There was no answer at the door.

In the morning, as Joseph emerged from his suite for breakfast, he found Karl waiting. "Ah good," Karl said. "You're alive. Good. And also bad. Good if last night you were desperately ill. Bad if you have no dramatic explanation for your missed rendezvous. Amalee is both worried about your health and at the edge of a storm of indignation should you appear in perfect condition. They say the rage of a southern belle is a sight to behold."

Joseph clapped his hand to his head. "My God! I forgot!"

"You forgot?"

Joseph took Karl by the arm and led him to a quiet corner of the great saloon. "Karl, the most wonderful thing has happened to me. Can I tell you? Will you keep my secret?"

Karl smiled. The truth was in the boy's manner. "Keep your secret? My dear Joseph, till the last breath leaves my body. Who is she?"

"That I cannot tell. It's a question of honor. I shall never reveal her name, and you must promise to never try and discover it. I must have your word on this."

"I swear on the head of my sainted mother," Karl said. "But you must tell me how it was that you found and bedded a woman between dinner and midnight. That I absolutely must know."

"I'm sorry but I can't tell you that either. But Karl, it's so wonderful! You can't imagine!"

"I could try. You're in love?"

"Those aren't big enough words. In love. Karl, I don't know the words. God, I love her!" Then Joseph's face darkened. "Help me. She's married. What shall I do?"

"Married. Of course. The princess is the only single young lady onboard."

"She hates her husband. He is a brute, a drunkard who beats her. How shall I save her? I don't know what to do."

Karl's eyes darted past Joseph's shoulder. "There's Colonel Soulé. With your permission, I suggest we consult him. In these matters he's the most senior."

Joseph nodded and they crossed the great saloon and explained his mission to Colonel Soulé.

"*Formidable!*" Colonel Soulé saluted Joseph. "You continue to be a man after my own heart. This is wonderful, but very serious. The most important thing, of course, is to continue the *affaire* with *éclat*. The second most important thing is for the husband never to find out. On such a small ship the *scandale* would be impossible. In this case you would be on the wrong side of a duel. And, with the fat prince already your enemy, it would be a disaster. *Absolument désastre!* So you must be very careful."

"But he beats her. I must save her."

"A noble ambition but, my young friend, not on the ship. Perhaps once the ship lands and you still have this passion, perhaps then there is the time and the space. But I warn you, as I have been warned before leaving on this journey, in America it is legal for the husband to shoot the lover of the wife—without the duel. Break down the door, find them together…barbarous but true."

"She is an American, then?" Karl asked.

"I didn't say. I can't. But what do I do?"

Colonel Soulé smiled. "Float away on the clouds of *l'amour*. But be very, very careful."

Karl sighed. "Listen to me, Joseph," he said. "This may be real love. But I have made enough ocean crossings to know that strange things happen on a ship. Take this romance for what it is. Yes, you are in love. Yes, the lady loves you. But understand a ship is suspended on a sea of fantasy between two landmasses of reality. Make no decision about what will happen after the ship docks. That will be a different time."

"But…"

Colonel Soulé cut Joseph off. "Karl is right."

The five friends were at their usual places at breakfast. Like the other men, Fitzhugh-Reid's reaction to the news was one of amused admiration. His wife was shocked.

"Joseph von Ritter," Amalee said. "You mean to tell me that while that lovely girl was risking her reputation waiting in the night for you, you were with another woman?"

Joseph sat formally, as if he were at his own court-martial. "I didn't plan it. It just happened."

"I just guess it did," Amalee replied.

"You know what they called Napoleon?" Colonel Soulé interjected. "The Great Improviser. This hussar will one day be a marshal of armies."

"If some furious husband doesn't shoot him first," Karl added.

"Are you saying the lady is married?"

Joseph nodded.

"Well, you are a rapscallion!" Then Amalee smiled. "But there still is the question of the princess' honor."

"I'll do anything." Joseph said.

"Good," Amalee said. "I'm afraid you won't be able to join your comrades at fencing for a few days. You also must not appear for the constitutionals. I shall inform the princess that you've been taken with an indisposition. Something from an old battle wound."

As the table ate and plotted, the ship's movement changed. It was imperceptible at first, a sharpening of the gentle roll, a slight hesitation in the bow as it reached the bottom of a pitch before it rose again. But by the conclusion of the meal the diners found they had to take hold of chairs and rails as they made their way to the deck for the morning constitutional. Once there, they discovered a chill in the air, and husbands and servants were sent below for shawls and cloaks. The sky faded from the normal azure to a hazy gray. A wind came up and the sea appeared darker. Flecks of white dotted waves whose rounded shapes were becoming craggy. Joseph dutifully went to his suite to begin his house arrest.

When he opened his door, Mrs. Bussey was waiting for him. "Your valet let me in. Augustus is working on his papers. We have two hours, my precious."

Mrs. Bussey appeared in Joseph's suite every afternoon and every night. Since Joseph knew nothing of sexual practices, he didn't know that some of the joyful acts in which he lost himself were considered by the world beyond his cabin to be perversions, and he had no idea that his endurance was beyond anything Mrs. Bussey had ever experienced.

When the others of the five friends understood why they saw their youthful companion only at mealtimes, the men were amused and somewhat envious. Amalee was scandalized and thrilled.

With each day the weather worsened. The ship plowed on in increasingly rugged seas, rolling in ever-wider arcs so that the huge paddle wheels began rising out of the water, causing the whole ship to shudder as if it would break apart until the paddles once again dipped into the sea. The morning constitutionals were attended now by only the hardiest men. The fencing was suspended. Seasickness overcame a majority of the passengers. Meals were sparsely populated, while the ship's servants brought bouillon and dry biscuits to the cabins of the afflicted. Two days from New York, cold black rain drove the remaining passengers below. Only Amalee and Karl showed up for meals.

Joseph, although desperately ill with motion sickness, rallied himself for his nights with Mrs. Bussey. The daytime assignations had terminated with the rough weather.

On the next to last night at sea, as they lay side by side in near exhaustion, Mrs. Bussey said, "I will miss you, my precious."

Joseph stared at her, the full import of her words slowly seeping into his numbed mind. "What do you mean?"

"The day after tomorrow we shall land. We shall never see each other again."

"No!" Joseph leaped to his feet. "You must run away."

"My precious, it's impossible. We shall dock at six in the morning. We'll go directly to the train for Buffalo. We spend the night there and the next day we travel to St. Louis. It will be impossible for me to escape."

"Why?"

"To do so requires money. I've none. How would I hire a cab to take me to the train? Or pay for a ticket back to New York? And once in New York, how shall I live? It's impossible."

Joseph laughed, "Money is the difficulty? I have all the money in the world. Tomorrow night I shall give you enough money to be free forever."

"Joseph, my precious. Would you?"

Joseph smothered her face with kisses. "You'll never have to worry about money again."

The next evening Mrs. Bussey appeared at midnight, three hours later than usual. "He didn't start drinking till late." She started to cry.

"Show me." Joseph was weak with his days of motion sickness, his extravagant sexual exertions and lack of proper nourishment, but he knew that if she was marked again he would find Bussey and kill him.

"No. He didn't beat me. Oh my precious, love me until I no longer have thoughts of him."

They made love, then after collapsing exhausted in Mrs. Bussey's arms Joseph, hardly conscious, was jolted by a searing pain at the back of his head. He was dragged by his hair from his love and slammed to the deck.

"I could kill you," Aaron Augustus Bussey said.

As Joseph turned, Bussey's booted foot kicked the air out of him, cracking two ribs. By the time Joseph regained his breath, Bussey was pointing a pistol at him.

"You have been fucking my wife," Bussey said. "We are in American waters now. No court in this country would convict me if kill you. But I don't think I will. What I'll do is ruin you. I'll divorce this whore. I'll name you as the correspondent. The New York papers will eat it up. You'll be ruined in America. Your own embassy will disown you."

Impostor! Jew! Joseph thought. He would spend the rest of his life in prison. He would never see his parents again. Perhaps they would hang him. He tried to focus on Bussey's words.

"Whatever hopes you have in America are dead. I'm going to sue you, Mr. Baron. I'll take every penny you have. And as for this bitch, I'll see to it that she ends up on the streets. A nickel whore. I can do that."

"You must not hurt her."

Bussey stunned Joseph with a kick to his head.

When Joseph woke he saw Bussey standing over Mrs. Bussey, her head held by her hair cruelly twisted. She was dressed. In Bussey's other hand was the alligator bag. He gestured with it toward Joseph. "Maybe we can settle this out of court."

Joseph nodded dully.

"Good. Here's the deal. I take the money in this bag and we're even. But if you say one word about this settlement, she's a nickel whore and you're ruined. Deal?"

Joseph nodded.

"I didn't hear you. Do we have a deal?"

"Yes," Joseph whispered.

"Didn't hear you!"

"Yes!" Joseph shouted.

"Yes, what?"

"I give you all my money. You will protect Mrs. Bussey."

"One other thing. I am a hunter. Every time I shoot a prize animal, I nail its skin to my wall. I want your fancy black uniform and that fur hat and that saber. You have any objection to that?"

Joseph looked at the floor. "No."

"I didn't hear you. What did you say, boy?"

"No!" Joseph shouted.

"Good." He turned to Mrs. Bussey, who flinched. "Pack it up."

Joseph watched as Bussey hauled his wife to her feet and shoved her to the closet, where she brought out Joseph's suitcase and filled it with his uniform and busby. She also gave him Joseph's saber.

Bussey took it to the porthole. "We don't need this junk to weigh us down, do we?" Then he threw the saber into the sea.

"Just one other thing. Money buys you out of the trouble, but not my honor. You've been fucking my wife, boy." He grabbed Joseph by the hair and beat him senseless. Joseph did not see or hear the Busseys leave.

Back in their stateroom, Bussey dumped the contents of the alligator bag on their bed. "It's so much more than I thought," he said. "Figured the servants were lying. No one carries this much money. Look at it." He turned to his wife fondly. "I couldn't have accomplished it without you."

"I loved how you smashed him," she said simply.

Bussey gently removed her clothing and they made love on the piles of Joseph's money.

At four in the morning, Wissenkopf let himself into the cabin to prepare his master for the six o'clock docking and the seven o'clock disembarkation. Instead he ministered to Joseph's cuts, contusions, and swellings. One eye was already bloating shut and several ribs were cracked. Joseph forbade him to call the captain or the ship's doctor.

"Allow me to summon your friends, Herr Albert, Colonel Soulé, Mister Fitzhugh-Reid...."

"No," he told Wissenkopf.

Now to his misery was added loneliness. He could never see these friends again. Without his money the masquerade could not continue. If they found him in his present state and penniless, they would write to the non-existent Breitensteins for help and discover his fraud—that he was a Jew. For the first time Joseph wept, not for his wounds, nor his pain, nor the loss of the money, but for the lies he had told.

And then Joseph thought of God. Could the God of the Jews have done this to him out of spite? No, he decided. It happened because it happened. There was no God.

Joseph asked Wissenkopf to tell his friends that it was with great regret that he had needed to hurry off as soon as the ship docked.

At seven the passengers disembarked. At ten, when the crew was given shore leave, Wissenkopf helped Joseph from the ship. The rainstorm that had overtaken them at sea was pouring torrents of icy sleet over the city. Wissenkopf bundled Joseph into a hansom cab and wrapped him in one of the ship's blankets.

"To the St. Nicholas Hotel," Wissenkopf said, per Joseph's instructions. The cab pulled away. As it rounded the corner, Joseph shouted to the driver.

"*Halte! Stoppen!*"

"You say to stop?"

Joseph answered in English. "Not St. Nicholas Hotel."

"Where to then?" the driver asked.

"I have no money."

The driver climbed down from his seat and looked at the battered form in his carriage. "No fucking sailor joke on me!" he roared. "Out!" He reached in, pulled Joseph out of the cab, and dropped him into the gutter.

BOOK TWO

THE MOUNT OF THE LORD

*"It is not thy duty to complete the work,
but neither art thou free to desist from it."*
—*Rabbi Tarfon, Pirke Aboth II:21*

§13

Stunned, joseph lay inert where he fell, the sharp chill of the gutter water soaking through his clothes. Around him the world was gray: the rain, the sky, the streets, the buildings, the people. Joseph's body shook with numb cold. He was in pain. A thought occurred to him. He needed help. Where was his Poppa? Dark forms under umbrellas darted by. People hunched over in rain-soaked wool or slick oilskins hurried up and down the narrow sidewalk. In the street, wagons clattered and rumbled, their noise merging with the shatter of the rain. No one gave more than a glance at Joseph crumpled in the street.

"Help me," he said. No one heard. Perhaps, he thought, he should sleep for a while and think later. Joseph closed his eyes.

Hercules, who had seen humans lying in the roads before, watched him. Fallen humans always interested him. Humans were so powerful, and yet some were not. The one behind him on the wagon, the one with the uncertain hands and the cursing voice, was not powerful, even though he sat on the high seat and held a whip. Yet the one crumpled on the street, with his eyes closed, was powerful.

Joseph first became aware of the warm breath against his face, and then the sound of a thin, shouting voice. It was in English. Joseph recognized the tone but not the words. When he looked he saw a horse inches from his eyes.

"Get on with it, yuh dirty bastard! Gee-up! Who the fuck told you to stop! Gee-up goddamn your soul to hell! Gee-up!" Hercules hated the whip, but he had long ago learned not to be afraid of it in the hands of the one on the wagon, the man called Skilley.

Joseph watched the great gray start forward and instinctively recognized that his life depended on following that horse. He struggled to his feet. The pain in his chest tore him apart, his head was on fire and his legs wouldn't move. But he forced himself to lurch after the empty wagon clattering over the cobbles ahead of him.

Hercules heard him coming. Through the sound of the rain he listened to the crumpled man's faltering footsteps and knew the man would fall again. Hercules stopped. The skinny man up on the driver's seat automatically launched into his litany of curses. While he was doing so, Joseph stumbled into the wagon, even before he realized it had stopped. He grabbed the tailgate to keep from falling and it came down, dropping him to his knees. His whole world compressed into a single thought. He had to climb into the wagon. With the last of his strength he clawed his way into the dry darkness of the wagon and pulled the tailgate up behind him. He lay his face on the rough planks of the wagon floor and felt the vehicle lurch ahead. The last thing he heard before he passed out was the rumble of the iron shod wheels on the cobbles.

Cully Brannagan understood that there were only two kinds of people in the world: those you used, and those who used you. To the former he was whimsically merciless. To the latter he was engagingly servile. With his natural charm and artful words, his victims only realized their error after the fact. Fortunately for the world, Brannagan's voracious ambition was limited by a meager imagination. Cully Brannagan hadn't it in him to aspire to be mayor of New York City. He did, however, want to own a piece of the mayor of New York City.

During his fifteen years in New York, Brannagan had built himself a comfortable teamster business with sidelines in horse swindling and politics. In the latter he had risen from a seller of the odd few immigrant votes to a mid-sized vote merchant. He could, and did, deliver on demand of Tammany Hall as many as eight thousand votes each election. The votes had been nearly all Irish, but of late there had been an ever-increasing number of Germans. Many were immigrants just off ships, many were former immigrants who owed their meager well-being to Brannagan's intercessions with Tammany Hall, and others were recently deceased. In return for his efforts Brannagan was awarded the unofficial but powerful title of Boss of the Sixth Ward, which included the notorious Five Points area, Misery Row and Murderer's Alley. His livelihood, Brannagan Cartage & Co., was on a list of select enterprises doing business with and for the City of New York. Brannagan Cartage & Co.'s invoices to the city fathers were never closely examined and always paid in full upon receipt.

Brannagan's place of business and Democratic headquarters for the Sixth Ward was a large stable, wagon-yard, and barns on Baxter Street in the Five Points district. The stable, dark and rat-infested, was four stories high with ramps for the horses to move from floor to floor. It reeked of horse urine and manure. The little ventilation came through the great double doors on the stable yard. In cold weather when the doors were shut, only a small amount of air entered through the cracks in the wooden walls. That just a few horses died there was due only to Brannagan's greed. Sick animals couldn't be worked to death. He could tell when they were on the verge of illness and, if he couldn't quickly cure them, he doctored them to keep them well-looking just long enough to swindle unsuspecting buyers.

Now Brannagan glanced up from his desk and watched as Skilley backed in his wagon, unhitched Hercules, and led the horse across the yard to the stable. There was something about Hercules' movement that bothered Brannagan. The old horse was going to be sick. Twenty-two years was a good lifespan for any horse, but Brannagan would regret the loss of Hercules who could do the work of a team. Brannagan would have to start thinking about setting up Hercules to sell to a sucker or, failing that, the renderers. Then something else caught his eye. The empty wagon jiggled slightly. Brannagan had seen that before too. One of the street rats had crawled in, probably hoping to hide until night when he'd sneak into the tack room and steal whatever he could.

Brannagan closed and locked his roll-top desk, for he was careful about his private business and, smiling expectantly, pulled on a gum coat and ambled over to the wagon. On the way he picked up a heavy oak wheel spoke. But one look inside the wagon told him he wouldn't need it.

"Skilley!" he shouted. "Skilley, you horse's hind end. Get Mick and drag your dirty ass over here. Now!" Skilley and Mick, a burly teamster, came on the run. Brannagan pointed into the wagon.

"Now what do you make of that?"

"A dirty skug," Skilley said. "I don't know how he got in me wagon, but out he goes. Come on Mick, we'll drop him over the wall."

Brannagan liked Skilley's ever-present meanness. "You'll do nothing of the kind," Brannagan said. "Now just look at him and tell me what you're seeing, you sod."

Skilley squinted to show that he was looking, but he had no idea what he was supposed to see.

"The boots," Mick said. "Look at them boots. He's wearing fine boots."

Brannagan smiled his approval. "That's using yer old block, Mick. Tiz fine boots he's wearing. And what else?"

The two teamsters studied Joseph's unconscious form. Skilley, to look as though he were actually thinking, scratched his head. Then strangely enough, a thought appeared. "You want we should pull his boots off, Boss?"

Brannagan spoke softly, as to a favorite but retarded child. "Not just yet, darlin'. Do you not see the way he's dressed?" He waited until both sets of eyes looked into the wagon again and swung back to him without any understanding. "He's a Dutchman, by the clothes, from South Germany. But for the boots, a peasant I'd say. But for the boots..."

There was little Brannagan understood better than immigrants. And here was a brand new voter, lying in the wagon, dressed like a peasant and wearing gentleman's boots, much more interesting than most of the voters. "Go and fetch me Dutch Wagner."

Someone was shouting in German. "What's your name?" the voice said. "Wake up! Who are you?"

Joseph smelled a sour stable. He opened the only eye that would. Two men were watching him. One was a giant with a huge chest, green eyes, and flaming red hair; the other was smaller, powerfully built, with a flat nose and puffy ears. "What's your name?" the second man rasped in rough German.

"Von Ritter," Joseph mumbled.

Dutch turned to Brannagan. "You're right about them boots. He got a 'von' in front of his name. Maybe could be a gentleman. A fucking aristocrat."

"Yeah? Ask the little darling who done him."

In German, Dutch growled, "Who beat you up?"

Joseph's mind cleared enough to understand that he had to be careful. "I don't know. From behind. Took all my money."

Brannagan next asked Dutch to find out what ship he was off, and whether or not he had family in America.

"No family," Joseph said. "I'm alone." He knew he couldn't give them the name of the *North Sea*. If he did, they could ask about him, he'd be discovered, and they'd send him to prison. Joseph struggled to recall the name of the other shipping company in Bremen. "From New World." He closed his eye, pretending to faint again. He heard the man translate for the giant.

"He's alone. Came on one of the New World ships."

"Then he's been here a week. The *Dutchland*. Went back yesterday, didn' it?"

"*Ja*. On the morning tide."

"We get any off that rotten tub?"

"Nah. Not many. They was most of 'em contracted for. Went right on the cars. Shipped west. Farmers." Dutch spat in contempt.

Brannagan smiled. "That's right. 'Twas a bunch of contract farmers, wasn't it? The lot of them signed for working the new lands." A dirty grin appeared on his face. "You know what I think? I think this little bugger's gone and weaseled out of his contract. Can yuh imagine, a nice looking lad like that cheating an honest contractor out of his fare to the New World. Oh, tiz a wicked, wicked world indeed." Brannagan turned to Dutch. "Ask him if he's a farmer."

Dutch shook Joseph until he opened his good eye. Dutch asked the question. Joseph painfully propped himself on his elbow and looked past the two men. Beyond them he saw the old horse that had stopped for him. Joseph guessed the larger man was the boss. To him, in his best Georgia-accented English, he said, "Horses. I know horses." The effort exhausted the last of his reserves. Joseph collapsed back into his fever.

"Well, now," Brannagan said. "Ain't this me lucky day! Horses, he knows. And just listen to the beautiful English the lad spouts. And him with an obligation for his passage. Tiz only fair he should pay what he owes. Well, I say tiz worth the risk of fixing him up a bit. Only enough though to see what we got here." Brannagan calculated it to the penny—time, medicine, effort. If the boy was useless, he could always be sold back to the contractor from whom he had escaped.

Brannagan moved Joseph to a bunk in the tack room near his office at the end of the row of stalls. The room was filthy but reasonably dry and warm. While Brannagan was willing to spend time and a small amount of money on medicines, believing that Joseph could speak English, he wasn't willing to spend much on Dutch Wagner's translations and so, while Joseph lay in a delirious fever, Brannagan missed bits of biographical information that he would have valued.

Brannagan tended Joseph as he did a costly horse. He dressed his wounds, applied poultices, and worked liquids down the boy's throat. After three days the fever broke, and by the end of five Joseph was aware of his surroundings.

When Brannagan realized how little English Joseph spoke, he once more sent for Dutch who was one of most expensive teamsters. Brannagan hated paying Dutch wages for anything but driving. It angered him that the boy had fooled him with his English. Dutch's wages would have to be added to the forty dollars for the trans-Atlantic fee that Brannagan now believed was rightfully his.

"Tell the little darling about me contract," Brannagan said.

Joseph was pleased he could understand as many words as he did. He now looked to the German whom they called Dutch to see how many he had guessed correctly.

In German, Dutch said, "You listen to what I say. Mr. Brannagan is the boss. In the old country he would be like a count, who decides who goes to jail or who gets hanged. He owns all this, but also he owns the police. Even judges do what he says. He's very powerful. He knows that you ran away from the contractor who paid your passage to America. He's now paid that contractor for your services. He has also paid for your food and bed and medicine. He pays for me to talk to you. You will have to work for him till you pay back all that money. You understand what I say?"

"You mean I work for no wages?"

"You get wages, but he takes out what you owe him. For a while you get nothing left over. You understand?"

"For how long a while?"

Dutch enjoyed telling the aristocrat his new fate. "The contract is usually for three months," he said. "The others, the peasants who were honest and didn't run away, they work for three months for their passage, and then for another year for money to buy their own land. Then they'll be Americans working only for themselves. You, who tried to cheat—and I know how aristocrats like to cheat—will work for nothing. Boss Brannagan says that he pays you wages, but you will see nothing of wages. He'll charge you for your bed. He'll charge you for your food, for your clothing, for everything. He'll charge you for the air you breathe. The charges will always come to more than your wages. And wages? You will be cheated there too. Because you already have no choice, even the sum he'll lie about paying you will be less, much less, than he'd pay if he were just hiring a free stable boy. You have no choice. If you're very lucky, you'll be a slave for only a few years."

"But what happens if I refuse?"

Dutch had been hoping Joseph would ask this. "He will beat you worse than you have ever seen. Perhaps he will beat you to death. They say he has done it before. But if you live, after the beating, he'll take you to the police. He'll tell them that you've stolen money from him. They'll put you in prison for ten years. I've seen him do this and worse."

§14

JOSEPH STOOD ON THE LARGE ROCKY PROMONTORY, ENGULFED IN impenetrable blackness. In the distance a small cloud, at first puffy white, began to grow and then move toward him. He was desperate to run but around the rocky pinnacle was only a void, an emptiness more dreadful than the cloud sailing toward him. As it came closer, the cloud billowed into roiling grays; the closer it came, the darker and more violent it grew. It was going to take up all the space in the universe. Joseph was unable to breathe. He was at the moment of his death. Then, at the last possible instant, the cloud exploded. Joseph ecstatically sucked in clean fresh air. But in the distance the exploded fragments became hundreds of tiny little white clouds, immediately beginning to grow and churn into the awful grays. And as each cloud grew it seemed that it alone would occupy all the space there ever was. The clouds filled the universe and pressed against Joseph's eyes and nose and mouth. He thought he was going to burst into a million fragments. Then, with a scream, he was violently thrown from the rock.

Joseph woke as he hit the planks of the tack room floor. He was blinded by the light of a lantern, behind which loomed a huge dark figure. Then he recoiled with pain as a booted toe dug into his healing ribs. Someone was yelling.

"Get out of it, you lazy scut! Time to earn your keep!" Brannagan loved shouting in the morning.

Joseph was too disoriented to understand all of the words. He remained still. Then an arm reached out from behind the light and, grabbing his hair, jerked him to his feet.

"*Bitte,*" Joseph wailed in German.

Brannagan's huge hand emerged from the darkness and rocked Joseph's face. "None of your Dutch talk. From now on you talk English. Say it in English."

Joseph understood. He had to speak English. What was the English word for *bitte*? "Please," Joseph said. "Please."

Brannagan smiled. "Well now, there's a darlin'. I knew you could do it if you put your mind on it. Now say, 'Good morning, Mr. Brannagan.' "

Joseph understood he was expected to say something but before he could, another slap jolted his head.

"Say, 'Good morning, Mr. Brannagan.' "

He was supposed to say something. What?

Another slap. "Good morning, Mr. Brannagan."

The words came out of him as if they themselves had willed it. "Good morning, Mr. Brannagan." It was a near-perfect imitation of Brannagan's Irish lilt.

Brannagan laughed. "Well then, you can speak English if you've a mind to do it. Now put your clothes on and be quick. Time is money. Money is time." He held up Joseph's smock and said, "Shirt." When Joseph didn't respond he cuffed him again.

Joseph said, "Shirt."

Brannagan handed Joseph his pants. "Trousers."

"Trousers." He pulled them on and looked around for his boots. Neither the smock nor the trousers mitigated the chill in his body.

Brannagan handed him a crude pair of hard and dirty shoes. Joseph looked at them and handed them back, for which he received another slap.

"Put 'em on."

Joseph remembered the English words he needed. "Not mine. Mine good boots."

"Ah, yer boots is gone, darlin'. They was a perfect fit for Dutch so you gave 'em to him for helping you with the difficulties of speakin' English. I know 'twas expensive them being such fine boots an' all, that's why I've taken it upon meself, busy as I am, to teach you proper speakin'. I'll deduct me lessons from yer wages. Now get these shoes on and start earning your keep. Say shoes."

Joseph, in spite of the fuzziness in his head, understood most of what was said and instantly repeated the word. He then sat on the bunk and pulled them on. They were too large and cold. When he stood up he was nearly overcome by dizziness and hunger. He looked up at Brannagan and croaked, "Hungry. Please food."

Another slap rocked his head. "Hungry is it, you lazy little beggar! You'll eat when I say and not before. And before I say, you'll earn your breakfast." He grabbed Joseph by the arm and marched him out of the tack room and into the stable. By the dim illumination of three oil lanterns hanging from the ceiling, Joseph saw another figure waiting for them. Twitchel, the seventeen-year-old stable boy, the product of generations of inbreeding, had skin and hair so pale it seemed all the color had been deliberately bred out of him. Tall and too thin, he moved like an ungainly bird.

"Twit, you idiot, this is Joe, your new assistant." Brannagan laughed at his joke. "Assistant stable boy, assistant idiot." Twit laughed too although he did not know why.

"He says he knows about horses. So you go on and take him now and get all these fed." And to Joseph, "There's thirty horses to feed before you get to eat. Say, 'thirty horses.'" Joseph was slow in replying and Brannagan cuffed him again. To Twit, he said, "He's a Dutchman. We're teachin' him English. You tells him a word, he don't say it back, you cuff him, you get that, you idiot?"

Twit nodded. "I say a word, then he's supposed to say it back an' ifin he don't I whack him." Then his face crinkled in a thought. "What word?" he asked.

"Ah Twit, you got less brains than the horses in the stalls. You pick up a pitchfork, you say pitchfork and make him say back to you. Do it now. Lemme see you do it once so I can see you do it right." Brannagan handed Twit a pitchfork.

Twit studied the fork for a moment and then, turning to Joseph, said, "pitchfork," and handed it to him.

Joseph took it and said, "pitchfork," whereupon Twit slammed his fist into the side of Joseph's face. Joseph fell to the floor.

"No!" Brannagan laughed. "O'bejazus. That's the best you done yet. Glory, what a fuckin' idiot! If he says it right, you don't whack him. You got that?"

Twit smiled. "He says it right, I don't whack him. When do I whack him?"

"When he says it wrong, or he ain't fast enough sayin' it back to you. I'll show you once more. You mess up this time and I'll slam you so hard you'll go through the wall. Now watch." Brannagan jerked Joseph to his feet and again handed him the pitchfork. "Pitchfork," he said.

Joseph replied, "pitchfork."

Brannagan smiled at him. "Good lad." He turned to Twit. "See he said it, so no whack. You got that?"

Twit nodded. "He sez it an' no whack."

"That's right. But if he don't, that's when you whack him. But no fist. Open hand. No fist. If you hurt him he can't help you work. You got that?"

"Whack him with my open hand."

"And when do you do that?"

Twit's brow contracted.

Brannagan sighed. "I'll show you." He turned to Joseph, "Say, 'Abracadabra-oppseedaisy-arounshegoes-anoutshecomes.' "

Joseph stared uncomprehendingly, and Brannagan, making sure that his pupil Twit was observing, slapped Joseph with his open hand. Next he pointed to the manure in the first stall. "Horseshit."

"Horseshit," Joseph repeated.

Brannagan smiled. "See? Easy as pie. Now get them fucking horses fed. And when you're done bring this one to me office for his feeding." He turned and went out into the still-dark morning.

Twit stared at Joseph, and Joseph looked back with near non-comprehension. "We goin' to the barn for hay now," Twit said. "You say it."

"We goin'." Joseph couldn't remember the rest.

Twit slapped him and said, "C'mon, folly me."

"Folly me," Joseph mumbled, and shambled after Twit.

Feeding horses in New York wasn't different from feeding horses in Bavaria. With Twit leading the way, saying words and slapping Joseph when he did or didn't repeat them properly or quickly enough, they moved hay from the barn to the thirty stalls.

.Twit, who had lived his seventeen years at the bottom of the human hierarchy, had never once dominated another living creature. With each slap delivered to Joseph, Twit felt himself enlarged. By the end of their first hour, Twit had taken to booting Joseph at odd times for only the true pleasure of it.

Their first chore completed, Twit delivered Joseph to Brannagan's office. Brannagan saw the boy's fatigue and, taking him from Twit, closed the door on the stable boy. Gently he led Joseph to a bench near the stove. "There now, lad. You've had a hard time of it, haven't you? And I bet you're hungry."

The warmth of the room seeped into his body. Brannagan poured a steaming mug of coffee from a chipped white enamel pot on the stove and held it out to Joseph. As Joseph clutched at it, Brannagan withdrew it and said, "coffee."

"Coffee."

Brannagan smiled and held out the cup. Joseph seized it and, ignoring the scalding pain in his throat, drank. Then another smell commanded Joseph's attention. Brannagan, at the stove, had taken the lid off a pot. He filled a thick pottery bowl with steaming porridge and repeated the exercise. "Porridge."

"Porridge," Joseph answered.

Brannagan handed it to him with a wooden spoon. Joseph didn't look up again until the bowl was empty. He looked up and held it out to Brannagan. "Please."

Brannagan nodded in approval. "Since you asked so nice, and in English, I'll give you a bit more."

Joseph felt more than hunger. He felt tender gratitude.

When Joseph had licked the bowl clean, Brannagan took it from him, went to a peg on the wall and unhooked an old wool jacket. "Winter's coming on, and any fool can see you're cold. So I'll rent you this nice warm jacket. Don't worry about the cost. I'll deduct it from your wages. At night after you've had your supper, you leave it here in me office and each morning you come for it, and if you've been a good lad, I'll rent it to you for another day. And oh, I'll be wanting you to leave your shoes here at night too. Here by the stove, so they'll be nice and warm for you in the morning."

Brannagan watched as Joseph pulled on the coat, which was too big, and then he handed Joseph back to Twit. For the next twelve hours Joseph, cuffed and kicked by Twit, pumped and hauled water, curried horses, mucked out stalls, and moved mountains of manure.

The more Joseph worked the less Twit had to. During that twelve hours Joseph ate twice; both times like breakfast from Brannagan's hand, and both times barely enough to sustain him. Yet the gratitude Joseph had begun to feel to the Irishman grew with each meal, just as by the third day of his labors, he began to feel something else: hate. His hate, as unreasonable as his gratitude, was directed toward Twit. With each command, slap, or kick, Joseph's hate deepened.

In the weeks that followed, Joseph ate every meal in Brannagan's warm office, and always from Brannagan's hand. It was never enough food for a boy worked to exhaustion twelve or fourteen hours a day, and so Joseph was unable to focus his mind on his situation. But he was comforted by his love for Brannagan who took care of him and who taught him English. And he was sustained by his ever-festering hate for Twit.

One morning, after a night slightly warmer than most, Joseph woke and knew his spirit had returned. He was still weak and exhausted, but he could think clearly. He lay on his hard bunk and reveled in his rediscovered ability to think. He thought about food: the food his mother had made; the sumptuous meals at Count Wehdel's; the breakfasts, lunches, teas, and dinners on the ship. He relived every taste. He thought about his father and working the horses with him on sunny spring days. He thought about the hussars and his friends on the ship. And as he lay in his bed he felt tears running down the side of his head. He would never see his parents again, nor the wonderful people he had met on the ship. And when the crying was done he thought about Twit, and how one day he would beat Twit into a bloody pulp. But to his surprise he found that he didn't hate Brannagan. He was afraid of him, but he didn't hate him. Brannagan was tough, a hard man, but also a kind man.

With the recovery of thought came the understanding that escape was necessary. He rose in the dark night, dressed and quietly walked to the office door to retrieve his warm jacket and his shoes. The door was locked. Joseph turned and ran quickly out of the stable. He was on the dark street. There the damp sidewalk chilled his feet. Joseph ran to the corner, turned left, ran several more blocks, turned right, ducked into an alley, ran to its end, turned right onto another dark street and left at the next corner where he saw activity. He then slowed to a walk and moved toward some lights. It was a river, and at the covered wharf directly in front of him fishing boats were unloading their catch by the glow of oil lanterns. Joseph noticed for the first time that it was raining. He was shivering again.

On the street in front of the wharf Joseph saw men warming themselves by a large bonfire. He slowly worked his way toward them, prepared to run at the instant of danger. But no one paid any attention to him and he was able to approach close enough to feel the heat. The cold rain fell harder. The men, all of whom wore oilskins or gum coats, stared at Joseph, who drifted onto the wharf under the protection of the roof. Down the wharf's center were two rows of tables marked by signs indicating the names of the fishmongers, who were now bargaining with the fishermen for their catch. Nearby, Joseph saw something he desperately needed: a wool blanket draped across one of the tables. Above the table the sign read, "Moses Cohen. Fresh Fish." Joseph looked around. No one was watching. When he was absolutely sure he was unobserved, he ducked down below the table level and carefully began working the material off. Slowly, ever so slowly, it came. Then it stopped. It was stuck. He tugged again. It didn't move. Joseph raised himself up over the edge to look. There an angry man in a black suit was holding the blanket with both hands. Two large sailors in oilskins stood on either side of him. They were grinning. The man in the black suit said, "*Gonif!*" It was Yiddish. "Thief!"

Joseph instinctively replied in Yiddish. "I must have it! I'm cold!"

The man was astonished. His face changed from anger to compassion. "A Jew?" he asked in Yiddish. "You are a countryman? A Jewish boy?"

Joseph shook his head violently. "No!" he shouted. "I'm not a damned Jew!" He grabbed the blanket from the man's hand and ran. The two sailors started after him, but the man stopped them and called after Joseph. "So that you should not have the sin of stealing," he said, "I give you the blanket!"

Joseph ran up a dark alley, turned at its end, and ran right and left until he was sure he hadn't been pursued. Exhausted, he sank into an arch of a doorway under a portico, wrapped the blanket around his body, and fell asleep. His last thought before he closed his eyes was that he had become a thief.

The sun in his face woke him. He was damp, cold, stiff, but most of all he was hungry. He had to find food. The street was lined with wooden buildings, some only one story high, others two and three. No two roofs were alike or aligned. Some had their entrance at street level, others had stairs leading to doors five or six feet above the sidewalk. Near the eastern end of the street the morning sun glinted off a row of red brick houses three stories high with white window frames and cornices. At the corner was a tall building of six stories.

The street was just now coming to life. A carriage pulled to the portico under which Joseph was lying. Two men in dark suits descended and started toward the doorway. They paused when they saw Joseph. He quickly rose. "I work," he said to the men. "For food work. Horses I know."

The first man opened the door quickly while the second raised his walking stick. "Get out of here," he said, "or I'll have the police on you."

Joseph turned and ran.

The next street was busier. White-roofed omnibuses drawn by horses and filled with people rumbled by in both directions. The buildings were covered with signs. The smell of fresh bread caught Joseph's attention. He turned and saw a boy in a white apron rolling a baker's cart loaded with fresh-baked goods down the street. Joseph walked after him. The boy, aware of Joseph, walked more quickly, throwing anxious glances in Joseph's direction. Three blocks away the boy stopped in front of a restaurant, McBride's, where a man with a drooping black mustache came out to unload the bread. The boy whispered something, and the man turned to Joseph. "Hungry," Joseph said. "Food. Work I can do. Horses I know."

"Beat it!" the man said. "None of you Dutch here!"

Over the next few hours Joseph met rejection wherever he solicited work. Once, when he ran forward to hold a nervous horse for a coachman, the man slashed at him with his whip.

By noon gray clouds had covered the sun and chill winds blew down the streets. Joseph's feet were bleeding. He began to imagine he was on the deck of the ship, ready to join his friends for a meal. When he fell, he didn't see the people hurrying around him. He saw only the filthy rags he was wearing and knew that if he didn't eat he would lose his mind. He remembered where the boy took the bread. It was, he understood, a restaurant. Carefully rising to his feet Joseph concentrated on the sidewalk, on who he was, and what he was going to do. He was Franz Joseph von Ritter Baron von Britenstein, and he was going to get food.

McBride saw him coming. He watched as Joseph studied the restaurant. Just as McBride suspected, the boy next disappeared into the narrow space between the restaurant and the building beside it. McBride looked around. Except for the two waiters and four busboys, it was empty—the quiet time before the Tammany gang arrived for their supper. McBride went into the kitchen. "Ma," he said to the large woman at the stove, "Send one of the boys on the run over to the precinct and bring back a couple of the officers."

When she was gone, he took an iron skillet from the rack above the stove, positioned himself behind the door and waited. After a while the back door opened slightly. Through the crack, McBride saw the street rat peering into the kitchen. He waited. The door creaked open and the boy ran to the bread basket. He snatched a loaf and turned for the door.

"Gotcha, you little thief!" McBride slammed the iron skillet into Joseph's head.

When Joseph opened his eyes, four people were peering down at him: McBride, McBride's mother, and two policemen.

"What's your name, boy?" the first policeman asked.

"Von Ritter," Joseph answered. His head was throbbing.

"I told you 'twas. The one as belongs to Brannagan," the first policeman said to the second.

"Do you work for Mr. Cully Brannagan?" asked the second policeman.

"Yes," said Joseph. "Mr. Brannagan."

§15

Brannagan horse-whipped Joseph with precision and without anger. "Tiz for your own education, lad," he said. "You'll be a lot better off for the understanding you get from it."

Brannagan kept at his work until Joseph's cries were steady and the responses to each lash sharpened. At last, when he knew Joseph was ready, Brannagan made Joseph repeat after him, "When you owe Mr. Brannagan money, there is no place you can go to hide from him." Although Joseph's back was torn and bloody, his deepest wound was his humiliation.

At the end of the disciplinary session Brannagan rubbed ointment on Joseph's welts and tenderly bandaged his feet. Joseph was then allowed a recovery of five days on his cot in the harness room, with hot meals personally brought by Brannagan himself.

Joseph spent the five days thinking. He was a fool to run before he was ready. He had to accept that there was no escape. For now. Brannagan controlled the police. Joseph would go to prison if he attempted to escape again. He decided to pretend to be his slave, to speak English and learn about America. He'd earn enough money to go far away. But to do this he needed more food than Brannagan allowed him, not to work so hard and more sleep. He also needed warm clothes. He was, after all, Franz Joseph von Ritter Baron von Britenstein!

When Brannagan had decided Joseph was sufficiently recovered he took him back to Twit. "Twit, you idiot," he said. "Your assistant idiot is back."

After Brannagan left the stable, Twit handed Joseph the pitchfork. "Say, 'pitchfork,'" he said.

Joseph took it from him, and said, "Pitchfork." Then he drove the tip of the handle into Twit's stomach. Gasping for air, Twit fell to the floor. Joseph dragged him into an empty stall and waited until Twit's breathing returned to normal. Twit looked at him with terror.

"Who is boss, you *oder* me?" Joseph asked.

"Mr. Brannagan said I was to be…" Twit gasped.

Joseph back-handed Twit across the face. "Who is boss? You *oder* me?"

Twit had no answer.

Joseph slapped and backhanded him, snapping Twit's head against the wooden partition of the stall. "Who is boss?"

"You!" Twit screamed.

Joseph pushed Twit to the floor and, knee on Twit's chest, took hold of his hair. "You must do everything what I say." With his free hand Joseph slapped Twit's head from side to side. "Everything what I say. Yes?" He asked the question with each slap. "Yes?" Slap. "Yes?" Slap. "Yes?" Slap.

"Yes!" Twit screamed. "Yes." He was crying. Brannagan, watching from the shadows, congratulated himself on his excellent judgment.

At breakfast that morning Brannagan said, "I don't care who does what so long as the work gets done. You kill Twit and you'll have to do his share too. You get me drift?"

Joseph felt a glow of pride. Mr. Brannagan had seen him and had approved.

"From now on you can keep your coat and shoes in your own room." He smiled at Joseph and, unasked, poured more coffee into his cup. "And another thing," Brannagan said. "No more Dutch name. From now on you're just Joe Ritter. A fine American name. It's the one you'll be voting with."

To Brannagan, Joe Ritter, Joseph thought. But he would always be Franz Joseph von Ritter Baron von Britenstein. "Good," he said. "I am Joe Ritter." He smiled.

In a matter of days Joseph had trained Twit to do the hardest work and put in the longest hours. Work continued for him as well, some of it heavy but none of it mentally taxing. There was still the problem of his perpetual hunger. Brannagan insisted he take his three meager meals in the office with him. There was never enough.

Then one day Joseph discovered Twit brought his midday meal with him in a tin pail. Joseph took the pail. With Twit watching in mute despair, Joseph ate half the bread and cheese. "You're lucky," he told him. "Your Momma gives you food when you go home."

Joseph turned and went to get a cup of water from the trough pump. When his back was turned, Twit muttered to himself, "She don' give me but a cup of soup. An' that ain't got nothin' in it."

Since half of Twit's food wasn't enough to satisfy Joseph's hunger, soon he was taking all of it. Twit made no objection. In fact, Twit stopped speaking except for the occasional mumbled monosyllable. Joseph saw but refused to give any compassion for the pain in Twit's eyes. To himself, he thought, this is how it works in America.

Because Joseph no longer worked punishing hours, he no longer fell into exhausted sleep moments after his meager supper. The first time he stayed awake into the early part of the night, he discovered he was the only one who slept in the stable. Except for the horses he was alone for the first time since he left the ship. Alone, and with that came the ache of loneliness. He tried to push it away, but it remained. Then he remembered Hercules, the gray Percheron who had saved him.

The moment Joseph looked at Hercules he could tell he was sick. But before he examined him he spoke: "I'm your friend. My name is Joseph. Thank you for saving me. What a good old horse you are. Come, sniff my hand. See? It's my smell. Joseph smell." He bent down next to the horse's nostrils and softly blew his breath into them. Hercules sighed. "I'm your friend," Joseph said. "Let me touch you. You helped me, and now it is my turn to help you." Continuing to speak gently to the animal, Joseph lightly ran his hands over its body. At the hock joints Joseph's fingers confirmed what he already suspected: bog spavin. The horse's joints were filled with fluid. If untreated, a bony substance would form and Hercules would be forever crippled. Joseph had no doubt as to what Brannagan would do with a crippled horse.

Joseph began his cure: massaging Hercules under the tongue and around his gums, working his fingers around the back glands in the neck and the horse's joints, all trying to stop the production of the fluid in the joints and begin a natural draining.

Hercules, feeling Joseph's hands, knew he was safe. The bad feeling in his joints was already easing. So when Joseph stopped touching him he rubbed his nose against Joseph's hand, and then lowered himself to the floor and fell into his first deep sleep in many nights.

Joseph rose early the next morning to check on Hercules. The horse was still sick but Joseph detected a slight improvement. He worked on him for over an hour. And when Skilley came in to lead Hercules out for his day's hauling, Joseph told him to take another horse.

"Who the fuck are you giving orders to? You Dutch skut!"

"Horse is sick. Not work today."

"Get out of me fucking way!" Skilley tried to push past Joseph.

Joseph kicked him in the groin. Skilley went down, wailing and skittering around the floor. A moment later Brannagan, Dutch Wagner and the other drivers appeared in the barn.

"What the fuck is going on?" Brannagan demanded. Since Skilley couldn't yet talk, Joseph stepped forward.

"Mr. Brannagan," he said. "When I tell Skilley horse is sick, he not listen. Is not good for horse to work."

Brannagan backhanded Joseph, knocking him to the floor. "I'll decide about when horses can't work. Skilley you horse's ass, get up and take that animal out to your wagon."

From the ground Joseph said, "No!"

Brannagan, amazed and delighted at the defiance, was preparing to kick in Joseph's ribs when Joseph scuttled out of the way. "I can make good horse from sick horse!"

Brannagan withheld his foot. "And how would you do that?"

Joseph turned to Dutch Wagner and spoke in German. "Tell him that in the old country I grew up training horses. Tell him I know many ways of curing horse diseases. If he will give me two weeks with this horse, I'll have him cured and healthy and strong. Tell him this horse has bog spavin. I need seaweed and molasses and comfry leaves. If he'll get me these things, I'll cure this horse."

Dutch replied in German, "I'll tell him, but if you're lying, he'll beat you into sausage stuffing." He turned and translated Joseph's words to Brannagan.

Brannagan smiled. "Bog spavin," he said. "I thought it was. And I never seen anybody cure it. And he can, can he now? Amn't I not the greatest judge of immigrants as ever there was? Sure now wasn't I right in me going to all the expense and care in the training of the lad?" He turned to Joseph. "Okay, two weeks. He's cured, he goes back to work. He's sick an' tiz to the glue factory he goes." He turned to Skilley, who was painfully climbing to his feet. "Skilley, till Hercules is all cured and fit, you use Rosie. Now back to work everybody. I'm not paying good wages for you to be standin' around."

Skilley left, but as he passed Joseph he muttered, "I'll do you for that."

Dutch heard it and in German said to Joseph, "Watch your back, Herr Aristocrat. Watch the dark places too. He's a sneaky one that." He laughed. "He has a knife."

"Enough of that Dutch jabber. Back to work or I'll be dockin' your wages," Brannagan said.

Two weeks later Brannagan examined Hercules and found the horse sound. "Come on then," he said to Joseph. He strode to his office, Joseph following. Once inside he was thrilled to find Brannagan holding his old pair of boots.

"They was pinching Dutch's feet so he sold 'em back to me." Brannagan said. "And I'm giving 'em to you for what you done for me horse. Never let it be said that Cully Brannagan is an ungrateful man." He handed the boots to Joseph. "And somethin' else. You're no longer a stable boy. You still got your chores to do, but from now on your gonna see to the health and well-being of me horses. And if you do good, Cully Brannagan will treat you good. And to show you I'm a man of me word, you come with me now."

Brannagan led Joseph out through the front doors and into Baxter Street. The buildings lining the street were an undistinguished architectural hodgepodge. Some constructed of brick, some wood frame, some one or two stories high, some a few feet taller or shorter. None were as tall as Brannagan's collection of buildings. The one trait shared by all was neglect. Paint peeled from the wooden structures, bricks and mortar were missing from the others. This was the main street of the notorious Five Points. Its inhabitants, Joseph noted, were dressed as badly or worse than he was.

"Look at 'em, will you? The dregs of the earth," Brannagan said. "Now remember what I'm telling you. There's two kinds of people in the world, them as eats and them as is eaten. But you figured that out with Twit, didn't you? I'm telling you this 'cause I'm giving you a choice, and if you're as smart as I think you are, you'll grab on to it. The choice ain't about if you'll work for me or not. You owe me a fortune and that makes you mine whether you will or no. But you can choose if you wanna be one of me gang like Dutch, or shit, like Twit. If you go along and are a good lad, you'll pay off your debts to me in no time flat, and then you'll be getting good wages."

Joseph, never far from his fear of Brannagan, was thrilled at the offer. "I do it."

Brannagan laughed. "Good lad. I knew you had a head on them Dutch shoulders. You can consider that you just enrolled in the great Brannagan university of life. Why from what I'll be teaching you, by the time you're a man you'll make yourself a millionaire. You'll be thanking me all your days."

They had come to a squalid second-hand clothing, dry, and stolen goods store. Brannagan led Joseph inside. "A man of your position can't be running around in dirty old clothes from the old country, especially them as never gets washed," Brannagan said. "I'm staking you to some new duds. Don't worry, it'll come out of your wages, which I've just increased ten cents a day." He turned to a pale man who scuttled forward from the dark recess of the shop. "Feeney, this here's me new right-hand man, a Dutchman, but the soul of Erin is in him. We got to fix him up with proper duds."

Brannagan bought Joseph two brown wool shirts, two dark gray wool trousers, two pair of tan wool stockings, two sets of winter underwear, a pair of sturdy work shoes, warm leather gloves and a heavy gray wool jacket. Joseph swelled with pride in having earned Brannagan's generosity.

Over the next weeks Joseph examined every horse in the stable. For some he recommended diet changes, for others different harness. Some he massaged, some he touched. All responded. As the horses became better mannered they worked harder and, to Brannagan's joy, ate less. In light of these miracles Brannagan allowed Joseph to convince him to hire more help so that the stable could be completely cleaned, emptied of all the old musty straw, and every board scrubbed with lye soap. Brannagan even paid for wagon loads of sawdust for the stall floors and water barrels for each stall so the horses could drink whenever they wanted. He balked when Joseph examined the stored hay and suggested that it was poor quality and should be thrown away, but consented to purchasing additional green alfalfa to mix with the poor hay. Brannagan openly exhibited pride in his protégé and Joseph basked in that warmth. Their meals together continued, with Brannagan instructing Joseph in English, and Joseph telling Brannagan some of what he knew about horses. Joseph wasn't sure when it happened but the meals now satisfied him. It had been weeks since he had been hungry.

Joseph had found a kind of equilibrium: not happiness, but a precarious kind of balance. Most of his days were spent doing the thing he loved best—working with horses. It did no good to think about his past or to worry about the future. He could do nothing about either of them. It was enough that he had the horses. Especially Hercules. At night, when the horses came in from the day's hauling, Joseph personally took care of the big Percheron.

Hercules loved Joseph. Joseph talked to him in a way that made him feel good. Sometimes when Joseph talked Hercules remembered the place where he had been foaled and had grown to be a colt: all legs and eating, the green fields, the sweet clover, and how he ran with the other colts. He hadn't remembered any of that before Joseph had come to him to make him not hurt in the joints anymore. Joseph talked to him like none of the other men. Joseph made him feel safe. For a long time Hercules had known he was in danger. Ever since he came to this stable he had known he had to be careful or something bad would happen. Now he was safe because Joseph had told him to trust him, and he did.

One afternoon some weeks later Dutch drove Sam, a draught horse of mixed bloods, into the yard with the complaint that he had gone lame. Brannagan told Joseph to examine the horse.

"Tiz rheumatism," Joseph said to Brannagan. "Tiz what the Gypsies call the Flying Lameness. I can stop the hurtin' for a few days, maybe a week. But for a true cure the poor beast got to be in a pasture. I gotta work on 'im every day for months."

Brannagan laughed. "Not on me payroll. You get him free of pain so's he looks good and we'll sell him to a sucker from upstate. You know, there's a fella's got a museum downtown on Ann Street, says there's a sucker born every minute. Well, I got me own special supply."

Horse traders often did such things to one another but Joseph considered it dishonest. Still, things were different in America. All that mattered was survival. Joseph knew what Brannagan would do if he opposed him. Besides, this might not hurt the horse. The horse would even be better off with a new owner. The new owner might properly treat the disease.

Joseph massaged the horse three times a day and changed his diet to good hay and an increase of oats and bran. He mixed chopped celery plant, watercress, parsley and comfry with the oats and gave the horse a brew of lightly boiled nettles every day. By the end of the week Brannagan was delighted to find Sam pain-free.

The following day, Sam was tied behind a buggy. Brannagan ordered Joseph up on the seat and handed him the reins. "Now let's see how you drive."

It had been so long since he had driven a horse—and the streets were so crowded with vehicles—that Joseph could pay only a little attention to his surroundings. As they neared their destination he could smell the river. Brannagan instructed him to stop at a large, dilapidated livery stable.

"Read me the sign," Brannagan said.

Joseph read the weathered brown letters: "Josiah Whitman. Horses Bought, Sold, and Boarded."

Brannagan clapped him on the back. "Well done, lad. Now here's how we work this. You lead the horse inside. Whitman's waiting for you. He'll give you a stall and then you're on your own. There's a Dutch farmer, name of Vanmater, from up the Hudson's comin' in. Wants a good strong pulling horse. He'll ask for you by name. Your name's Kelly. You got that? Patrick Kelly. Say it back."

Joseph said, "Me name's Patrick Kelly."

Brannagan nodded. "You'll tell him you're only selling this fine animal 'cause your daddy's took sick and there's all your poor starvin' brothers an' sisters and you got no choice. If you can get tears a running down your mug it'll help. You ask him for sixty dollars, and he'll offer thirty. You'll go on a while about what a fine pullin' horse this is an' all that stuff. When the two of you is in the thick of it, in I'll come. I'll look over the beast and I'll offer sixty dollars, and you'll tell the Dutchman you're in a great agony. You need the money for your poor sick Da and the starving babes an all that. Tiz tricky lad. You got to know how far to go. And just so we understand each other, you lose him and I'll teach you to not make that mistake again."

Joseph could feel the threat in the scars on his back.

Within the hour, Vanmater, a tall, grave farmer in a dark brown coat, arrived and asked Joseph if he knew the whereabouts of a Mr. Kelly.

"I am Patrick Kelly," Joseph answered.

After Vanmater left with the horse he had been swindled into buying, Brannagan came back into the stable and pocketed the fifty-five dollars from Joseph. Then to reward him for his effort, he took Joseph to Josie Martin's Ballroom in the basement of a large brick building on Cow Alley off Worth Street. Cow Alley was the filthiest concentration of whorehouses, gambling hells, and opium dens in New York City.

Josie Martin's Ballroom was a low-ceilinged, unpainted, smoke-filled cellar. Her clientele were the riffraff of New York, the hard nucleus of the mobs that periodically erupted in the riots which so unsettled the city.

"Two of the best!" Brannagan ordered at the bar. The bartender filled two glasses from a bottle he kept under the bar and handed them over to Brannagan who passed one to Joseph. Brannagan didn't pay for the whiskeys, nor did the bartender expect him to.

"Drink up," Brannagan told Joseph. He downed his own whiskey in a gulp. Joseph did the same, burning his throat. His eyes watered but he didn't cough. Mostly he felt pride. He had showed Brannagan what he could do and now Brannagan was drinking with him.

Brannagan refilled the glasses and, after they had once again drained them, led Joseph into the ballroom. Although it was crowded and noisy, a corridor instantly appeared for them.

A large woman in dirty green silk floated into their presence. Her greasy black hair was parted in the middle; below it were tiny black eyes and only the thinnest hint of unsmiling lips.

Brannagan shouted over the noise of the room. "Meet me new right-hand man," he said. "Joe Ritter." He turned to Joseph. "Tiz our hostess, Josie Martin. Kiss her hello."

Joseph was unsure he heard correctly. The woman had a dark mustache above her ungiving mouth.

Brannagan, his eyes glinting, slammed his fist into Joseph's shoulder. "I said, give her a great kiss now!"

Joseph quickly did as he was told. As he did she emitted an eerie shriek of laughter.

"Oh, what a beauty he is," she screeched at Brannagan. "I could have him for me supper. Look at his cream flesh. God, I could eat him here!" She reached out with a dirty white glove and pinched Joseph's cheek. Joseph turned crimson, and she shrieked again. "God, he's blushing! Don't you worry, laddie. You're safe. I'm finished with men and boys."

A waiter in a filthy apron brought them two more whiskeys. Joseph imitated his mentor and downed it in a gulp.

"Josie, we'll have Flossy," Brannagan shouted.

She shook her head. "She's busy."

Brannagan smiled. "Then unbusy her. Me'n the lad'll have another of them fine whiskeys an' then we're comin' up." He reached out and took her chin in his hand and lifted her head. "You got that?"

Never taking her unblinking eyes from his, she nodded carefully. "Good."

"Ten minutes," she said.

"Five," Brannagan said, and she hurried off.

Brannagan turned to Joseph, "She's shit, Joe," he shouted. "I've eaten her and shat her. Like the rest of them is here. Eaten and shat. You'll learn. You learn. Joe? Did you ever think there was God?"

Joseph shook his head. "There is no God."

"Ah, but you're wrong. I'm the God here, and to prove it I'm gonna take you into the gates of paradise. Come on." Brannagan led Joseph through a back door and into a courtyard reeking of garbage and human excrement. Joseph, his mind swimming in an alcoholic haze, followed Brannagan up a set of stairs to the second floor and into a dark, smelly hallway. Brannagan pushed open the first door to the right.

In a narrow room lit by only a candle, a buxom naked girl lay on a rumpled bed. Grinning, Brannagan turned to Joseph.

"Me first."

§16

In THE WEEKS THAT FOLLOWED, BRANNAGAN USING JOSEPH'S GIFTS increased his activity in the horse-swindling game, buying ruined animals for pittances and doctoring them to sell at grossly inflated prices. Aside from his duties as a healer, Joseph always played the unfortunate boy forced to sell the horse in order to feed his starving family. No one ever suspected his innocent face or tears.

Along the way Joseph picked up new bits of information about horses from Brannagan. Most of the tips involved cheating. For instance, one day Brannagan purchased a twenty-four-year-old, worn-out horse for three dollars and turned him into an apparently well-fed, sound eight-year-old by reworking the animal's teeth; grinding them to smaller, narrower sizes and bleaching off their old-age stain—a trick done with arsenic. Brannagan showed Joseph how to reshape the incisors by drilling cups into them and, just before the sale, painting youthful small black dots into the cups. He sold the animal for forty-eight dollars. Two days later the horse collapsed and died. For his part in the swindle Joseph was rewarded with another night at Josie Martin's.

Just as he cut himself off from so many of his own unpleasant feelings, Joseph shut himself off from any questions about his new profession. He knew only that all the good things that came to him—the food, the whores, the whiskey, and the warm clothes—resulted from Brannagan's approval. Each day he sought that approval, and with each such effort became less sensitive to the world.

And because excess lived in Joseph's nature, it now presented itself in the crafts of swindling and licentiousness. Joseph became Brannagan's ideal companion in wickedness. They became such a successful team that Brannagan bought Joseph a flashy brown and orange checked jacket along with a green cotton shirt and an orange tie for Joseph to wear on their nocturnal visits to the whorehouses. Joseph became so focused on this life that he failed to see the minute daily changes at the stable: in Twit, who was growing incrementally weaker; or in Dutch Wagner, whose smile was increasingly full of contempt. And he failed to note Skilley's mounting hatred.

One night Joseph was asleep in his bed in the tack room when an unusual noise in the stable woke him. Hercules was whinnying. Joseph quickly lit a lantern, pulled on his pants, slipped into his shoes and ran out to investigate. The noise had changed to a rasping cough. The horse was choking. Joseph raced to the stall where he found Hercules rearing and tugging against a noose with a slip knot around his neck. Someone had tied him, snubbed the rope to a corner post, and had set a burning lantern swinging at the horse so that Hercules in terror continually reared back, drawing the rope ever tighter around his neck. Joseph blew out the lantern, and rushed to untie the horse. Hercules charged forward and bumped Joseph to the side, preventing his neck from being slashed. The blade opened a wound along his jaw. Someone, invisible in the darkness, was trying to kill him.

He instinctively grabbed the knife wielder's arm and bit into the wrist. The knife went flying into the stall. A horn-hard fist smashed into Joseph's face and he fell back. Before he could recover, a figure loomed out of the darkness and kicked him. Joseph rolled away from the blow and grabbed the foot, throwing his assailant to the floor. Then both men were on their feet. The other man attacked, fists rapidly driving Joseph back into the stall. Hercules, already ter-rified by the noose, his eyes wide and ringed with white, reared and jittered around the stall, bumping the fighters. His hindquarters hit Joseph and knocked him down. As Joseph struggled to his feet, he finally saw his attacker: It was Skilley. And Skilley had recovered his knife. Now, taking no chances, he advanced slowly, bouncing on the balls of his feet, deliberately moving the knife back and forth. Joseph backed into a corner of the stall.

"I'm gonna cut you slow, you Dutch scut," Skilley said in a quiet monotone. "I'm gonna cut your arms, and then when you're too tired to keep 'em up, I'm gonna stick this here knife in your belly." The knife slashed out, and Joseph knew his arm had been cut open. "That's one," Skilley said. He made a feint to the right and slashed Joseph's other arm. "Two," Skilley said. "The next'll be your balls." Then he violently lurched forward, but the move was not of his own volition. Hercules had kicked him in the small of his back, snapping his spine, catapulting him into the rear wall of the stall. The knife flew out of Skilley's hand. Joseph raced to retrieve it. When he turned back to Skilley, Hercules bumped Joseph aside and, rearing up, smashed his great round Percheron hooves into Skilley until there was only pulp where there had been a head.

In order to avoid any embarrassing questions, Brannagan didn't let the police talk to Joseph. They recorded Skilley's death as an accident.

The doctor who bandaged Joseph's wounds told him the cuts on his jaw and arms would leave scars but that, unless he contracted lockjaw or gangrene which were fatal, he would recover. Brannagan added the cost of the doctor to the sum Joseph owed him.

Joseph recovered quickly. Still, before he was quite ready, Brannagan had him out in the stable-yard learning the rudiments of knife-fighting. "You're nothing if you can't handle a shiv," Brannagan said. He flipped a short stick from hand to hand. "Tiz a great weapon, the shiv. If you do it right, tiz silent death. And there's no rules, lad." He suddenly leaned forward and jammed the stick in Joseph's belly. Joseph grunted and fell to his knees. In a flash Brannagan was forcing him to the ground, poking the stick's point into Joseph's neck. "If you can sneak up on a man and take him from behind, tiz better than the fight." Brannagan laughed and pulled Joseph to his feet. "Always remember in a face-to-face fight, man-to-man, heroic like, you kin get hurt. And there's none of your fine-folks mercy. No mercy, lad. You kill him or he'll sure as hell kill you dead yourself. So the first thing you learn is no mercy. Say it."

"No mercy."

"You didn't say it like you meant it. Now damn your eyes! Holler it!" He whacked Joseph across his face wound, opening the scab and making it bleed.

"No mercy!" Joseph shouted.

Brannagan reached into his belt and flipped another short stick at Joseph. "Now see if you kin hit me."

At first Brannagan was surprised when Joseph, his fencing skills coming into play, started to drive him back. "Ah, the fancy gentleman stuff. Pretty it is."

Then Joseph lunged, Brannagan grabbed his wrist, and kicked him in the groin. Joseph went down howling. Brannagan was on top of him with his stick digging into Joseph's neck. "None of your fancy shit!" he said. "And no mercy. Tiz kill or be killed, lad."

They worked every day. Joseph's natural skill with weapons made him as good as his master in only two weeks. The course included all the dirty tricks of street fighting as well as the blade.

One day Brannagan said, "Now we'll see how good you are." They drove a light rig over to Cherry Street. "The Dead Rabbits is me gang," Brannagan explained. "They do what I tell them. Simple things, like protecting me polls on election days. They also keep the Bowery Boys, a nasty gang from uptown, from interfering with what goes on in Five Points. Good lads for throwing a riot, the Dead Rabbits is. But there's this boyo, Slobbery Grimes. A nasty ungrateful hulk of a scut. Good street fighter. A brute with a shiv. He runs the gang for me. Only lately seems like he thinks he's running it for himself. He's not as good as me with the shiv. Nowhere as good as you are. Now I can't fight him 'cause I'm the big boss. 'Twould be undignified. But you, Joe me boy, you're gonna cut him to ribbons. Make an example of him to whoever I pick to run the Dead Rabbits when he's croaked."

While Brannagan talked, Joseph felt excitement, fear, pride and further inside, self-loathing.

The Dead Rabbits headquarters were in four tenements on Cherry Street. When Brannagan and Joseph arrived seventy members of the gang were amusing themselves by charging a toll to any vehicle entering the street.

As soon as they saw Brannagan they gathered around him. "Shut your gobs!" Brannagan yelled. Their noise lessened. "This here is me personal assistant, Mr. Joe Ritter," he said. "And this here is ten dollars that says he can cut the ears off Mr. Slobbery Grimes."

At that moment, instead of looking at Joseph, the gang's eyes turned to the steps of the tenement headquarters. There Joseph saw a very large man, perhaps twenty years old. He was dressed like the others, in dirty sweater and gray, red-striped pants, but there the resemblance ended. Unlike the other Dead Rabbits who were skinny or undernourished, Slobbery Grimes was thick and muscular, with bulging shoulders and arms. His brown hair protruded from above a nearly nonexistent forehead. Two huge ears stood straight out from his head like handles on a silver trophy.

"Slobbery," Brannagan said, "the important thing about being a boss of me gang is to remember that tiz me you answer to, and tiz my bidding you follow." He smiled. "Now for you to stay boss of the Dead Rabbits," he continued, "you're gonna have to live through this fight. And to do that, you're gonna have to beg me for mercy." Brannagan turned to Joseph. "Okay, Joe," he said, "cut the fucker's ears off."

Joseph took off his coat, which he then held dangling in his left hand. In his right he produced his double-edge, nine-inch blade and, crouching, started moving toward the thick man. The Dead Rabbits made a circle in the street and watched in silent fascination. A nearby metropolitan police officer made a hasty withdrawal.

Grimes took a huge knife from his belt. He shambled down the tenement steps, never taking his eyes from Joseph's. Joseph watched him carefully. Grimes outweighed him by at least fifty pounds and was taller. Joseph's advantage was speed, both of foot and mind.

Suddenly Grimes shot forward and his long knife drove at Joseph's body. Joseph evaded it and, as Grimes thundered past him, he pivoted behind him. With a bending stroke he cut just below Grimes' bulging calf muscle, cleanly severing his Achilles tendon. As Grimes crashed to the ground, Joseph kicked the large knife from his hand and with the same movement rolled Grimes on his back. He finished with his knee on the huge boy's chest and his knife at his throat.

"Remember what I said, Joe me boyo," Brannagan said. "No mercy. Cut his throat."

"Mercy!" Grimes' voice was hoarse with horror.

Joseph looked at Brannagan for instructions.

"Mercy is it?" Brannagan asked, taking in the whole gang. "Tiz an arrogant man who found me orders too onerous to obey, and now he's begging for mercy?" He walked to Grimes and placed the sole of his dirty boot just above his mouth. "Lick me boot."

Grimes licked the filth off Brannagan's boot sole. Brannagan smiled and looked around at his minions. He then turned back to the terror-stricken face under the knife. "The church says contrition is good for the soul," he said. "Are you truly contrite then?"

"Yes."

"Louder."

"Yes!"

"Yes, what?"

"Yes, I am truly con-con-trite."

"And...?"

"And I beg for mercy."

Joseph put away his knife.

The story of Joseph's victory over the Dead Rabbits' leader made the round of the underworld. It also made him a feared personage. The girls at Josie Martin's thought his facial scars romantic, and the denizens of Five Points regarded them as proof that Joseph was a dangerous plug-ugly. Joseph's response to all was to swagger and bully. The more he bullied, the more people were afraid of him. The more people were afraid of him, the more Brannagan laughed. And as always, because it delighted his mentor, Joseph continued to cuff, kick and humiliate Twit until one day in early March when Twit didn't appear at work. Later a young boy came by and said that Twit had died. Joseph forced any emotion away. He was an eater, not the eaten.

Later that month, Joseph was working in the warehouse when Hercules returned from a fourteen-day trip to New Jersey with Dutch. Only later did Joseph walk to Hercules' stall. There he saw Brannagan holding up one of Hercules' huge front hooves. Brannagan looked up from his examination. "Look at this and tell me what ails him."

However insensitive Joseph had become he'd never lost his love for Hercules. First he scratched Hercules' head between the eyes and pulled gently at his ears. Then he examined the horse's front hooves. What he found shocked him. "Oh Hercules, me friend," he whispered. He turned to Brannagan. "Tiz the—Oh Jazus I don't know the word in English—founder! Tiz the founder he's got."

Brannagan nodded. "Tiz that. Founder. And how bad?"

Joseph continued his examination. "There's a turning of the coffin bone. I can feel it. And there's cracks around the top of the hoof where it touches the coronary cushion. Oh that fuckin' Dutch! The bastard never once looked at the poor beast's feet. Every step for him is agony." He stood and put his arms around Hercules' neck. Hot tears splashed down his face and into the shaggy coat.

Hercules sighed. He felt chills and fever at the same time, and his feet hurt worse than he could ever remember. He hadn't been sure he was ever going to return to his stall, but he had known that Joseph was waiting for him and Joseph would take this hurt away.

Joseph wiped his eyes and walked away from the horse, indicating with his hand for Brannagan to follow him. When they were standing by the door Joseph whispered, "Tiz gone too far. There's no cure now. The poor beast'll have to be destroyed."

Brannagan held Joseph's eyes with his. "There's no killing for me horses. They earns their keep or they get sold, either to a sucker or to the glue factory. Now did the Gypsies, great thieves they are, ever show you how to fix up a founder to sell to a sucker?"

Joseph shook his head.

Brannagan smiled. "First you use your herbs and stuff an' get his fever down, and then another lesson from the great university of Brannagan. I've got some stuff, and not from any fuckin' Gypsies but good Irish Tinkers, as'll take the pain out of his feet for a couple hours so he'll walk normal like. Just long enough for the sucker to get him home before he goes lame."

Joseph was stricken. "But if we do that," he said, "and the sucker don't take proper care, tiz a horrible painful life he'll have."

"And the money's ten times better than the glue factory. So what you'll do is, cut the white line to drain it. Trim the hooves an' square 'em up. I got me stuff as will hide the cracks." He gave Joseph a conspiratorial wink. "You do that and you'll get your first real cash. A nice cut of the fat profit when we fob off this old nag." He slapped Joseph on the back.

"I won't," Joseph said.

Brannagan smiled. "I've been noticing lately that you've got too big for your britches—which I bought for you. 'I won't,' you say to me? Did you not remember you're mine?"

"You don't own me! I've done all your bidding an tiz a fortune you've made off me. I don't owe you nothing no more and I'll not let you hurt Hercules."

Brannagan remained calm. "You won't now, won't you?"

Joseph stood his ground. Wasn't he the terror of Five Points?

Brannagan sucker-punched Joseph. The beating was short and without mercy. When Joseph woke, Brannagan was kneeling beside him. "Don't you never again say 'I won't' to me!" He put a knee on Joseph's chest and lifted Joseph's head by his hair. "Now this is the way you done it to Twit, wasn' it?" He began slapping Joseph's face from side to side. "I own you, Joe." Slap. "I own you, the same as if you was a nigger on a plantation." Slap. "You can have a good life here so long as you remember who owns you." Slap. "Now say it." Slap. "Tell me who owns you."

"You do."

"An' who's that?" Slap.

"Mr. Brannagan."

"Mr. Brannagan what?" Slap.

"Mr. Brannagan owns me."

Brannagan stood and lifted Joseph to his feet. His eyes danced as he put both his thumbs against Joseph's Adam's apple and squeezed. "Do you plan to fix that horse for me?"

"Yes," Joseph rasped.

"Good. Now gimme your boots. And you put all your fine clothes in me office tonight."

That night Joseph dreamed of the clouds again and woke in a sweat. He needed to go to Hercules. But when he tried to open his door he found it was locked.

For the next four days he was allowed out of his room only to treat the sick horse, and he was fed once a day. But the beating, the starvation, the humiliation and the imprisonment affected him differently than in the past. Joseph allowed his rage to flow into revenge fantasies. And as Joseph worked through those fantasies a thought intruded, a thought he desperately tried to push away. It was of Twit. Only by clinging to his rage and his determination never to allow anyone to humiliate him again could he drive the vision of Twit away.

On the fifth day Brannagan opened Joseph's door, all smiles and good humor. Joseph pretended to be chastened. Tossing Joseph his good clothes and boots, Brannagan said, "Tiz a grand job you did on that nag. And now you're going to see the results of your fine work." He led Joseph out into the yard where a buggy was waiting with Hercules tied to the back. "Look 'em over an' tell me if you can see any sickness."

Hercules was glad to see Joseph. Joseph would stop the fearful hurt in his feet. But Joseph didn't stop to look or touch him in the good way he always did. Hercules became afraid.

Joseph examined Hercules' hooves without petting or talking to the horse. The hooves appeared sound, but he knew better. He could feel it in his fingertips. He turned to Brannagan. "Tiz fine he seems, but the horse is in agony. I doubt he'll make it to where your takin' him."

"You better hope he does. He don't, you don't. Get in."

With each step Hercules was in more pain. Something was wrong. He hadn't been led behind a wagon like this since he was a colt. But Hercules thought of Joseph and walked in spite of the pain.

They pulled out of the yard, turned right on Baxter, left on White Street, crossed Center Street and turned right again at Broadway. For a moment Joseph's concern for Hercules was jolted away by the spectacle before him. They were in an endless canyon of clean, well-cared-for buildings that spoke of prosperity: buildings five and six stories high with bright glass, tinted banners and colorful awnings. Broadway was straight and long and presented Joseph with a stunning panorama of wealth. The wonder of it! A city so vast it had no end. The bright, warm sun glinted off the buildings, making all their colors seem newly painted. New York was huge. It dwarfed Bremen. With Joseph's appreciation of the city's size, a germ of an idea took root. New York was too big for Mr. Brannagan to own all the police.

They turned left at Waverly Place and came to Washington Square Park, a large pastoral space with a beige parade ground surrounded by lawns of green grass. Groves of tall trees bearing the tender first leaves of spring shaded well-dressed pedestrians. Hercules stumbled and fell. Joseph instantly jumped off the buggy and ran to the horse's side. People turned to see the accident. Brannagan knelt beside Joseph.

"Oh, the dirty beast. Is he bad hurt?"

Joseph examined Hercules. "No. Tiz the pain. He can't walk another step. What is it you have, you told me, makes the pain go away?"

"Tiz costly lad, an' I don't have much."

Joseph noticed that Brannagan was throwing nervous glances at the curiosity seekers drifting over from the crowd. "He'll never get up without we give him some of the stuff," Joseph said.

A well-dressed gentleman carrying a gold-handled stick walked through the crowd. "You there!" he shouted. "What have you done to that horse?"

Brannagan scrambled to his feet, his manner deferential. "Tiz nothin' sir. The poor beast stumbled. The boy's a grand doctor for the animals. We'll be having the poor beast on his feet in a minute."

"You better. I'll not have you Irish trash mistreating horses. You understand?"

"I'll do that, sir. The poor dear horse is fine. See the boy is fixin' him now." He quickly knelt and handed Joseph a jar of salve. "Rub it in right there at the top of the hooves," he whispered. "Be quick."

Joseph did as he was told. And when he touched the salve in the jar he was astonished to find that his fingertips went numb. But that didn't keep him from noticing Brannagan's servile behavior. So Brannagan was not a prince in this country. He controlled only his little district.

Hercules felt the pain disappear. Joseph had helped him, just as he knew he would. Hercules got to his feet. He was puzzled, though, when he tried to nuzzle against Joseph and Joseph pulled away.

Brannagan turned right on Sixth Avenue and left on Twelfth Street. Although he had said nothing to Joseph, he muttered constant curses. Then, halfway down the block on the right side, Joseph saw a red and gold sign that read, "Dooley's Fine Livery Stable."

Brannagan brought them to a halt. "There'll be a slight complication here," he said. "Dooleys' not one of me regular places. Respectable Irish he is, the scum-sucking sod. Tiz how come I use him from time to time. He gets a higher class of sucker. You go in. You give him the story, and you don't let on you're coming from me. And in case you got any ideas about anything, old Dooley finds out you're connected with me, and he has a close look at the animal— he's a man as knows his horses—you'll be in jail before you can blink your eyes. You got that?"

Joseph nodded.

"You do the sucker, give ten percent of what you get—and it better not be less than fifty dollars—to Dooley for the use of the barn, and you bring me the rest here. Now get."

Joseph got down from the buggy. He untied Hercules and led him toward the stable. There was no way out. He was consigning Hercules to hell.

§17

UNLIKE BRANNAGAN'S STABLE, DOOLEY'S WAS CLEAN AND SMELLED of fresh hay and well-tended horses. The hallway, flanked by stalls, led out to a sunny wagon-yard where Joseph caught a glimpse of gleaming carriages.

Phineas P. Dooley looked up from his desk, slowly rose from his seat and came forward. He was a short, round man wearing an old-fashioned, black claw-hammer jacket, a white shirt and a cream-colored vest with a heavy gold chain draped across an ample stomach. Dooley's face was framed by long, gray side-whiskers and a carefully slicked-down thatch of salt-and-pepper hair.

An eater or to be eaten? Joseph asked himself.

"This must be young Master O'Connor," Dooley said. Joseph thought the smile on Dooley's face was exactly right for business with a stranger—welcoming, but not extravagant.

"Yes," Joseph replied. "Ryan O'Connor. And this is me poor Da's horse."

"May I have a look?"

Joseph bobbed his head and watched as Dooley, without giving offense to Hercules, opened the horse's mouth and examined his teeth. He then tenderly touched Hercules over his body much in the same manner as Joseph.

He knows horses. Be careful, Joseph warned himself.

As Dooley reached to examine the diseased front feet, Joseph sought to distract him. "Me Da says I gotta get best dollar for him."

Dooley looked at the hooves, then slowly straightened his body and peered at Joseph. "A Belfast boy, are you?"

Joseph nodded shyly. "Yes. Belfast."

Dooley studied Joseph a moment longer. "A fine horse. Now why would your father wish to sell such an animal?"

Joseph saw the look of compassion on the man's face and interpreted it as weakness. To be eaten, he thought. He launched into his poor-sick-father-and-starving-family routine.

When he stopped, Dooley asked, "Does your father not know about the Free Society of Loyal American Hibernians?" As Joseph had never heard of them, he shook his head uncertainly.

"We are an organization of Irish Americans dedicated to the furtherance of democracy, the education of the Irish ignorant, and philanthropic works for the Irish poor. If your father is an honest tradesman, perhaps we can help him keep this fine animal."

Joseph improvised quickly. "The doc says me Da is dying and so me Ma needs the money for the horse."

"Ah, pity. I'm sorry, lad. It's hard to lose a father." Dooley brought his mind back to business. "I have a client, a peddler of dry-goods in the rural areas. This appears to be just the animal he's searching for. If the horse is well-mannered I'll deal for him. Now walk the horse the length of the hall and trot him on back to me, if you would be so kind."

As Hercules walked beside Joseph he felt a hint of the pain in his feet that had so troubled him, but he knew things were all right. Joseph had made it go away before and he would do it again. He tried to walk with no concern. Joseph felt it too. He stole a quick glance at Hercules' feet and knew the pain was starting again. To hell with the damned horse, he raged to himself. Eat or be eaten!

When they returned, Dooley nodded and said. "Good. A fine looking animal. Nice easy gait. Now let's take him out to the yard and see how he stands for harnessing and how he backs up to a wagon. Then we'll take a small drive around the village. Does that suit you, young Ryan O'Connor from Belfast?"

"No, sir. It does not." Joseph was astonished to hear himself talk. "Me name's not Ryan O'Connor, it's..." But even now, Joseph could not be Gershomsohn, nor a Jew, nor a hussar aristocrat. Stripped of all pretense, he wanted merely to be himself, with his own name. He reached for the only one that made sense. "Ritter," he said. "Joseph Ritter. And I ain't from no Belfast, and this here poor beast is me friend Hercules and he's got founder so bad as the only thing is for him to be put down before the stuff Mr. Brannagan made me put on his feet wears off and he's in an agony of pain."

Dooley's massive eyebrows shot up. "Brannagan is it? Cully Brannagan?" Joseph nodded. Filled with the shame he had suppressed for months, he looked at the ground and cursed himself. Dooley studied him.

"I knew you were not from Belfast, just as I knew that in spite of that terrible Dublin way of speaking you have that you're not Irish." He put one hand on Joseph's shoulder and with the other he tenderly lifted Joseph's chin so that they looked each other in the eyes. "Tell me, lad. Tell me what's happening. With you, the horse and Cully Brannagan."

Whether the kindness was honest or not, Joseph couldn't restrain himself. Weeping, raging, disbelieving, he recounted everything that had happened to him from his arrival in America. "And I don't care if I do go to prison. I won't let me friend live in the torment that's waiting when the medicine wears off them poor diseased feet. Oh sir, I beg you, give me a pistol and let me put him down before the pain comes to him again."

Dooley turned, went into the harness room and returned with tools and a bucket of water and a brush. "Show me," he said. He handed the items to Joseph who took them, pried off Hercules' two front shoes, cleaned the wax out of the cracks in his hooves and gently rotated the foot.

"Here," he said to Dooley. "Do you know how to feel and see if the coffin bone's turned?"

"The coffin bone?" Dooley's eyebrows contracted, then rose. "Oh, the dropped sole. The way most people know about it is to shave down the sole of the hoof and look for bruising. There's another way, but the truth is I thought I was the only one in New York City who knew it. An old man showed me how to do it many years ago...." He studied Joseph with great interest. "I've never known anyone else who could tell. How do you do it?"

"I don' know zac'ly. You got to have the feel, to sense it. It's in me hands."

Dooley stared at him for a moment, then turned and examined the horse. When he was done he was breathing hard, but not from exertion. "Oh, the bad, bad man." He turned and went to his office. When he returned, he handed a pistol to Joseph. "There's apples in that barrel. Give him one and lead him to the wagon-yard. We'll let him go while he's eating."

Joseph, his heart pounding, fought to hold back his tears. He fed his friend the apple and led him to the wagon-yard. Outside he was unaware of anything but Hercules' eyes. Joseph brought the horse to a halt and slipped a feed bag over his nose and mouth. Hercules loved the sweetfeed. It had been a very long time since he had tasted something so good. He sighed happily.

While the horse ate Joseph gently touched him, stroked him, pulled at his ears and whispered to him of green fields. When at last he felt Hercules was completely relaxed, he quickly raised the pistol and, pointing it to a spot in the center of the forehead, squeezed the trigger. Hercules dropped in the instant.

Joseph stood with the pistol at his side. It was not the first time in his life he had committed this act of kindness. But as always he felt that when the horse died he had taken some of his own life as well. "Nicely done, lad." Dooley's voice was compassionate. He took the gun from Joseph and gently led him back into the stable. Joseph was dimly aware of men moving behind them, and a team and a tilt wagon being backed up to Hercules.

"My men will take care of him. Now for Brannagan. Joseph, you have committed no crime. You have no indenture contract with Brannagan. There is nothing that makes you his slave. This is

America. You will not go to prison. Would you like to leave Mr. Brannagan's employ?"

Joseph, unable to trust his voice, nodded.

Dooley's face was unreadable. "Good. Where's Brannagan now?"

"At the top of the street."

"Are you up to fetching him?"

Joseph nodded again.

"Then get him and bring him to me here."

Joseph ran out of the stable, turned left and right and found Brannagan waiting in the buggy. "Mr. Brannagan!" Joseph cried. "Come quick! Tiz Mr. Dooley! Oh, tiz a great sum of money!"

Brannagan had to wait for traffic to ease before he could make the turn on Sixth Avenue, but when he did he trotted down Twelfth Street and brought the buggy to a stop inside the stable. What he saw in the shadowed light did not please him: Dooley, with a gun in his hand and Joseph standing behind him.

"Where's me horse?"

"Dead," said Dooley. His tone was deceptively tranquil. "It was a cruel thing you were about to do, Cully Brannagan. But this fine young man did the right thing and shot him."

"I'll shoot him!" Brannagan roared. He started to jump down from the buggy, but Dooley raised the pistol.

"Stop right there. This isn't your ward. You own no police here. I'll shoot you—and the boy and a dozen Hibernians will back me up when I say you attacked me." Brannagan sat down. Joseph was amazed. Dooley was more powerful than Brannagan.

Dooley continued speaking, his voice sheathed in iron. "I have been waiting for a long time for this moment. At last you've given me the opportunity. And not me alone. Down at the Hibernian Hall, all the boys have been waiting for this."

"Fuck you and all the Hibernians," Brannagan muttered. But he didn't move.

Dooley continued as if he hadn't been interrupted. "Brannagan, you are an embarrassment to all decent Irishmen in this good country. It's you and your like who are responsible for the 'No Dogs Or Irish Allowed' signs. It's you and your like that give support to the Know-Nothings and their hatred of us. I could go on for a while with a bill of particulars, the long list of the criminal things you do that harm us all, but I am sure you got my drift."

"Fuck your drift," Brannagan growled.

"Now, we know there is nothing we can do to you in your own ward," Dooley continued. "More's the pity. The poor folks there will have to go on suffering you. But the rest of us don't. So here is the ruling of the Hibernian Council. As you may know, we are not without influence at Tammany Hall ourselves. Any time you want to match votes with us, we're ready. The ruling is, as long as you confine your crimes to your ward, you are left alone. But if you attempt to do business in any part of the city outside of your ward, excepting City Hall, or at any time do harm to or cheat any member of the society, or any of our customers and friends—and from now on this boy is our friend—then look to yourself. We have the charges. We have the judges. You will be prosecuted and you will go to jail."

Brannagan paled and kept his mouth shut.

"Now back that rig out of here and return to your sewer," Dooley said. Joseph stared in wonder as Brannagan, now a mere mortal, silently backed the buggy into the street and drove away. When he at last turned, Joseph found Dooley looking at him. It made him afraid. If Dooley could crush Brannagan with such power, what could he do to him?

"I liked the way you handled your horse. Where did you learn about horses?"

"In Germany." Putting as much respect as he could into his voice, Joseph replied. "Me father bred and trained horses for the cavalry."

"Did he now?" Dooley studied the boy carefully. "And why did you leave?"

Joseph, who was afraid of Dooley, ventured a part of the truth. "I got me in trouble with an aristocrat," he said. "We fought, and I won. His family was to have me in prison or killed. I came to America."

Dooley laughed. "Forgive me, Joseph, but it's amusing to hear such a brogue coming from a German country boy."

"It was the only way I learned English."

"Well, if that's what you accomplished in six months I am sure you can fix it in less, though it will be a shame to lose the mixture. Now lad, I have an idea of you. But you tell me what is it you can do around a stable."

Slavery again! Joseph thought. But his instincts told him that truth was the way out. "Anything, sir," he replied. "Me Da says I'm the best trainer he ever saw. I can ride and drive. I can drive anything. I've even driven six-up, sir."

"Have you now? And what's the secret of driving six horses?"

"You only have to drive the lead pair. The rest follows." Dooley smiled. Joseph wanted to trust him. But Brannagan had an even warmer smile.

"And I know a lot about curing, and not just stuff Mr. Brannagan showed me about cheating cures for selling, but I know real stuff with herbs and the like. If I'd had Hercules before he took so bad, I could of fixed his founder."

"Really?"

"Oh yes, sir. And I can cure most colic, and worms, and hives, and sores, and swamp fever, and cuts and all kinds of foot problems, and I can mend harness an'...."

Dooley interrupted. "Enough. I believe you. I've seen enough to suspect the horseman you say you are. I can always use another good hand. You start with general work, grooming and mucking out, and some harness cleaning and repair. I'll watch you do some work with the horses and see how well you drive. An ordinary hand gets eighty cents a day. When you drive you get a dollar a day and can keep your tips. I have a high-class clientele. Many people choose not to keep their own horses and carriages. We drive customers to and from their businesses. We take ladies on errands and for visits to each other in the afternoon. Good drivers with a sure knowledge of horses and the city are extremely hard to come by. There's a manner about you that I think will do. And if you know horses as well as you say, you shall have a fine future here."

"Tiz in your debt I am," Joseph said.

"If you do the job I expect from you, we will neither of us owe the other. Good work for wages is a fair trade. Do you have a place to live?"

"No, sir. I slept in the tack room at Mr. Brannagan's."

"Oh, the bad man," Dooley sighed. "Well, it so happens that I know of a place. Not far from here, on Bank Street, between Fourth and Bleecker. Mrs. Clymer's. A lovely boarding house, and only last week she told me that they have a small room in the attic that they've just fixed up."

"I've no money," Joseph said.

"I'm sure she'll trust you for your first week. Come hitch up Sugar and drive me over there. Let's see how well you can do these things." Dooley watched as Joseph introduced himself to Sugar, a dark bay mare with a white blaze, touched her in his special way, and harnessed her to a light carriage. Joseph then took the reins and, on Dooley's instructions, drove out into the city traffic. As they passed Bedford Street, Grove Street made a gentle curve to the right and ended at the red brick edifice of St. Luke's Chapel. They then pulled up before a row of elegant brick Federal-style houses. All but one was freshly painted, red with false mortar lines of white. The one house with weathered paint was where they stopped. What kind of place was this? Joseph wondered. He tied Sugar to the iron hitching post and followed Dooley up the eight steps to the front door.

Their knock was answered by a plump, middle-aged woman with a cotton cap trimmed in pink. Her flaxen hair, which was drawn up under the cap, also seemed pink. Only her eyes were of another color, cornflower blue, and they exactly matched the blue silk ribbons on her collar. She smiled with pleasure. "Why, Mr. Dooley. How nice to see you. Won't you come in?"

Dooley smiled back at her. "Thank you, Mrs. Clymer, but I came just to introduce you to Mr. Ritter. Mr. Ritter is now in my employ and requires a room. It occurred to me that you still had the small room in the attic."

"Why, so we do," Mrs. Clymer said. She smiled at Joseph. "It's a lovely little room and it only costs two dollars a week."

"He can afford it," Dooley said, "but he'll not have that sum till his payday at the end of the week."

"Fine," she said and turned to Joseph, "I'm sure Mr. Clymer will have no objection. Won't you please come in?"

As Mrs. Clymer closed the door, Joseph studied the pink woman carefully. An eater or to-be-eaten? He turned his attention to the hallway in which he stood. A trap or a prison? It was narrow and white, and from the back of the hall a stairway rose to the floors above. Beyond the stairs a windowed door flooded the space with light. Two small portraits in gold frames hung opposite each othe, and several whiter-than-the-wall rectangles, where paintings had once hung, were visible. Joseph also observed that although the waxed dark wood floor gleamed, something was missing. He noted a darker spot where he assumed a carpet had once lain. These people had come upon hard times. Good. They most likely were not eaters. He relaxed, but only a little.

"This way, Mr. Ritter." Mrs. Clymer led him up the stairs.

The little attic room seemed filled with spring. Paper printed with pale green leaves and pink blossoms lined the walls. A flowered quilt covered the thick, soft-looking bed. An oval hooked rug in the middle of the room appeared to be strewn with rose petals. For a moment Joseph forgot his dark suspicions and was delighted. This room was so fresh. Why were they giving all this to him? What did they want? He turned to face Mrs. Clymer.

Although she didn't enjoy talking about business, Mrs. Clymer tried to act professionally. "Bridget will change the bedsheets on Saturdays. Breakfast is served from six in the morning till seven-thirty, although if you must leave earlier than that, I am sure we can accommodate you. Did Mr. Dooley explain to you that for two dollars a week, we cannot afford to serve breakfast, and dinner and supper? Dinner and supper would have to be four more dollars. I am so sorry." She peered at him with a stricken look on her face. "Will that be all right?"

Joseph stared at her speechless.

"Oh, I know it isn't. I'll speak to Kate, that's Mrs. Finnigan, our cook. Perhaps she can save a little from supper each day for your return."

Joseph thought she might cry. Although he was still puzzled by all this friendliness, he assured her it was splendid.

"Well then, that's all settled. We're very pleased to have you as a guest in our house, Mr. Ritter," she said, and quietly left the room.

Joseph remained standing until he heard her footsteps descend the narrow stairs to the floor below. Then he went to the door. It opened easily. Next he sat on the bed. It was wonderfully soft. What terrible thing, he wondered, was going to happen?

§18

JOSEPH HADN'T SEEN CLEAN SHEETS IN NEARLY SIX MONTHS. HE slept for eighteen hours. When he woke, his body was rested and he could think clearly, but his spirit was still hiding in a deep and safe place far within. Joseph dressed, went downstairs and ate an enormous breakfast, during which he was polite but guarded to the Clymers and the other boarders. Afterward he walked to Dooley's stable. While the streets were cleaner here than at Five Points, and the buildings nicer, he wasn't sure this part of America was any safer.

After a few hours of observing Joseph, Dooley was confident of his decision. He outfitted Joseph in coachman's livery and the following day began teaching him about the city.

Nearly all of Dooley's business came from the golden Fifteenth Ward, bounded on the south by Houston Street and on the north by Fourteenth Street and stylish Union Square. The ward then extended west to Sixth Avenue and east to Fourth Avenue, although there were fashionable homes and fine old names as far east as Second Avenue. Within these precincts lived some of New York's best families: the Beekmans, Roosevelts, DePeysters, Goodhues, Duers, Joneses, Kings, Lorillards and the Schermerhorns. The wealthy August Belmont had recently erected his Italianate palace on Fifth Avenue just above Washington Square, while the more adventuresome were building their mansions uptown at Gramercy Park, where respectability so far north was ensured with the move of the exclusive Union Club to its new building on the corner of Fifth and Twenty-first Street.

Astor Place and the immediate area had become the "Athenian Quarter," for here were located New York's great libraries, including the Astor and the Mercantile. Book shops and art galleries, where one could purchase the latest in European culture, opened in the former mansions of the rich who had moved uptown. The Grand Opera was currently located at the new Academy of Music on Fourteenth Street.

The sight of this wealth reawakened Joseph's ambition, but his determination to become an American aristocrat was hardened by his experience in Five Points. As he looked at the mansions of the rich, he swore to himself that one day he would live in one of them. He was Franz Joseph von Ritter Baron von Britenstein. One day they would all know it.

There was no more knowledgeable guide in New York than Dooley. He pointed out the homes of their customers and expounded on their habits, relationships and idiosyncrasies. He pointed out the private haunts—the restaurants, the theaters, the shops, the best routes, and how to drive to all of them so as to avoid the jammed city traffic. In two weeks Joseph was driving Dooley's clients by himself. In four weeks, due in part to his aloof, aristocratic manners, Joseph had become among the most popular of Dooley's coachmen.

One night Joseph was unable to sleep. He rose, lit a candle and, taking it to the tall dresser, extracted a sheet of paper from those he used to practice his English writing. While standing, he wrote in German:

> Dear Poppa and Momma,
>
> I know you must be very worried about me, and for that I am sorry. I have had a very bad time. I was foolish and lost all my money. Poppa, you were right about that. I did not think much about money but now I do. I am well. Although I lost the money I did not starve and I am not hurt. For six months I worked in a stable in New York City for a very bad man. But I ate, and I learned the language. I did not write to you during that time because I was lost, to me as well as to you. But now I am myself again.

He wrote about New York and Dooley's stable and he told them about his nice room at the Clymers, but without mentioning anyone's name or address.

> It is odd but here in New York, even though I drive everywhere, I have not yet come across the Jewstreet and I have not met any Jews. No. I am wrong. I saw one. He was on a wharf and he shouted at me in Yiddish of all things! Maybe the Jews of America do not know yet that Yiddish is no longer fashionable.
>
> America is a cruel and hard place but there is also something about it I am beginning to like. I am not sure what it is but I think I will make my fortune here. One day you will be proud of me.
>
> Your loving son,
> Joseph

By the terms of the postal treaty between the United States and Great Britain, all mail destined for Europe had to pass through a British port. Another agreement between the American Congress and the Collins Steamship Line required all mail bound for Europe from New York to leave once every month.

Joseph mailed his letter to his parents from the post office at Nassau and Liberty streets. His timing was perfect. The next day the Collins steamship Orion carried it to Liverpool; it took eleven days. From there the letter was carted to the Royal Post Office in the center of that city, and then routed to the Royal Post Office in Southampton, where it was again sorted and this time taken by steamer to the port city of Hamburg. This was accomplished in the space of two days.

Joseph's letter then traveled from Hamburg by stagecoach through the cities of Braunschweig, Magdeburg, Halle, Leipzig, Weimar, Kulmbach, Bayreuth, Nurnberg, and Regensburg, arriving five days later at the Royal Post Office in Munich where it was intercepted by an agent of Prince Gotthold von Exing, patriarch of the family and privy chancellor to His Majesty King Maxmilian II of Bavaria.

After reading Joseph's letter, the prince allowed it to continue to its destination. He then ordered his postal spies to watch for a reply from Joseph's parents. The prince also dispatched orders by courier to his agent in Paris, commanding him to leave immediately for New York in order to engage an assassin to watch the Nassau Street Post Office.

Being a civilized man and wishing to shed no innocent blood, the prince imposed a severe condition on the thousand dollar fee to be paid for Joseph's death. His agent was to release the money only upon the unmistakable proof of a photograph of Joseph taken after his death and identified by the prince's nephew Baron Otto von Exing.

The prince noted with distaste that the alias on the return address of Joseph's letter was a childish "Mr. Thunder." The prince also noted that distaste was what he felt about the whole affair. His exiled nephew's behavior was distasteful. Hiring an assassin for a Jew was distasteful. Reading other people's mail was distasteful. But he reassured himself that the preservation of honor required the distasteful experience of distaste.

Jakob and Rebecca rejoiced in hearing from their son. She wept; he pretended he had never been worried. Later Jakob rode over to Schloss Falkenbrecht and showed the letter to the count who was upset. "I have no doubt this letter was intercepted," the count said.

"You think the von Exings still search for Joseph?" Jakob asked.

"They will not stop until the insult to their honor is avenged."

"But even in America...?"

Von Falkenbrecht held up the letter. "Now they know he is there. They will have their agents watch the mails." The count examined the postmark. "When Joseph comes to the Nassau Street Post Office to collect your letter, they'll have him."

"Then I must not write."

"You must write. Joseph needs to hear from you. But here in Europe, I shall be the post office. Bring your letters to me. I'll send them by courier to my cousin in Paris. He will then mail them to Joseph with his return address in Paris. My cousin, the Duke de Lignon, will forward Joseph's letters here to me by courier, bypassing the official post and thus the von Exing mail spies. We must warn him." The count paused, "And he will need a new code name. Tell him his letters will be addressed to M. Henri Duport."

"But if they are watching the mails they will see Joseph when he asks for this letter."

Von Falkenbrecht shook his head. "I don't think so. Mail across Germany is slow. Across the sea is slower. Finding an assassin is also slow. We shall be ahead of them."

"An assassin? But I thought they would use the police."

Von Falkenbrecht was gentle. "America is not Europe. The von Exings have no power there. They will attempt to kill Joseph and that is what we must tell him. I'll send a courier tonight. I also suggest you write a loving letter to be sent by normal mail, one they can intercept and pass on. That is the one their agent will await."

By listening to his passengers' conversations, Joseph quickly realized that his Irish brogue was an impediment to his advancement. He secretly began auditioning the accents of his wealthy clients, and soon selected that of Mr. Winfield Lawrence Fall, lawyer and social leader. Joseph drove Mr. Fall, who was a compulsive talker, to his office every morning and home every night. Joseph's brogue was slowly replaced by a perfect imitation of Mr. Fall's fluid upper-class drawl. To improve his vocabulary, Joseph enrolled in the free night school for immigrants run by the Thomas Paine Society. Over the next few months he made rapid strides in learning to read English. There too, thanks to the efforts of a dedicated teacher, Joseph discovered how to use the libraries and to browse in the book shops.

At the stable, he remained guarded in his behavior and prepared to fight at the slightest insult. None, however, were offered. Dooley hired good, hard-working and reasonable people—like himself. At first Joseph regarded this decency with suspicion. Dooley, perceiving this, took every opportunity to explain that not all of America was Five Points. Most of it resembled what he was now seeing. As the weeks went by, Joseph began to slowly accept this. But he wondered whether if Dooley and the Clymers knew he was born Jewish, would they still be so nice?

The warmth of this new, genial world healed Joseph each day. He occupied his mind with his job, the horses, the city, his customers, speaking English correctly, and books. Every spare moment was spent in the libraries and bookstores clustered around Astor Place. No matter how tired, Joseph always read for at least an hour every night before sleeping. He kept books under his driver's seat and read while waiting for his clients. At first he escaped into the romance of novels, and later of poetry.

One morning at breakfast, as Mrs. Clymer heaped a third helping of ham onto his plate, Joseph realized that he ate more than any of the other borders and that Mrs. Clymer, although constantly worried about money, never hinted he was eating too much. Not only didn't she want anything from him, she was giving to him! And from that idea his thoughts wandered to Dooley and the others at the stable. They treated him with the same kindness. The truth came to him as gently as the fresh spring breeze wafting through the open kitchen window. The nightmare was over.

Once James "Funeral" Wells seemed a good man. Some said he went bad because of a bad woman. Others thought his ruination resulted from gambling. But those few who knew him well during his years as a New York policeman accepted that evil had always lived in him. Funeral Wells was addicted to other people's pain. He acquired the nickname "Funeral" when as a police officer it was noted by his associates that a high number of those he arrested never arrived at the police station. Considering the endemic crime, the faulty justice system and the weakness of the police force, Wells' techniques made him a hero to his fellow officers. Wells was especially feared by the Dead Rabbits and their uptown rivals, the Bowery Boys. But Funeral Wells committed one serious error of judgment. One night he arrested a young man for disorderly conduct on Greene Street, the most notorious thoroughfare in America. Two blocks west of Broadway, running from Canal to Eighth Street, Greene Street was lined with shabby red brick buildings, every one of which was either a brothel or a dance hall, or both. At the lower end were the filthy whorehouses catering to sailors off the ships docked in the Hudson River. In the middle of the street were the brothels accommodating the clerks and small tradesmen. The houses of assignation at the north end prided themselves on their upper-class clientele. An aging whore, her face beaten and bloody, had run to Wells to report a disturbance at the Forget-Me-Not, a squalid establishment one house from Canal Street. Wells proceeded to the house and found a disheveled young man running amok. Because of the Forget-Me-Not's location, Wells assumed the young man to be a person of no consequence, and he quickly and easily subdued the offender without doing much harm. For his own pleasure, and to entertain the ladies, he continued to subdue the young man until the victim had several broken bones and had lost his right eye. The boy turned out to be the scion of one of the more powerful families in New York.

After his dismissal from police work, Funeral Wells chose a prosperous life of crime: bank burglary, forgery, and the confidence and banco trades. His greatest success was in the private spy business. Wives hired Wells to spy on their husbands and their husbands' mistresses; husbands hired him to do the same to their wives. This naturally led Wells into the blackmail trade. When hired by a lender to collect a debt, the debt was always promptly repaid in full with compounded interest and newly added late charges. But it was in his skill as an assassin that Funeral Wells took his greatest pride. That kind of work didn't often come his way, but when it did he found it monetarily and personally rewarding.

On April 7, a friend on the police force sent a note telling him to go to meet a man with a French accent at a room in the Albion Hotel. There he was given a hundred-dollar retainer and the conditions for earning an additional nine hundred dollars. He wasn't told for whom he was working and he didn't care. The thousand dollar fee was the largest he'd ever been offered for a single killing. And he was amused by the demand for a photograph to be taken of the corpse.

§19

On THE FIRST WARM SPRING NIGHT OF THE YEAR, JOSEPH SAT BY his window at the Clymers and considered his circumstances. He decided that nothing but his own ignorance could keep him from succeeding. He was prepared to learn everything about upper-class American behavior. And when his English and his American behavior were perfect, when he had saved enough money for a good horse—thereupon Joseph fell into a reverie of uniforms, prancing horses, flashing sabers, banners and flags snapping in the wind. And then he heard a voice. At first he thought it was his mother's. It said, "If I am not for myself, who will be for me? And if I am only for myself, what am I? And if not now, when?"

He recognized it as a quote of Rabbi Hillel from the Sayings of the Fathers. Joseph was surprised that he thought of it in his mother's voice; it was his father's favorite quote. Still, he was glad it had come to him. He would be for himself, but not like Brannagan was for himself, no eat or be eaten. Eat or be eaten was contrary to everything his father had brought him up to be. Eat or be eaten was a Brannagan obscenity. He would be for himself, and he would be for others too. For the first moment since Aaron Augustus Bussey had beaten him senseless on board the *North Sea,* Joseph felt the prospect of being himself again was possible.

One day, as Joseph drove Dooley's grays back to the barn, he was surprised to find himself thinking of his Atlantic crossing. It wasn't something he normally allowed himself to do, for at Brannagan's those memories had been too painful. But now he luxuriated in thoughts of Karl Albert, the Fitzhugh-Reids and Colonel Soulé. He saw again the amusement in Karl's eyes the time they first met and relived some of their outrageous conversations at the table. He had begun to think the crossing had all been an illusion; now he knew it was real and one day he would see his friends again. What would Karl say to his adventure in the lower depths of Brannagan's world? What would Colonel Soulé think of his scar? And the Fitzhugh-Reids? He feared they would understand none of it.

The photographer was afraid of Funeral Wells. He had good cause to be. He tried to keep his shaking invisible while waiting for Wells to speak.

Wells didn't bother to look at the photographer. He was fooling with the large camera. "When I tell you to," he rasped, "you will close up for a day or two."

"But this is the busy time. The sun..."

"You may have to close for a week. Short notice." Wells experimented with taking the lens cap off and putting it back as he had seen photographers do.

"What kind of photograph did you want?"

"A corpse."

Dooley came out of his office as Joseph brought the grays to a halt. "Emmanuel Loeb," Dooley said. There was no mistaking the sly amusement in his attitude. "Special for you. My very best customer. He's been traveling. Lives at 6 West Sixteenth Street, on the corner of Sixth Avenue. You pick him up in an hour when he has finished his dinner. He always drives home for dinner, him and his son, each to their own families, and back again to Wall Street. That's where you'll carry him, to his banking house on Wall Street. E. Loeb & Sons, number six. Six is his lucky number. He's a jolly sort but don't let that fool you. As hard as iron he is. He likes to go fast. Faster than I'll drive. If he takes to you, and I suspect he will, you drive him every day. Tips like a Russian prince."

The Loebs' home occupied ten city lots; five on Sixteenth Street and an adjoining five on Seventeenth Street. Emmanuel Loeb, the patriarch of the clan of two married sons, a bachelor son and an unmarried daughter, thought his mansion much too grand and his grounds outrageously imperial, but excusable in that they were an excellent real estate investment and would one day support ten fine houses on which he would make an enormous profit. He considered the establishment an extravagance at variance with his concepts of republican simplicity, but he also understood that life was a paradox. Besides, Emmanuel Loeb was not a man who could deny Hanschen, his wife, the home and gardens she wanted. For their own good, for the good of the Republic, in the name of ethical behavior, he would deny them many things he considered too luxurious. A fine carriage with drivers and footmen, for instance, was a too aristocratic public display for America. But if Hanschen required such things as drawing rooms, front parlors, back parlors, a music room and formal gardens, then he gave them to her.

Loeb considered the mansions lining Fifth Avenue from Washington Square up to Twenty-third Street an ostentatious show. The houses were so overwhelmingly grand that they had, he thought, a discouraging effect on the poor. Therefore, in light of these beliefs, he had his own house built four lots back from Sixth Avenue and rejected his architect's pleas for Italianate embellishments of columns, balustrades and cornices. The result was a large, plain brown house. And although he refused to own coaches and horses, Loeb constructed a long low stable, coach house, and servants' quarters along the Sixth Avenue side of his property. Only in consideration for his neighbors' esthetic sensibilities did he allow his architect the pleasure of decorating the building's facade—the same brownstone as the mansion—in a unpretentious version of the Greek Revival style. An eight-foot masonry wall surrounded the entire property.

All in all, not counting the servants' apartments above the unused stable, the mansion contained twenty-six rooms. Its running water came from the Croton Reservoir at Forty-second Street. It had central heating, bathrooms with washstands, tubs and flush toilets on each of the bedroom floors. The art on the walls consisted of portraits of the men Emmanuel Loeb thought the greatest the world had seen since Moses: George Washington, Thomas Jefferson, John Adams, Sam Adams, Benjamin Franklin, John Jay, James Madison, and Alexander Hamilton. Above the drawing room fireplace hung framed copies of the Declaration of Independence and the Constitution of the United States of America.

The paterfamilias himself was much like his house—formidable on the outside but filled with a comfortable tumult inside. He wore a full, neatly trimmed, dark but graying beard with a luxuriant mustache that swept past his mouth in carefully tended curls. He laughed easily and often. His temper was legendary and feared by all, especially his three sons. Most of all he loved his family. At his life's center was Hanschen, his wife. Next came his children and grandchildren. Then came his country, America. His love of eating and drinking, and making money followed. Among the things not loved were those that interfered with his pleasures. He also and most particularly loathed the emperors, empresses, kings and queens of Europe and all the nobility surrounding them.

Joseph pulled under the portico of 6 West Sixteenth Street and waited. Mr. Loeb opened his own front door and then, in spite of his age, he rushed down the stairs, pausing by Joseph who was holding open the coach door.

"You are Joseph?" he asked. "The one Dooley brags about?"

"Yes, sir."

"Joseph, do not open doors for me."

"Yes, sir."

"For my wife, open doors. For my daughter, open doors. For me, do not open doors."

"Yes, sir."

"Now we will go to the palace of my millionaire son. Fifth Avenue, between Thirteenth and Twelfth. Fifth Avenue he lives. Why not? He has a rich father. For him you will open the door. He will expect you to bow. Don't do it. It is not American."

The carriage swayed under Loeb's weight. As soon as he was settled, Joseph set off at a slow trot.

"So you should understand, Joseph, I hate wasting the time going places. You go as fast as you can without killing anybody. When my son Mayer gets in he will complain of the speed. Be respectful, but don't slow down. Understand?"

"Yes, sir." Joseph smiled and put the horses into a medium fast trot. As traffic generally moved at a decorous walk, this necessitated maneuvering in and out and around everything in the street.

As they pulled up to 32 Fifth Avenue, Loeb said, "Good! I like the way you drive. It will give Mayer a heart palpitation. Can you drive faster?"

"If you please, sir."

Loeb smiled. He had bright white teeth. "And I will tell you something else, Herr Ritter." Loeb switched to German, which he spoke with an accent not unlike Joseph's father. "Herr Dooley tells me you are from Germany. This is so?"

Joseph was instantly on his guard. He nodded.

"Good," Loeb said. "Sometimes it is easier for me to think and speak in German. Herr Dooley is a fine man but he suffers from too great a desire to live. He refuses to drive me at the speeds I require. He assures me that you have no such concern for your life. The best time at this hour from here to my bank is thirty-seven minutes. Normal time is about forty-five minutes. For each minute you get me from here to there under thirty-seven minutes, I will pay you the sum of one dollar. If, on the other hand, you are the cause of an accident in which I or my son or anyone riding with me is injured, I will refuse to pay you anything and charge Dooley for all costs. For every minute over thirty-seven minutes I will deduct ten cents from your tip. Fair?"

"It's more than fair," Joseph grinned and replied in his impeccable German. "Herr kind sir."

Loeb's eyebrows shot up. "Such elegant German? So tell me Herr Ritter, there is a 'von' perhaps before your name, back there in the old country? A 'von' perhaps? Is it von Ritter?" Although his smile remained, his tone was not nearly as friendly.

"No, sir." Joseph had heard the switch in tone. "I am of humble birth." This was true.

"So? With that beautiful aristocratic German?" The word "aristocratic" was tinged with ice.

"My uncle was a professor of classical German at Heidelberg. He became ill and came to live with us. It was he who educated me."

"And your father?"

"A horse trainer, sir."

At that point a liveried servant opened the front door of 32 Fifth Avenue and hurried before the emerging figure of Mr. Mayer Loeb. Mayer wasn't as large as his father, wore side whiskers and mustache, and had none of his father's humor in his serious face.

The senior Loeb signaled Joseph to stay on his seat. Mayer's servant opened the door to the carriage for his master, who paused briefly to view the equipage with some slight distaste. "Really, father, when I have an excellent coach…"

"I know. I know," Loeb replied. "Joseph, earn your fortune!"

Joseph put the horses into a medium trot, found the hole in the traffic, and urged them into an extended trot. Mayer groaned. "Father, you didn't offer him money for minutes?"

"I did. The minutes are worth more to us than the money."

"And if we get killed?"

"So we get killed. Now," he said, "Vanderbilt comes today. Are you ready for him?"

"Yes. We can outbid him if you wish."

Joseph, focused on his driving, paid no further attention to his two passengers. Avoiding Broadway, he cut over to Fourth Avenue which merged into the Bowery where traffic was less dense and genteel. Joseph drove so aggressively that some openings were long enough for him to actually gallop the horses, bringing outraged oaths from other drivers.

When Joseph pulled up in front of 6 Wall Street, he turned to Loeb and asked, "How did I do, sir?"

Mayer's face was pale and wet, but Loeb calmly took his gold watch from his waistcoat pocket. "*Gott in Himmel!* Twenty-two minutes! From now on you drive only me." He reached into his pocket, counted out fifteen dollars, and gave them to Joseph.

It was Joseph's turn to be astonished.

Loeb smiled. "Now don't think that you get this sum every time," he said, "The new record is now twenty-two minutes. The deal is the same, a dollar a minute for everything under the record, now twenty-two minutes. But now also I think we raise the stakes. You pay me fifty cents for every minute over twenty-two, and one dollar for every minute over thirty-seven. Do we have a deal?"

"We have a deal, sir."

Because Joseph was now Mr. Loeb's exclusive driver, he had more time than ever for reading. His primary interest was American fiction, but for reasons he didn't understand he also read the Torah in Hebrew with English translations. He told himself this was the best way to improve his English vocabulary.

He had discovered the bilingual texts quite by accident when one day he had raced Loeb to a noon conference on Christie Street. As Loeb sprinted into the building, he shouted back, "An hour at least. Go eat something."

Joseph looked around and saw a store with a sign in both English and Hebrew: "S. Roth. Books and Religious Supplies." Fascinated, Joseph dismounted, tied the horses to their standing block, and entered the store. It was dark and cluttered with glass cases containing phylacteries, prayer shawls, embroidered velvet bags, bronze and silver menorahs, and goblets of varying sizes all inscribed with Hebrew characters and devices. But books predominated. They were stacked in the shelves, piled on tables, and covered the merchandise cases. The store's owner, a wizened man in a white beard and a black hat, looked up from a book and addressed him in German.

"So, Mr. Coachman, you understand German maybe?"

Joseph smiled and replied in the same language, "I need the Holy Scriptures."

"Need! Of course you do. We all need. Did not the sages, blessed be all their names, say 'Great is the Torah which blesses those who practice it'...."

Joseph switched to Hebrew and corrected the old man. "Great is the Torah which gives life to those that practice it. The exact words and meaning are 'gives life.' " He smiled.

The old man didn't. "So, Coachman, you are a teacher? Who asked you? A pisher is such a great sage! You are maybe the Rambam? Blesses I said, and blesses it is! You are maybe the Messiah come to Christie Street to save me from ignorance?"

A large man emerged from the shadows. "Schmuel," he said, "the boy is right." He held up an open book. "Pirke Aboth, section six, paragraph seven."

The old man snatched the book and held it very close to his eyes. Then he looked up. "So maybe you are the Rambam," he said. "So Rambam, what kind of Torah you want? A small scroll, fresh from Jerusalem? A book printed in Germany with a silver binding? You want big? I got big. You want small? I got small. So? Nu?"

"As cheap as you have," Joseph said. "In Hebrew, and if you have it with Hebrew and English alongside, it would help."

The other man stared at him. "Excuse me," he said. "I know you? We have met before? I am Moses Cohen, cantor of the Emanu-El temple. We have met?"

"Cantor?" The old man snorted. "He says cantor? He is the finest hazzen in America. You would think they would pay him enough, those reform Jews, so he would not have to sell fish to eat!"

"Rabban Gamaliel," Moses Cohen said, "the son of Rabbi Judah the prince, said: 'An excellent thing is the study of the Torah combined with some worldly occupation, for the labor demanded by them both makes sin to be forgotten.' So Schmuel, let me be a hazzen and let me also sell my fish."

While the two men amiably argued, Joseph studied Moses Cohen. Something was indeed familiar about that red face and hair. What was it?

Moses Cohen realized Joseph was staring. "So. We have met?"

"No, sir, I don't think so. I'm Joseph Ritter."

"Perhaps you have been to our services? Heard me sing?"

"No, sir."

"You belong to a congregation?"

"I do not."

"So, in that case you must come and see us at Emanu-El. You come Friday night, come early and ask for me. I'll introduce you to those who study the Torah...."

"Thank you, sir," Joseph spoke as politely as possible. "But I couldn't do such a thing."

Moses Cohen chose not to press the matter.

The old man came back with a set of five books. "See? Cloth bindings, the cheapest I have. Five volumes, printed right here in America. Not so good, but cheap. See? Here Hebrew, here English."

Joseph negotiated the price of the first volume and offered to purchase another each week until he had the whole set, if the old man would save them for him.

"Save?" asked the old man. "What am I, a bank? I would give if it were the old country, but here I hardly make a living. Rambam, how can you take only one volume? What if you have to look in another book for something. Impossible. Take all five. Each week you come and pay for one more volume."

Joseph blushed with gratitude. "Thank you," he said. He noticed that Moses Cohen was watching him very carefully. Joseph paid and quickly left the shop.

"I've seen him before," said Moses Cohen.

"Such a scar on such a sweet boy face you would remember. You remember the scar?"

"No..."

"Then believe me, him you never saw before."

Back at his coach Joseph carefully stowed the five volumes under the driver's seat and, taking out James Fenimore Cooper, lost himself in The Deerslayer.

"What is this? A reader?" Loeb was standing beside him.

Joseph put down the book.

"Did you eat something?"

"No, sir."

"A man who would rather read than eat? Most interesting." Loeb reached up and took the book out of Joseph's hands. "Aha, a novel. Why do you read this romantic stuff?"

"To improve my English."

"Improve? Already you speak like a founding father."

"Vocabulary, sir. When I find words I don't understand, I remember them and look them up in Mrs. Clymer's dictionary."

"Commendable. I like ambition. What else do you read?"

"Novels by Washington Irving, Herman Melville, Edgar Allan Poe. Poetry by Mr. Walt Whitman." He was careful not to mention the scripture under his seat.

"And about your new country? What about histories of America?"

"It didn't occur to me, sir."

"Then let it. You are living in the greatest country man has ever known. Perhaps it would be better for you to spend your time reading about that than all this romance. Now, schnell. As fast as you can to the bank."

As Loeb heaved himself into the carriage, Joseph turned to him, "Sir?"

"Yes."

"I have an idea for going much faster."

"You do? Tell me."

"You see, sir, the problem isn't the speed of the horses but the size of the carriage and two horses. If we had a small, light, two-wheeled buggy and one small fast trotting horse, I could get through many more spaces."

"It is logical. Go on."

"The problem is, sir, that perhaps there is, in being transported in such a small vehicle, a certain loss of dignity."

"Dignity?" Loeb repeated. "To hell with dignity. You know where to purchase this buggy and such a horse?"

"Mr. Dooley does."

"Yes, but I asked if you do. Do you?"

Joseph paused. Loeb saw the hesitation and pressed on. "Do you know where to purchase this buggy and horse for me?"

"I could find out."

"Then by all means find out."

"Excuse me, sir, but really this is something that Mr. Dooley should do."

"He knows more about horses than you?"

Joseph's youthful pride wouldn't let him lie. "No, sir. But he knows more than most. He's the one to do this for you, Mr. Loeb."

Loeb hid his amusement. "But if I go to Dooley, he gets the commission, not you. After all, it's your idea."

"Mr. Loeb, I work for Mr. Dooley. Forgive me. It's not my intention to tell you how to behave."

"Why not? All my children do."

"The proper thing," Joseph continued, "would be for Mr. Dooley to buy the buggy and horse. Then you can continue the present arrangement, and hire them from him."

"And what if I choose to buy you this buggy and hire it back from you? Put you in business for yourself?"

Joseph caught his breath and spoke quickly. "Oh thank you, sir. That's kind of you to offer such a thing. But I couldn't do that, sir."

"Do you have a contract with Dooley?"

"No, sir."

"An oral agreement to be employed by him for the rest of your natural life?"

"No, sir. But..."

"Then you can do it. Settled! You give him fair notice, purchase the buggy and horse, and you are in business for yourself. That is the American ideal."

Joseph wanted to accept. "Thank you for the offer, sir, but I couldn't do that. It would be dishonorable for me to leave Mr. Dooley."

"Dishonorable?" Loeb studied Joseph for a moment and then nodded. "So. Now, Joseph, a change of plan. We do not go back to the bank. Slowly, you understand me? We shall proceed slowly to Mr. Dooley's establishment. The way I would expect you to drive a very old and very frail grandmother. I feel like talking and when you drive fast you don't talk. Will you talk with me?"

"Yes, sir."

They proceeded at a leisurely pace.

"This difficulty out of which Mr. Dooley helped you, did it have to do with the scar on your face?"

Joseph was determined to tell as much of the truth as he could, and to remain silent about what he couldn't say. So he told his story, but eliminated the hussars, the gambling and drinking, the ship on which he crossed, and the friends he'd made on board. Under Loeb's probing, Joseph slowly revealed he had been robbed of his money. He talked about how he had dreamed of starting a great stud farm, and how instead he wound up with Brannagan. Loeb knew of Brannagan and of Five Points and was impressed that the boy had survived with only a single scar. But when Loeb probed into Joseph's family history, Joseph lied. While he was no longer a hussar, he still didn't want to be a Jew. Instead he said he had come from Poppenlaur and, being a boy, was unable to refrain from bragging about his wise, loving mother and his father, the best horse trainer in Bavaria.

Once Loeb found that Joseph was undefended when it came to the subjects of his father and horses, he kept the boy at it until he understood that Joseph was hiding some sort of military mystery. But Emmanuel Loeb, a man who had started with a pack on his back, peddling on the roads of rural America, was a fine judge of character. He respected the boy.

Dooley was surprised by Loeb's decision but proud of Joseph's success. He refused to take any compensation for Joseph's imagined contract with him and insisted that Joseph receive the commission on the purchase of the horse. He said, "Joseph will choose the team and I the carriage."

Loeb was puzzled. "Dooley, I am purchasing only a buggy and a small horse. I am not an emperor or an Astor to have a carriage."

"I put it to you this way, Mr. Loeb," Dooley said. "Your aversion to owning such things is well known. It's also well known that Mrs. Loeb has the opposite feelings about a carriage. Now you, sir, are a man of logic. Do you think for one moment, once Mrs. Loeb discovers you have purchased a private conveyance for your own use, she won't be severely disappointed if she doesn't have one for her own use?"

The logic was irrefutable. "What's life," Loeb said, "if not change?"

And so it happened that Joseph Ritter moved up another notch.

§20

"MR. THUNDER? DO YOU HAVE A LETTER FOR MR. THUNDER, PLEASE?" The clerk glanced at Joseph and went back to the pigeonhole boxes. He returned in a moment. "Came in this morning," he said. Joseph took the letter and walked quickly toward a quiet corner just as Funeral Wells strode past and entered a door marked "Postmaster."

Postmaster Alpheus P. Stockwell had done well in his previous four years, but he had no illusions about Franklin Pierce's ability to win his party's renomination. He had barely five more months of pocket lining left, and so he was happy to accommodate Mr. Wells.

"In the next month," said Wells, "a letter to a Mr. Thunder will arrive. I want you to hold that letter and inform me of its arrival. I wish to be present when Mr. Thunder takes delivery." He handed five silver dollars to the postmaster.

Joseph was puzzled by the Paris return address and the crest of a French duke on the letter addressed to Mr. Thunder. The thick envelope contained two letters. On the first Joseph immediately recognized his father's bold hand. The second bore the von Falkenbrecht crest. Joseph first read the letter from his father.

My Dear Son:

Your mother and I rejoice in your good health. We are both well, and now that we know you are safe we are happy.

I will write you another letter that will come much later. That one will be filled with news of us and of the horses. This one must be short. A messenger stands here, ready to race with it to Paris. Your mother and I pray to God that it reaches you in time.

Count von F. believes that your letter was intercepted by the von E. swine. Now they know where you get your mail, they will send an assassin. You must immediately go to another city.

When you write to us, send your letters to the Duc de Lignon whose Paris address I enclose. He will send it to Count von F. who will bring it to us. We are blessed in the friendship of this good man. You will use the code name of Henri Duport on your return address.

I have written another letter which is intended to be intercepted by the von E. swine. It is addressed to Mr. Thunder. Do not ever try to claim it. That is the one they will watch.

Joseph, I know you. You will wish not to run from the assassin. America is a huge place and the von E. swine are not powerful there. Your mother and I want you to go from where you are. Change your name again. Make a new life. But whatever you decide to do, remember, you are my son and I am proud to be your father.

A horse is a horse. By now I hope you have learned you do not have to be a Christian to live with honor.

Your mother and I kiss you
Poppa

The second envelope contained a letter from von Falkenbrecht.

My Esteemed Baron von Britenstein:

When you left Europe, you did the prudent and honorable thing. I understand that in America all are equal before the law. Therefore, I do not expect you will waste the hours Stumpf and I have spent training you. Do not run from where you are. Stay and defend yourself. Now it is a question of my honor as well as yours. If the von Exings send an assassin I expect you to find that creature and kill him, since the von Exings are doing a dishonorable thing. You may destroy their minion in any fashion you choose. When you have dispatched the dog, write to me. Perhaps then I can do something here to bring an end to this stupidity.

Even if men are all equal in America, which I doubt is possible, you are still Baron von Britenstein. It is an old and honorable title. Do not dishonor that name or my belief in you.

Von Falkenbrecht

Joseph folded the letters and put them in his pocket.

Fannie Loeb, the youngest of the four Loeb children by ten years and the only daughter, was her parents' favorite child. Fannie was not a beauty in the accepted standards of her time. Although she had an excellent figure, her mouth was too wide, her nose too aquiline, and her eyes too big.

Hanschen didn't think it was Fannie's looks that were standing in the way of a good marriage but rather that men weren't attracted to educated women. Fannie, encouraged by her father, knew five languages: English, German, Hebrew, French and Italian. She constantly read books in all of them. Hanschen tried to counter-

balance the books by teaching her daughter the proper feminine
social skills: small talk, working needlepoint, playing the harp, and
ballroom dancing. But Fannie preferred to read.

As Hanschen watched Fannie grow into a young woman, she
worried about a suitable marriage. There were enough eligible and
wealthy bachelors of good German Jewish families, and Loeb had
often talked about a proper alliance with another of the great
banking families in their "crowd." But for her special daughter,
Hanschen allowed herself to dream of more. She wanted Fannie to
marry a Rothschild.

Fannie's brother Nathan, the youngest and most brilliant of her
siblings, who lived a wicked bachelor life from his splendid apartment in the St. Nicholas Hotel, had always been her best friend.
When she was ten, and Nathan twenty, he began escorting her on
"adventures." He took her to see the ships in the harbor, to eat at
her first ice cream saloon, and to visit the Gypsies at a New Jersey
fair. Nathan brought her to A.T. Stewart's Emporium, to Columbia
College, and to Barnum's Museum. He took her on her first pony
ride, on her first steamboat excursion, and out to her first restaurant.

On March 18, 1856, Fannie turned sixteen and the appropriate
party was given by her family. But it was Nathan who gave her the
best present. The following night he arrived at the Loeb mansion
and told Fannie he was taking her out for dinner. He warned her
not to dress too elegantly. "We're going on an adventure," he said.

"Where?" she asked. "What? What are we going to do?"

"Have you heard of Charlie Pfaff's restaurant?"

"Where the Bohemians meet?" Fannie was amazed. "You
propose to take me there?"

"I do."

"But what if people recognize me? Momma will hear."

"Fannie." Nathan raised a finger to his lips for silence. "Momma
will hear nothing. We're going to another planet. A place where no
one from Momma's crowd has ever been or ever will be."

"Why are we going there?"

"Before it is too late, I wanted you to know another world."

"Too late for what?"

"If you are not married by the time you are twenty, you shall be
an old maid. Momma will never permit that."

"And you?"

"I want you to be happy," Nathan said. "I want you to know all the world and marry for love."

"And if I loved a Bohemian? Would you accept that?"

"If he loved you, yes."

"Nathan," Fannie said quietly, "Must I get married right away?"

"What will you do if you don't marry?"

"I don't know. Sometimes I think I want to be an adventuress and have many lovers. A prince..."

"A title? Father would never approve."

"Not a title. Magic. I want smart, beautiful men, just like you." Then she blushed.

"What about your ambition to sing in the opera?" he asked. "Or to dig a canal across Central America?"

"That was when I was a silly little girl. Oh Nathan, I love Momma, but I don't want to be like her. Am I a bad girl?"

"Dear baby sister," he said, squeezing her indulgently, "you're the most good of the good."

Charlie Pfaff's cellar restaurant, on Broadway just above Bleecker, was headquarters for a group of poets and painters called the "Bohemians." They scandalized all of polite society. Most frequently seen there were: Walt Whitman in his rough blue-gray suit and open shirt, occasionally reading his poetry; Junius Booth the actor, declaiming the classics after his second bottle; and Ada Clare, poet and writer, who brooded. All New York considered Ada Clare to be an abandoned woman because of her open affair with the great pianist Gottschalk, friend to Chopin and pupil of Berlioz.

To Fannie's amazement, not only did her brother know these people, they liked and respected him. And from the first moment she talked with them, they found her to be a kindred soul, too.

Dinner with Nathan at Charlie Pfaff's became a weekly event. One night, Fannie and Nathan sat at the crowded long table in the alcove at the far end of the cellar eating sauerkraut and sausages. An argument about slavery was raging. A poet from Massachusetts was saying that even if freed, the blacks would never be accepted by white America. The only solution was to send them all to Nicaragua where they could own plantations and coal mines. A mulatto painter from New Orleans agreed to the first part of the proposition but said that colonization would be impossible: you couldn't ask four hundred thousand free American Negroes to leave their native country. The only real solution was to forbid blacks to marry blacks and offer federal grants of land out west to each interracial couple in each generation until there were no blacks left.

Fannie looked up in the middle of the argument and saw Ada Clare sitting by herself at a small table she often took when she chose to avoid the general discussion. She was smoking cigarettes and drinking wine. Fannie went to her table. "Miss Clare?"

Ada Clare, elegant, slender, her ivory skin set off by the black she habitually wore, shut off her contemplation of suicide and smiled with pleasure. "Fannie. Do sit down, honey." Her husky voice revealed a trace of her southern origins.

Fannie sat down. "I hope I'm not interrupting," she said. "I mean, I hope I'm not stopping you from thinking up a new poem or story."

Ada laughed. "Smoke?" She offered Fannie a cigarette and quickly withdrew it. "No, I know. No tobacco. No alcohol." She stared at Fannie for a long moment. "Are you sixteen yet, Fannie?"

"Last month."

"And do you have a beau?"

Fannie shook her head. "No."

"Why?"

"All the suitable young men are so…"

"Dull."

Fannie smiled. "Oh, much worse."

"Tell me."

"When I am with them, I feel like I'm…"

"Suffocating?"

"Yes!"

"And here in Bohemia?"

"The most wonderful exciting people!"

"But so far no beaus."

Fannie smiled and shook her head. "I'm not really looking. You see, I don't intend to marry."

"Ah. And what is it you wish to do?"

"I don't know. That's the problem. You see, I don't know a great deal. I mean I know a great number of things. Languages, and literature, and how to play the harp; but none of it is any good to me because all I know from it is that I don't know about life. Do I sound like a fool?"

"No. You sound astonishingly wise. Why are you telling me this?"

"I have read your poems and stories. They're so beautiful, and wise, and…"

"Wicked."

"Oh no! They're pure!"

"Polite society thinks they are wicked."

"Well, they're wrong! They're wrong about so many things."

"You think so?"

"Oh, I'm quite sure."

Ada resisted an impulse to grab Fannie and hold her to her bosom. Instead she smiled and asked, "What are they wrong about?"

"About money and love and marriage."

"Especially love."

"You must know more about love than any person in the world."

Ada smiled, "So I'm told. And it's probably true. I'm an authority on the subject." She posed importantly. "I see a question. Ask and ye shall be enlightened."

"Can it be personal?"

"Yes."

"Is it very painful to be an abandoned woman?"

Ada Clare laughed so loudly that all conversation in the restaurant momentarily paused. Fannie blushed.

Then Ada looked at the child at her table with warmth. "Fannie," she said, "I'll tell you the truth and it shall be yours all your life. That they," and with a gesture she indicated the wide world beyond Bohemia, "consider me abandoned is of no consequence whatsoever. As you've already perceived, their glittering, materialistic lives are dreary beyond bearing. But they do serve a natural function, for I believe the Creator put them here. They build our railroads and canals, and they see to the care of governments and sewage. But I think your question was about something else. I think you were asking me what it is like to love in utter abandon. If I write the truth in my poetry."

"Isn't truth beauty and beauty truth?" Fannie asked.

"There is only one kind of true love. It's passionate. It's total. It can only be experienced with utter abandon. When it happens nothing else matters. I'm not sure that it comes to everyone. Perhaps it does but most push it away. They say all the world loves lovers, but that's only in fiction. The world only loves the idea of lovers. The world demands that lovers live by laws currently in fashion. Woe to the lovers who love outside those conventions. Woe to the unmarried lovers. Woe to the adulterers. Woe to the lovers of the same sex.

"Is the true passion worth all that woe? Yes! It always is. Always! It always is. Never doubt or forget this. You give your life to it not knowing if you will live happily ever after like a fairy tale, or die in despair." Ada reached out and, taking Fannie's hand in hers, stared into her eyes. "Be courageous, Fannie. Let yourself be open to whatever you feel. When your love comes, give yourself to it. Hold nothing back."

"Yes!" Fannie said. For years she had hoped someone would tell her exactly this. "I shall! When my love comes I shall abandon myself to it. No matter what follows!"

"And now the hard part. Like all art, love requires discipline. Are you prepared to study love?"

Fannie nodded her head and locked eyes with the poetess again. "I am."

"Will you defy convention?"

"Yes," Fannie whispered. "What must I do?"

"Are you a virgin?"

Fannie blushed crimson and looked at her lap. "Yes."

Ada Clare reached out and raised Fannie's chin to make their eyes meet again. "I can stop now…."

"Please don't."

"A great love may only come once in your life. You must prepare for that moment as a young artist prepares to be Michelangelo. First the artist studies the lives of the great ones that have gone before. I shall give you some books. In the early years the study is all technique, until it becomes second nature, forgotten by the thinking mind and at the service of the soul. Then, and only then, you will be ready for the great *passional* experience. You must be not only experienced in the arts of love, you must become a supreme practitioner of erotica. The ecstasy you give shall be returned a thousandfold."

Fannie was near faint with excitement, "How…?"

"What I'm going to say now is considered very wicked. But it's the truth, and if you follow my advice you may lose everything—family, friends, everything—and become an abandoned woman. If you do as I say, the risk is your life. The prize? You may win the great passion. Shall I go on?"

"Please."

Ada leaned close. "Not even your enlightened brother Nathan will approve of this. You may never share this with him. Agreed?"

"It shall be our secret."

"You must give up your virginity. Men pretend they like virgins. They don't. The losing of your virginity will be a painful, messy business. Find a man, not in your own circle. I know that is almost impossible for a girl of your circumscribed life. Perhaps it will be someone who frequents this place. I shall look. Perhaps it might be a servant in your parents' household. Servants are the traditional way. One can always give them a sum of money and dismiss them. When you have found your practice lover, you seduce him."

Fannie's eyes had never opened wider. "How?"

"Later. You'll come to my apartment and we shall speak of these intimate and delicious things. When you've found the man, come to me and I'll tell you what to do. And what is equally important, I'll tell you how to avoid pregnancy."

Joseph, who couldn't afford a pistol, knew much about knives. One day on his lunch hour, he went to a shop on Bayard Street, where he purchased a nine-inch, dagger-shaped blade. Because it had no guard and a thin handle in its scabbard, it fit inconspicuously into the side of his boot.

§21

L OEB NOW DECIDED THE COACH AND TEAM WOULD BE A WONDERFUL surprise for his wife and daughter. Joseph was to be a surprise as well. Therefore, Joseph wasn't allowed to move directly to the Loeb coach house, but was to remain at the Clymers' until all was ready.

While Loeb did not believe in livery for servants, Hanschen did. Their compromise was to dress employees in well-cut, dark materials, making the Loeb staff resemble en masse a Quaker congregation. During the time it took for Loeb, Joseph and Dooley to find the horses and carriage for Hanschen, Joseph was outfitted in several changes of Loeb non-livery. The only difference between his dress and that of the other household servants was his black boots and his top hat with a silk blue and white cockade above the band—Hanschen's favorite color combination.

To draw the eight-spring landau Dooley had purchased for Hanschen, Joseph selected a pair of elegant white Andalusian geldings. The horses were beautiful but too docile for their previous owner.

The landau intended for Hanschen was painted with twenty coats of hand-rubbed, dark blue lacquer. It shone like a mirror. Dooley had the seats re-upholstered in the same pale blue as the landau's trim. He also asked his painter to add an intricate monogram to the doors. He knew this would outrage Loeb, but he also guessed he was doing his old friend a favor in the long run. Hanschen would be thrilled.

When at last everything was ready, Joseph drove the glimmering rig from Dooley's stable to 6 West Sixteenth Street. Pulling through the gates, he drew up before the front door of the mansion. After a while he saw Loeb peer at him from a window. Moments later, Loeb led his wife and daughter out onto the steps. Both were blindfolded with silk scarves.

In German, Hanschen said, "But why must I come outside to see my present? Is it a willow tree for the garden?"

"Soon my love. Soon you shall see," Loeb said.

Then with a clumsy, loving flourish, Loeb removed the scarves.

"That?" Hanschen asked, "That's my present?"

Loeb put an arm around his wife's shoulders. "It's yours."

She stared in silence. Joseph watched her eyes move from detail to detail. Then in English she said, "The Seligmans will drop dead!"

"Momma!" Fannie said. She burst out laughing. But her laughter was cut short when she looked from the carriage to the coachman, for what she saw there was far more interesting than the horses. Taking Ada Clare's advice, she had considered the household servants: Iverson, the butler, and Hooks, the footman, were both old and married. The three gardeners were dirty, and too far beneath her. But now her father had hired this young stalwart. She blushed at the thought.

Joseph looked briefly at Fannie, took in her deep, dark eyes, her pale skin and raven hair, and thought, "I hope she likes the horses."

My God, Fannie was thinking, I'm going to be an abandoned woman!

"And this is the famous Joseph Ritter of whom you have heard me speak," Loeb said. "Joseph, may I present my wife, Mrs. Loeb, and my daughter, Fannie."

In a gesture more military than servile, Joseph cocked his head and touched his hat. "I am honored."

He speaks beautifully, Fannie thought. And how well he carries himself. But he is very young. He couldn't possibly teach me what Ada Clare said I must learn.

Hanschen looked at Joseph. "Mr. Ritter, no fast driving we shall have. What you do with Mr. Loeb is one thing. But with me and my daughter, no fast driving. You understand?"

"Yes, ma'am."

"Except," Fannie said, "when I am in the carriage without my mother." Fannie knew she was talking too fast. "Then I want to go as fast as father." She wondered, could they see how breathless she had become?

"Absolutely not," Hanschen said. "Mr. Ritter, you understand."

"Perfectly ma'am."

Fannie stepped forward and ran her hand over the nearest horse. "In that case," she said, "Joseph shall teach me to drive."

Joseph found this a silly request. Women didn't drive horses.

Loeb laughed. "It wouldn't help," he said to his wife. "Joseph has selected these animals for their beauty, not their speed. Is that not so?"

"It's true, Mrs. Loeb," Joseph said. "These horses are beautiful and strong, but have no spirit."

"Good."

Loeb opened the door. "Now shall we go to Heckman's Ice Cream Saloon and show off?"

Although Heckman's Ice Cream Saloon was on Broadway, south of Bleecker, they first drove up Fifth Avenue to the newly fashionable Murray Hill neighborhood, specifically to pass the Seligman mansion. Then they wound their way back downtown past the homes of all of Hanschen's friends. Throughout Joseph was completely unaware of the pair of dark eyes carefully studying his back.

A few days after, Joseph found a small Standardbred trotting horse for Loeb's racing cart. "She's called Daisy," he said. "Not much to look at, but I can make a world-beater out of her."

Cully Brannagan looked up from his desk and scowled. "Well, well, if it ain't me old pal."

Funeral Wells closed the door and shot the bolt. He then pulled up a wooden chair and sat opposite Brannagan. "Two things," Wells said. "One, I want you to keep a closed wagon handy, day and night till I say I don't need it anymore. I come by, no notice, and get it when I need it. How much?"

Brannagan smiled. Wells wasn't a man to involve himself in petty crime. If there was dirty work, it was for big money. Maybe a piece might come his way. "What for?"

"My business. How much?"

"Five dollars a day."

"One."

Brannagan laughed. "C'mon, me boyo. We both know tiz for something dangerous you need me wagon for. Four fifty. Never a penny less. An' damages. You pay for any damage to me wagon, for which you'll give a deposit of fifty dollars, and another fifty for the well-bein' of me horse. Poor beast exposed to shooting and what not."

"Done."

That Wells accepted this deal only convinced Brannagan there was indeed serious money in Wells' scheme. "And tell me darlin', what was the second thing you said you'd be needing?"

"I'm looking for somebody. I'll pay five dollars to the tip that leads me to my man."

"Has he got a name?"

"Joseph Gershomsohn, although he's using Thunder as a name too and God knows what other name. He's a Jew kid and they say he's real good with horses." Wells then went on to describe the boy.

Brannagan knew instinctively that this was his Joe Ritter. He also knew that Wells wouldn't be looking for Joseph unless there was real money in it. He'd always thought Joe was special. A gentleman in peasant clothing, who spoke fancy German. Why shouldn't the money come his way? Who had a better right? Didn't he care for Joe when the boy was sick? And what return did he get? The boy had repaid his kindness by stealing his horse. Wells would never tell him how to turn Joe into a profit, but Joe would. It was just a question of starving or beating it out of him. The easy part was that he knew where Joe was. The kid was driving for Dooley.

He smiled at Wells. "We'll keep an eye out for him," he said. "Five dollars for the tip-off, did you say?"

Iverson showed Joseph to his quarters above the coach-house and stable. The apartment consisted of a sitting room, a bedroom, a kitchen, and something Joseph had never seen before: indoor plumbing.

After completing the tour, Iverson led Joseph back down the stairs to the stable and coach house. The beautiful Andalusians and Daisy, the ugly trotter, occupied three of the twelve stalls, and the racing cart and landau two of the six spaces for coaches.

The next morning, a spring day with the first heat of the summer in it, Joseph raced Loeb to his office and set a new speed record. Mayer, who refused to ride in the little cart, appeared a half hour later. Loeb then sent Joseph back to the house to take his wife and daughter for a morning shopping expedition and a round of afternoon social calls.

Joseph waited by the front door for the ladies to appear, thinking about the best routes to the destinations he guessed they would visit. But he was also fretting about Fannie. What if she persisted in wanting to learn about the horses? It wasn't right. Horses weren't for women to drive or ride. Except on some paintings in Schloss Wehdel, he had never even seen a woman on a horse. There had to be a reason for that.

At exactly ten o'clock Iverson opened the door, followed by Hanschen and Fannie. Hanschen was wearing light blue dimity and an embroidered grenadine shawl.

Fannie, who had been awake nearly the whole night planning for this moment, paused briefly in the hall, took a deep breath to calm herself, and then floated through the front door in a frock with peach shadows and golden highlights. She stopped to allow the morning light to filter through her straw bonnet and illuminate her face. Joseph appeared as he had the first moment she saw him, almost gentlemanly, if he hadn't been sitting on the box with that ridiculous cockade in his hat.

Joseph moved directly to her mother. "Good morning, Mrs. Loeb," he said. He glanced briefly at Fannie. "Miss Loeb." He saluted and opened the door to the carriage.

That magic hadn't happened disappointed Fannie. Hadn't she been seductive enough?

"Good morning, Joseph," Hanschen said. "Slow we will go?"

"I'll drive at the stately pace used by Queen Victoria's coachman when she reviews the guards, Mrs. Loeb."

Hanschen paused and looked at him. "Stately pace I like."

Joseph, pleased with himself, helped her into the vehicle. He then turned to assist the daughter, but Fannie didn't take the extended hand.

"I'd like something more like a chariot race in the coliseum," she said, helping herself inside.

Joseph laughed politely and thought, what a strange girl. He closed the door, mounted the driver's seat, and started the horses into their elegant walk.

"Joseph," Hanschen said. "First we will go to Spring and Prince Streets on Broadway." She then wanted to talk with her daughter. But Fannie's eyes kept returning to Joseph's back. Had Joseph understood her desire? Did he see how beautiful she was? He gave no indication. Could he feel what she felt? Her spirits now plunged to deep despair. And now, too, she considered some practical questions. How could she ever spend time with him? Joseph's life consisted of driving her family. When he wasn't driving, he was caring for the horses. If she went to his apartment, he wouldn't let her in. But she needed to spend time with him. How? How?

Then she thought of a way.

So did Cully Brannagan.

"You remember Joe Ritter?" he asked Slobbery Grimes, once again the undisputed bully of the Dead Rabbits.

"Yeah. I remember him."

"Well, you start watchin' Dooley's. When you see Mr. High an' Mighty Joe Ritter, you wait till four of you can get him alone at night when nobody can see you and..."

Grimes interrupted, "We stick a shiv in 'im?"

"No, you stupid scut! You grab him and you make sure nobody sees you so he disappears off the face of the earth, and you bring him here to me. If I ain't here when you come, you lock him in the tack room. You think you can do that, darlin'?"

§22

JOSEPH'S SECOND NIGHT AT THE LOEBS' HOUSE WASN'T AS PEACEFUL as his first. As usual he read until his eyes wanted to close, but when he put out the lamp he suddenly was as awake as if it were morning. He couldn't stop thinking about the von Exings. But this was America. There are no aristocrats here. Perhaps the von Exings could buy some of the police, but at least here he had a chance.

Here there were millions of immigrants. Here he could make the life he wanted. And one day, when he was rich, he could buy as many police as the von Exings. And when he was rich he would seek out Otto von Exing. He would challenge him and kill him. It was a question of his Jewish honor.

The word surprised him. His *Jewish* honor? Was that it? He could not be Jewish until he had killed Otto von Exing? Nonsense, he thought. If that were the case he would have to kill millions of Christians who humiliated and persecuted Jews every day. He would never be Jewish again. But then if he wasn't Jewish, what was he? Certainly not Christian. He would, he decided, be just himself; living without the Jewish God but not without Jewish honor.

There was only honor, he reasoned. If a man could live with honor he would fulfill the best hopes of mankind. Of that Joseph was sure. He had behaved dishonorably in succumbing to Brannagan. But honor could be recovered by honorable deeds. One had to admit to one's dishonorable acts and then struggle to right the wrong.

Then Joseph thought of death. Death was the price of dishonor. Life consisted of honor or death. Was he afraid of death? What had the poet Walt Whitman written? "Has anyone supposed it luck to be born? I hasten to inform him or her it is just as lucky to die, and I know it."

His mind finally at rest, Joseph fell asleep.

On Thursday morning of that first week, Loeb descended from his racing cart and turned to Joseph. "I'm changing our arrangement. No more bonuses for speed." Loeb held up both hands, "I know. I know. We had a deal. I'm a man famous for the sanctity of my word. But in this case it is a question of lives or deaths. Yours, mine, and God knows whoever else is foolish enough to get in our way. Setting a new speed record is at an end. We shall establish Monday's record as our norm. That is fast enough for me.

"But will you lose by this? No. I pay for my mistakes. From today on you will receive a hundred percent increase in salary, and at the end of each year that I'm still alive and uninjured you will receive a six-month bonus. Agreed?"

"Agreed."

"Good. Also on Monday while the family takes the train, you will drive the servants up to our summer cottage in Riverside. Hooks will show you the way."

"Yes, sir."

"We'll stay there for the summer."

Joseph noticed that whenever he drove Hanschen and Fannie, Fannie stared at him. It made him uncomfortable. He also observed that she smiled often, perhaps not at him but as if she had some kind of secret. He decided that if one looked at her enough, one could see she was pretty.

In the hours he wasn't occupied with driving he practiced knife-fighting. He then calmed down for sleeping with an hour or two of reading.

At the end of his first week Joseph made an astonishing and unpleasant discovery: the Loebs were Jewish.

Friday afternoon, E. Loeb & Sons closed at four instead of the usual seven. Joseph drove Loeb to his home and was told to put up the horses. He was then instructed to reappear at the front door the following morning at nine to drive the family to temple.

Temple? Joseph wondered. Were the Loebs Greeks? Did some Greeks still worship their old gods in temples? Would it be a temple dedicated to Zeus? He recalled the block Loeb had mentioned and recollected that there was some kind of church there. Well, he thought, it would be interesting to see what these Greeks did on their Sabbath.

The weather in New York was beginning to heat up and the evening shadows offered only a small relief. Joseph and the stable boy, who was called Moon, bathed the horses. When they were finished, Moon went to work polishing and waxing the landau. Moon was a pleasant young man, ignorant but with an instinct for horses that Joseph respected.

Joseph stood in the stable entrance-way to catch a faint breeze coming from the Hudson River. He was not surprised to see that Iverson and Hooks were setting a dinner table under the vine-covered pergola at the center of the garden, where large weeping willow trees kept it shaded all day. Seven children were playing, supervised by two nannies who periodically called out to them in German. Joseph guessed that these were Mayer and Isador Loeb's children.

Loeb and Hanschen led Fannie and her brothers and their wives from the house in festive spirits. Loeb then clapped his hands and summoned his grandchildren to gather around him and Hanschen.

Next, as if making magic, Loeb raised both his hands. Silence fell on the crowd and he began to sing. To Joseph's utter amazement, the song's words were in Hebrew. It was Lecha Dodi, a traditional song welcoming the Sabbath.

At the end of the song the children sat at the far end of the table with their nannies and mothers, while Hanschen pulled a shawl over her head, lit the Sabbath candles and in Hebrew sang the blessing.

Joseph looked away from the candles and his eyes came to rest on Fannie, who smiled at him.

Joseph quickly stepped back into the shadows of the stable. Leaning against the wall, he fought to control his emotions. The Sabbath! Shabbes! Why did this make him ache with emptiness?

That night Joseph lay in bed, his eyes wide open, pondering his discovery. How could the Loebs be Jews? They were millionaires. Everywhere he drove them, people—Christians—tipped their hats to them. How was it possible for Jews in America to live like this? Were there other rich Jews?

The next morning, Joseph waited with the carriage by the front door. Loeb emerged first, wearing an elegantly tailored black suit, a gray tie and a tall silk hat. Hanschen was dressed in a dark shade of blue silk matching her carriage's lacquer. Her crinoline skirt was so wide that, had Joseph not learned about such things from the whores of Five Points, he would have thought it impossible for anyone else to ride in the carriage with her. He didn't see what Fannie was wearing, as he refused to look. She appeared to him only as a rose scent.

"Gut Shabbes, Joseph," she said as she walked past.

He kept his face blank, as if he didn't understand her. Loeb laughed. "It's Jewish. It means have a peaceful Sabbath. Keep it till tomorrow and may it be a blessing for you in your church. Now take us to ours. Temple Emanu-El. Twelfth between Third and Fourth."

Temple Emanu-El, built of New York brownstone, had a square belltower with a spire rising from its center like many of the churches Joseph had seen in the city. This made it taller than all the buildings around it. Joseph wondered if this meant Jews were allowed to build taller structures than their Christian neighbors. A large, arched wooden door stood at the base of the tower and above it was an even larger stained glass window composed of two interlocked frames of diamond-shaped colored glass supporting a circular frame just below the window's peak. There was no mistaking the design in the center of that round window. It was the Mogen David, the Shield of David.

The street filled with carriages dropping people at the temple's entrance. Some of the carriages were as grand as the Loebs' and some of the horses almost as good-looking as the Andalusians. Joseph had never seen so many well dressed Jews. He carefully and politely worked his carriage to the front door. As they descended, both Mr. and Mrs. Loeb were too occupied with greeting friends to hear Fannie tell Joseph, "I am counting on you to teach me to drive."

"I don't know if I can do that, Miss."

"You'd be surprised at what you can do."

What did she mean by that? Joseph wondered.

After Fannie had glided into the crowd and through the doors of the temple, Joseph remounted the carriage and moved it to a position from which he could watch for the Loebs when they reemerged.

Temple Emanu-El, he thought. The words were Hebrew and meant "God is with us," but these Jews were like no Jews Joseph had ever heard about: riding instead of walking to shul. But it wasn't a shul, he reminded himself. It was a temple. There was much he had to find out, and he knew he had to be careful. He was exactly where the von Exings might be looking for him—with Jews.

Joseph carefully looked about him. The last of the congregants had entered the temple and their coachmen were either waiting by themselves or gathered in small groups chatting. No one was paying any attention to Joseph. He relaxed his vigilance for a moment and missed the large man who walked up to his side. A powerful arm reached toward him.

"Gut Shabbes, Reb Joseph!" Moses Cohen shook Joseph's hand. "So, Reb Joseph, you drive the Loebs," he continued. "Very nice. But there is a reason they are in shul and you are not? The Loebs do not let their servants observe Shabbes?"

Joseph stepped down from the coach.

"Please, Mr. Cohen," he said quietly, forcing Moses Cohen to draw very near. "My life depends on no one knowing that I am born a Jew. Please do not give me away."

"Your life?" Moses Cohen looked at Joseph carefully. Why was this face so familiar? "So serious? Your life?"

"It is dangerous for me to be seen here among Jews."

"So? And the Loebs? They are not Jews?"

"I didn't know they were Jewish until last night."

"And they don't know you're a Jew?"

"No one does but you and Mr. Roth at the bookstore. When I came there I behaved foolishly. I had forgotten I was being hunted."

"Hunted?"

"Will you keep my secret?"

"Your life? This is true?"

"I swear."

"You swear? Will you also swear you have not committed a crime of murder, incest or idolatry?"

"I committed no crime. But I must warn you. Although born a Jew, in my heart I'm no longer so. I don't believe in the God of the Jews."

"Not just God? You say 'the God of the Jews?' You're talking of more than one god?"

Desperate and exasperated, Joseph answered angrily. "This is not idolatry. I'm speaking of..."

"I know. I know. Although Shabbes is a good time for discussion, this isn't the right place." Moses Cohen struck his head with the flat of his hand. "*Ach*! I know you! On the wharf. Last year. A cold night. The street rat who spoke Yiddish and denied he was a damned Jew. You took my blanket."

Joseph remembered too. "And you removed my sin by giving it to me. Will you save me again?"

When Moses Cohen spoke it was more to himself than Joseph. "We have a new rabbi," he said, "who thinks it is the rabbi, not the hazzan, who must conduct the service. A new thing. A rabbi like a minister. And what is it, this service? No *tallis*. Men and women mixed. A choir, also mixed. They read the service in English and even more in German—no Yiddish there. Very high class, and only a little Hebrew. He thinks it is only for the hazzan to sing what is in Hebrew. Still I worship here instead of with the traditional Jews, because here there is something important to learn. So it is with you. You think it's by accident that you stole my blanket? That I met you again in Roth's store? That we meet now? That I am, for the first time in my life, late for the Shabbes service?

"I live at number 7 Clinton Street," Moses Cohen continued. "Come this evening, after sundown. We will have supper and talk.

Now I must hurry. They are all in there praying and I am, after all, the hazzan."

He hurried toward the temple.

At the completion of the Shabbes services, Joseph drove the Loebs home. Iverson and Hooks had once again set the table under the pergola; Joseph watched from his window, taking care that Fannie couldn't see him again. But he could see her. Look how the children cling to her, he thought, and how her father beams at her. What an odd person she is. Drive horses, indeed.

At the conclusion of the meal Loeb read from a small book he took from his pocket: "We hold these Truths to be self-evident, that all Men are created equal, that they are endowed by their Creator with certain unalienable Rights, that among these are Life, Liberty and the Pursuit of Happiness—That to secure these Rights, Governments are instituted among Men, deriving their just Powers from the Consent of the Governed, that whenever any Form of Government becomes destructive of these Ends, it is the Right of the People to alter or to abolish it, and to institute new Government, laying its Foundation on such Principles, and organizing its Powers in such Form as to them shall seem most likely to effect their Safety and Happiness."

Loeb closed the book reverently. "So, who can say this from memory?" he asked his grandchildren.

Mayer's two sons, seven and six years old, raised their hands. Isador's six-year-old daughter tentatively raised her hand too, then pulled it down. Fannie saw the movement and cried out, "Do you know it, Rose?"

The child nodded.

Fannie turned to her father. "The boys always say it. This is the first time Rose has tried. Let her say it."

"Rosie, do you think you can say the Declaration of Independence?"

"I memorized it," she said.

"I read it to her every day," said Bella, her mother. "And each day she has a new line memorized. She's very smart. Like her father."

Loeb beamed, "So, say it to grandpoppa."

When Rose had finished, she sucked in such an amount of air that her eyes crossed. Loeb snatched her up into his arms and covered her with kisses. "So why is it," he asked, "that on the Shabbes we go to temple and read a portion of the Torah, and then come home and read a portion of the Declaration of Independence and from the Constitution of the United States?"

This was Loeb's ritual moment, as surely as opening the ark in temple was God's. The children listened patiently, with affection and respect to the repetition they knew so well.

"Because," Loeb spoke in the rhythm of Hebrew prayer, "they are connected. Because from one came the other. Because one is the seed and the other the tree that gives the fruit. Because from Moses bringing the law at Sinai to Jefferson at Philadelphia there is a direct line. Because America is the New Jerusalem."

Joseph, listening from his window, looked at Fannie again. Her hair was loose and softly combed to fall around her face and curl over her shoulders. Every time he saw her, he saw something more beautiful about her. Joseph wrenched himself from the window. He tried to read but nothing engaged his attention. It made him furious. He needed to do something physical. He couldn't race Daisy. He had to be on duty if called. Besides, she wasn't his horse. How stupid, he thought—what if the von Exings come? I have done no sword drill for nearly a year. He cut the handle from a broom and began his saber exercises.

§23

MOSES COHEN'S APARTMENT WAS ON THE TOP FLOOR OF A RAM-shackle wooden structure with a hat store on the first floor and a book bindery on the second. Joseph assumed the attic was another bookstore, for the large open space and all the furnishings were covered with books. Still, from the scrubbed wooden floor to the shine of the leather bindings of the books, the room had a meticulous air of order and of safety.

"Come in, Reb Joseph," Moses Cohen said. "It's a little late but I have saved the Havdalah service for you. I know. You don't believe in God, blessed be his name." He was wearing a worn maroon dressing gown and a small round silk cap embroidered in gold threads. He took Joseph's arm and led him to a cluttered table.

Joseph started to speak, but Moses Cohen raised his hand for silence. "So humor me," he said. "An antediluvian Jew. Even though you don't believe. Help me end my Shabbes so at least the God of Moses Cohen, may he ever be patient, will not be angry with him."

"But I'm not a believer. I…"

Moses Cohen interrupted. "To be a Jew you don't have to believe, you have to do," he said. "So for tonight, don't believe, just do."

He immediately began the end of the Sabbath service and picked up an intricately woven candle with multiple wicks. He lit it and handed it to Joseph, and in a hauntingly sweet voice sang the blessing of the liquor. Next he sang the blessing of the spices and handed Joseph a small gold and jewel encrusted box. Joseph, not hiding his surprise at the box's splendor, sniffed its spicy contents and handed it back to Moses Cohen, who also sniffed.

Moses Cohen then sang the third blessing and placed his hands before the burning candle to create an effect of light and shadows. Taking their little silver cups in their right hands, they held them aloft while Moses Cohen sang of the light and dark, the holy and profane, Israel and all other nations, and the Sabbath as different from the other six days. They next drained the cups which were filled with schnapps. The alcohol caught Joseph off-guard and made him cough. He could feel its effect on his body. To his astonishment he found comfort in the ceremony, in the room, and in Moses Cohen.

To complete the service they sang the lilting Ha-mavdil, a song of distinctions. When it was completed, Moses Cohen saw Joseph's eyes return to the spice box and he smiled. "Such a splendid spice box, eh? Worth a king's ransom and here it is in the fishmonger's house. And if I told you that once it belonged to King Solomon? If I told you that King Solomon presented this very box to my ancestor and from then on every generation of our family has revered and protected it? I know. I know you would say to revere this object was idolatry. Am I correct?"

"The box makes no difference. It's all idolatry."

"Everything?"

"It doesn't have to be gold. It's in the attitude. If there are printing presses, then to have scribes hand-letter Torahs and if they make one mistake at the very end of a sheet, for them to do it all over again—that is idolatry. If the point of the spice box is to smell the spices, then to make it in gold and jewels is idolatry."

"You're saying that King Solomon was idolatrous?"

"Did he not build a big fancy temple? Why wasn't God's tent enough? How is Solomon's temple different from the Greek and Roman temples?"

"But God told him..."

"Which god?"

Moses Cohen laughed and picked up the box. "So Reb Joseph, when is it idolatry and when is it respect? And when is it a miracle?"

"A miracle?"

"You also don't believe in miracles? Even little ones?"

"No."

"If I told you that never, since the time of Solomon, has anyone placed spice in this box, and yet every Sabbath it smells as rich as the first Sabbath? You would believe it?"

"No."

"And if I told you that in every generation of my family we have kept records, and that never once has anyone ever put spices in the box?"

"And was your family dispersed by the Romans?"

"Yes."

"Did they wander for generations always robbed, tortured and killed for being Jews?"

"Yes."

"And you love a God whose miracle is putting spice in a box? Where were your God's plagues on the goyim? Did your God murder the first born of the Spanish for their Inquisition? How come the oceans didn't rise up to sweep all of our murderers from their lands? Do the Bavarian nobles have boils for the ghetto? Why are we in New York instead of under our fig trees in Jerusalem?"

"Perhaps we are where the Creator of the Universe, may he watch over us forever, wants us to be. Perhaps it is all *beshert*, preordained."

"Perhaps the God of the Jews, if He existed ever, died when the Second Temple was destroyed."

"Perhaps the Unknown cannot be known."

"Meaning?"

"It was Akiba who said, 'Everything is foreseen, yet free will is given; and the world is judged by grace, yet all is according to the amount of work.' God made us, but He made us with free will. It's not so much that God is hidden but rather that He is hiding. We can choose to seek Him out or not to. It's for us to do the work."

"And if there's no God there? If there's no God of anybody there?"

"If! If! If you argue like a child I shall have to stop calling you Reb Joseph. If! Where did the miracle of man come from? From where the earth? From where the sky and the stars? If we could fly to the stars and beyond them to the end of the universe, what would we find? When we die, what is there? Heaven? Hell? Reincarnation? What? How?

"Look at the relationship between a flower and the bee and tell me you know the answer. How the flower? Why the bee? Unless you tell me you think there is a mystery, I have made a mistake and there is no point to our meeting every Shabbes to argue these things."

"Every Shabbes?"

"First things first. Do you feel the mystery? Do you wonder at the how and the why?"

"Yes. But that does not mean there is a God."

"But it also does not mean that there is no God. Yes? You give me that little crumb?"

"A mystery I will concede."

Moses Cohen looked to heaven and, in Hebrew, chanted, "I thank thee O Ruler of the Universe for this little victory of reason." He smiled at Joseph and continued in Yiddish. "So it is agreed. We shall meet here every Shabbes and do the Havdalah together and then we shall argue. We shall argue in Yiddish...."

Joseph interrupted in English. "Not Yiddish. It's the language of the defeated Jews."

"And Hebrew is for the sacred texts. German?"

"German will be satisfactory."

"What? You agree to the language of the oppressors? We shall speak English, the language of the new land."

"Good. English. You really wish me to come every Shabbes?"

"I do."

"Even though I'm no longer a Jew?"

"Jew. Not Jew. What's important is a man's relationship with God. If you're an atheist, you already have a powerful relationship with God because to be an atheist you must wrestle with the question of God."

"I won't be able to come every Shabbes till after the summer. On Monday we go to the Loebs' summer cottage."

"So we'll start when you come back. Now tell me as much as you wish about why you are hunted and, while you do, I'll light a fire under Moses Cohen's famous Manhattan fish chowder."

"Can I trust you with my life?"

Moses Cohen turned to him. "And I, you with mine?"

Still feeling awkward, Joseph asked, "Will you give me your solemn oath never to reveal what I am about to tell you?"

Moses Cohen sighed. "No, I will not. You wish to tell me. Tell me. How I maintain your secrets is between me and Hashem. I know. I know. In Hashem you don't believe. For now it's enough that I do. You wish to tell me? Tell me. You do not wish? Don't. Should I go this night to Emmanuel Loeb and tell him his coachman is a renegade Jew who is being hunted? That will still be my decision to make even if you tell me your story."

Joseph said, "Leviticus 19."

Moses Cohen laughed, and in Hebrew quoted the verse: " 'You shall love your neighbor as your self.' But Reb Joseph, who is my neighbor? The Loeb family who I have known for years, and who are founders of our temple? Perhaps they're in some danger from you who have already attempted to steal from me. You are a Jew who does not wish to be a Jew. You forsake God. What if you're from the dark side? Oh, God in heaven, smell that fish chowder! A few more minutes. A few more minutes, you'll taste, and you'll think the Messiah is here in the soup pot. So tell. Do not tell. It's for you to decide. Not me to make promises."

Joseph said, "My name is Joseph Gershomsohn." And he then told Moses Cohen every detail of his life. While both men ate their soup, Joseph spared no detail of the months with Brannagan and his internal shame over Twit. He talked until midnight. When his tale ended, Moses Cohen asked, "And from me? What do you want?"

"To keep my secret. But if the von Exings kill me, to write to my parents and tell them what has happened."

"You think that's why you have told me this story? So that I'll write to your parents when you are murdered?"

"Yes."

"I think it's more."

"What?"

"Do I know everything? I don't know. But I think it's more. What it is, we shall see or we won't see. So Joseph Gershomsohn, be easy in your mind. For now your story is safe with me."

"For now?"

"Who can know what will be?"

Joseph pursued another matter. "I don't understand what I learned today."

"What? Understand?"

"The Loebs. How can Jews be so rich? How can there be so many rich Jews to come to the shul? Please, Mr. Cohen, tell me what is happening here?"

"First," Moses Cohen said, "in America, everybody calls everybody by their first name. It has something to do with no kings or nobility. So you call me Moses, and I'll call you Joseph. Reb Joseph when we argue Talmud. Second, the Loebs are only big Jewish millionaires. The Seligmans are bigger millionaires, also possibly the Loeb cousins, the other Loebs. The Schiffs maybe as rich, but not the Lewisohns. Richest of all is Mr. August Belmont, who used to be Shoenberg, and who, like you, has decided not to be Jewish. To be a Jew in America is different than to be a Jew anyplace else in the world. But of these matters you must ask the Loebs. Emmanuel Loeb comes to shul—excuse me, temple—prays, fears his God, but his Torah is the Declaration of Independence and his Talmud the Constitution."

"What are they?"

Moses Cohen stared at Joseph for a moment. "You, I suspect, will be very interested in them. Ask Loeb about them. And ask about his letter from George Washington."

"The man who made America?"

"Ask Loeb. About America, ask Loeb. With me we will talk about God."

"But what is this shul they call a temple?"

"In Germany you heard of the reform Jews?"

"A little. My father thought it was another version of the old problems. We read Spinoza. My father called us Spinoza Jews."

Moses Cohen laughed. "The Spinoza who wanted to replace all the old religions with a universal morality?"

"Yes. But it is more complicated than that."

"Simpler it couldn't be. I think I would like your father. About some of these things Spinoza was right." Moses Cohen saw that Joseph was going to start another debate and raised a restraining hand. "We'll save Spinoza for another time. Now I'll tell you about Temple Emanu-El. I go there because of Ezekiel 18:31: 'Make you a new heart and a new spirit.' Judaism survives on change as much as tradition. Our constant is to rethink ourselves in terms of human freedom and moral responsibility. Before, did I say to you that to be a Jew you don't have to believe, just do? Do enough moral responsibility and you will believe. But we're talking about Ezekiel. New. Not change for the sake of change, but change as in growth. For now, you don't believe in God. I do. If God is hiding, then the way to find Him is in constantly making a new heart.

"This temple is possibly a new heart, a place of change. It's a new thing, unique in history, an American invention.

"You believe that revelation is a constant? *Ach*! I forgot. You're a Spinoza disciple. You don't believe in revelation or redemption. But at the Temple Emanu-El they believe that revelation is a constant. Again Ezekiel. Revelation didn't happen once only at Sinai. After all, were there not also the epochs of the holy books, and then of the sages? The Talmud was once only oral—forbidden to be written, and was it then not written? Are not many of the strict laws to do with rituals in the temple, and there is no temple? So in this American temple, they're making a new American kind of Judaism. That's why I go there. To be a Jew is to be curious."

"So they're creating a new Jewish God."

Moses Cohen laughed. "Perhaps," he said. "Perhaps a special God of the American Jews. A God who chews tobacco and never misses the spittoon. Look how you are looking at me! You're thinking, 'Moses Cohen, the fishmonger hazzen, is playing games with me.' Only a little game. You think you are the first Jew to think that there is more than one god?"

"I don't know. My father liked the idea."

"The idea is in the holy scriptures many times. In Genesis 14:18 Abram comes to Malkhi-tzedek, king of what was to become Jerusalem and accepts from Malkhi-tzedek the blessing of their God who was called 'El.' So at least then, if we accept that the scriptures are the word of God, there were two Gods. The God of Abram and Malkhi-tzedek's El. There are other mentions of El as separate from Hashem. Go study your texts. Find how many times El is not Hashem. And when Abram went to Egypt? They did not have many gods? Not Abram's God. Not El. But gods. Then came Moses and the tablets: 'Thou shalt have no other God before me.' God acknowledges other gods. Look in the Cabbalah there is the tradition of the two Gods, God the Unknown and the Seferot—God the lesser administrator. So you see, Reb Joseph, you can still be Jewish. It is in fact almost necessary to question everything to be a Jew. Tell me who, who in the tradition does not question? To question is to be Jewish."

"And you are a hazzan? What are Jews about if not the One God? What kind of Jew are you?" asked Joseph.

"Like you. A Jew who asks questions. I've been waiting for a Jew like you."

"I'm not a Jew."

As Joseph was leaving, Moses Cohen said, "In the Midrash it asks, 'Who is a Jew?' And it answers. 'One who testifies against idols.' Good night, Reb Joseph."

After Joseph left Moses Cohen's apartment, he walked across town to visit Dooley. Dooley answered Joseph's knock in his night-shirt.

"What is it lad? What's the trouble?"

"I've done a stupid thing," Joseph said. He told him about the letter and the von Exing assassin.

Dooley led Joseph into his sitting room. "It's not a total disaster, Joseph. You didn't use your new name, so if they come to me they'll be asking me about a boy named Thunder. You've broken no American law and we don't ship people back to the old countries for old country justice. I suspect those looking for you will be sending some sort of private agent. But it makes no difference. I'll tell them you worked for me, and then you left to run off to the California goldfields. Let them go looking across the breadth of this vast land. The boys in the stable will back me up.

"As I see it, your big problem is Mrs. Clymer. You can't ask a nice respectable woman like Mrs. Clymer to tell a lie. It isn't in her nature."

"Then what shall I do?" Joseph asked. "She knows I'm at the Loebs. Besides, I don't have time to go there. I must drive to the Loebs' country house for the summer on Monday."

"The country place. That's good. So here's what you do right now. Run over to the Clymers. Hammer on the door and wake them all, excited like. When Mrs. Clymer comes down, tell her you came to say good-bye. Tell her you're leaving in the morning for the goldfields in California to make your fortune. You'll be doing her a favor. Then she won't have to lie."

Joseph thanked Dooley and ran all the way to Mrs. Clymer's so he would be out of breath when he got there. He hammered the brass knocker until a light appeared in the windows above him. Mrs. Clymer's head emerged from her bedroom window. Mr. Clymer was standing beside her. "What on earth is going on?" she asked, looking down at the street.

"It's Joseph, ma'am. I'm sorry to wake you, but I couldn't leave without saying good-bye and thank you for all your kindness."

"Leave? Where? Dear me. This is all unusual. We were sleeping."

"Yes, ma'am, but I'm leaving in an hour and I wanted to say good-bye."

"That's very nice of you, Joseph. Good-bye." She started to pull her head back and poked it out again. "Leaving? Where are you going?"

"I am going to the goldfields in California to get rich."

"Well, thank you for coming Joseph. Good luck and God speed." As she withdrew her head from the window, Mrs. Clymer turned to Mr. Clymer, "What a dear young man. Can you imagine? Waking the whole street to say good-bye?"

Exhausted from his day with Moses Cohen, and pleased with himself for the ease with which he had set his story with Mrs. Clymer, Joseph failed to pay sufficient attention to his surroundings. He heard a wagon rumbling up behind him and, along with it, running footsteps. He turned too late.

§24

BEFORE JOSEPH OPENED HIS EYES HE BECAME AWARE OF A FAMILIAR smell. Why was it so dreadful? In the distance a small cloud started to gather and move toward him. He opened his eyes. He was still in the dark, but it was a familiar darkness. His body understood before his mind and he broke out in a cold sweat. He was on his old bunk in Brannagan's tack room. Now he remembered more. He'd been walking away from Mrs. Clymer's when someone came up behind him. Brannagan had him kidnapped. He tried to rise but the shooting pain in his head kept him down. Still, he forced his body to sit up on the edge of the bunk. After a while the pain subsided. Then he stood swaying uneasily in the blackness. He willed himself not to fall.

A dim light shone through the cracks in the door. Joseph remembered the lantern hanging to the right, by the entrance to the stable yard. He could hear the horses as they moved about in their stalls. The place stank the way it had before he and Twit had cleaned it up.

His eyes, now used to the dark, could make out the familiar objects in the tack room. If he was to fight his way out, he would need more than the knife in his boot. Brannagan must not have been present when he was brought to the barn, he thought, or he would have taken the boots and discovered the knife. He must have been kidnapped by the Dead Rabbits. If it had been Slobbery Grimes, and Grimes was still with Brannagan when he came for him, he knew he was no match for the two of them.

Groping with his hands, feeling the bridles hanging on the wall, he found one made of heavy leather, studded with brass, with an iron curb on the end of it.

In the other room he heard voices.

"Where's me darlin' Joe?" It was Brannagan. His voice was thick with whiskey.

Joseph saw the bulk of the man blocking the light outside the door. He waited silently.

"C'mon, Joe, me good lad. Wake up and tell old Cully how glad you are to be home again."

Joseph controlled his breathing and crouched into a position from which he could attack the moment the door was open.

Brannagan spoke to someone next to him. "If you killed 'im, I'll rip your hide off."

The padlock on the door opened and Brannagan stepped into the room. Joseph lashed out with the bridle. It raked across Brannagan's head and he reeled backward. With his knife in front of him, Joseph followed, but Slobbery Grimes was standing between him and escape. Grimes, who saw the blade in the hand that had already once crippled him, stepped back. Brannagan, his face bleeding, stepped between Joseph and Grimes.

"Didn't I once tell you, Joe? No mercy? You should've used the knife when you had the chance." To Grimes he said. "You, you stupid ox. Stay out of it. This fight's between me and me darlin' Joe. Now will you lend me the use of your shiv."

Grimes handed his long knife to Brannagan. "Kill the little fucker."

Brannagan turned to Joseph. "Oh no. I'll not do you in, lad. But I'm gonna hurt you. I'm gonna hurt you real bad. I'm gonna hurt you till you'll be pleading to tell me why a certain party thinks there's money in grabbing a Jew kid named Gershomsohn."

Joseph had expected it. Gershomsohn. He assumed a fighting stance and backed away from Brannagan. Brannagan followed a quick feint with a lunge. Joseph swung the harness at him again, and Brannagan grabbed it, jerking it from his hand. "That's what I was expecting you to try," he said. "It's just the shivs now, Joe. Do you have the guts, Joe? Can you come up against your old teacher, Joe? If you put your knife down now, I promise to only hurt you a little." He slashed with his knife.

Joseph saw the move in Brannagan's eyes a flash before it happened. He leaped out of the way. There was Brannagan's weakness! His eyes. He had to keep watching Brannagan's eyes and he had to keep Brannagan distracted. Joseph counterattacked with a feint to Brannagan's face and a kick to Brannagan's shin.

Brannagan howled. "Oh, you dirty scut!" The smile was gone from his face. He feinted right and lunged left. Joseph again saw the move by watching Brannagan's eyes; he remained untouched. He slashed out and opened a deep cut along Brannagan's left arm. Blood oozed onto Brannagan's coat. Brannagan paused and looked at it. "Jazus!" he screamed. "No one cuts Cully Brannagan!" With a roar he launched a series of slashes and thrusts. But Joseph backed away, parrying the thrusts and avoiding the cuts until, seeing his opportunity, he opened a seam in Brannagan's forehead. Blood gushed into Brannagan's eyes, temporarily blinding him. "You scut!" he screamed. He threw his huge bulk at Joseph, who sidestepped him. It was Joseph's intention to make the same move he had once done on Grimes: bend down and sever Brannagan's Achilles tendon. But as he spun by Brannagan he came face to face with a woman. The woman abruptly raised her hand. Joseph stumbled, struck Brannagan in the neck with the tip of his knife and a channel opened between Brannagan's fourth and fifth vertebrae. Brannagan spun around and fell to the ground.

Joseph turned back to face the woman. But she was gone. With his blade pointed at Grimes, Joseph backed into the stable yard and ran out the front gate.

Grimes approached Brannagan carefully.

Brannagan was moaning. "Jazus! Mary Mother of God! Oh Jazus! Jazus!"

"Are you hurt bad?" Grimes didn't come too close.

"Slobbery lad. Oh Jazus! I can't move me arms or me legs! Jazus! Jazus!"

Grimes edged closer. "You can't move your legs or arms?"

"Get me to me feet! You fucker! Oh Jazus, I can't feel nothin'. If I can just stand up. Get me to me fucking feet, you scut!"

Grimes tentatively toed one of Brannagan's legs. "Didja feel that?"

"What? I don't feel fucking nothin'!"

Grimes kicked the leg, this time so hard it jumped six inches. "Didja feel that?"

"Fuckall. Get me to me fucking feet or I'll bash yer stupid face in!" Instead Grimes stood with his boot heel in Brannagan's hand. Brannagan rolled his head and stared at his palm. "What the fuck are you doing?"

"Do you feel this?" Grimes jammed his boot heel down until he knew he had crushed all the bones. Brannagan felt nothing.

"Fuckall! I don' feel nothing! Oh Jazus! Jazus!"

Grinning, Grimes reached out and retrieved his knife. He put it to Brannagan's throat and cut just a little. Brannagan screamed.

"Okay, that one you can feel. Now beg me for mercy!"

"Fuck off!"

Slobbery cut a little deeper.

"Mercy! Fer the love of fucking God! Mercy! You slimy fucker!"

Grimes stuck the knife point in Brannagan's eye. Brannagan screamed. "Beg me for mercy or I'll dig your other eye out too," Grimes said. "Beg me real nice. Beg."

"Oh Jazus, Slobbery. Mercy. Mercy. Sweet Mary Mother of God, Mercy! Oh I beg you, don't put me other eye out. Mercy. Mercy. Mercy.

Grimes stood and put a filthy boot sole over Brannagan's mouth. "Lick it."

Brannagan licked it.

"Lick it clean."

Brannagan licked it clean.

Grimes put the blade close to Brannagan's remaining eye. "Beg me for mercy again. But this time nicer."

"I beg you, Slobbery. Dear sweet lad. I beg you. Please darlin', mercy. Mercy!"

"Wasn't you the one that said no mercy?"

"There's money. Money in me safe. Mercy an' tiz yours."

"How do I get in?"

Brannagan told him.

Grimes went into the office and emerged a few moments later his pockets filled with money. Grimes jammed the last bills into his cap, pulled it on his head and started for the door.

"Help me up, you fucker!"

"Help yourself up." Slobbery Grimes took the oil lantern and smashed it against a post and ran out. Months of dry straw crackled into flame. In minutes the building was engulfed. Brannagan's screams were drowned out by the fire's roar.

It was dawn by the time Joseph reached Dooley's house. Dooley fed him breakfast and listened to his story.

"It's Sunday now," Dooley said when Joseph was finished. "You stay here and rest up. Tomorrow you're driving up to the Loebs' country place. You'll be safe there for the summer."

§25

IN NEW YORK CITY, WHERE SOCIAL TRENDS MATTERED, THE SELIGMANS were the social leaders of the wealthy Jewish community. But Emmanuel Loeb, unintentionally, was the first to lead the others to country homes. Three years earlier he had gone up to Riverside looking for a rare copy of the Declaration of Independence, printed by John Dunlap on the eve of July 4, 1776. The copy's owner sold it to him along with the colonial house he and his family had occupied for a hundred and fifty years.

Hanschen, who came to see the house the following weekend, liked the land and the long, sloping view of the river. But she thought the house too small and too plain, and wanted to enlarge it for their children and their families. Loeb, however, refused to have it altered. Instead he engaged local artisans to build three close duplicates of the house in suitable locations within a short walking distance of the original. Loeb promised Fannie that when she married she, too, would have her own house there.

The first summer the family was in residence their friends came to visit. Within a year many had purchased land of their own. The Seligmans built a Regency-style manor house, the Lewisohns chose the popular Italianate, the Schiffs a cottage in the Gothic Revival style; within three years Riverside had been established as the fashionable Jewish summer place.

The train ride to Riverside took thirty minutes, but Joseph's drive, over rutted and primitive roads, required a half day. This gave him time to think about his fate. Brannagan was dead. Had he killed him? No. Brannagan had fallen, but he was screaming obscenities when he fell. And that woman. Was she really there? Again, no. It was a trick of the mind. It was the same face he had seen in the synagogue in Dittelheim when he had put the Torah on the floor. Why did he see the same face twice? It must be a trick of the mind. But why? She didn't look like anyone he knew. The oddest thing was that he couldn't recall the face. But there were far more important things to think of. What had Brannagan said? Someone was looking for a Jew named Gershomsohn? That was why Brannagan had kidnapped him. He thought there was money to be made. The assassin had come to Brannagan but Brannagan didn't give him any information. Joseph was sure of it; he knew Brannagan. A wave of elation swept over Joseph. He had beaten Brannagan! Beaten him in an all-out fight. He would beat the assassin too. No one would ever again take away his freedom!

Once at the Loebs' country house, Joseph placed his Andalusians in charge of the stable hands and returned to the city by train that night. He drove up Daisy and Moon the following day.

Loeb considered the best part of his one vacation week a year the hours he spent with his wife, his daughter and his grandchildren. His sons he saw every day at work. Nathan, whom he loved best, didn't return his affection and had run off to Staten Island for his own summer vacation. Loeb often thought about the reasons for this and could find none. Had he offended Nathan? He must have but couldn't recall what he had done. On the one occasion when he tried to discuss it with him, Nathan evaded him. It was humiliating. He knew he had done all that a father could honorably do. Now it was up to the son. Loeb looked at the uninhabited house he had built for Nathan and the family Nathan didn't have, and he sighed.

With his daughters-in-law Loeb was dutifully loving but not close. He found them superficial. They were good wives to his sons and excellent mothers to his grandchildren. For that he was grateful. But he confined his conversation with them to the mundane.

With Hanschen he could talk about anything but finance. Business frightened Hanschen. So the highlight of his annual week of vacation was the hours he spent in conversation with his daughter, as he did now.

"Which is the wise choice?" he asked. "Do we acquire a small established railroad in Indiana? Or do we, for the same money, build a new and much longer railroad in Kansas?"

Fannie considered his question. "Poppa," she said, "that would depend on whether Kansas comes into the Union as a free or a slave state."

"Fanschen, this is business not politics. It's not a place for your abolitionist ideas."

"But Poppa, you're an abolitionist too."

"Against slavery, yes. But an abolitionist? A revolutionary? No. It's possible to oppose slavery and not destroy the country, which is what will happen if the radical abolitionists ever become a political majority. No, my child. Now we're discussing only business."

"And if I showed you that in this case of your Kansas railroad they were the same?"

"Show me."

"I studied the 1850 census. The statistical tables show that the North has surpassed the South in commerce and manufacturing...."

Loeb interrupted. "I don't have to read the census to know that."

"The figures show that the North surpasses the South in agriculture as well."

"Really?"

"Yes. The average value of an acre of land in the North is five times that of the South. Poppa, slavery is inefficient. If Kansas comes in as a slave state, your railroad land will be worth one fifth the value of the same land if Kansas comes in as a free state."

"These census figures," Loeb asked, "you have them?"

"In the city, Poppa."

"Good. I'll look at them."

"And something else."

"Tell me."

"I studied the annual reports of as many of the railroads in the slave states as I could. Not one of them showed an operating profit."

"Really?"

"And a random look at the same number of free state railroads shows that nearly all of them were in profit. Oh, look Poppa!" Fannie pointed at Joseph, who was coming up the drive with the racing cart. As soon as Joseph saw them watching, he gave Daisy a slight signal with his two middle fingers and Daisy's walk changed into an elegant, slow trot.

"How beautiful!" Fannie said. "Poppa, I want to learn to drive. Will you ask Joseph to teach me?"

"Absolutely not."

"Please? It would be a good thing for me to learn this summer. And I may never have another chance to learn from an expert."

"Under no circumstances," Loeb said. "It isn't something a lady should do. Your mother would never approve."

But Fannie knew that, while he was a fierce disciplinarian with his sons, Loeb couldn't resist her demands. It took only a little wheedling to gain his approval.

Later that afternoon, while Joseph was practicing his swordplay with his broom handle, he looked up to find Loeb and Fannie staring at him. "What are you doing?" Loeb asked.

Caught in military activity, Joseph almost brought himself to attention. He stopped just in time.

"Physical exercise, sir. Something to keep the arms and hands strong."

"It looks like dueling. Are you practicing dueling, Joseph?"

"It is like dueling, sir," Joseph said. "But it's really for the hands and arms, to keep them strong and supple for fast driving."

"And where did a peasant boy learn such a thing?" Loeb asked.

"From a hussar who lived near us. My uncle insisted I learn it when I was young."

Loeb had an unpleasant feeling that Joseph was lying. Before he gave it more thought, Fannie stepped forward.

"Joseph, my father says that I may learn to drive. Will you teach me?"

Joseph looked at Loeb.

"You may give her a lesson or two," Loeb said, now uneasy about having given Fannie his permission. "Let us see how she does."

"Please," Fannie said. "I so want to learn."

"I shall be happy to teach you, Miss Fannie," Joseph said, but he was apprehensive. What if she got hurt? Loeb would never forgive him. "Do you have any experience with horses? Do you ride?"

"Once. On a pony." Fannie smiled and shrugged apologetically.

"Joseph," Loeb said, "you shall have your hands full with this one. I promise you."

"Once?" Joseph asked Fannie.

"When I was little. My brother took me on a pony ride at Battery Park."

"And," Loeb interjected, "she was terrified of the horse. She cried all the way around the circle."

"Oh, Poppa, please. You must go away or I'll be too nervous with you watching to learn a thing. Please, Poppa?"

Loeb looked at Joseph. "Be careful," he said. But then he left.

Joseph didn't know what to do. Fannie did. She and Ada Clare had discussed it in detail.

One of the white Andalusian geldings stood in the cross ties. Joseph now went to him, scratched his forehead, caressed his eyes and his nose, and turned to Fannie.

"This is Paco," Joseph said, using his most formal voice. "Paco is always on the right." He waited a moment for a response and, when none followed, continued. "Before you can learn to drive, you must learn about horses. Have you ever spent time just being with a horse?"

"No."

"Miss Fannie..."

"Please call me Fannie."

"I don't think that would be proper."

"Why?"

"I'm your father's coachman."

"Don't be silly. Call me Fannie. I insist. Please say it."

"Fannie," Joseph said.

"Good."

"I've never..."

She interrupted. "You didn't say my name."

"Fannie, I've never taught anybody how to drive."

"Then I'll be your first pupil. How shall we start?"

"First, I must teach you about horses...."

"You said that." Fannie kept her eyes on his.

"Yes," Joseph answered. "Many people think that you control a horse by pulling on a rein."

"That is what I thought," she said.

"But that's wrong. The best way is to help the horse do what you want by causing him to think it's all his idea. You get him to want to do what you want him to do. Does that make sense?"

"Oh, yes." She was sure he wanted to kiss her. What would it be like—her first kiss?

"Good," Joseph said. "The way we start is how horses like to be touched. Then ground training. Then we'll have to get a training cart." A thought occurred to him. "Are you afraid of horses?"

"No."

"Good. Come and stand by Paco." He moved away from her. "Right here," he said. "Like this. Be sure you're comfortably balanced on your feet, and breathe quietly." Joseph demonstrated what he wanted, and then stepped aside.

Tentatively, for Fannie discovered she was indeed afraid of the horse, she reached out and touched its forehead. Then she quickly withdrew her hand. "I'm afraid," she said. Joseph suppressed astonishment.

"But if you teach me about horses, then I shall not remain afraid. I'm a very good student. I promise you I am."

Joseph thought for a moment. "Yes, you're right to be afraid. It's a natural reaction. The horse is huge and powerful. But Paco is a very gentle horse." Joseph spoke in the soothing tone he used for frightened horses. "See how he likes his ears pulled." He matched his action to his words, stroking the horse's ears from the base to the tips. "Good old Paco. Good Paco," he crooned. In a moment the horse, eyes drooping, was asleep on his feet. Joseph turned to Fannie. "Are you really afraid?"

She nodded.

Joseph gently took her fingers in his hand; when he did Fannie looked into his eyes. She found reassurance in them, and something else. She was sure he was experiencing the same excitement she was. She felt him tremble. He placed her fingertips against Paco's neck.

"Just feel his fine coat."

She did.

"Close your eyes."

"All right," she said.

When Joseph spoke again his voice was barely above a whisper. "Feel him. Feel not just with your fingers. Feel with your being. Feel how he is at rest. How he trusts you. Feel him."

But a moment later Paco stamped a foot and Fannie bolted in terror. Instinctively Joseph reached out to protect her. Fannie, instead of pushing him away, put her arms around his back. Now it was Joseph's turn to be terrified. He removed her arms and backed away.

"Miss Fannie, I beg you, for your well-being do not come near me. Give up this idea of lessons. See me only when in the company of your parents and when I am with the coach."

"I could not possibly do that," Fannie said. "You've promised to teach me. I shall hold you to your promise. If you teach me, I'll not ask you to tell me your secret." There was a secret. She was sure of it.

"My secret?"

"Does it have to do with dueling? You didn't fool Poppa with that story about strengthening your hands for horses. You were practicing dueling."

"Please, I beg you. Don't ask me."

"You're quite right, of course. It isn't any of my business." She changed the subject. "I'm too frightened of horses to ever learn to drive."

"What shall we do?" he asked.

Fannie smiled sweetly at him. "Why, you'll teach me to become unafraid of horses." Before he could answer, she added, "It's been a delightful lesson. Thank you so much." She ran toward the house.

Joseph sat down on a tack box, stunned.

Later, laying naked on his bed, Joseph was thinking of honor. He was sure that honor required he not allow Fannie to become his friend—he refused to entertain thoughts of anything else—because of the danger from the von Exings. He would never place her in harm's way. He thought bitterly about von Exing, and in doing so realized that once the Loebs returned to the city in the fall, he had to leave them.

He heard a creak on the stairs leading to his room. He ignored it. Then he heard another. He simultaneously gripped his knife and blew out the candle. After a moment, he sensed someone standing on the other side of the door. He silently moved to a position from which he could attack. The latch slowly lifted and the door opened. Joseph drew in a breath, let it out halfway, and held it.

"Joseph?" Fannie whispered.

Joseph shoved the knife under a chair. "Fannie?" he asked.

She stepped into the room and ran into Joseph's arms. My God! she thought. He's naked!

In the moonlight his body looked like the copy of Michelangelo's David that Ada Clare had shown her at the museum. How beautiful, she thought. Her hands lightly slipped from his shoulders and her fingers caressed his chest.

Joseph gently took them away. "Fannie, I love you," he said. He meant it, although this was the first time it had occurred to him.

"And I love you." Ada had told her she would have to say that if the man said it first.

Later, back in her own bed, Fannie thought over the preceding hours. Had there been the pain Ada Clare said she would experience? None that she could remember. Quite the opposite. It had been wonderful.

Joseph sat on the edge of his bed and watched the eastern sky lighten. What have I done? he thought. Oh God, what have I done?

The arrival of the Loebs became the start of the official summer season: at-homes, teas, dinner parties, socials, picnics, hay-rides, boating and croquet. Fannie loathed it all. She was looking forward to a grand tour of Europe, ostensibly to find a husband. Once there she would meet and fall in love with a great composer. She would inspire him. They would live on a lake in Switzerland. He would drown in a storm while working on his greatest symphony. She would be a tragic figure in black until one day a wild young revolutionary would rescue her. She would help him topple the kings of Europe. And meanwhile there was Joseph, and all the nights of the summer.

Brannagan's death displeased Funeral Wells. Now he had to find another supplier for his wagon, and there was no one else he could trust to look for Gershomsohn. So he did it himself. Starting at the Battery, he systematically worked his way uptown from livery stable to livery stable.

§26

Fannie came to joseph's room the next night, and the night after that, and the night after that. Joseph lived in a state of innocent bliss, while Fannie allowed herself ninety minutes in his room each night. She had calculated the precise amount of sleep she needed so as to not cause her parents worry over her fatigue. Then one night a strange thing happened. They talked.

"I've dishonored myself with your father. I'll have to leave."

Fannie panicked. She couldn't lose him now. "There's no dishonor," she said. "My father approves."

Joseph was amazed. "He knows?"

Fannie was surprised she had said such a thing. Now it had to be defended. "Well, not about you, specifically," she added. "But about having a lover," she improvised. "You know I support the cause of equal rights for women, and Poppa approves. Why, he's even planning for me to be a full partner in the bank. He doesn't want me to marry any of those awful suitors you've seen. Momma likes them, but not Poppa. He believes his daughter should have the same rights as his sons, and he told me when I was ready that I should take a lover. It was very difficult for him to say that. But he's a man of strong convictions and he thought it important for me to be as world-wise as my brothers. But he warned me to only pick a lover who was worthy. The only condition he made was that I was to be discreet. He said he wanted to never know about my lover, and we must honor that. Right?"

Joseph, so willing to believe her, nodded.

The following day, Loeb greeted Joseph with his usual warmth and Joseph no longer felt duplicitous.

When Loeb's vacation ended he began his daily commute to Manhattan. Each morning Joseph raced him to the train station and on their way they flew by the carriages of Loeb's neighbors. Loeb gravely tipped his hat to each of them. They tipped back and shook their heads at such eccentric behavior.

That first day, when Joseph returned to the stable, Fannie was waiting for her lessons. He was astonished by her costume—white

Turkish pantaloons gathered at her ankles beneath a short, hooped skirt. "The pantalettes are called bloomers," Fannie explained, "after a great woman, Mrs. Amelia Bloomer. She invented them to free women from the constraints of our unwieldy costume. Mrs. Bloomer has pointed out that our cumbersome clothing makes it difficult to do practical things and therefore contributes to our enslavement by men. Don't you agree? Isn't this practical as well as beautiful?" She spun a little pirouette. The idea of the enslavement of women had never entered Joseph's mind.

"And don't you think the bloomers are charming as well as practical?" Fannie asked. "Of course, I only wore the hoops under the skirt to show how the costume looks in its more formal state. However, since we're going to be working with the horses, they'll be in the way." She reached under her skirt and loosened the ties, causing metal hoops to fall to the ground and her skirt to cling to her hips.

"Please, Fannie," Joseph said. "Put the hoops back."

"Why?" she asked. "Won't it be easier to work with the horses if I am unencumbered?"

"Fannie, we promised. During the day, we must do the work. Please."

She laughed. "Very well then. For now." She reached down and picked up the hoop cage. "There. Respectable as I shall ever be."

"Fannie," Joseph said. "Can love just accidentally happen between any two people or is it preordained? Is it *beshert?* Destiny? Were we born to love each other?"

"Did you say beshert?" Fannie asked. "Joseph, are you Jewish?"

"I was born a Jew," Joseph said tentatively.

"Why do you say 'born a Jew?' Can one stop being a Jew?" She didn't wait for an answer. "I suppose in America anyone can do what they wish. Particularly if they have a father like mine. Oh, Joseph, you're Jewish. How nice!" And in Hebrew she quoted from the *Song of Songs:*

> O give me of the kisses of your mouth,
> For your love is more delightful than wine.
> Your ointments yield a sweet fragrance,
> Your name is like finest oil—
> Therefore do maidens love you."

Joseph, also in Hebrew, quoted another verse:

> "I have likened you, my darling,
> To a mare in Pharaoh's chariots.
> Your cheeks are comely with plaited wreaths,
> Your neck with strings of jewels.
> We will add wreaths of gold
> To your hoops of iron."

She blushed. "Not even Moses Cohen speaks such beautiful Hebrew," she said. "And he's our hazzan." And then she burst out laughing. "Hoops of iron? You made that up."

Over the next hours the two young people engaged in their first serious conversation. Joseph, true to his resolve, spoke nothing of Dittelheim, von Falkenbrecht, the hussars, the ship, Brannagan or the Clymers. Instead he talked about horses and God, and his hope for one day creating the greatest equine breeding establishment in the world. But Fannie only wanted to discover his romantic secret. Why a Jew was practicing dueling? Had he been in any castles?

Then Fannie spun her own tales of adventure with Nathan and her favorite poets. She didn't mention Ada Clare.

One morning Hanschen saw her daughter leaving the house in bloomers and she forbade her to wear them again. Fannie did as she was told, but that night modeled the costume for Loeb, who laughed and arranged a compromise. Fannie was permitted to wear the pantalettes for her horse lessons but not off the property, nor if they had visitors. The driving lessons themselves were torture. Fannie recognized she had no aptitude, but the lessons were essential to continue her dalliance. Besides, Ada had told her a properly abandoned woman should know how to drive horses.

While Fannie never was able to overcome her fear of horses, she learned how to approach them, to touch them, pet them, and to groom them. She also learned how to hide her fear of them from Joseph. She did this by fooling the horses, burying her fear so deep that the two Andalusians were completely taken in.

Although Joseph and Fannie were together each morning from Monday to Friday, never more than an hour was spent with the horses. The rest of the time was devoted to discussions solving the great questions: What is happiness? What is beauty? What is truth? Joseph astonished and enlightened Fannie with his views of God, gods, and Jews. Fannie opened Joseph's mind to abolition and women's rights. And once done with these issues, they read poetry to each other.

Fannie developed some small skill in her work with the horses, but she had no talent for it. Joseph was disappointed. He accepted her perseverance as her gift of love to him, but Fannie's technical ability was no longer sufficient. She lacked the essential rhythm to drive safely. Joseph concluded that it was her intellect blocking her instincts. Later, when the two of them were reading poetry to each other, Joseph decided to try something new.

"You know more verses of the *Song of Songs?*" he asked.

"By heart?"

"Yes."

She laughed. "Not all eight chapters."

"How many do you know?"

"The one I quoted to you, and a few more."

"In Hebrew?"

"Naturally. Do you think I'm a barbarian?"

"No," he said. "But I have a game."

"Good."

"Tonight you must study them in Hebrew."

"But what about us?" she asked. "The nights are ours...."

"Just for a little bit. I swear to you, my love, the nights without you will be torture. But we'll have our whole lives together. Now, the most important thing is for you to be safe. If, God forbid, you should have an accident, your father would stop our lessons and we would lose everything. Please. For only a week, perhaps even less, just learn the first ten verses. We'll say them in Hebrew. Tomorrow, when you're driving, I'll say the first two lines of a verse and you must finish it correctly."

"When I am driving? But why?"

"You'll see. Can you do it? You said you were a brilliant student."

"I never said such a thing."

"No. But it's what you meant."

She laughed again. "When?"

"Whenever you talk about what you read and what you learn from it. Will you study the verses?"

"Yes, but I'll miss our nights."

"I will too," he said. "It's a sacrifice we must make. I need to know you're safe and I promised your father the same thing."

The plan worked as Joseph had anticipated, although Fannie's Hebrew was not as fluent as his. She studied late into each night for the rest of the week, and each morning, when she drove around the enclosed field, she had to concentrate on both the verse and the language. Whenever Joseph corrected her Hebrew she felt humiliated and forgot to worry about her driving. Paco noticed it immediately.

Fannie generally didn't train on the weekend mornings. On Shabbes it was not permitted, and Sundays she liked to sleep late and spend time with her father. This Sunday, however, she rose early and went to the barn.

Missing her at breakfast, Loeb strolled down toward the barn, where he could hear the couple before he could see them at work. What he heard stopped him before he turned the corner.

In Hebrew, Joseph shouted: "Ah you are fair, my darling. Ah, you are fair, with your dove-like eyes."

Fannie shouted back: "And you my beloved are handsome, beautiful indeed."

Joseph responded: "Awake, O north wind, come O south wind. Blow upon my garden, that its perfume may spread."

And Fannie said: "Let my beloved come to his garden and enjoy its luscious fruits."

Loeb hurried around the corner to see his daughter driving the horse and cart in a smart trot. When Fannie saw her father she drove the cart over to the fence. "Joseph is Jewish, Poppa," she shouted as she drove past.

Loeb nodded. "So it appears." Fannie was in love, Loeb thought. She was in love with Joseph. God in Heaven! What about Hanschen? But he knew the answer. A catastrophe! Not a Rothschild, not a Seligman nor a Sachs, not a Jewish millionaire—but a coachman. Hanschen would never survive the humiliation.

And that's why she did it this way, Loeb thought. My God, what a child. She picks a coachman, which is crazy, but since it is Joseph, it is not so crazy. But what is her first thought? To elope? To run away thinking only of her happiness? No, Loeb decided, Fannie was trying to protect her mother.

Loeb stared at Fannie in wonder. Why not Joseph? He was an exceptional boy. He had manners like a German prince. If Joseph's last name had been Seligman, Hanschen would have considered it a perfect match. The boy didn't have any prospects or money. But if this romance was as serious as it appeared, prospects and money could be arranged. He could bring Joseph into the firm and teach him the business. Who would care if the boy had started as a coachman? Did anyone care that he and the Seligmans had started as peddlers with packs on their backs?

But Hanschen? Loeb signaled to Fannie, who stopped the cart, handed the reins to Joseph and ran to her father.

"This, my Fanschen, is a very large surprise," Loeb said. "Come, we shall walk a little."

"A surprise?"

"What? I am blind? You think I don't know how your mind works? Oh Fanschen. The coachman."

"Joseph?" Fannie asked.

Loeb nodded. "A unique young man. You brought me to the meadow so that I was to discover that he is Jewish and that you love him. But for one little obstacle you wish to marry him. Correct?"

Fannie was appalled. But to deny her father's erroneous conclusion would be to start him on the road to suspicion.

"Yes," she said demurely. "It'll break Momma's heart." Well, she thought, that was certainly the truth. "Poppa, will you help us so that Momma will not be wounded?" She wondered how she was going to get rid of Joseph when the summer was over without arousing her father's suspicions.

"I'll think about it," he said. "And Joseph? He loves you?"

"I think so, but his honor won't let him speak of it. He says that he's the coachman and that it wouldn't be right. He says that I'm too young and that it would dishonorable for him to permit anything between us but a childish friendship, and that if I insist on more he will leave our service and go to California. Oh Poppa, he is a very moral man. I know that if he suspects you or Momma disapprove he will go away. And Poppa, if he does go away I shall follow him." She burst into tears. Tears always affected her father.

"Shhhh," Loeb said. "There, there. You love him. That's all I need to know. If he is worthy of you…"

She interrupted. "Oh, he is. Poppa, he's even Jewish."

Loeb continued to stroke her hair. "So it appears."

"Appears?" She took her head from his chest and looked up at him. "Why do you say appears?"

"Fanschen, he speaks Hebrew like the hazzan. But there are gentile aristocrats who study Hebrew with their Latin and Greek at the great universities." Loeb was thinking of Joseph's dueling. And was ever a Jew such a horseman? "Did he tell you he was Jewish?"

Fannie thought that if Joseph had been lying about being Jewish, she could later discover he was a Christian and break off their relationship. "Yes," she said. "I asked him and he said yes. But he said he no longer believes in the God of the Jews."

"He said, 'God of the Jews?' Not God?"

"Poppa, you don't believe in God."

Loeb was slightly taken aback. "Of course I believe in God. Don't I go to temple?"

"The One God?"

"Of course."

"The same God the Christians and the Muslims say is theirs as well?"

"What they think is their business. We know that there is only one God, and that is Hashem."

"Joseph thinks there are more than one, and that the Christian God is the most powerful right now."

Oy, Loeb thought. "Fanschen, is that why he went to the Episcopal church with the servants?"

"He told me about that. He did it to see what it was like not to be Jewish."

"And now will he come to visit the God of the Jews at our temple?"

"No. He is angry with the Jewish God."

"He is angry with God." Loeb couldn't restrain himself. He laughed, which is what Fannie had hoped for.

"So," Loeb said. "We have a Jew who is angry with God. He is a Jew unlike any we have ever seen. We know nothing about him, except that he is an expert with horses. Do I like him? Yes. Do I respect him? Yes. Do I trust him with my daughter's safety? Yes. Will I permit him to marry my daughter?" He paused and looked into her eyes. "Fanschen, we don't lie to each other," Loeb said. "I don't know the answer to that question. But I promise you I will let nothing or no one hurt you or your mother. Do you understand that?"

"Yes, Poppa."

"I offer you the following deal. For the rest of the summer, you and Joseph may continue your time together. I trust your discretion to see to it that your mother doesn't have the slightest suspicion about your feelings for Joseph. Do I have your word on that matter?"

"Yes, Poppa."

"Now tell me," he said. "There is too much we don't know about Joseph Ritter. Who are his family? Has he told you?"

"No. He's told me that he'll answer no questions about his past."

"And you do not find that odd?"

"I trust him and when the time is right he'll tell me everything."

"So now I'll tell you my part of our bargain. I shall not grant to him, as you have, his desire to remain a mystery. Monday I'll have him come to the city with me. We'll go to our house and there we'll have a man-to-man talk. As I like and respect him, I don't anticipate this talk to be anything but friendly. If he chooses to remain a mystery, I shall write to my agents in Germany by the next steamer. They'll be instructed to find out everything they can about Joseph Ritter of Poppenlaur."

"He is from Poppenlaur? Where is that?"

"In Bavaria, a river town. This much I had from Joseph when he came to work for me. He also told me his parents died, which is why he came to America. There was some talk of an uncle who was a university professor. This is the deal. If Joseph is who we believe him to be, I will help you with your mother so that she will happily consent to your marriage. But if I discover that Joseph Ritter is not who he says he is, I shall forbid this marriage. Will you accept that deal? Will you shake hands?"

Perfect, Fannie thought. She knew Joseph was lying about something important. Now she could continue the romance and then, when her father forbade the marriage, she would obey. That would guarantee an immediate trip to Europe—her grand tour! Fannie grabbed her father's outstretched hand and squeezed it. "Oh, Poppa," she said. "Oh thank you, Poppa."

"But, Fanschen, the news I get from Germany may not be what you want to hear."

"How can it not be? I know him. He is pure and good."

The following morning Iverson informed Joseph that Mr. Loeb wanted him to accompany him to the city. He was to hitch up the carriage so that one of the grooms could return it to the stable. Joseph did as he was told, although he had a strange foreboding and as a precaution took along all his cash. He also took the passbook for his savings account at the Merchants Bank of New York.

On the train Loeb rode in a private car where he knew his coachman couldn't. Instead, Joseph took a seat in the chair car and continued to wonder why he had been so summoned. One half hour later he met Loeb on the platform of the Hudson Line Station in New York. "Get a hansom," Loeb said. "We'll go to Sixteenth Street."

Joseph did as he was told. They rode in silence to the Loeb mansion, where the maid, who alternated with the other servants watching the town house, admitted them. This was the first time Joseph had entered the front door. Even with dust covers over the furniture, the house was warm and friendly. Loeb led Joseph to the large drawing room where he closed and locked the sliding doors, crossed to two chairs by the fireplace and, pulling off the dust covers, indicated that Joseph take a seat.

"Joseph," Loeb said. "We will start this meeting with what we know to be true. I know you're a young man of impeccable honor, and a brilliant horseman. You have told me that you come from Poppenlaur, that your father was a horse trainer, that your parents, may they rest in peace, are dead, and that your Herr Professor uncle educated you. Beyond that I know nothing. What do you know about me?"

Joseph was confused. "You are a kind and fair man."

"What else?"

"You are rich."

"How rich?"

"I don't know. Millions?"

"Yes, millions. What else?"

"You have a wonderful family."

"More."

"You are an American kind of reform Jew."

"Good. Anything else?"

"This meeting is about Fannie."

"Good. You don't disappoint me. What about Fannie?"

"You're concerned that she is infatuated with the coachman."

"The coachman?" Loeb asked. "You know me better than that."

"Please forgive me. You're concerned that she loves me."

"And you? Do you love my Fannie?"

"With all my heart, sir."

As he said the words aloud, Joseph knew that never had he loved so deeply. He also saw the pain his words caused in Loeb's eyes. He loathed himself for not having left the day after that first night.

"But don't be afraid, Mr. Loeb, I have already made the decision to go away."

"You would do that to Fannie?"

"It would be best for her, sir."

"How old are you, Joseph?"

"Sixteen, sir."

"So young. I thought at least two years older. And you are Jewish? Truly?"

"Yes, sir."

"Can you prove it?"

"I was bar mitzvahed."

"Where?"

"Poppenlaur," he said, which was a lie, but a necessary one. And then Joseph recited the most sacred of Hebrew prayers, "Shema Ysrael, Adonai Elohaynu, Adonai Echod. Hear O Israel, The Lord our God. The Lord is one."

Loeb nodded. "Tell me about Poppenlaur, about your father and mother, about your family."

The temptation to tell his story was strong, but he decided to say nothing until he was out of danger. "Mr. Loeb, I cannot. I beg you to not ask me about these things."

Loeb suddenly thought of Nathan, his youngest son. He didn't understand why he was estranged but he felt the pain. He wouldn't let such a thing happen to Fannie. He glanced up at the wall above the fireplace. There, behind glass, was his precious Declaration of Independence. In America, all were innocent until proven guilty. So be it for Joseph. But what was the boy was hiding? All Loeb knew was that it had nothing to do with criminal behavior. Both Joseph and Fannie were too young to consider matrimony. He had time to get to the bottom of the secrets. Today he would dispatch a message to his agents in Bremen. In a month, he would have some answers. In the meantime, the children could enjoy their summer romance.

"Joseph," Loeb said. "Fannie loves you. We both know that. I can put a stop to this. But if I do, it will cause great pain and as yet I am unsure that is necessary. You know I like you, Joseph. From what I know about you I would be proud to have you as my son-in-law. So, I'll make a deal with you. Will you deal with me?"

Joseph was astonished by Loeb's words. "Yes, sir."

"First, understanding that both of you children are so young, I want your word that you will not attempt to marry without my express permission—which I shall not grant for at least two more years. Do I have that from you?"

"I agree," Joseph said, for he also knew he was too young to marry.

"But you may have the summer to play," Loeb continued. "To protect Mrs. Loeb from the shock, I will need to prepare her. The two of you are to remain absolutely discrete."

So, Fannie hadn't lied to him! Loeb did approve of the affair. "Yes, sir."

"When you and I are finished here," Loeb said, "I'll go to the office and you'll go to Dooley and rent, for the summer, a heavy wagon of some sort, and a docile horse for Fannie to drive. Take it up to Riverside. Except in an enclosed field, you are never to let her drive alone. Is that agreed?"

"Yes, sir."

"If the summer continues as we are planning, when we return to the city, you'll find me a good replacement coachman. You'll then come to work at E. Loeb & Sons, where you'll begin to learn the business."

"Sir? You mean the banking business?"

"This is a time of huge economic expansion. You are coming to it at just the right moment. I mean to make your fortune."

"I can't do that," Joseph said. "I'm a horseman. I've saved every penny. Soon I'll be able to begin my own stud. That's what I want to do."

"You think you can support my daughter with a horse farm?" Loeb asked.

"Yes, sir. I do. I'll breed the finest horses in America."

"Joseph, you want a horse farm? You can have one. It's something the rich do for pleasure. But from horses no one makes millions. You come to work for me. You'll learn to make your millions, and you can play with all the horses you want. But first you learn the business. That is part of our deal."

"I am a horseman."

"I understand," Loeb said. "Will you at least agree to this? Without giving up the idea of going into the horse business, but with the understanding that you should know what this family does. At the end of the summer you will come to E. Loeb & Sons, for just one year, enough to learn how to manage the considerable fortune that will be Fannie's. Do you not think you owe her that? To learn to manage her fortune?"

The proposal made Joseph uncomfortable. But it was a fair request. He couldn't expect Fannie to live the life of a farm wife when she was an heiress. But it made him intensely uncomfortable.

Loeb saw Joseph's indecision. He said, "When we return to the city you'll come to work only five days a week. Come Shabbes and Sunday, go to the country. Look at horse farms. Study the breeds. Buy some horses. On the day of your engagement, one year from the time you join the firm, I shall buy the two of you any farm you choose, provided it is not too far away. It will be your engagement present. Do we have a deal?" He stuck out his hand.

Joseph took it and they shook.

"Now, tell me why you decided not to be a Jew."

Without mention of the Judengasse of Dittelheim, Joseph recounted his version of the history of the Jews and their ineffectual God. Loeb listened quietly. When at last Joseph had finished a litany so familiar to Loeb that he could have mouthed the words along with the boy, he nodded. "So," he said, "now tell me why you came to America."

Joseph chose to tell as much truth as possible. "I got in trouble. I'm not at liberty to tell you all the details, but a certain baron was going to kill a rabbi in a Jewstreet unless the rabbi said Jesus Christ was the only true Messiah. For that the rabbi was prepared to die. I wasn't prepared to let him. I defeated the baron in single combat, on horses, with sabers. I made him say, 'Jesus Christ is not the Messiah.' "

This story was beyond anything in Loeb's experience as a Jew or a man. It explained the dueling practice in the barn, but something else was wrong. He still had to protect his daughter if Joseph was not what he seemed.

"Who was this baron?" Loeb asked.

"I can't tell you, sir. Not yet. Trust me."

Trust him? Loeb wondered. To make such a desperately complicated decision he found himself in the unaccustomed position of being uncertain. Fannie's happiness was at stake. Loeb gambled on his instinct that Joseph Ritter was real.

"Joseph," Loeb said, "this is very strange. I ask you to make another promise. I ask you to promise that if you are unable to resolve your trouble, and you choose to leave, you will first come to me so that I may see if I can help you. Will you promise me that?"

"Yes," Joseph said.

"So you came to America to run away from trouble?"

"Yes."

"You did not know what America was?"

"How do you mean, sir?"

"A good place for Jews. A place where you could remain a Jew. You did not know that?"

"No. Is it?"

Loeb laughed.

"You have seen Jewstreets here?"

"No. Do they exist?"

"You really don't know about America? About the Declaration of Independence? About the Constitution?"

"I know Jews here can be rich like you and your friends."

Loeb walked over to look at his framed Declaration of Independence. "Come here, Joseph. Read this."

Joseph did. When he finished, he turned to Loeb and repeated: " 'We hold these Truths to be self-evident, that all Men are created equal, that they are endowed by the Creator with certain inalienable Rights, that among these are Life, Liberty, and the pursuit of Happiness....' Does this mean us too? Does this mean Jews as well? Is that why you can be a millionaire?"

"It's more than money. This is our country. When we become citizens of this country it becomes ours as well as it is any man's. For the first time since the scattering of the Jews we are not guests in someone else's country. Here we can be fools as well as millionaires. Here we can be as right or as wrong as anybody else. Here we are all equal owners. You want to see something? Look." He showed Joseph another framed piece of writing. "This is a letter written to the Jews at the beginning of America. It was written by George Washington, the man they call the father of this country. He was the first president. Read." Joseph read the letter:

> To the Hebrew Congregation
> Newport, Rhode Island,
> August 17, 1790
>
> It is now no more that tolerance is spoken of, as if it was by the indulgence of one class of people, that another enjoyed the exercise of their inherent natural rights. For happily the government of the United States, which gives

bigotry no sanction, to persecution no assistance, requires
only they who live under its protection should demean
themselves as good citizens, in giving it on all occasions
their effectual support.... May the children of the stock of
Abraham, who dwell in this land, continue to merit and
enjoy the good will of the other inhabitants, while everyone
shall sit in safety under his own vine and fig-tree, and there
shall be none to make him afraid.

George Washington

Loeb said, "Now there are people here, like the Know-Nothings,
who are against foreigners, the Irish and the Catholics, and also us
Jews. In America it is their right. They can be against us and we
can be against them. Here, in America, they can't put us in Jewstreets. They can't tell us how to make a living or how to worship
God. This...," Loeb said, tapping the glass covering the Declaration
of Independence, "is why you came to America. So you could be a
Jew. So that you could marry Fannie." His eyes moistened, and he
surprised himself by reaching out and hugging Joseph. Then he
pulled away.

An hour later Loeb arrived at his office, where he sent a packet
by messenger to the captain of the next ship leaving for Bremen,
along with a cash gift and a request to deliver the packet to the
offices of Klostermann & Co.. The letter contained instructions to
send a man to Poppenlaur and make inquiries in the Jewish community about one Joseph Ritter. The agent was to also investigate
any story of a young Jew who humiliated a baron in a horseback
duel by making him say, "Jesus Christ is not the Messiah."

Joseph next went to visit Dooley, who was glad to see him. "I
have something you need," Dooley said. He opened a drawer and
took out a polished oak box. Inside were a derringer and accessories.
"Do you know how to shoot?"

"I do," Joseph said.

"Take this," Dooley handed the pistol to Joseph. "It fits easy in
your pocket. Never go out without it, even in the country. You
promise me that?"

"Yes." Joseph hefted it in his hand.

"Good. Have you ever used one?"

"No."

Dooley showed Joseph how to charge the barrel with powder and shot. "It isn't good at more than a few feet. One shot is all you get."

"You ever know Dutch Wagner?" asked Paddy Muldoon of Muldoon's Freight Company of Funeral Wells. "The one as worked for Brannagan, God curse his soul. Gone west he has, Dutch. But he was telling me about this kid was Brannagan's shadow. German kid, a regular tinker for doctorin' horses and the like. And a great danger with a knife, this kid was, and speaking English with the same sweet brogue as Brannagan, may he burn in hell for all time."

§27

"SMELL THAT?" MOSES COHEN DREW IN A HUGE BREATH THROUGH his nose. Joseph did the same and smelled the same clean, sweet scent. Behind them, among the dripping tables covered with crushed ice at Moses Cohen Fresh Fish, a small crowd of women were competing for the few remaining aromatic flounders, mackerels and smelts.

Moses Cohen and Joseph were sitting at the very end of the pier by the East River, their legs dangling over the black water. "Fish," Moses Cohen said with enthusiasm. "They wonder why such a fine hazzen, such a great scholar sells fish? Look." He indicated the activity all along the dock. "Not yet noon and it's all gone. I get here at four and my day is done by twelve. A fulfillment of the sage's admonition for the Torah scholar. Work eight hours in the real world, study eight hours, and sleep eight hours. Fish is the perfect business for the scholar. And so, Reb Joseph, how's life in the country?"

Joseph couldn't tell him everything, but he did say that he and Fannie loved each other and, per Loeb's proposition, were to be married. Moses Cohen registered no surprise. Fannie Loeb and Reb Joseph. What could be more natural? That, without question, was beshert.

Then Joseph said, "I've come to ask you to do me another service."

"Ask."

"If the assassin should kill me, please tell Fannie and Mr. Loeb everything."

"So easily you can say, 'if the assassin should kill me?' "

Joseph shrugged. "How else can I do it? He's been hired to kill me. I can't pretend that he's not there, can I?"

"No." Moses Cohen wondered, was Hashem punishing Joseph for desecrating the Torah? "So what will you do about this assassin?"

"I'm safe for the summer, perhaps longer if he believes I've gone to the California goldfields. He doesn't know I work for the Loebs. He might continue to watch the Nassau Street post office for my mail, and I'll not go there. He might search the Jewish community here in the city for me. In September, when we come back to the city, I'll tell the Loebs I must go away for a while. Then with Mr. Dooley's help, I intend to hunt down this assassin."

"How?"

"I'll send a letter to Mr. Thunder, collect it, and then the assassin will follow me."

"And?"

"And what?"

"When you find the assassin, what will you do?"

"Mr. Dooley says his friends can make him go away."

"If they can't do such a thing? If this assassin still wishes to kill you?"

"Then I'll kill him."

"You can do such a thing? You think you can kill a man?"

Joseph nodded. "When I fought von Exing, I knew that if he didn't do as I told him I would have killed him. He knew it too, which is why he humiliated himself."

"But that was in the heat of battle."

"And this? A man is taking money to kill me. What should I do? Should I run all my life?"

"To save a life? Yours or the assassin's? Perhaps both? Maybe the answer is yes."

"Have you read this Declaration of Independence?"

"The American Declaration of Independence? Of course I have read it."

"It says that in America we are all equal. I don't have to run away from any man. If I am an American and I obey the laws, then no man may make me run away. There are no princes here. If the von Exings can order a murder of an American in his own country, then this Declaration of Independence is a meaningless paper."

"The police can protect you."

"How? Will a policeman be with me every moment? The police can do nothing till after I'm murdered. Then they can see if they can bring the murderer to justice. No, I must defend myself. And even though we Jews haven't done it for centuries, do we not have laws and sayings about defending ourselves?"

Moses Cohen nodded sadly, "It's spoken of in many places. We're obligated to defend ourselves but, like the laws regarding the sacrifices in the temple, they have fallen into disuse. The first that comes to mind is in the Babylonian Talmud, Sanhedrin. I forget the number: '...It is permitted to kill a potential murderer if this is the only way in which the life of his intended victim can be saved.' " He stared at Joseph. "So young to carry such a burden."

"How old does a Jew have to be to defend himself?" Joseph asked. "They murder babies because they are Jews. Why do they want to kill me? Because a von Exing was defeated in fair combat? No. Because a Jew defeated him. I'll defend myself. Will you do what I have asked of you?"

"I shall."

Joseph left. On his way north he stopped at the Astor Place book shop and purchased a copy of the *Federalist Papers,* which included the Declaration of Independence and the Constitution of the United States of America. He also purchased Tocqueville's *Democracy in America,* as well as a history of the United States.

Joseph used the half-day drive to Riverside to become acquainted with the seventeen-year-old bay Morgan gelding, Junius. The horse was exactly what Loeb wanted for his daughter: dependable, placid, lazy, and steady. Joseph couldn't get the horse to spook or shy, or move at a gait faster than a poky trot.

He tested the horse and his new derringer at a small farm, explaining to the owners that he was bringing to Riverside a horse that had to be absolutely safe for his employer's daughter. The horse had to be able to remain calm during hunting season, so he asked permission to put the horse in the pasture and shoot the gun. Interested, the farmer agreed.

Once in the pasture, Joseph walked twenty yards from Junius and fired the derringer into the ground. Junius looked up momentarily and resumed cropping grass. Joseph was surprised by the nasty sting the derringer created in his hand. For his next shot, Joseph walked ten yards closer to Junius. This time he took a stronger grip on the little pistol and fired. Junius again paid no attention. Joseph repeated the process, walking closer to the horse with each shot and varying his grip until he found exactly the right feel for the gun.

For the remainder of the journey he practiced handling the derringer, testing its weight, and seeing how quickly he could pull it out of his pocket. Dooley was correct that it fit into his pockets, but he was wrong about its usefulness there. It was too heavy and caused the pocket to sag, which gave away its presence and made it difficult to extract. Joseph tried placing the derringer in his waistband at the small of his back where it didn't chafe or get in the way. This worked well, and for the remainder of the drive to Riverside he practiced quickly drawing it from there.

The moment Funeral Wells ambled into Dooley's stable, Dooley was aware of something wrong. The man smelled of violence. Dooley rose from his seat at his desk and casually rested his hand on his Blackthorn cudgel. "Good morning, sir," he said. "Is there something I can do for you?"

"Perhaps you can," Wells said. He saw the cudgel and hoped the coachman would try to use it. "I'm looking for a boy." He showed Dooley his old police badge.

Dooley respected the law but was too Irish to warm to the sight of a badge. He nodded.

"A German boy. Immigrant. They say he's good with horses. Name is Joseph Gershomsohn. A Jew kid. I heard he might be around here."

Dooley allowed his face to contract in thought and then brighten. "Joe? Maybe you're talking about Joe the Dutch kid? But his last name was Thunder. He was good with the horses." Dooley let go of the cudgel.

"Not too tall, dark hair and eyes?"

"Sounds like Joe all right."

"Where can I find him?"

"Somewhere between here and California."

"He went to California?"

"Gold fever."

"He went to California?"

"Going to pick gold up off the ground," Dooley said. "Too itchy to be a millionaire to wait till he earned enough to pay his passage."

"When did he leave?"

"About a month ago. He said he was going to write. You give me your address and I'll let you know direct when I hear from him."

"Yeah, but if he's gone, then he's gone and that's that." Wells stalked out of the barn. If the old coachman wasn't lying, he was out nine hundred dollars. He could never find a kid crossing the continent. But if the coachman was lying, Gershomsohn had been warned and was hiding.

The following morning while sweeping the front stoop, Mrs. Clymer looked down and saw a strange man tipping his hat to her. "Excuse me, ma'am," he said. "Am I speaking to Mrs. Clymer?"

"You are." The man made her uncomfortable. She decided that although the attic room was still vacant, if he asked she would tell him it was taken.

Funeral Wells smiled and displayed his old police badge. "We're looking for a German boy. First name is Joe or Joseph. We understand he's staying with you."

"Oh, dear, I do hope Mr. Ritter isn't in any trouble."

Ritter, Wells thought. Good. "Oh, no ma'am. He's come into a bit of money, an inheritance from an uncle in Pennsylvania. The lawyers asked us to see if we could find him. It is the Joseph Ritter who worked for Mr. Dooley that we're talking about?"

"Oh, yes. He lived here."

"He doesn't live here now?"

"He went to California. To the goldfields."

"Do you know when he left?"

"Oh, some weeks ago."

"Do you know where he was heading first?"

"He didn't say. Inherited money?" Mrs. Clymer sighed. "Oh, how sad to have missed him."

"Yes."

"Oh, dear." Then Mrs. Clymer added, "You know, after he left Mr. Dooley's employ he went to work for the millionaire, Mr. Emmanuel Loeb. You might inquire there."

Wells tipped his hat again and left.

§28

W HEN JOSEPH TOLD FANNIE ABOUT HIS CONVERSATION WITH HER father she pretended to be delighted. And with the arrival of Junius, Fannie argued, there was no longer any risk involved with her driving and therefore no longer any need to study her verses. They resumed lovemaking that same night and continued every night thereafter, while every morning they met for driving lessons. Soon Fannie was handling the reins confidently.

Over the next weeks, with Joseph sitting decorously beside Fannie on the seat of the heavy wagon, they explored the roads and lanes in the surrounding countryside. Fannie discovered she was speaking with Joseph in a way she had never done before with a man other than Nathan. She told him about her childhood, her deepest secrets, and her wildest hopes. In turn Joseph told Fannie about challenging God, about how he took the Torah and placed it on the floor of the synagogue, and about his parents, whom he still pretended were dead. He also told her about von Falkenbrecht, although he didn't name him, and his duel with von Exing, but he didn't name him either.

The duel on horseback was the most romantic thing Fannie had ever heard. She felt sad over Joseph's lost fortune on shipboard—he didn't mention his infatuation with the tragic Mrs. Bussey—and was in near despair about his time in Five Points. She tenderly touched the scar on his jaw and told him it was a symbol of noble suffering.

Funeral Wells didn't get off the train at Riverside but went one stop further to Yonkers. There, as Mr. Wellington, a recent widower seeking solitude in his time of mourning, he rented a room and a saddle horse from a local farmer. The following morning he rode south toward Riverside.

Hanschen had been surprised and then delighted when Loeb told her that Joseph was Jewish, and from time to time Loeb made sure Hanschen became aware of the boy's many talents. Soon Joseph became a subject of conversation with Hanschen and her friends, who were impressed by Joseph's excellent English, his impeccable manners, his aristocratic German and the rumor of his flawless Hebrew. That Joseph kept his background a mystery only deepened his aura of romance. Some said he was a Rothschild cousin escaping a scandal in Europe. Myra Schiff, just back from a trip to Germany, said that Sophie Mendelssohn, the granddaughter of the Jewish philosopher Moses Mendelssohn, and cousin to composer Felix Mendelssohn-Bartholdy, had had a tragic affair with the crown prince of Prussia, and that their illegitimate son had disappeared from Europe after a duel. Was this Joseph? There were also enough rumors of relations to other great Jewish families of Europe to make Hanschen suggest that Joseph be invited to share the Friday night Shabbes dinner.

"It's a shame," she said to her husband. "A fine Jewish boy with no place to go for Shabbes dinner." Then she surprised Loeb by asking, "Perhaps also you think I have not noticed?"

"What?"

"What? Oh liebschen. I know you think I am foolish."

"Only about foolish things. About life, never. I didn't think you would fail to see it."

"She truly loves him?"

"She does."

"And she didn't tell me because she thinks my foolishness was more important to me than her happiness?"

"She knows you love her, and she loves you so much she wanted me to help prepare you so you wouldn't be hurt."

Hanschen sighed. "You prepared me well. You're right—about a coachman, without such preparation I could have been foolish. So now tell me everything."

When Loeb had told Hanschen all he knew, she went to her daughter and the two of them wept in each other's arms. To Fannie's uneasy relief, they agreed that the secret would be maintained until the fall. Still, in her most private thoughts, Hanschen was positive Joseph Ritter was a Rothschild.

In egalitarian America it was only slightly less difficult than in class-conscious Europe for a family such as the Loebs to invite their coachman to dinner. Loeb consulted the butler, Iverson. Iverson, who had fled England to escape its rigid class structure, understood. He assembled the staff and explained that Joseph's invitation to the

Sabbath dinner was another strange Jewish custom. The Old Testament required them to give their Jewish servants a proper Sabbath. Yes, Joseph had pretended to be a Christian because as a new immigrant he didn't understand that, in America, Jews weren't persecuted. The staff was to hold no grudges, and none did except Hooks, the footman. Hooks never had liked Joseph and now had an excuse for his hatred.

Both Fannie and Loeb had reminded Joseph to enter the house by the front entrance, as this night he was their guest. As he approached it, a carriage pulled up at the front door and a tall thin young man leaped down. He bore a striking resemblance to Fannie. It was Nathan. He saw Joseph and extended his hand.

"Joseph," he said. "I'm Fannie's brother Nathan."

Joseph took his hand. "A pleasure, sir." He was touched by a sadness in Nathan's eyes.

"I'm happy for both of you," Nathan said. "At least I think I am. I count on her good judgment. A quick warning—beware of my brothers Mayer and Isador and their wives. They are much too bourgeois for this. They're afraid of Poppa, but they'll be watching for a chance to save themselves from the humiliation of having the coachman for dinner."

"Thank you, Mr. Loeb."

"Nathan."

"Thank you, Nathan. I'm in your debt."

"Not at all, sir. We're to be brothers. Shall we go in?"

Loeb was astonished and deeply pleased to see his youngest son. He guessed he had come in answer to a summons from Fannie. It made him happy and at the same time he tasted bile. Nathan was present to protect his sister, not to see his father.

By prearrangement, Fannie and Joseph only glanced at each other. The brothers Mayer and Isador and their wives mustn't know, or so would the whole world.

Loeb spoke. "Gut Shabbes, Joseph."

"Gut Shabbes," Joseph replied. They shook hands.

Loeb turned to Nathan and spoke in German. All family gatherings were conducted so. In a house filled with non-German-speaking servants, it provided intimacy and privacy. "Gut Shabbes, Nathan, my son." To the astonishment of the rest of the family, Loeb reached out and hugged him. Taken by surprise, Nathan was unable to summon his anger. He hugged his father back and whispered, "Gut Shabbes, Poppa."

Loeb then turned to the room and said, "This is a special Shabbes. Nathan is home. Our family is all together. And Joseph is here. Among our friends, to entertain a servant," he had thought carefully about the use of that word and decided the evening would only succeed if total candor were applied, "is an unusual thing. If it's not to result in confusion, we must all of us understand the special conditions of this situation. What we are doing is a Jewish tradition. The Torah commands that we celebrate Shabbes with our Jewish servants. It's something Reform Jews, especially in America, should observe. Tonight, Joseph is our guest. Each Shabbes he will be our guest. I have invited him to temple...."

Mayer and Isador and their wives became uneasy. In the house was one thing. But in public?

Loeb continued, "...but he has declined."

The relief in the faces of the two elder sons and their wives was apparent. Joseph didn't care. He loved Fannie and she loved him. Was there anything else in the universe more important?

Loeb turned to Joseph and spoke in English, for what he was about to say was important for the family as well as for the servants, who he knew would be listening. "Tonight, Joseph, you are our guest and our friend. But at the end of the Sabbath you will be our coachman. You understand that?"

"I do. And I am grateful for the kindness you show me."

"So," Loeb returned to German, "now the sun has set. Let's go to the table." He took Hanschen's arm. But Hanschen first turned to Joseph.

"Please," she said, "walk with us." Her smile was warm and welcoming. Joseph went to her side, and the children followed their parents in order of birth. First Mayer and Cora, then Isador and Bella. Nathan, who came next, took Fannie's arm and gave it a conspiratorial squeeze.

The room they entered, tiny by comparison with the palatial establishment at Sixteenth Street, could accommodate eighteen at table. Hanschen, respecting if not quite understanding her husband's reverence for the house's colonial architecture, had left the room much as she found it. It was simply illuminated by candle-light from brass wall sconces and a matching brass candelabrum with twelve candles. A Jacobean table surrounded by Queen Anne chairs was set for sixteen. In addition to the nine adults and the five children of Mayer and Isador old enough to eat with the family were two nannies, both German-Jewish.

But in the table setting Hanschen had her way. The table was covered with a fine silk cloth trimmed in Liege lace, and the Rosenthaler china from Germany was of the same gold encrusted pattern designed for the electors of Brandenburg. Heavy sterling silver cutlery, used only for Shabbes dinner, was cast in vines and flowers entwining around and through a Star of David at the center of which were the Hebrew letters for Loeb. Of these there were seventeen pieces at each place setting; four forks (paté, fish, fowl, meat), five knives (for all of the above plus one for butter—the Loebs didn't keep a kosher house), one soupspoon (being a warm June night, there was only to be one chilled soup), three sherbet spoons (sherbet between courses had been recently introduced to New York Society by Mr. August Belmont's new French chef), a small fruit knife and fork in gold, and a separate knife and spoon for desert. Antique silver wine goblets for the *kiddush* stood next to the crystal from France and Germany, appropriately tinted glasses for three white wines, clear for two reds, beside the thick sweet ceremonial *kiddush* wine, and two champagnes.

It was as grand as anything Joseph had ever seen at Schloss Falkenbrecht, except this was a Jewish table.

The family took their assigned places and stood while Hanschen lit the Sabbath candles and, with one hand covering her eyes, recited the benediction. Then all but Loeb sat. He raised a silver goblet and recited the *kiddush,* the blessing of the wine. He then took one of the two loaves of bread, a braided *challeh*, broke off a small piece, and passed the remainder around the table for each to do the same. He next asked Joseph to recite the blessing. As he did, Joseph nearly cried.

After eating his bread, he looked down at his plate to retain his composure. What had his father said? To be Jewish was to be part of a people, not a religion. These simple blessings over the light, the wine, and the bread had nothing to do with God. It was a ritual of a people reminding themselves of themselves.

Next the servants, led by Iverson, brought in the first course and the room echoed with casual talk. Then the conversation became serious. The Loebs were vitally engaged in the life of their country. Two issues were inflaming the land. They were intertwined: the question as to whether Kansas was to be admitted to the Union as a slave or free state, and the tumultuous election of 1856.

Two state governments were confronting each other in the territory that had become known as Bleeding Kansas: the pro-slave legitimate government under the territorial governor, Wilson Shannon, who had been sent out by President Franklin Pierce, and an irregular government elected by the resident free-soilers and headed by Charles Robinson of Lawrence. On May 20, a posse of pro-slavery men led by a federal marshal crossed over the Missouri border, burning and pillaging the free-soil town of Lawrence. The situation was threatening to ignite a national civil war.

Meanwhile, three parties were running candidates in the presidential election. Two of the men were sectional. The Democratic party, dominated by the South but strongly supported by northern businessmen, had nominated James Buchanan, whose record in state and national government made him the most experienced man ever to run for the office. The Republican party, representing the more radical north, nominated John C. Fremont, the famous explorer and honored military man. And a coalition of the nativist Know-Nothing party and the old conservative Whigs had joined forces to run Millard Fillmore, who from 1850 to 1853 had served as the thirteenth president of the United States and favored compromise with the South. The Abolitionists, not a major force, were supporting Fremont.

All sides were represented at this table.

Mayer, a supporter of the New York Democratic party, started the discussion. "As Isador and I were preparing to leave the office this afternoon, a message arrived from our correspondent in Kansas," he said. "There has been another outrage."

"More of your good Democratic border ruffians crossing from Missouri to murder decent people in their beds?" Fannie asked.

Mayer didn't often catch his sister off-balance. When he did it gave him pleasure. "It seems a free-soiler, a Mr. John Brown, instructed personally by God, along with four of his sons and his gang, raided a pro-slavery town and murdered a number of innocent citizens in their beds. It will be in the evening editions of the papers."

"If they were pro-slave," Fannie said, "then they weren't all that innocent, were they? Perhaps Mr. Brown had tracked down some of the villains who sacked and pillaged Lawrence. Really, Mayer, it tries my mind to understand why two such decent and intelligent men as you and Isador can support the party of the South, the party of slavery and aristocratic privilege."

"You know what will happen if the Democrats lose?" Isador asked. "South Carolina, Virginia, Georgia, Alabama, Mississippi, and perhaps all of the South will secede."

"I know that's what you and Mayer and many of our practical friends of the business world believe," Nathan said. "But you're wrong. You're wrong to believe these cavaliers of the South have the ability to bolt the Union. You're wrong to support the Democratic party, a misnomer if ever there was one. And, most importantly, you're wrong to believe that, by appeasing these bullies, you will avoid a civil war."

"Mayer, Isador," Fannie said, "It's not too late to correct your folly. Neither of you believe in slavery. It's nothing for Jews to support. Join the Republicans. Fremont can win. Help us."

"Us?" Mayer asked. "Have I missed something? Has there been a constitutional amendment for women's suffrage? Are you now a member of the Black Republicans? Will you vote in November?"

Fannie laughed. "Not yet, dear brother, but beware of 1860. Women shall have the vote, and when we do, then see if you can still go on doing the practical thing instead of what is right."

"The southern gentlemen are not all bullies like Preston Brooks," Isador blurted to Nathan. Less than a month before, Preston S. Brooks, a congressman from South Carolina, took offense to a speech made by Massachusetts Senator Charles Sumner entitled, "The Crime Against Kansas." It contained passages Brooks considered insulting to his cousin, Senator Andrew P. Butler. On the following day, Brooks entered the nearly empty Senate chamber, struck Sumner on the head with his gutta-percha cane, and beat him to the ground. Brooks immediately became a hero all across the South. The House of Representatives was unable to muster the required two thirds majority to expel him but, because of the number of northern representatives voting against him, Brooks felt insulted and resigned. Senator Sumner never fully recovered from the attack.

Fannie started to answer Isador, but Nathan put a hand on her arm. "Allow me," he said, and turned to his brothers. "You're quite right. We've all seen the southern gentry. Elegant, well-mannered, cultured—and yet they honor this Preston Brooks as the best of them. My God, they're giving him a testimonial in Charleston this very week! If you help those people elect Buchanan, he, like Pierce, will be their bumbling apologist."

"Isador, Mayer," Fannie said, "you think you'll forestall a civil war by compromising with these creatures? When has appeasement ever worked? If you win, your Buchanan will be their willing prisoner. For fear of his masters he'll bumble us into civil war. I don't understand how the two of you can be so blind. My God, haven't you heard your fellow Democrats say that if Fremont is elected he'll never live to get to Washington? They're openly talking about killing a president-elect."

"Nonsense," Mayer retorted. "Hotheads."

"And when the hotheads murder the president, will they too have a testimonial dinner in Charleston, or Richmond?" Fannie turned to her father. "Poppa, you're the boss. Make them support the Republican cause."

Loeb turned to Joseph, who had been listening to the debate with little comprehension. "And you, Joseph?" he asked. "What do you think of these matters?"

Fannie caught her breath. What if he were a Democrat?

Joseph smiled. "I'm sorry, but I don't understand much of what you say. I don't read the newspapers. But I think abolition is a good thing. We who were slaves in Egypt can't possibly support such a thing as slavery."

"You aren't a citizen yet," Mayer said. "You can't vote."

"No," Joseph replied. He didn't tell them Brannagan had made him appear before a judge who gave him citizenship so that he, and all the others just off the boat, could vote. Only after he had read the Constitution did he realize his citizenship was fake, and he had burned the papers.

"Then there's really no reason for Joseph to know these things," Isador said.

"But I want to know them," Joseph said. "I've been studying America. The Declaration of Independence. The Constitution. The Federalist Papers. I just haven't caught up to the present time."

"All of my family," Loeb said to Joseph, "is opposed to slavery, both as believers in the Declaration of Independence and as Jews. But Mayer and Isador see the greatest threat to the Declaration of Independence in the dissolution of the Union. Nathan and Fannie agree with them but believe that a Republican victory will call the bluff of the secessionists. They think that, at most, South Carolina will attempt secession, but that it can be easily contained and brought back into the fold.

"I agree with both and with neither. The danger of a great civil war is real. The victory of either Republicans or Democrats will bring us dangerously close to such a catastrophe. Should the Republicans elect their General Fremont, South Carolina will secede, which if a solitary act can be contained by a blockade. But if South Carolina should be joined by Georgia or Virginia in a Southern Confederacy, we shall then have two courses of action, both disastrous: a great civil war or dissolution of the Union. For America, a catastrophe—but for us Jews, a loss greater than the destruction of the second temple."

"There are other things in which this family is united," Nathan said. "While my father and two older brothers accept the legality of the institution of slavery, all of us hate it. We hate it as much as we love the institution of democracy. Yes, Joseph, like you, we the children of Israel, who come to Passover each year and recount the story of our own slavery and the great exodus, must be opposed to this pernicious institution. But as Jews who have fled from the Europe where social injustice flows from an aristocratic system, we especially mistrust aristocrats. The South is dominated by them."

Joseph thought of the Fitzhugh-Reids who were, he knew, gentle and refined.

"Joseph, it's so obvious," Fannie said. "Slavery corrupts everything. It's created a whole class of people who are wealthy from no effort of their own. Why, if the South were able to secede, it would become an American oligarchy. This election isn't just about Kansas and slavery and secession. It's about the fact that all people," she looked at Mayer, "men and *women,* are indeed created equal."

"Enough political talk," Hanschen said. "The children must go to bed and there are songs to be sung." All this talk about aristocrats made her uneasy.

Herr Wunderlicht, acting on behalf of his esteemed clients, Mr. Emmanuel Loeb of New York and Klostermann & Co., found no Jewish families in Poppenlaur. All the local Jewish families in the district lived in Dittelheim, where no one knew of any Ritters. And when Wunderlicht discretely inquired about the rumor of a duel between a Jew and a nobleman, he was met with silence. But he was too good an investigator to accept that as a denial. In fact, he thought it might be confirmation. Wunderlicht's next stop was the magistrate who, out of fear of the von Exings, said he knew nothing of any such duel, but suggested Wunderlicht ask Count von Falkenbrecht. It took two weeks for Wunderlicht to arrange the interview with von Falkenbrecht, for he had to send to Bremen for an introduction to the count from a nobleman who was in debt to Klostermann & Co..

Von Falkenbrecht received Wunderlicht in his bedroom, as he was ill. Von Falkenbrecht didn't like the man's look and refused to offer him a chair. From his seated position in bed, he asked the reason for the visit.

Wunderlicht explained himself. Did the count know a Herr Joseph Ritter? Was Herr Ritter a Jew, and did that Jew, Ritter, fight a duel with a nobleman?

Von Falkenbrecht assumed that Wunderlicht was a clumsy agent of the von Exings. "Von Ritter?" he asked. "You want to know if Franz Joseph von Ritter Baron von Britenstein is a Jew?" He snorted with contempt. "You waste my time and insult my name. Herr von Ritter is my nephew. He is the fourteenth Baron von Britenstein. He is an officer in the Royal Wittelsbach Hussars. His Majesty has forbidden dueling among officers. There was a rumor of an affair of honor. I tell you this only because I will have no hint of dishonor for von Britenstein, who is currently on leave and traveling in America. The story has it that a duel on horseback took place. Lieutenant Baron Otto von Exing resigned his commission and is, I believe, currently residing in Egypt. You are to understand that any duels that may or may not have been engaged in between these gentlemen is not the affair of anyone else. You may go."

Later, thinking over the conversation, von Falkenbrecht realized that if Joseph had been Baron von Britenstein when he defeated von Exing, the von Exings would have accepted defeat. Jew or gentile, von Britenstein was a noble title. Too bad he had not conferred it upon Joseph earlier. Then the solution came to him. He called for his secretary and dictated a letter to his cousin, the king.

§29

Late saturday morning, joseph took the train to new york City and arrived at Moses Cohen's just as the hazzan was returning from services at Temple Emanu-El.

"Gut Shabbes, Reb Joseph."

"Gut Shabbes to you, Reb Moses."

"Such a hot day. Shall we walk and talk? We can go and sit by the river. Perhaps there'll be a breeze."

As they strolled Joseph related the events of his Shabbes dinner with the Loebs. "It's amazing," he said. "They act as if this country is theirs."

"Why not? It is. And mine. And yours. Everybody's." Moses Cohen paused and looked at Joseph. "So you've decided to be a Jew?"

Joseph nodded.

"And about God? You've made a decision about God?"

"I still think there is more than one. You know in Exodus, the Song of the Sea..."

"Chapter fifteen, verse eleven. 'Who among the Gods is like you?' " Moses Cohen said. "Yes, in the years until the prophets, the Jews believed their God was a God among many but more powerful than all the other gods. It was the prophets who changed it to the One God."

"What if the God of the Jews came to America with these German Jews?"

Moses Cohen laughed. "And back there, they're praying to a God who lives in New York? About that I don't know. But what you're saying is that God draws his strength from man. You're saying that because the Jews spent eighteen centuries as a weak and helpless people, their God became the same way?"

Joseph nodded. "What if in the biblical times, when we Jews were so primitive and so weak, the God who picked us out to be His had to use all those violent means, the floods and famines to train us? But as the centuries went by we learned more and became stronger and stronger. And why was God so afraid for man to eat of the tree of knowledge? Because we had the capability of becoming as smart as He. And what if, because of His training, that very thing has happened? And at the same time without realizing it God became dependent on us? Don't forget from the very start God was constantly demanding that we love Him. Isn't it obvious? *God needed our love.* Maybe God didn't know it was going to happen. But what if the first time Adam looked at God with love in his eyes and said, 'Thank you Lord,' God was trapped? What if man's love was an instant addiction?"

Moses Cohen laughed again.

Joseph pressed on. "What if the God of the Jews doesn't know everything? What if He made a mistake? What if God, not realizing that His strength was linked to the strength of His people, allowed the Romans to destroy the temple and disperse the Jews only to teach his stiff-necked people yet another lesson? He'd done it many times before. But this time He didn't realize how He had become so dependent on his Jews, and because they scattered and became weak, He found Himself equally weak. To his horror He discovered He was weaker than the Roman gods, weaker than the new Christian God, and then weaker than the God of Islam. He was unable to protect his Jews. Once His lesson in humility was taught, he found he was unable to return them to power. This time the lesson was for Him. The more weak they became the more weak He was."

"Until, you are going to tell me," said Moses Cohen, "God came to America with the Loebs. And now God is a millionaire. Yes, Reb Joseph, you have come to the right country."

"But Moses, don't you see? It's perfectly logical."

"And the poor Jews of Europe? They no longer have God in residence?"

"I haven't thought that out yet. Maybe there is more than just the one God of the Jews. We Jews are so proud of 'and God remembered.' God forgot His people in Egypt for four hundred years? Four hundred years, and he just forgot? Is this the same God who sent them to Egypt because things were good there? What if it were two different Jewish gods? One sent them there, and was overwhelmed by the Egyptian gods, or died on His own. Then, four hundred years later, a peopleless God stumbled on us and decided to try the Jews."

In spite of Joseph's youth, Moses Cohen took him seriously. "Perhaps you are not discussing several Jewish gods," he said, "but different attributes of the One God. You know the Cabbalists have many symbols for God. They use one that has always appealed to me. It's an upside-down tree. The roots, God, are above the clouds and can't be seen. Man, having never seen roots, cannot even imagine them. But we can see the branches and the leaves and the fruit. All of them seem to be separate things, yet all are of the same tree. Perhaps as the Loebs and their crowd came to America a branch of the tree grew in this direction. Perhaps, because here the soil is better for Jews to grow in, here the branch has richer fruit."

Their discourse went on until sundown, when once again Joseph shared the Havdalah service with Moses Cohen. After their fish chowder Joseph took the last train to Riverside.

The next morning while taking their early drive, Fannie said, "My mother adores you. You know what she said when we were alone last night? She came into my room and sat on my bed, just like when I was a child. She said you were a fine young man and even if it turned out that you were not a prince or a Rothschild, she thought you would make me happy. And Joseph, you do."

Fannie felt odd saying this. After her mother had left her last evening Fannie had wept without knowing why. She changed the subject. "What do you think about our Shabbes dinner discussions? Aren't they grand?"

He nodded. "I was surprised to learn that your father and brothers aren't abolitionists. From what you told me I just assumed all Jews would be."

"Well, in their hearts they are. At least Poppa is. It's the hardest thing for him to reconcile about America. But slavery isn't mentioned in the Declaration of Independence, and it's the law of the land. Washington and Jefferson owned slaves. The most they can do is take the commandments in the Torah and give them a modern interpretation. They're all working for legislation that would make some of its worst practices against the law, like selling families apart from each other, and to prevent cruelty and concubinage and all the other abuses."

In the days and weeks that flew past, Fannie brought newspapers along on their drives. Joseph read to her as they drove and they discussed the issues.

One Saturday he and Moses Cohen spent the whole day in study of the holy scriptures, the Talmud and other writings of the rabbis, preparing an annotated, classical Jewish argument against slavery. The following Friday night Fannie brought the discussion around to Noah's curse on Ham and could hardly contain her joy when Mayer fell into her trap.

"The southern biblical argument, which is a sound one," he said, "is that the Negro was condemned to slavery four thousand years ago by Noah's curse on Ham and his descendants, the African race."

Joseph took a breath and plunged into his first family discussion. "Forgive me," he said, "but that's not quite correct. The curse was Noah's, not God's. And Noah has never been regarded as a Jewish saint, at least not by some of the most authoritative of the old sages. The first planter of the vine was a drunkard, and this particular problem arises because he got drunk. There are those scholars who say that Noah was only regarded as pious in comparison to the corrupt people God was about to destroy, the best of a bad lot."

Mayer understood that Joseph was showing off to gain family respect, but he held off further judgment until he saw the result. Loeb quietly waited.

Joseph continued, "The Hebrew word bedorothav, which translates to 'in his generations,' is attached to Noah's list of virtues. It is attached specifically to compare him to his contemporaries— people so bad God had to destroy them all. When Noah the drunkard made his curse, it was not against his third son, Ham. There's no mention of Ham in the curse, and forgive me if I remind you that the curse is Noah's, not God's. And the curse is not, as some people think, for all of Ham's descendants, but only mentions Ham's fourth son, Canaan. There is no authority for the doom of his other sons or his race. And what of Ham's African race? There's no mention of an African race in Genesis. And are Ham's descendants the 'meanest of slaves'? Hardly. Look at Genesis 10. Ham's son Cush founded the land of Cush, which is believed to be the cradle of all civilizations this side of India. His second son, Misraim, was the ancestor of the Egyptians. His third son, Nimrod, founded Babylon. He was also the ancestor of the Assyrians of Nineveh. And Ham's son, Canaan, the one who received Noah's curse? Canaan had nothing to do with the African race. His descendants lived in Syria or possibly Palestine. If the southern slavers look to the Torah for justification, they will not find it there." Joseph paused, and surprised himself by saying, "I've been a slave. Not in the sense that all Jews were slaves in Egypt. I was a real slave in America."

Joseph then told the story of his life with Brannagan. When he
finished, he said, "Mr. Jefferson wrote the Declaration of Independence
out of an understanding of natural law. In natural law we are
all descended from one set of parents, Adam and Eve. In natural
law all men are born free. You cannot imagine how grateful I am
to have come to America, even with my experience with Brannagan,
and how deeply grateful that I have come to the Loebs."

At the Riverside Inn, Funeral Wells, known as Wellington,
bought an occasional round, talked of horses and his recently
deceased wife, and ingratiated himself with the locals. It took no
special effort on his part to become friendly with Hooks, the Loebs'
footman. Hooks drank too much and talked too much. Wells learned
that the Loebs' coachman was really a Jew, and that the Loebs had
him to dinner on Friday nights. Wells knew he'd found his man. The
next weeks he spent spying on Joseph and Fannie on their morning
drives. It didn't take long to discern a regular pattern in their choice
of lanes. They were obviously secret lovers. The more quiet and
tree-lined the road, the more the couple liked it. So did Wells, and
he picked his spot. It was near an abandoned farm with a tumbledown barn.

§30

DID IT ONLY SEEM THAT THERE WAS A HINT OF FALL IN THE LATE
August breezes? Joseph sensed a small change in the horses'
behavior and saw a slight lengthening of their hair. He could also
smell a change in the morning air. The Loebs were planning to
return to the city in only one week. One more Shabbes, and seven
more days of his drives with Fannie, and then it was time to deal
with the city and the assassin.

Four days before the move the air turned heavy and wet. Loeb
seemed out of sorts, and he left the carriage and boarded the train
without speaking to Joseph. As Joseph turned the rig he thought he
saw a man staring at him from the window of the Riverside Inn.

Fannie was waiting for him at the house. When they drove out
of the Loebs' gate, a cool breeze came out of the northeast and
Fannie shivered.

Joseph felt the hard metal of the derringer squeezed against his back by his belt and a cold sweat instantly covered his body. He was bitter. He would have to go to the city and find the assassin. And then an even greater terror gripped him: He would lose Fannie.

Fannie had been thinking she had to end the affair. She had learned the art of love. It was time to go to Europe and find her great romance. But when she looked into Joseph's eyes she saw pain. She suddenly wanted to comfort him and to protect him. She loved him. How was that possible? He was just an experiment. But she loved him. Was that what she had cried about last night?

"Oh Joseph," Fannie whispered. "I love you."

He nodded. "I know."

She was amazed. "How do you know?"

"You told me that first night."

"Joseph," she said, "I've been false. I used you for my own selfish ends. I wanted to become a woman of the world and so I used you to teach me about love. I lied to you. I was going to go away from you next week. I didn't care if it wounded you. I said I loved you when I didn't. But now I do."

He took both of her hands in his and said, "We're beshert. We've always been destined to be lovers. If there's such a thing as reincarnation, then we've been lovers in all our past lives, and will be in our future lives. If the Messiah comes, it will be because of our love. Fannie, my beloved, you have never lied to me. You have only not looked deep enough into yourself. You've always loved me, as I have you."

For the first time in her life Fannie felt whole and safe. She felt no pretense. She was Fannie and he was Joseph. It was the most tender of miracles.

"Next week," she said, "you'll no longer be Joseph the Loebs' coachman, but Joseph Ritter of the banking establishment of E. Loeb & Sons." She sat up. "Oh, Joseph, next week our real life begins! Nathan has found you a lovely place to live, and he's going to take you to his tailor, and he's already made plans for us to go to Charlie Pfaff's where you will meet Mr. Walt Whitman. Do you like art?"

"There is a castle in Germany where I saw my first paintings," he said. "Wonderful pictures of great battles. But I've been so busy learning about America that I haven't had time to learn more."

"I'll teach you," Fannie said. "It will be a gift from me to you.

"There is so much I want to tell you," Joseph said. "I can no longer live with secrets between us. Fannie, will you swear on our love never to reveal what I am about to tell you?"

"I swear."

Joseph told her of Dittleheim, his real name, about his parents and von Falkenbrecht, and about the von Exings.

"The assassin is waiting for me in the city," Joseph said. "But I have friends there. They'll help me find him before he finds me." He looked directly into Fannie's eyes. "If they can't make him leave me alone," he said, "I intend to kill him."

Meanwhile, Funeral Wells, watching them both from the cover of the woods by the narrow lane, considered his luck. He was lucky that these lovers always took the same roads. He was lucky that a deserted old farm was nearby. But luckiest of all was that the girl turned out to be the daughter of a millionaire. Wells planned to kidnap her, receive a small fortune for killing the Jew, and then another fortune for the girl's ransom.

Wells stepped out from behind a tree, pointed his pistol at Fannie and said, "Stop, Miss, or I'll shoot you dead." And to Joseph, Wells said, "Herr Joseph Gershomsohn, I bring you greetings from Bavaria."

Then Wells' luck ran out. Joseph shot him in the center of his forehead. Wells' last thought was: "The damned Jew has a gun."

"Fannie?" Joseph asked. Taking her shoulders in his hands, he turned her face away from Wells' corpse.

"The assassin?"

"Yes. He called me by my real name."

"My God," she whispered. "My God."

Joseph stared into her eyes and saw that she wasn't going to faint. Now he had to protect them both. It was daylight and the body was bleeding like a fountain. Joseph looked around and saw a tumbledown barn.

"Fannie," he said. "Listen to me. There are things I must do now. Will you be all right if I leave you for a few moments?"

"Yes," she whispered.

He checked her eyes and believed her. "All right," he said. Taking the reins, he drove the wagon just past Wells' body, and then handed the reins back. "Keep Junius still. I'm going to tie the body to the rear axle. We'll drag it to that barn."

Joseph climbed down, took Junius' halter from the back of the wagon, and walked to the corpse. Blue flies were beginning to swarm at the bloody head. He went to Wells' feet and turned them toward the wagon, then hitched the halter around them and tied the end of the rope to the center of the rear axle. Returning to the seat, he took the reins and drove up the overgrown path to the tumbledown barn. Wells' body left a bloody trail behind them. There was room enough behind the three partially standing walls to hide the horse and wagon.

As they entered, Joseph thought he saw something near the foundation of the collapsed farmhouse that might be useful. He stepped out of the shadow of the barn, walked over and pulled some warped planks from the top of a well. He dropped a stone into it. It took a long time for the stone to hit the dry bottom. A gust of wet wind stirred the long grass around him. The sky was darkening quickly. Joseph ran to the barn. Fannie was still seated in the wagon. Joseph untied the body from the axle and went through its pockets. He found a wallet with a police badge and a card identifying Funeral Wells as a detective. He returned the items to the wallet and put it in his pocket. As he turned to grasp the body by the legs, he looked up and terror nearly slammed him to the ground.

A woman was standing in the shadows of the ruined barn. She was weeping. Joseph looked quickly over to Fannie who was staring straight ahead; she hadn't seen the woman. Joseph looked back, but the woman was gone. He leaned against the wagon and closed his eyes. It had been his imagination. There was no woman. Yet he knew he had seen that woman before. But he had no time to think. He had to hide the body.

Taking the corpse by the legs, Joseph dragged it toward the well. It was difficult. Rain started to fall. The body was heavier than he expected, and the footing was slippery. Then Fannie was beside him. She attempted to take one of the booted legs from Joseph.

"You mustn't," he said. She ignored him and took the leg.

With two of them dragging the body the work went quickly. After dropping the corpse into the well, Joseph took some stones from the rubble of the foundation and began dropping them also. At first the stones hit the well's bottom with a soft sound, but soon there was only the noise of stone on stone. Fannie helped Joseph to replace the planks covering the well, and the two started back to the barn. The rain now fell in solid sheets, soaking them to the skin and washing away the blood in the grass.

The old-fashioned wooden wagon top gave them little protection for the remainder of the storm. Fannie put her head on Joseph's shoulder and wept.

The storm passed and the sun returned. Junius' coat steamed and the couple felt their wet clothing grow warm.

"Joseph," Fannie said, her voice quiet but firm. "You shall not go away."

"I must."

"If you do, these awful people will have won. They will have assassinated each of us. If a terrible thing like this has happened to the two of us, I believe it was intended. It is a test of our love."

Joseph nodded, for Fannie was correct. He would never leave her. The chances of the body ever being found were slight. But there was a complication.

"He was a policeman."

"How do you know?"

"I found his badge." He showed it to her.

"Throw it in the river."

"Yes. But his comrades will come looking for him. If we are ever discovered, it'll not only destroy us but your family as well. We must protect them. Promise me, Fannie, that you'll never tell anyone about this. Not your father or mother, not Nathan. No one. Ever. Promise me."

"I promise."

§31

THEY DID NOT SEE EACH OTHER THAT NIGHT, AND THE FOLLOWING day, as Loeb mounted the racing cart for the run to the station, he told Joseph that Fannie was suffering from a bad cold. Hanschen was keeping her in bed.

Joseph was glad to have the time alone. He'd killed a man. He'd squeezed a trigger and a man's face had exploded in a spatter of red. If there really was a God, and the Bible was true, then that man was made in God's image. Did God weep when he killed that man?

Joseph didn't. The man had come to kill him for money. Instead, he had killed the man to save his and Fannie's lives, to save the life they would have together. But what if Fannie never wanted to see him again?

"So. What is going on?" Loeb asked Hanschen as they were preparing for bed. "I've seen my Fannie with a cold. Runny nose, swollen eyes—a more dismal sight there never was. A cold she does not have. So what's going on?"

"I don't know," Hanschen replied. "She just lies in bed and stares at the ceiling. She doesn't read. She doesn't talk. She eats something of what I put in front of her, but with no interest."

"So...?"

"Perhaps they are having their first quarrel."

"A fight? I don't think so. My Fanschen fights like a tiger. What is going on is not from a fight."

"I should have said lovers' quarrel. Liebschen, we've never seen our daughter in love before."

"So, what do we do?"

"We wait. If on Shabbes she doesn't come to dinner, then I'll ask her to tell me. If it's serious we'll send Joseph away."

Fannie lay in her bed, trying to think her way out of her confusion. She knew she was frightened, but a man had been hideously killed before her eyes. Was she frightened of Joseph who had so quickly killed? She knew she should hate the assassin. But why then did she hate Joseph too? He was a hero. Why did she think she hated him?

Joseph didn't see Fannie until that Shabbes dinner, the last of the summer. When they met in the parlor, she looked at him briefly and then averted her eyes. The look gave away nothing. Fannie was pale but otherwise had no sign of the cold he had been told was afflicting her.

Joseph was confused and hurt. She hadn't wanted to be with him. He stood mute, unable to take his eyes from her. When asked questions by family members he answered in monosyllables. He allowed himself to be led to the table. He said the blessing over the bread, answered questions, barely ate, and could not keep his eyes from drifting to Fannie's empty face.

No one at the table but the self-absorbed Isador was unaware of the tension. The meal ended early.

Later that night Joseph, unable to sleep, lay on his bed and considered the emptiness of his life. Never, not even in the worst of the Brannagan days, had he felt so worthless. When he finally fell asleep the cloud dream appeared. He was standing on the promontory and the little clouds began to fill the universe until he thought he would suffocate. Then, wet with sweat, he was awake. Someone was coming up his steps. It was Fannie.

"Forgive me," she said. Weeping, she threw herself into his arms. "I'm a coward."

"It's over," he said. "We're safe now and we'll always have each other. There. There. Shhhhh."

Her weeping lessened. "Joseph, you killed a man."

He continued to rock her in his arms. "He was going to kill us. But it's over now. We're safe."

"Joseph, I'm a coward. I tried not to love you."

"But you couldn't do it. We shall love each other till the end of time."

"Don't you see? I was tested and I failed."

"But you're here with me now."

And there they stayed, like children sleeping quietly in each other's arms. Just before dawn, Fannie ran back to her room.

The following day, Joseph asked Loeb for permission to accompany the family to temple. His attendance had nothing to do with God. It was to be with Fannie. Loeb, surprised and uneasy, asked Joseph to wait on the porch and went up to his room. Hanschen was just pinning on her hat.

"Joseph has asked to come to temple."

"So the lovers' quarrel must be ended," Hanschen said. She started for the door. "Come."

They walked to Fannie's room, where they saw that she too was dressed for Temple. "About some things women always know more than men," Hanschen said to Loeb. To Fannie she said, "Fanschen, my darling, your Joseph has asked to come to temple with us."

"Oh please, Poppa, let him."

"Of course he may," Loeb said. But Fannie looked pale. Something wasn't right.

"Poppa?"

"Yes?"

"Monday, when we return to the city, you will keep your promise?"

Loeb was startled. He always kept his promises. "Which promise, my Fanschen?"

"Joseph will start right away at the bank?"

He nodded. "I've already told Dooley." Perhaps, he thought, Fannie was nervous about Joseph's introduction to their friends, so he turned to Hanschen. "If Joseph comes to temple with us this morning," he said, "this is the time to start his new life. He'll sit with us. I suggest you tell Mrs. Seligman that he's no longer our coachman and will come to work in the bank this week. If I know her, she'll have the word out before the Torah portion is read."

Hanschen was delighted. "Oh, the look she'll have on her face! You know they all think he is a Jewish nobleman." She looked at Fannie. "Is he?"

Fannie, still grinning, shook her head. "No, Momma. He's just like us."

Hanschen took her daughter's arm. "So for a while we'll let them think he is royalty. It'll make the change from coachman easier." To Loeb, "Nathan knows. But have you told Mayer and Isador?"

"Not yet. I'll tell everybody now." He sent some of the servants to the other houses to call his children. As the family gathered, Fannie went out to Joseph who was standing beside the carriage. She took his arm and led him toward the stairs to the porch.

"Poppa is telling them all now," she said.

At temple Hanschen whispered the news to Mrs. Seligman, and the whole congregation knew about it by the reading of the Torah portion.

Monday, while the family traveled back to the city by train, Joseph drove down the staff. In New York he accepted Dooley's congratulations and turned the racing cart over to him. In the afternoon Nathan showed Joseph his new room at the St. Nicholas Hotel, and then took Joseph to his tailor, where they ordered a suitable wardrobe for a young businessman. From there they went to a shop that sold ready-to-wear clothing. That night Joseph dined with Nathan who reported that Fannie couldn't join them. Exhausted by the change of houses, she had taken to her bed at an unusually early hour. During dinner Nathan outlined their upcoming social schedule: the opening of an exhibition of western paintings the following night, theater the night after that, then an opera with a late stop at Charlie Pfaff's, and so on. Joseph wondered when he would be alone with Fannie again.

On Tuesday, Nathan took Joseph to the bank. Joseph was surprised by its lack of opulence. The ground floor was a plain, open space filled with dark desks at which men in dark suits were already at work. On the second floor were the offices of Loeb and his three sons.

"You'll begin by spending time with Nathan," Loeb said. "You'll join him for all of his meetings, where you shall sit quietly and listen to everything he says, watch everything he does. Take notes. Put down on paper any questions you may have. At the end of the day we have a meeting: Mayer, Isador, Nathan and I. You'll attend this meeting, at which you may ask your questions."

And so Joseph followed. He wrote very little on his paper, as nothing interested him. Joseph's utter lack of aptitude was immediately apparent to Nathan, who sympathized and tried to think of some other way to involve Joseph. But by the day's end Joseph's attitude was obvious to Loeb as well as his other sons. That, combined with what Loeb now saw as Fannie's forced gaiety, gave him a sense of foreboding.

Nathan, always the first to leave, hailed a hansom. When both he and Joseph were seated he said, "It's deadly dull and you already hate it."

"Forgive me Nathan," Joseph said, "but I don't really hate it. I don't understand it, and I'm afraid I never will. I'm a horseman. It's all I really know how to be. But I promised your father. I shall make every effort to do well at banking."

"We'll find something," Nathan said. "And if we don't then you'll have a terrible year of boredom which is little enough to pay for the hand of the fair Fannie."

"I promise not to disappoint any of you. I'll learn this business."

"Enough of that. Have you ever been to a gallery for the opening of a painting exhibition?"

"Never."

"Tonight you shall make your debut. We must hurry home and dress. Poppa and Momma are bringing Fannie at eight, and we must be there to greet them. Poppa hates these occasions, but Fannie and Momma love them. Tonight all of Momma's crowd will be there."

Meanwhile, as Loeb was preparing to leave his office his secretary knocked and entered. "Excuse me, Mr. Loeb," he said, "but a ship's officer from the steamer *North Sea* is here. She has just arrived from Germany. He's brought a packet from Klostermann & Co.."

After they had walked through the bronze doors of the Astor Place gallery, Joseph saw that in this huge room all the gentlemen were wearing outfits similar to his black and white evening attire, while the ladies were shimmering in bright colors and jewels. Joseph had never encountered so many elegant people in one room before, and it seemed to him as if Nathan knew all of them. Glasses were raised to him. People greeted him from every direction.

And then Joseph saw the paintings on the walls. Landscapes framed in gold, unlike any places on earth he had ever seen. Yet they were familiar. It wasn't that the paintings' rich colors were so familiar, but the shapes. Where had he seen them? Why were they so important to him?

Then he had a sense of bright blue and red and gold moving toward him and he was seized by strong arms.

"Baron! *Mon cher* Baron von Britenstein."

He was being kissed on both cheeks. When the face withdrew he saw Colonel Soulé. They embraced again.

"But this is *fantastique*. Where have you been, you bad man?"

Before Joseph could answer, Soulé shouted across the room. "Karl! Come look and see. *Mon dieu,* we have a ghost."

Fifteen feet away Joseph saw Karl Albert in black tie and glistening chestnut beard, surrounded by adoring patrons.

"Joseph," Karl said. He walked over and hugged him. "My God. Risen from the dead!" Then, looking him in the face he said, "We have much to talk about. Tonight, when this is over." He turned to Soulé. "Colonel, don't let him out of your sight. Guard him with your life." Then, taking Joseph again by his hand, he turned him to the crowd immediately surrounding him. "My dear friends and patrons, allow me to present Herr Franz Joseph von Ritter Baron von Britenstein. Baron, Mr. and Mrs. James Astor, Mr. and Mrs. Hobart Van Rensaleer, Mr. and Mrs. George Tempelton Strong, Mr. and Mrs. Emmanuel Loeb, and their fair daughter...."

Loeb, who had only just shown up at the party from his office, glared at Joseph. "My family and I already know the Herr Baron," he said. "Fourteenth Baron von Britenstein, nephew of the famous hero of hussars, Count Rupprecht von Falkenbrecht, cousin to the king of Bavaria."

Frozen in horror, Joseph heard the words but saw only Fannie who was staring at him with loathing. Loeb, his voice flat and hard, continued. "We hope the Herr Baron was amused by his little adventure with us."

Joseph turned to Fannie. "Fannie, you must believe..."

"Baron, you shall never speak to, or see my daughter again," Loeb said. He gathered his family and they left the gallery.

BOOK THREE

OUR SACRED HONOR

"Everything is foreseen, yet free will is given."
—Rabbi Akiba, Pirke Aboth III:19

§33

"BEHOLD THIS CUP OF WINE. LET IT BE A SYMBOL OF OUR JOY tonight as we celebrate the festival of Passover!"

Joseph, brandishing a silver chalice, gazed at the happy faces assembled at his table. Nearest him were Fannie and their three young sons. Around the rest of the table he had carefully arranged his brothers-in-law and their wives and children. To his immediate left was Nathan. Next to him, opposite Fannie and the children, sat Karl Albert and Colonel Soulé who were witnessing their first Jewish ceremony since the wedding. At the opposite end of the table, next to Loeb and Hanschen, was Moses Cohen.

On this March 25, 1861, Loeb's family was gathered in the formal dining room of Liberty Hall, Joseph and Fannie's newly completed house. Although the style had passed out of fashion more than a decade earlier, Joseph and Fannie had elected to build their mansion in classic Greek Revival. It was, Joseph thought, the architecture that best represented the ideals of democracy.

Although the mansion and 640 acres of land had been a wedding present from the Loebs, the successful horse business was Joseph's doing. He had named it Thunder Farm after his boyhood pet who now lived there as well. The horse, the foundation stallion upon which the enterprise had been built, had been brought over from Germany and presented to Joseph as a wedding present by Count von Falkenbrecht.

Joseph was a success. He had become what he knew, even with the gift of a title, he could never have been in Germany—a person of consequence. When his name frequently appeared in the newspapers it was usually followed by the phrase, "the celebrated horseman."

During Joseph's toast Fannie stared at him. He's perfect, she thought. He's perfect in every way. And yet I hate him. No, she decided. Not hate. I don't hate Joseph. How could I? I love him. But If I love him, why do I hate him?

Concerned about his still-youthful appearance, Joseph had grown an extravagant hussar mustache which swept down past his mouth and, with the aid of wax, stuck out past the sides of his head. True to his promise to Fannie, he had also grown a beard that left the scar on his face visible. It was an "Imperial," starting just below his lower lip and blossoming to an inch and a half width at the promontory of his chin. It then fell two inches to a perfect point. Fannie, who at first thought it adorable, now found it particularly annoying.

A fool, she thought. Pompous. Selfish. Fool.

Joseph's jet black hair reached past the tops of his ears and almost touched the collar of his tailored coat. Fannie had come to loathe his hair as well.

No woman, she thought, not Eve, Ruth, Héloise or Juliet—My God, not even Ada Clare!—could ever have loved her man more. So why did she feel such rage? Oh, why had Ada Clare disappeared? They said she had gone to Paris to be with her lover. It had been more than two years and there had been no word of her. Fannie, wondering if she might be going insane, longed for her mentor.

Fannie had become more beautiful. And to her uncomprehending terror, more lonely. Weren't children supposed to fulfill a woman? How could motherhood be so solitary? The angular lines of her adolescent figure had softened, and the large features of her face, which had seemed odd on the child, were in perfect harmony with the woman.

Joseph checked his notes, which he and Fannie had painstakingly prepared over the last few weeks, and turned to the two Christians.

"Karl," he said, "you and the colonel are my first and dearest friends in the new world. Your presence here gives special meaning to this, our first occasion to entertain in our new home."

Everyone smiled politely.

Loeb was amused by Joseph's formal tone and hoped it, as well as the ridiculous mustache wax, would disappear in the not-too-distant future.

"We are indeed fortunate," Joseph continued, "to have Christians at our table. Your presence requires us to explain each step of this evening's ritual perhaps in greater detail than if we were Jews alone. And thus…"

Nathan interrupted. "And *thus?* Have you been taking speechifying lessons from the Reverend Beecher?"

Except for Mayer and Cora, the resulting laughter was equally good-natured, and Joseph nodded graciously. "And *thus*," he said, "by inducing us to do so, you present to us the opportunity to know ourselves better."

Loeb and Moses Cohen allowed their eyes to meet in a bemused look.

Joseph glanced at Fannie. How radiant she is! Then he plunged ahead. "Please do not make the common error of supposing that this is a religious service," he said. "It isn't. On this night we engage in a joyful recounting of our history. To be a Jew is to remember. On this night we remind ourselves that we are not a race, nor even a religion, but rather a people. Passover is the oldest, in fact the very first of the Jewish festivals. Can you imagine? We have been celebrating it for 3,173 years. The Last Supper was a Passover seder and by then the Jews had been observing it for 1,279 years. For some Jews it remains a religious festival, for others it is a celebration of three wonderful things."

"Four, Reb Joseph," Moses Cohen said. "Four. The tradition is that on Passover things come in four." He turned to the Christians. "It's also a tradition that the seder table is for discussion of everything. We discuss meaning, fact and fancy. Even we argue. Now I am arguing." He turned back to Joseph. "Four. In the seder we drink four glasses of wine. They symbolize first, freedom. We drink four cups for freedom to reign in all four corners of the earth."

"The earth is round," Nathan said.

"It's a very old tradition," Moses Cohen shot back. "Second, we drink four cups for the four seasons. Freedom should reign in every season of the year."

Loeb interrupted, "See, here, Reb Moses. Here is where you make your mistake. For Joseph and Fannie there are only three seasons. They have only spring, spring, and spring."

Karl Albert raised his glass. "Then let us have five cups," he said. "The first to toast their example to us all. To Joseph and Fannie! To romantic love. May they exist always in eternal spring!" He was about to drain his glass when his eyes met disapproving looks from Mayer and Cora. He lowered the glass. "Forgive me my heathen manners. Four cups." He saluted with his glass and put it down.

Joseph, his pomposity slipping, smiled at his friend. "Thank you, Karl." He turned to Moses Cohen. "Please continue your lecture."

"My lecture? Continue? Of course I will continue. Third, we drink four cups to remind us of the four empires that oppressed us in the olden times. We drink them to say let tyranny be gone from the earth. And," he looked at Joseph, "the fourth, for those of us antediluvians who still believe in the One God, blessed be He who rules the universe, the four cups are in remembrance of the four promises He made to us." Moses Cohen chanted them in Hebrew, and then translated them for their guests. " 'I will bring you out from Egyptian rule. I will deliver you from bondage. I will redeem you with outstretched arm. I will take you to be my people.' Four, Reb Joseph. Always four. Also coming up are the traditional four questions."

Joseph nodded. "I stand corrected, but only in the old ways. You traditionalists mired in the dark past may have your four. But you see, Fannie and I, being modern Jewish-Americans, combined the ideas of spring as rebirth with the concept of redemption." He looked back at Moses Cohen. "More efficient. The first cup is a symbolic gesture to indicate a rejoicing at the coming of spring, the symbol for renewal."

Fannie, sensing the mood of the room, thought she might try to curtail Joseph's speech. She jumped out of her chair and gave Joseph a hug. "Isn't this a wonderful seder!"

By allowing the seder to take place at Joseph and Fannie's house, ostensibly as a house-warming, Loeb was once again indulging his daughter. He was surprised to find Christians present. He had taken Moses Cohen aside to discuss it. Was such a thing permitted? Moses Cohen had said, "Perhaps to not have Christians at the seder table is the sin. Doesn't the Haggadah have specific instructions about strangers?" He quoted, " 'The stranger that sojourneth with you shall be unto you as native among you, and Thou shalt love him as thyself; for ye were strangers in the land of Egypt: I am the Lord.' Leviticus, 19:34." Moses Cohen nodded, and gave Loeb another quote from the Haggadah, "And, Exodus 23:9: 'And a stranger shalt Thou not oppress, for ye know the heart of the stranger, seeing ye were strangers in the land of Egypt.' "

Loeb shook his head. "For how many years have I read these passages at the seder table? And I forget." He sighed. "Tonight, my friend, I think we shall hear a lot of talk about the strangers. Especially the black strangers in the land of the Pharaoh, Jefferson Davis of the Confederate States of Egypt."

"Interesting people, your daughter and son-in-law."

"Oy," said Loeb.

Joseph continued, glancing at his notes. "It's an unusual thing for Christian friends to be invited to a Passover seder, even friends as dear to us as you are. But this is America." He looked up. "I know that what I'm about to say will sound to some like heresy. But it isn't. Fannie and I believe it comes straight from the Tradition. If you want to argue about it, we're ready to defend our position."

"So tell us already," Loeb said.

Joseph nodded, took a deep breath and said, "In America, before we are Jews and Christians, we are Americans. First Americans, then Jews and Christians. What I'm saying is from the covenant at Sinai, when the Jews brought the first humanitarian law into the world. From the Jews were born the Christians who refined and amplified those laws. Then together, taking what we learned from the Greeks and Romans, we Americans through the genius of Thomas Jefferson and the founding fathers, created the Declaration of Independence." And Joseph now read that document, and then continued to read from his Haggadah.

Then he said, "Passover celebrates the birthday of the Jewish people. So in America, the New Jerusalem where we are not guests but equal owners, where it seems that the covenant, the idea of freedom and justice for all is being fulfilled more than in any place in the history of man, we might ask ourselves if it's still necessary for us to remain Jews or Christians. Here, for the first time since the founding of the Christian faiths, we live in equality with each other." He looked at his Christian friends. "Perhaps the Declaration of Independence was beshert. When I first understood it, I thought America was the promised land. If that was the case, I thought, why must we stay Jews? Why do you have to stay Christians? Why not just be Americans? But then I came to see that America is imperfect—more promise than perfection. That we as Jews and you as Christians have more work to do to perfect it." He stopped and waited for others to speak. Instead there was silence.

"What? No arguments?" Fannie asked.

"I am sure discussion and argument will follow," Loeb said. "But for now, since you are conducting a seder that's even strange to me, we're content to let you go on for a while longer."

Joseph did. "You see, the Know-Nothings were wrong to try and stop immigration. Because America grows stronger by the influx of immigrants. We each bring to America the best of our cultures. And so it is with this festival Passover—the Hebrew word is 'Pesach'— with *Pesach,* we Jews present to ourselves and the rest of the world our symbol of Emancipation. We were slaves and we were the first in history to be emancipated."

Now, Loeb thought, comes the abolitionist argument with Mayer. He settled back to enjoy the fireworks. But Cora kicked Mayer's ankle under the table and he remained silent. Still, Mayer could not help thinking that a seder was no place to talk about black slaves.

Joseph proceeded. "Passover is our yearly summons to freedom. Because of Exodus we Jews are obligated to champion the cause of all oppressed and downtrodden people. So it's the tradition that with this first cup of wine we drink to freedom."

Joseph raised his glass and chanted the prayer in Hebrew because it was less offensive to him to say the words, 'Blessed be Thou Oh Lord Our God Ruler of the Universe,' in Hebrew where they seemed a mere ritual incantation, rather than acknowledgment of such a knowable supreme being.

Then they all drained the glasses of thick sweet wine, the taste of which was a shock to the two Christians, who hid their reaction. It occurred to Colonel Soulé that perhaps if this noxious liquor were called something other than wine, one might have felt less revulsion. Inwardly he groaned with the knowledge that he had to drink three more cups.

Joseph proceeded through the ritual foods: the green herbs symbolizing the coming of spring and the rebirth of hope, and the traditional unleavened bread, the *matzah* of affliction.

When the blessings were said and the foods tasted, Joseph continued: "The Jews, always living in exile, dreamed of a restoration of a great Jewish state linked to the coming of the Messiah. But now there is this extraordinary place where, for the first time since the fall of the second Temple, we are not in exile. No Messiah is coming to save us. Rather, America gives us all the opportunity to perfect ourselves and America. That perfection will be the Messiah. We shall all be the Messiah."

At this point Colonel Soulé shouted, "To America!" and downed his glass of wine, whirled and smashed it into the fireplace. The group was astonished; Hanschen was appalled. The glass, an Irish crystal goblet, had been a wedding present from the Seligmans.

Fannie, realizing disaster was approaching from an entirely new direction, rose, lifted her glass and shouted, "To America!" She drained it and flung it into the fireplace. Joseph, Nathan and Loeb quickly did the same, followed by the others. And Cora was happy because this was Fannie's best crystal.

The moment had come for the participation of the children. The youngest asked the four questions in halting Hebrew and English.

Then came the traditional retelling of the story of the exodus. When they came to that part where drops of wine are spilled to commemorate the ten plagues, Joseph explained: "The tradition here asks us to each spill ten drops of wine from our glass. We do so by dipping a finger into the wine and letting a drop fall on the little plate by the glass. Each drop symbolizes a lessening of our pleasure in our freedom by the suffering the Egyptians went through so that they could let us go. The plagues are: Blood, Frogs, Lice, Flies, Cattle Disease, Boils, Hail, Locusts, Darkness, and the most horrible of all, the Death of the First-born. But tonight I should like to change those words to these." Dipping his finger into his wine glass and letting the drops fall into a plate, he chanted: "Slavery, South Carolina, Mississippi, Florida, Alabama, Georgia, Louisiana, Texas, Rebellion, Civil War."

Joseph next came to the passage where the Jews being pursued by the Egyptian army arrived at the Sea of Reeds.

Moses Cohen stopped him. "In the Haggadah it merely states that God opens the sea and we crossed. So simple it wasn't. According to the Tradition, the Jews stood there in terror of the dark sea and in the distance was the great dust cloud of the coming Egyptian armies. They could see destruction approaching. Trembling with fear, they looked at the water. Was it not better to be recaptured than drown? Where was the hand of God? Then Nachshon ben Amminadav, a prince of Judah and the ancestor of the great King David, leaped into the sea. Only then did the others follow. In they walked deeper and deeper until it was soon apparent they would drown if they went further. Then and only then, when they had bravely gone as far as they could by their own efforts, did God part the waters for them."

Joseph read on about the Egyptians who, when they started to cross the sea, were covered by the waters. "Then the ministering angels began to sing a song of praises before the Holy One, but God rebuked them, saying, 'My children are drowning, and you sing praises!' "

Next came the first of the joyful songs sung at the feast table. The second ritual cup was drunk and, to his astonishment, Colonel Soulé found he was becoming accustomed to the wine's sweet taste.

The meal was then served and the conversation turned to the subject on everyone's mind: the breakup of the Union and the possibility of war.

Loeb and Joseph remained uncharacteristically silent. Loeb, because he knew beyond a shadow of a doubt that a great national catastrophe was about to descend on them, and Joseph, because he was elated by the prospect of war.

Fannie was saying, "Of course they're fools. They've read too much Sir Walter Scott. If there really is a war, they'll lose in a matter of weeks. The slaves will rise in a great moral rebellion. The southern cavaliers will not only have to fight us, but there'll be four million slaves at their back."

Moses Cohen shook his head in disagreement. "When we were slaves in Egypt, it was not the Egyptians' armies that held us in place but rather—to our eternal shame—that we had learned to endure it. Our chains were in our minds. No, the slaves will not rise up. If there is a war, God help us all."

A servant handed Joseph an exquisitely wrought golden goblet inlaid with lapis Hebrew letters.

"This," said Joseph, "is the cup of Elijah. I'll pass it around and each of us shall spill a little of our wine into it until it is full. Then it will remain here on the table for him to drink." The cup was passed and filled a little from each glass. When it was returned to Joseph, he placed it on the table and rose. "And now if you'll all come with me, we'll open the front door for Elijah.

"The Prophet Elijah," Joseph continued, "is the messenger of one of the ancient Gods of the Jews. If Elijah comes through the door, it will be to announce the coming of the Messiah, the beginning of the era of happiness." Joseph opened the door and a man was standing there.

It was Sergeant-Major Stumpf.

§33

Sᴇʀɢᴇᴀɴᴛ-ᴍᴀᴊᴏʀ (ʀᴇᴛɪʀᴇᴅ) sᴛᴜᴍᴘꜰ ʜᴀᴅ ᴄᴏᴍᴇ ᴛᴏ ᴀᴍᴇʀɪᴄᴀ ɪɴ November of 1856 with Count von Falkenbrecht. Count von Falkenbrecht had come to America with Fannie, Hanschen, and Joseph's parents.

Within a week of the art gallery incident, Fannie, confused and battered, had been hurried aboard a steamship bound for the austere home of her Tante Augusta in Germany, with Hanschen as an escort. Exhausted by the emotional storms of the previous week, Fannie slept for most of the next three days and nights. During the few hours she was awake, she wept. At dawn of the fourth day she awoke to find the ship in violent motion. Wrapped in a heavy wool boat cloak, she climbed up the stairs to the deck where two stewards told her the captain had ordered all passengers to remain below. She swept past them. As she did a chill blast of North Atlantic gale nearly pitched her off her feet. Fannie clutched at the storm rope rigged across the deck and worked her way forward. A high sea was running, and the ship labored up and then slid down the huge waves.

Fannie came around the deckhouse just in time to receive the direct force of the ocean rolling across the deck. Instinctively she clutched at the storm rope. It held and the water surged over her, tearing her cloak away. This saved her life for, had the cloak held to her shoulders, the weight of the wet wool combined with the sea's power would have pulled her over. Fannie, who had thought she wanted to die, clutched the safety rope with all her strength. Then when the ship once again began to ascend a wave, she fell to the deck and was dragged to safety by two sailors who brought her to the captain's cabin, placed her in a chair and covered her with a blanket. The captain was upset. He informed her that when he ordered all passengers to remain below, it was for their protection. He had never lost a passenger and it wasn't his intention to do so on this voyage. Fannie laughed.

The captain was startled. "The girl is hysterical," he told the sailors. "Fetch the doctor."

Fannie stopped laughing as abruptly as she had started. "No sir, I'm not hysterical. I'm quite well, I assure you. You see, I wanted

to die—and just a few moments ago I thought I was going to die—
and now I'm alive. When I was about to die I didn't think about
me, but of Joseph. I knew, in that moment, Joseph would never lie
to me. Never. I knew it, and I wanted to live, and to live I must be
true to my love."

Count von Falkenbrecht looked up from the note his butler had
just handed him. "Show the ladies in," he said.

Hanschen was intimidated by the great hall with its shields,
banners, dead animals and portraits of war, but Fannie was ecstatic.
It was exactly as Joseph had described it. So was Count von
Falkenbrecht.

He came forward and kissed each lady's hand. "Dear ladies,
welcome to Schloss Falkenbrecht. Won't you please sit here?
Perhaps you might take tea with me?" Within moments a tea service
was wheeled in.

Von Falkenbrecht kept up a practiced social chatter designed to
make the women feel at ease and allow him time to assess Fannie.
After the tea was served, he said, "This is true?" He held up
Fannie's note. "You are Joseph's fiancée?"

Fannie nodded. "I am. We were to be married this June."

"Were?"

"We are Jewish," Fannie said. She then related to him the events
following the arrival of the report from Klostermann & Co.'s spy.
When she completed the tale she said, "I intend to marry Joseph
even if he is an aristocrat. But if it turns out that Joseph is really
Baron von Breitenstein and not Jewish, my father will never accept
him. Can you tell us the truth?"

"My dear child, of course I can. And I shall. Joseph is legally
Baron von Breitenstein. He is also Jewish."

Jakob Gershomsohn saw them coming: the count on Thunder,
Stumpf riding the big Hanovarian, and the count's best city carriage.
He handed the mare he was training to one of his grooms, and
Rebecca, her hands covered with flour, came out of the house to
join him. That night Fannie slept in Joseph's bed.

Two weeks later the Gershomsohns, von Falkenbrecht and
Stumpf accompanied Fannie and Hanschen to New York. In June
of the following year Fannie and Joseph married.

During that time Joseph, through his racing and wagering, had become successful enough to start his horse business. He hired Sergeant-Major Stumpf as barn manager. The business prospered, and so did Joseph.

Now five years later, Stumpf stood in Elijah's place, equally startled by the crowd at the door as they were by him. Stumpf saluted and presented Joseph with an envelope.

"A telegram has arrived for the Herr Bank President."

Loeb took it.

Joseph took Stumpf by the arm. "Since you have come at the opportune time with a message, you may drink Elijah's cup of wine. Please come in."

Stumpf followed Joseph into the house. The family returned to the dining room and the children were sent to bed. Loeb then excused himself and went to Joseph's study. After ten minutes, Loeb, his message decoded, returned to the dining room and automatically sat at his place, momentarily preoccupied. The room silently awaited his attention. He looked up at his family. His face was sad and resolute.

"There will be war," Loeb said. "This communication is from my friend in Washington. President Lincoln has privately resolved to send a relief force to Fort Sumter. When a ship is found, 250 men shall be loaded aboard and sent to Sumter. There is no doubt but that when news of this reaches the rebel madmen in Charleston, they'll fire upon the fort. This result very well may be Mr. Lincoln's intention. Unlike the incident of the Star of the West, these shots will be considered by Mr. Lincoln as a declaration of war by the Confederacy. When Sumter surrenders, as it most certainly must, Mr. Lincoln will then call for seventy-five thousand volunteers."

"How long before they fire on Fort Sumter?" Joseph asked.

"Three, possibly four weeks."

"What are we going to do?"

"Poppa just said it," Mayer said. "The president will call for seventy-five thousand volunteers."

"Not the country," Nathan responded. "Us. The Loebs. What are we going to do?"

"Two things," Loeb answered. "First, Mr. Lincoln is asking for the volunteers for a three-month enlistment. In that he is mistaken. This will be a long and, I fear, bloody conflict. My information is that neither Mr. Lincoln nor his cabinet, excepting Mr. Chase, have any idea of the enormous costs involved in a protracted war, nor do they as yet have a plan for the financing of war. It's my view that much of this money will have to come from Europe. I'll go to Washington tomorrow where I'll make my views known. The government of the United States must issue bonds. We'll underwrite them to the limit of our capital."

Mayer was aghast. "But if the Union should lose the war, we'll be ruined."

Loeb nodded. "Next, this family, out of our own personal pockets, will finance the raising and equipage of a regiment of volunteer cavalry. My friend has arranged secret authorization to do so. Both General Scott and Secretary of War Cameron are opposed to the formation of cavalry regiments. General Scott because he believes that European-style cavalry is useless in the forested and fenced country of Virginia, and most especially because he has a contempt of volunteers. Secretary Cameron believes the war will be over in ninety days, and it takes far longer than that to train an effective cavalry soldier. But mostly he is opposed to cavalry on account of its expense—roughly ten times the cost of an infantry unit." Loeb looked up at the pale faces listening. Poppa Loeb was gone and in his place stood Emmanuel Loeb, businessman and banker. "Joseph, will you describe for us just exactly what a cavalry regiment is?"

"A regiment of cavalry consists of three battalions," Joseph said. "Each battalion has two squadrons, and each squadron is made up of two companies. The total is 1,278 officers and men. Each man requires a minimum of two mounts."

"And what," Mayer asked, "would this regiment cost?"

"Acceptable mounts could not be had for less than one hunded and ten dollars each, except of course for the private stock the men might choose to bring on their own. A complete enlisted man's uniform kit is twenty-five dollars, his weapons—carbine, pistol, and saber—can be had in Belgium for twenty-two dollars and fifty cents—tack another fifteen...."

Fannie was startled. "Joseph, how do you know this?"

"I asked him to find out," Loeb said.

Fannie looked from her father to her husband. "And you never told me?" How much more proof did she need? She was unimportant in Joseph's life.

"It was my wish," Loeb said.

"So far we're talking about a cost of 354,645 dollars," Isador said, in awe of the high numbers.

"I agree with Secretary Cameron," Mayer said. "Cavalry is far too expensive and, if it's too expensive for a government, it is certainly beyond our means. If it's true that an infantry costs ten times less, let us by all means raise a regiment."

"In the normal course of events," Loeb continued, "once Mr. Lincoln calls for his volunteers the costs will be born by the cities, counties, states and by the federal government. As each unit is formed it will be mustered into the army. By then it could be too late. Colonel Soulé, would you describe for us the condition of the cavalry, North and South?"

"Some months ago, Mr. Loeb, he has asked me to make this study," he said. "First, what small cavalry the United States Army has—five regiments of mounted troops—are undermanned, with poor horses and equipment. Worse, they are spread out from the Mississippi River to California and from Canada to Mexico. There are not all together nine hundred mounted officers and men. But even these small numbers will be less. Many are of southern birth and have already resigned to go to the South."

"My friend in Washington asks that we act, as a private matter, to form this cavalry regiment," Loeb said. "Let it even appear to be a rich man's folly. I've obligated us to finance this regiment and maintain it until the government is in the position to absorb it into the army."

"Are you saying we will have to not only arm, mount and clothe, but feed and house and pay these thousand men?" Mayer asked. "And for how long? How much are we talking about?"

"Then there are the additional costs of a minimum training period of twelve weeks," Joseph said. "In Europe it takes two years to train a good hussar and mount."

"But if it takes two years in Europe, why do you hope to do it in three months?" Fannie asked.

"We believe there are many veterans of the European cavalries," said Colonel Soulé, "who, like me, have come to be Americans, to live without kings. There are many Germans, Poles and Hungarians who have fought on the good side of the revolutions from 1848."

"How much money will this cost?" Mayer asked.

"We are putting up five hundred thousand dollars," Loeb said. "More if they need it."

"I am the eldest son," Mayer said. "I request the honor of contributing the largest share."

Loeb smiled. "And I am the poppa. First me, then you."

Isador looked over at Bella, who nodded. Isador then rose. "I claim equal shares with my brothers," he said.

"That's fair," Nathan said.

"Fannie and I pledge all we have," Joseph said. "But I'm afraid it will not equal your contributions. And I wish to be the first volunteer to serve. I'll take Thunder and offer all my stock."

"Come, Joseph," Nathan said. "It's one thing to offer yourself. We expect nothing less of you. But Thunder is your foundation stallion. He's worth a fortune. Without him you have no farm."

"Without the Union I have no farm. Thunder was bred for battle. I'll ride him to this war."

Loeb studied Joseph with sad eyes. "Colonel Soulé has been granted a leave of absence from the Regular Army and has been commissioned Colonel of Volunteers," he said. "He'll command this regiment. You, Joseph, will have the rank of captain and command of a company, which you shall be responsible for recruiting. Normally American volunteers elect their officers. In our regiment they will not. Since they shall all be Europeans, trained in the European traditions, they'll be led by experienced European-trained officers." Loeb turned to his three sons. "Mayer, you will go to London to open an office of Loeb & Sons. It will be your job to ensure that tens of millions of U.S. bonds sell to the British financiers. Isador, that will be your job in Germany. Nathan, Paris is your post...."

"I'm sorry, father." Nathan said. "Let Isador have Paris. I intend to serve in the regiment."

Loeb paused. One wrong word and he would lose him. "Nathan, I respect your desire," he said. "Allow me to point out to you that our country would be better served by you doing that for which you are best trained. This war can be lost for want of the money you will raise in Paris. It will not be won or lost if you fight."

"Nevertheless, father, I shall fight," Nathan said quietly.

Loeb started to speak, but Fannie wisely interrupted him. "Is there a name for the regiment? I have one! Let us call it the 'First American Hussars.' "

Colonel Soulé raised his glass, the fourth cup of Passover wine, and shouted, "The First American Hussars!" He knocked back the sweet wine and smashed the empty glass in the fireplace. The others followed suit. And that was end of Fannie's Irish crystal.

§34

WHEN THUNDER SAW THE GREAT MASS OF MEN, HE WASN'T AFRAID. When he smelled their excitement, he knew this was where he belonged. He was heated and yet he shivered. He wanted to charge into the men. In the same moment he felt Joseph's weight shift.

Joseph asked Thunder to rear. The great horse rose, pawed the air, snorted and plunged forward. The crowd cheered.

Shimmering in the blue and gold of his First American Hussar uniform, Joseph drew his curved saber and launched Thunder at a six foot wall of logs. Thunder soared over it, touched the ground and charged ahead. Joseph made four quick slashes: the first horizontally cutting a melon on a stick in half, the second splitting the next, and the third with a flourish cut a two-inch slice from the last of the melons. The spectators cheered again.

A band, also wearing the new uniform of the First American Hussars, struck up a cavalry march in an easy canter tempo. Joseph and Sergeant-Major Stumpf cantered their horses in time with the music and rode to either side of the flag-draped platform.

The music ended on a signal from Colonel Soulé, who now rose from his chair on the platform. "My fellow Americans," he said. "Permit me to present to you the celebrated horseman, Captain von Ritter. Late of the Royal Wittelsbach Hussars, and a fighter for freedom, democracy and the Union forever!"

Joseph made a graceful bow from his saddle while the band played a drumroll and a fanfare. He stood in the stirrups and raised his saber above his head. The crowd fell silent. Taking a deep breath, Joseph spoke to the throng.

"Your country thanks you for coming here today," he said. "There are those politicians..., " boos and catcalls from the crowd interrupted him, "...who still believe there will be no war. They sit in Washington trembling in fear that if they make one move to defend the Union while the South steals the property of the nation, the cavaliers will be offended and strike out at us." More boos followed. "So they make no preparations to defend the Union. And without the Union there will be no Declaration of Independence and no Constitution of the United States of America! Shall we, will we, can we let that happen?"

A storm of "No!" went up from the massed men and a group of Germans chanted, *"Die Freiheit! Die Freiheit!"* The same cry for freedom was shouted in many other languages.

Joseph waited for the noise to subside. "Make no mistake," he said. "Those secessionist traitors, those owners of human beings, intend to make war on the Union, on you and me and on all the ideas that brought us across the ocean to this great Republic. They call us the dregs of Europe, those princes of the plantations. They call us mongrels and scum. They, who believe in their divine right to own one race of humans, have declared us another less-than-human race—foreigners! Who are they? Gentlemen who are born to the glory of the Declaration of Independence and the Constitution, and who cast it aside as so much claptrap! And who are we? Scum who were born in servitude to kings and nobles, and who embrace these freedoms with our hearts and honor.

"If they war on us and win, will they think they can own us too? Why did we come here? We came to America for the astonishing idea of equal justice for all!"

The congregation shouted its approval.

Joseph continued. "We, the First American Hussars, shall be the cutting edge of the Union saber! Did you ride against the kings in Europe? So now ride to keep the southern kings from destroying America. Former cavalry officers report to Colonel Soulé. Former enlisted men report to Sergeant-Major Stumpf."

It was an option for all U.S. volunteer groups, North and South, to design their own uniforms. Joseph and Colonel Soulé, working with the most fashionable New York tailors, came up with a cross between the regulation cavalry uniform of 1857 and that of a modern European hussar. The basic color was blue: sky blue trousers with a dark blue jacket. The trousers were skintight and tucked into black square-toed cavalier-style boots. The fitted shell jacket was the same for enlisted men as well as officers, except for the facings. The officers' dress jacket was laddered with gold braid and lace in the hussar style. The enlisted men were decorated in the same manner except their braid was made of bright yellow wool. Regular army shoulder boards and arabesques of golden galloons rising from the cuffs of their sleeves indicated officers' rank. Non-commissioned officers wore yellow chevrons. The officers also wore black slouch hats, the right brim looped up and held by a golden regimental insignia, with a yellow and red plume on the left side. The enlisted men were assigned a traditional soft forage cap, stiffened with an inside liner to appear more like a shako. It was swagged with a yellow braid and topped by a yellow and red plume.

Officers and men both were armed with Prussian light curved sabers. The officers carried the Colt .44-caliber pistol, while the men were armed with Maynard breech-loading .35-caliber carbines.

For the previous two weeks the Loebs had waged an advertising campaign in every northern state with a substantial foreign population. The potential recruits poured into New York: former hussars, uhlans, dragoons, lancers, chasseurs, cuirassiers and even cossacks. Tents accommodating twenty men each were set up in the newly developed Central Park's sheep meadow. No man was taken at his word: they all had to prove themselves with horse and saber. Officers were selected first, then non-commissioned officers, and then enlisted men. The process took two more weeks, and it seemed at times as if the whole population of New York had turned out to watch the riding events.

The rusty soldiers quickly recalled the old discipline of their former trade, and by the end of three weeks the First American Hussars were able to parade down Broadway to the cheering of thousands. At Union Square they passed in review for the mayor and the city council. At Washington Square they took the salute from the Seventh Regiment, itself mobilizing for war. Then, from the docks at the foot of LeRoy Street, they embarked on barges towed by tugs to the New Jersey shore where they boarded special trains which carried them to Freehold, New Jersey. From there they rode past the cheering locals to Thunder Farm, where a camp had been prepared for them.

Joseph knew he was the happiest man in the world. The parade down Broadway was the beginning of the promised glory. On the train to Thunder Farm, he listened to the older officers complain about the ragged look during the parade, and agreed with them. He eagerly listened to their plans for ten hours of drill every day. They had the best horsemen and the most experienced officers in

America. The First American Hussars were going to astonish the Union and decimate the rebel armies.

On the following morning, April 14, the regiment woke to the news of the fall of Fort Sumter.

That the great war had started should have pleased Fannie as it did the cheering men outside her window. At last the slaves would be emancipated and an America free of sin would finally fulfill her dream. Instead she sat alone in her private sitting room, depressed. Joseph had dashed in with the news, kissed her, lifted her and whirled around the room, and raced outside to his men.

Fannie started weeping softly. Then, with increasing power, she was convulsed with sobs. Her anguish was not about the war, nor about the danger to Joseph, but about herself.

Leading A Company at a walk and in a column of fours, Joseph came through the woods into a large rolling field. Two hundred yards away the enemy was waiting. "Attention!" Joseph commanded. "Left into line, at a trot, ho!" His troopers, wearing white shirts in the hot sun, expertly flowed into one line facing the enemy and rode on. "Hold the pace!" Joseph shouted, "Dress to the guidon!" Then excitedly he commanded, "Gallop, ho!"

In the distance the enemy drew their weapons and started forward at a walk. Wrong, Joseph thought. They should come faster. Now we have them! Joseph raised his saber and pointed it forward.

"Bugler, sound the charge!" The company advanced to a dead run, but ahead was a split rail fence hidden by a small dip in the ground. It hadn't been there yesterday, Joseph thought. Thunder cleared it easily, as did the hundred horses behind him. They were moments from the enemy who were now coming at them in full charge. Joseph quickly sheathed his saber and pulled the white flour sack from his saddle. Now came the collision of two hundred horses. The troopers of B Company, wearing blue shirts and wielding red flour sacks, attacked with fury. The melee raged: men circling each other, taking and delivering whacks of white and red flour, leaving welts as well as color.

"Did you see?"

"Oh, my darling, it was heroic!" Fannie handed Joseph a mug of lemonade.

Gaiety swirled around them: troopers, cleaned up and in proper uniform, girls in summer dresses, flags and bright parasols, children running everywhere.

Joseph couldn't stop talking. "I looked back and saw it," he said. "The entire company jumped the fence at the same time! It was absolutely perfect!"

"Magnificent! Oh, how I loved it!"

"That's a lie! You are lying to me!" Joseph was astonished by the icy sound of his voice.

"What?" Fannie asked, startled.

Joseph stepped closer to her. He spoke quietly, with wobbly intensity. "All this enthusiasm, your big smile. It's false. Pretense. You think I am a fool? You think I don't know?"

The counterfeit happiness disappeared from Fannie's face. "Yes," she said. "I'm pretending. How good of you to notice. I hate your horses, Joseph. Did you notice that too? I hate your farm. I hate your soldiers. Perhaps you might have even noticed that I hate you."

"Hate me?" Joseph said. "How could I not know? You flinch when I touch you. You lock your bedroom door."

"Captain von Ritter?"

Joseph turned to the commanding voice.

"Sir." He saluted Colonel Soulé.

Colonel Soulé returned the salute. "You have lost your opportunity. I claim the first dance with this lovely lady." He bowed to Fannie. "*Madame.*"

"*Enchanté*," she replied.

"Forgive us, my friend," Joseph said. "But Fannie has promised to walk with me—something about the children."

"Of course." Colonel Soulé saluted and left.

Joseph took Fannie's arm and walked away from the crowd. From a distance they appeared to be the lovers all the world knew them to be. Arm in arm, Fannie and Joseph strolled down to the duck pond.

"My God, Fannie. What is happening to us?"

"You don't love me."

"I do. How can you think that? I love you! I always have. I always will. Fannie, you are all my world."

"And the children?"

"Yes. Of course. They too."

"And Thunder?"

"That's different."

"And the farm?"

"Different."

"And your regiment, the war?"

"Fannie, this is madness. The horses and the war have nothing to do with our love. I love you."

"Of course you do, Joseph. You love how pretty your wife is for all the world to see. You love how smart I am to impress your friends. You love what a good hostess I am for your palace, and what a perfect mother for your children I am. Oh yes, Joseph, you love me. Oh yes. Sometimes almost as much as you love Thunder."

"Fannie, I love you as I have always loved you."

"How much do you love me?"

He had never before seen her face look so hard and sardonic. "With all that I am."

"And with all that you have?"

"With all that I have."

"Prove it. Tomorrow let's sell the farm and all the horses, and leave for Europe. We'll find a villa on a Swiss lake and not come back until the war is done."

"You're not serious?"

"But I am. You love me? No, Joseph. You love everything better than me. You love your horses better than me!"

"They are what I do! I'm nothing without horses."

"You love war better than me. You don't care about the cause, the Union, abolition. Those are your pretexts. War is what you love, and now at last you have one. You can ride and slash and kill. Don't forget I know about you and killing. I was there. You love killing better than me."

Joseph turned and strode away.

Under the pretext of a need to live with his men, Joseph moved out of Liberty Hall and into a tent. That first night alone he wept bitterly, his face pushed into his pillow to muffle the sounds. Fannie and Joseph were separated as completely as if ordered by a court. Joseph only went to the house to see the children. On those occasions Fannie absented herself. They appeared together at public functions only to preserve the appearance of their union and to protect the family.

"Women?" Moses Cohen asked. "They are God's great mystery."
He was dishing out two plates of fish chowder.

"It's not by accident that the Shechinah is a woman," he continued. "God has chosen His feminine aspect to be the only way He speaks to us mortals. Why? I'll tell you why. Because God is the Unknown, and who better to speak for Him than women who are incomprehensible to men? Women are a puzzle for us to solve. When we understand them—may God let that happen in the next thousand years—we shall be a step closer to knowing God. Who knows? The Messiah may turn out to be a woman." He put a plate of chowder before Joseph. "Eat while we talk. It will make you feel better."

The soup was excellent but Joseph had to force it down.

"So Reb Joseph, tell me now what you feel. Not what Fannie does. What you feel."

"Now?"

"No. From the beginning."

"I've never loved as I loved Fannie. And I felt her love come back to me. Then things began to change. I've been doing a lot of thinking. I don't know when it started, but while we were still loving each other I began to notice things."

"Such as."

"Sometimes I would look at her and she was not beautiful. Nothing had changed. Her face, her figure were the same as I had always loved, but in those moments they seemed not beautiful. Once I found them ugly and ran out of the house."

"Where did you go?"

"To the barn. I saddled Thunder and rode the cross-country course as hard as I could."

"And when you came back?"

"I don't remember."

"She was beautiful again?"

"Oh yes, but..."

"But?"

"Something had changed. It was different."

"How?"

"I don't know."

"Joseph?" Moses Cohen spoke quietly, gently, but with authority. "You do know. Now you must apply to this the same intellect you use to understand God. You must be as unsparing of yourself, of Fannie, as you are to Him. Tell me, how had things changed?"

Joseph sat back in his chair and closed his eyes. After a while, the roiling confusion that had so numbed him began to recede. "We said 'I love you' to each other often. We reached out at odd moments just to touch each other. But it was as if we were on two rafts slowly being drawn apart by an almost-imperceptible current."

"How did that manifest itself?"

Joseph reached back into his memory. When he spoke again, it was with wonder. "My God. It was nearly two years ago. We began to be *polite* to each other. We became overly considerate of each other. Excessively solicitous. Reb Moses, this is very hard to say."

"Say it. You must hear the worst from your own mouth."

"We had been passionate lovers. And one day I realized that we had not made love for a very long time. It seemed to me that she was angry with me. I didn't know what to do to please her. Then it seemed she was angry with everything—me, the children, the servants, the house, everything. But there weren't angry words. It was looks, and the way she moved. And then I noticed that I was angry too. The house became oppressive to me. I spent more and more time at the barn." Joseph fell into reverie again.

"And?"

"I was working very hard. Very hard. She didn't understand that. I was building my horse business. For her it was easy. She had inherited wealth. But I had to earn mine. I had to fight for it. I was gambling large sums of money to make Thunder Farm a success. I was always so tired when I came in at night. So tired." He thought for a moment and looked up at Moses Cohen.

"Once I thought that I couldn't live without Fannie. I thought that if she were to die I too would die. Now we've been separated for three weeks. I'm living without her and I'm alive. It's amazing. I'm alive. I get up each day and train with my men. Do you know what's odd? In spite of this living death, I enjoy the training. My life goes on without her."

"And she?"

"I don't know. She spends more and more time here in the city."

"Joseph, do you love your wife?"

"I don't know. Yes. How could I not? This is the hard part. I only remember that I love her. But right now what I feel is hate."

In May of 1861, Lincoln asked for forty-two thousand more volunteers. Yet no one called upon Joseph's regiment to fight. The Confederacy declared war on the Union, and there was fear of an invasion of the North, and still the First American Hussars were not mustered into the army. General Butler seized Baltimore to keep Maryland from seceding, North Carolina seceded, and then Virginia. Union forces occupied Alexandria, and President Lincoln's flamboyant good friend Elmer Ellsworth died at the hands of the rebels. The nation mourned the martyr Ellsworth, and the people of Freehold, New Jersey, began to ask when their fancy hussars were going to save the Union.

In June came the first skirmishes between the North and South. A Union victory at Phillipi in western Virginia sent hearts soaring. The men of the First Americans began to wonder if the war would end before they entered it. Tennessee seceded. The First American Hussars continued to train. The local population grew less friendly. A nasty rumor surfaced: these European soldiers weren't going to war. They had been formed solely for the protection of the rich in New York City. With the Union defeat at Bethel Church, Virginia, children of the local farmers threw rocks at a troop of First American Hussars. In July the Union victories at Hoke's Run, Rich Mountain, and Laurel Hill, Virginia, were an occasion for rejoicing in town and gloom at the camp. When Lincoln called for four hundred thousand more volunteers, the locals turned openly hostile to the stay-at-home First American Hussars.

Nathan, appalled, stared at his sister. "Fannie, what have you done?"

"I have a right to be happy. Ada Clare was right."

"Ada Clare was an insane woman who ruined her life and those of others. I pray to God yours is not one of them. I want your promise that you shall under no circumstances see this man again."

"I can't promise that. I'll live my life as I choose."

"Fannie, are we not soul mates?"

"Of course. Otherwise I would have never told you."

"Then you know I've only your well-being in mind when I advise you."

"Yes, but you're a man, and men see things differently. You cannot possibly understand."

"Then why did you tell me?"

"Because we have always shared secrets."

"Because we have a special love and trust. Because you know that no matter what happens, I would always protect you. Fannie, I will allow no harm to come to you from any quarter, even from you. Do you love Joseph?"

"I hate him."

"I don't believe you."

"Why else would I take a lover?"

"You haven't taken a lover. You have behaved foolishly. You've come to me so that I can help you back to Joseph and a happy life."

"Joseph hates me."

"He does not."

"How do you know that?"

"As surely as I know that you love him, and that something has gone wrong and if we do not fix it now, it will destroy you. I'll not permit that. Look at me!"

She did, trembling.

"I want three things from you," Nathan said. "Will you give them to me?"

She nodded.

"First, your promise to never see this man again."

She nodded.

"Next, I want you to remember who your husband is. I want you to remember his sense of honor. Promise to never—do you understand me?—never tell Joseph of this adultery."

Fannie agreed.

"Now I want his name."

When morale was at its lowest, and Joseph and the men of the First American Hussars had come to believe they were forgotten and that no worse could happen, the Union suffered a colossal defeat at Bull Run.

Loeb went to Washington to see his friend, and the following day a telegram arrived from Secretary of War Simon Cameron, ordering the First American Hussars to report immediately to General McClellan in Washington.

"Good-bye, Fannie." Joseph did not kiss his wife. After he had hugged his children, he turned and left his house. He then rode with his regiment through Freehold, past the courthouse to the cheers of the citizens, and out to Monmouth Junction where they boarded the trains that would carry them to war.

§35

ON AUGUST 7, 1861 THE FIRST AMERICAN HUSSARS ARRIVED IN Washington City at the improvised military depot just north of the B&O Terminal. The temperature was ninety-five degrees and rising with thick, wet air. Although repeatedly warned by telegram, the staff at the depot was already operating well beyond its capacity.

The pandemonium reminded Joseph of his arrival in Bremen so many years ago. But now he was in a legitimate hussar uniform and had command over a company.

A staff captain rode up, saluted Colonel Soulé and announced that they were to parade up Pennsylvania Avenue and over to their camp on the other side of the city. Colonel Soulé returned the salute and turned to his adjutant. "Band forward," he ordered. The adjutant passed the command, and the band members rode their horses to the position between the command staff and color guard and A Company's First Battalion, commanded by Captain Joseph von Ritter.

"Colors!" ordered Colonel Soulé.

The national and regimental flags were uncovered and placed in their stirrup sockets.

"Sergeant Heffelstein." Colonel Soulé nodded to the bandmaster.

The bandmaster answered, "Sir!"

"Yankee Doodle."

"Yankee Doodle, sir!" He turned and gave the command to his mounted musicians.

Soulé raised his arm. "At a quick walk: column forward, ho!"

The command was repeated down the line, and on the operative, "ho!" the band struck up the song. The First American Hussars moved out of the railyards and toward Pennsylvania Avenue.

Joseph found Washington City a shock. Although wider than Broadway, Pennsylvania Avenue was crowded and busy. But things were all wrong. The still air was foul, reeking of sour whiskey and piss. Soldiers were everywhere, a drunken mob, staggering and shouting, cavorting with whores. Almost every other business was a saloon. The few men who bothered to look at the column trying to force its way up the avenue hooted insults.

The regiment came to a halt, blocked by crowds on foot and carriages and wagons. Colonel Soulé, his face set in anger, ordered the band to the rear. The music stopped and the column repositioned itself.

"Captain von Ritter," Soulé called.

Joseph rode to him and saluted, causing more drunken derision from the onlookers.

"They're Dutchmen!" shouted a drunken soldier.

"Hey, pretty boys. Where was you at Bull Run?"

"I hear them fancy horses make good eatin'."

"Who ever saw a dead cavalryman?"

Colonel Soulé spoke to Joseph through clenched teeth. "Captain von Ritter, would you be so kind as to take a platoon and clear the way for this column."

"Yes, sir." Joseph saluted and rode back to his company. He thought, were these people crazy? Didn't they realize that the First Americans were here to save the country? What kind of army were they? Where was discipline? No wonder they lost at Bull Run. He felt Thunder shiver beneath him. "First platoon," Joseph shouted, "in a column of twos, at a walk, follow me! Ho!"

A chorus of drunken "ho's" followed from the crowd.

Joseph led his platoon to the front of the staff. "Platoon," he commanded. "At a walk, right and left into line. Ho!" The thirty men formed a line from curb to curb.

The older, smarter foot soldiers, and the more sober, began to move away from the line of hussars. Those less wise remained to continue the razzing.

"Draw sabers!"

Now it was the hussars' turn to smile. The rattle of steel blades emerging from iron scabbards brought a momentary silence from the mob. More hurried away from the scene.

"Platoon, present sabers!" Joseph said. "Platoon, at a walk, forward, ho!"

With their saber hilts by their knee, blade pointing at the ground in front of their horses, they started forward. At first the mob couldn't comprehend what was happening. Then they became belligerent. A large Irish corporal in filthy, infantry blue strode up to Joseph, a cudgel in his massive fist. "Fuck you, Johnny Dutchman," he said. "And fuck all yer pretty boys!"

Joseph smashed the flat of his saber against the man's face, shattering his nose and sending the Irishman down in a spatter of blood. The crowd panicked, hurrying to the sides of the street. Wagons and carriages lurched out of the way.

Appalled, the staff captain, the son of a Chicago alderman, turned to Soulé. "Sir, this may be the way it is done in Europe," he said. "But Americans won't put up with this. We could have real trouble here."

"Thank you, captain. But drunken rabble is drunken rabble, no matter what their nationality. Is there no provost marshal here? Where are the military police?" Colonel Soulé turned in his saddle. "Draw sabers!"

The command was repeated down the line, creating an ominous rasp of steel.

"Present sabers!"

The sabers flashed up and then down.

"By a column of eights, forward walk! Ho!"

The regiment now maneuvered from four to eight abreast. The crowds moved away from them quickly.

"Captain von Ritter, return your men to your company!"

Joseph and his men wheeled and returned to position.

Colonel Soulé nodded his approval and gave the staff captain a quick glance. "Column! Prepare to advance at the trot!"

The command echoed down the line.

The staff captain was not happy. "Sir, I must prot...."

"Trot, ho!"

The movement was smooth and the sound of a regiment at the trot on a city boulevard became deafening.

"Column at the gallop! Bugler!" Soulé shouted.

The staff captain paled. "My God, sir!" he said. "You can't...."

"Sound charge!" And 1,278 horses and 390 mules pulling sixty-five wagons charged in perfect order down the main thoroughfare of their nation's capital.

The following day the First American Hussars were ordered to pass in review. This was an entirely different matter. A brief rain during the morning had cleared the humidity, and a fashionable crowd had gathered. Word of the previous day's adventure had spread through the camps, and thousands of soldiers joined the crowd. President and Mrs. Lincoln and most of the cabinet were in the reviewing stand along with General Scott and staff, and General McClellan and staff. Loeb, beaming with pride, stood with Secretary of the Treasury Chase.

But this was more than a review; it was an unprecedented demonstration of the hussars' talents. After they had completed their formal pass in review, they put on an exhibition of cavalry skills, platoon, company and squadron drills. Afterward, a staff officer summoned the First American Hussars' commissioned officers to General McClellan's headquarters. Joseph could hardly contain his joy. He had been summoned by his hero, the "Young Napoleon." And when he entered the great general's pavilion, he was not disappointed.

Thirty-four years old, short, handsome and energetic, George Brinton McClellan had dark hair and piercing gray eyes. Joseph was embarrassed to see that the great man wore a much less extravagant mustache and goatee than his own, and he decided to trim his the moment he returned to his tent.

At the outbreak of the war, McClellan left a successful civilian life to return to the army as a major general. His minor victory at Rich Mountain, just before the Bull Run disaster, lifted him to the command of the Army of the Potomac.

Surrounded by his staff of nineteen officers, including two French princes of royal blood, all of whom towered over him, he stared at the assembled hussar officers until, at last, he smiled. Joseph could imagine no more friendly smile in the world.

"My congratulations, gentlemen," McClellan said. "You have created a splendid regiment. I can think of none I have seen in Europe that is its match." Then, as if angry at himself for a breech of etiquette, he said, "Forgive me. At ease."

He continued, "As for your adventure of yesterday, you could not have served your country better. Colonel Soulé, although we have not met, I know of your excellent reputation at West Point." He extended his hand which Soulé shook.

"Thank you, *Mon Général.*"

The *"Mon Général"* did not go unfelt by the great man. It was McClellan, after all, who had coined the phrase "Young Napoleon" in reference to himself.

Next McClellan moved to Joseph. "Captain von Ritter," he said. "It's an honor to meet such an illustrious horseman."

Then McClellan strode to his desk, paused for a moment, and turned. His face had become grave. "Gentlemen, war is the greatest game," he said. "It's the game that may not be lost. Although you come to us as volunteers, I don't hold you in such low esteem. I know you to be, like all assembled here, professional soldiers. I thank God for that. As fellow professionals you will, I am sure, understand the grave problems facing me if I am to save this nation. I am required to create an army from this great mass of undisciplined volunteers. Never before in history has anyone ever created an army such as we require from civilians.

"Army regulations forbid the intermixing of regular army personnel and volunteers. Certain excellent officers, out of an honorable sense of duty, are sacrificing their careers by resigning their regular army commissions to reenlist with the volunteers. But there are not enough of them to train the vast force required. And gentlemen, make no mistake, trained and fit for vigorous campaigning this army shall be. I intend to march to Richmond. I shall march there the moment I have troops capable of doing so.

"Colonel Soulé, yesterday, you and your regiment demonstrated to me and to the government that you are capable of dealing with the first of our many discipline problems. I now appoint you provost marshal of Washington City. I authorize you to use any means you deem proper to empty the town of idle soldiers, to get them into their encampments and to keep them there; to close whatever saloons or houses of ill-repute you choose, and to rid the town of loose women and others who prey on the fragile morality and discipline of our volunteers."

The officers of the First Americans were aghast. Joseph was convinced he couldn't have heard correctly. Was McClellan telling them they were going to be policemen?

"*Mon Général*," Soulé started to object, "we are perhaps the only trained cavalry regiment in the Union army...."

McClellan cut him off. "Quite right. But we cannot invade the rebel territory until we have an army. One regiment of cavalry, no matter how superb, is hardly sufficient to take Richmond. You must be put to more immediate needs."

Soulé bowed his head in obedience.

"You may select half your staff from your own officers, but only from those fluent in English," McClellan said. "With the exception of your company commanders and their choice of sergeants, I have reassigned your men to serve as escorts for my generals."

Joseph was appalled. General McClellan was breaking up the best cavalry regiment on the continent!

McClellan continued. "It isn't easy to make a fighting army of a half a million men from mere volunteers. No one has ever done it. But I shall, no matter what the cost. My decision to turn your hussars into escorts for my generals is not, as you may think, frivolous. Americans don't take kindly to military discipline. To do so they must be impressed. When my generals gallop about with their First American Hussar escorts, wearing their splendid uniforms and on their superb mounts, those volunteers will indeed be impressed. Escort duty is as essential to me now as siege guns shall be when we take Richmond."

He turned to the company commanders. "Gentlemen," he said, "I'm exempting the company commanders and their first sergeants from this escort duty because you have all done superb work in training your men. I wish you to continue that excellent work. I therefore have the honor of breveting each of you as a major of volunteers. You'll have battalion command in all parts of the volunteer cavalry. Train those civilian-soldiers, gentlemen. Train them quickly. Train them well. Majors, I expect you to have them ready for me when I march to Richmond."

He paused, allowing a friendly smile, and added, "Thank you, gentlemen. You are dismissed."

§36

Washington City
August 12, 1861

My beloved Fannie:

I cannot accept what has happened between us. I don't know why it happened, or understand how, but I know we must bring this abomination to an end. Fannie, surely you must know that I truly love you. I pray that whatever I've done to alienate your love for me, I shall find a way to undo.

Please, Fannie, find a way back to me.

I write this in the fervent hope that you still have some interest in news of me. At least I'm confident that you'll be happy to hear of Nathan.

I've been breveted a Major. And Nathan is my adjutant. Imagine! I am to train a battalion of raw recruits, and I needed Nathan and so General McClellan—he is the greatest general since Napoleon the Great. They call him the Young Napoleon—assigned Nathan to me. I write this in haste as your father is leaving in moments and he promises to take this to you.

Oh my beloved, my beloved, my beautiful Fannie! I long for you, for us, the way we were. The way we can yet again be. Now in our separation I begin to have clearer thoughts about us. I resent this war that separates us, for I know now that if we were together, we could begin to heal this hideous breech.

Kiss our beautiful children. Tell them their father misses them.

Forgive me.
Joseph

In the headquarters tent of the Albany Invincibles, Colonel Pratt looked up from the orders to the new officers. "Well, that's settled," he said. "Come come, gentlemen, relax. What's the command? At ease." He stuck out his hand. "I'm Colonel Eli Pratt, Prattsville, New York, county commissioner, Green County, and member of the New York Assembly, temporarily on leave till we whip the rebel traitors."

Joseph recognized the colonel's smile as insincere. He extended his hand to shake the damp palm. "Major Joseph von Ritter, sir."

"Glad to meet you, sir."

Joseph introduced Nathan, and they all shook hands. Cigars were offered, but no liquid refreshment. "Teetotalers, gentlemen. The Albany Invincibles are teetotalers to the man," Pratt said. "The pledge was a requirement to join this illustrious regiment. You shall find us to be devout Christians here."

"Lieutenant Loeb and I are of the Jewish faith, sir," Joseph said in a respectful but authoritative voice.

"Well, I'll be hornswaggled! Hebrews! People of the book. You're the first Israelites I have ever had the pleasure of meeting." Pratt turned to his staff. "Any of you ever met Hebrews before?"

No one had.

The colonel raised his hand. "Gentlemen, does your religion forbid the taking of the pledge?"

"Sir, it does not," Joseph said. "From this moment on, we too shall imbibe no alcohol."

"Well done, sir. By gadfrey, we shall get along famously."

"Colonel," Joseph said, remaining formal. "We are most anxious to inspect the First Battalion."

"Eager, huh? I like that," Pratt said. "Soon as this rain stops we'll see if we can muster 'em out. But to tell you the honest truth, they don't like comin' out in mud."

Joseph was thankful that Stumpf wasn't present for this announcement. "Perhaps, sir," he said, "we might inspect the men in their tents."

"Yes. If that's what you want, you could do that. The men won't like it."

Joseph ignored this. "And of course we shall immediately inspect the battalion horses," he added.

"Oh, we don't have horses yet," Pratt said. "Maybe that's something you might help out with. Speak directly to General

McClellan?" By now Pratt had convinced himself that this connection to McClellan could be the making of his military career.

"Army? They're a mob! The Dead Rabbits have more discipline!" Joseph said. He was pacing furiously in the tent assigned as First Battalion Headquarters.

Nathan turned to Stumpf. "Have you ever seen worse? Ever?"

Stumpf rose from the camp stool. "Herr Major, what we got here is a catastrophe!"

"Is there a chance we could train them?" Nathan asked.

Stumpf nodded. "*Ja*. Maybe in two years."

"Considering the speed with which General McClellan is moving, I doubt we shall have two months." Joseph was positive destiny had brought him to this moment, the moment of his first military miracle. Clearly McClellan would present the nation with Richmond for a Christmas present, and now Joseph made up his mind he would lead the First Battalion of the Albany Invincibles into the traitor capital. "We'll start this minute."

"In the rain and dark?" Nathan asked.

"Sergeant-Major Stumpf," Joseph said, "you will pay my respects to all battalion officers and ask them to report here immediately."

"*Jawohl, Herr Baron!*" Stumpf snapped to attention.

Before Stumpf left, Joseph, in an imitation of von Falkenbrecht's command voice said, "Sergeant-major, we are now with an American regiment. You will never again refer to me as baron. You shall only address me in English when we are with the men and you will always call me major."

"Yes sir, major." Stumpf saluted, about-faced, and left the tent.

"Joseph, how are you going to do it?" Nathan asked.

"It's like Daisy."

"My father's trotting horse?"

"Yes. When I got her, she hated everybody. She was fast but didn't know how to use her speed. But I knew she was sound and had the potential to become the fastest horse ever. These upstaters are the same. They've come here at great personal sacrifice to save the Union. So we start with the good in these men. It's up to us to bring that good to the surface. They don't trust us because they don't know us. That's natural. Also it gives us the chance to let them get to know us as we wish to be known." Moments ago Joseph had seen insurmountable obstacles. Now he saw the greatest opportunity of his life. He thought of Gideon who started out to defeat the joint forces of "All Midian, Amalek and the Kedemites...spread over the plain as thick as locusts; and their camels were countless, as numerous as the sands on the seashore." And what about Gideon's forces? Joseph thought. He had thirty-two thousand men. But the God of those Jews reduced his army to only three hundred, saying to Gideon, "You have too many troops with you for Me to deliver Midian into their hands; Israel might claim for themselves the glory due to me, thinking, 'Our own hand has brought us victory.' Therefore announce to the men, 'Let anybody who is timid and fearful turn back, as a bird flies from Mount Gilead.' "

Joseph was sure this principle could be applied in the present. And after he had changed these untrained, undisciplined farmers into a formidable fighting force, he would get the full credit for the victories of the Fighting First. General McClellan had sent him here to accomplish this miracle. He would not disappoint him. And when the Young Napoleon saw the result, he would raise Joseph to the rank of brigadier. Too bad the U.S. Army didn't have the rank of marshal.

"We shall train these men, and we shall do it in two months."

"Where do we start?" Nathan asked.

"With respect. You can't train a horse for whom you have no respect. So the same is true with men. We must find a way to show these men we respect them. What they presently do they do from ignorance. So first let's see where they can be respected. When these officers come in they'll have assumed we are here to criticize them. They'll be resentful, belligerent. So our first task will be to disarm them."

All six captains and all twelve lieutenants arrived at the same moment. This indicated to Joseph that Stumpf had found them at a battalion meeting to which he and Nathan hadn't been invited.

Give or take a few years, the battalion officers were Joseph's age. That gave him some comfort. "At ease please, gentlemen," he said, but he saw no perceptible change in their positions or attitudes. Joseph pretended not to notice. "First allow me to compliment you on the condition of the battalion," he said. "In spite of the almost impossible conditions imposed upon you, you have managed to keep your men healthy. To appreciate the magnitude of your accomplishment in this one crucial matter, all you need do is visit the many other encampments. We all know the tradition is for the men to elect the noncommissioned officers, for the noncommissioned officers to elect the company officers, and for the company officers to elect the battalion officers. You are most likely angry because General McClellan has overridden your election of battalion officers and stuck you with us. Why has he done such a thing to the First Battalion of the Albany Invincibles? To punish you for some transgression? Hardly. It's because he has the highest hopes for this battalion. We have been sent to you because we know how to train a cavalry battalion and you do not. We must accomplish in two months what in Europe it takes two years to do. But can we, new and not-welcome officers, accomplish this alone? We cannot, gentlemen. While we possess the secrets of cavalry tactics and training, you are in possession of something perhaps even more valuable. You have the trust of the men. You know them. We don't. Therefore it's to you that we must look for the management of this battalion. In all such matters, we shall turn to you."

A captain stepped forward. "Captain Faragon, A Troop," he said. "You want some advice, major?"

"I do."

"You three get on your horses and ride back to the Young Napoleon and tell him we want the officers we elected fair and square."

"I am afraid I can't accommodate you, Captain Faragon. We follow orders, just as you must. But I'll make you a sporting offer. Give us two months. Except as discipline applies to training, you men run the battalion. But in all matters having to do with training you will unquestioningly obey our commands. If at the end of two months you do not freely elect us to be your battalion commanders, we shall resign our commissions."

The officers were knocked off-balance. So were Nathan and Stumpf.

"You mean that?" Captain Faragon asked.

"I do."

Captain Faragon turned to his fellow officers who nodded assent. He turned back to Joseph. "A deal, major."

"Excellent. We go to work immediately."

"You mean after breakfast, major?"

"No. Immediately. Please assemble the battalion. Those who do not wish to assemble may stay in their tents. The Lord said to

Gideon, 'Let anybody who is timid and fearful turn back....' Any man that doesn't appear in ranks will be discharged from the army as having declared himself unfit to fight. General McClellan has assured me that such men will never be permitted to join the army again. Dismissed."

The astonished officers shuffled out of the tent.

The battalion stood in a rough approximation of military ranks in front of the headquarters tent. As Joseph and Nathan came out into the rain, Stumpf called, "Attention!" Some of the men changed their position. Most continued to slouch.

"I am Major von Ritter," Joseph said. "This is Lieutenant Loeb. Sergeant-Major Stumpf you have already met." An unpleasant muttering arose in the ranks. Joseph ignored it. "We've been personally assigned to this regiment by General McClellan. The First Battalion, Albany Invincibles will be the finest cavalry battalion in the army. It is obvious that you men are tough and dedicated to the cause. But no matter how brave you are, unless you learn the cavalry way to fight, Johnny Reb will cut you to pieces.

"I promise you horses and all the proper equipment and, if you dedicate yourselves to the task, I promise you will learn to ride them and you will learn to fight from the saddle. You shall become known as the dreaded and glorious Fighting First.

"There will be an assembly sounded at sunup. Army regulations call for the flogging of men who absent themselves without leave. No man will ever be flogged in this battalion. Those who desert will be court-martialed for a capital offense and General McClellan assures me they will be shot. Dismissed!"

Although Loeb had worked another miracle in finding horses, it still took three weeks of Joseph's precious two months for them to arrive. During that time, while the other two battalions malingered, Joseph worked the First Battalion from sunup to sundown. The men, grumbling and complaining, were drilled on foot. They went from simple infantry commands to cavalry formations, forming columns of twos and fours and right and left into line as if they were mounted. They learned to respond to the bugle calls for each maneuver. They walked, they trotted, and they ran on command. And every daylight hour when they weren't drilling or eating they worked at improving the sanitary conditions of their camp. The other two battalions of the Invincibles, those still officered by their elected home-town cronies, observed the intense labors of their compatriots with derision.

Still, a huge upsurge in morale occurred when two weeks into the training the sabers arrived. After the men had achieved some small proficiency with the blade on foot, logs were cut and set up at horse height. The men sat astride them for basic instruction in the mounted saber.

The next arrival was the horses. Joseph had known from the first day of his command what the officers of the other two battalions were now discovering: although most of the men were farmers and knew how to take care of horses, they didn't know how to ride them.

While the officers in the other battalions simply ordered their men to mount the horses and ride, Joseph and Stumpf, with Nathan assisting, taught each man to touch his horse with Joseph's techniques. Next they showed the men how to properly saddle and bridle. Then, they showed the men how to mount and dismount. Next the saddles were removed and the men were taught to mount bareback. Once mounted, they were given a half hour each, four at a time, twice-a-day riding bareback lessons while Joseph, Stumpf, and Nathan controlled the horses with lunge-lines. All the men had to do was get used to sitting on a moving animal enough to feel the faint stirrings of self-confidence. By the end of the first day, no one was falling off.

At the other battalion drill fields, riderless horses ran in every direction. Steady streams of men limped to the infirmaries.

On the third day, when the men of the First Battalion were walking their horses in circles and figure eights without the aid of the lunge-lines, orders arrived from headquarters. In three more days General McClellan, the governor of New York and other dignitaries would arrive to take a grand review of the regiment.

Meeting in Colonel Pratt's Headquarters tent, the officers were in despair. Speaking for them was Major Wheelwright of the Third Battalion. "Colonel," he said. "I don't have ten men who can stay in the saddle for more than three minutes—and that's at a walk— and I'm including myself and all the officers. There's no way we can pass in any review in three days. No way at all."

Colonel Pratt produced a thin book. "Well," he said, "there's more than one way to skin a cat. Says here in this book that there's this kind of review where the regiment stands still and the officers doing the reviewing ride up and down the ranks. I think the governor'd like that. Fancies himself as a horseman. He just might like riding up and down ranks of smartly turned-out cavalry, with the Young Napoleon beside him and a trail of staff officers behind him. Question is, can we get away with it?"

Back at his own headquarters, Joseph told the other company officers the plan. Stumpf was positive they could keep their men in their saddles and the horses in place, but he added that, if there was to be a review, the men and horses must learn to present sabers.

Each horse was then shown the saber, and each horse watched as the men withdrew the sabers from the scabbards. The horses were comforted. The process was repeated for each eye. When Joseph was convinced the horses weren't afraid of the sabers from the ground, he began the same process with the mounted rider. Then Joseph gave the order to begin practicing the mounting and walking into line for the review. Over the next three days from sunup to sundown the men mounted, walked their horses from columns of four into ranks, and drew and returned their sabers from and to their iron scabbards.

The great day arrived. When the governor's party came into view, Nathan raced back to camp and alerted Colonel Pratt. The signal was given and all went well. The three battalions managed to mount with no mishaps and were lined up, waiting for the dignitaries to inspect them. The inspecting party arrived and took its position in front of the regiment. Colonel Pratt saluted them. "Draw sabers!" he commanded.

The sound of twelve hundred sabers rattling out of their scabbards, and the waving of glistening steel by the eyes of horses that had never seen such a thing, produced an astonishing effect. It was as if a bomb had exploded among the regiment. Horses leaped into the air. There were displays of rearing and bucking. Horses ran to all points of the compass, some still with riders clinging to them. All except for the horses of the four hundred mounted men of the First Battalion. There they stood: lines straight, swords at the salute, and grins on every face.

General McClellan, imperially oblivious to the pandemonium, walked his horse over to Joseph.

"Major von Ritter, is this battalion of yours capable of doing more than posing?"

"They can walk, sir."

"Walk?"

"Yes, sir." Joseph was terrified. Could they walk?

"Would you be so kind, sir, as to demonstrate?"

"Yes, sir."

General McClellan, avoiding a pair of runaway horses from the Third Battalion, made his way back to the governor's party.

"They can walk," he said to the governor.

Joseph commanded, "Battalion! Return sabers!" Four hundred sabers clattered back into their scabbards.

"Attention!" Joseph shouted. "By fours, column right. Walk ho!"

The troop captains repeated the command: "By fours, troop right. Walk ho!"

The lieutenants took up the call: "By fours, platoon right. Walk ho!"

To the astonishment of Colonel Pratt and his staff who had been considering their own courts-martial, the First Battalion moved off as if they were veteran cavalry. They walked around the parade ground in even ranks, executing nearly perfect corners.

"Form companies!" Joseph ordered. "Right oblique. Walk. March!" They then performed an elegant martial formation and came to a halt in the place where they had begun.

McClellan rode up to Joseph. "I shall address your men, major," he said.

"We should be honored, sir."

McClellan posed his horse toward the men. "Soldiers of the First Battalion," McClellan said. "I am aware of the difficulty you have had in getting your mounts. What you have accomplished in the brief period you have had them has been unequaled in all of the cavalry. I salute you!"

In his letter to Fannie that evening, Joseph related the events of the grand review and ended his letter:

Extraordinary event piles on extraordinary event. General McClellan has ordered me to take over the training of the whole regiment! While I continue to command my men of the Fighting First, Nathan has the training of the Second Battalion, and the general has returned Major Steigel of the old First Americans to train the third battalion. Stumpf moves from battalion to battalion making sure we adhere to the highest standards.

Fannie, you have not written me in all these weeks. Am I to assume that there is no hope of reconciliation between us? I cannot accept that possibility. In those moments before sleep each night I think of you—of us. I know we are beshert. Even if you do not write to me for this whole war, I shall return to you, my wife. I shall return and we shall struggle with this awful thing that has occurred between us. We shall tear it asunder and find our true love, the love this awful thing has obscured. Have no doubt my beloved, our love is as pure as when first we experienced it. We have only to search for it and we shall find it.

No matter what has happened, like Odysseus I shall return from this war and reclaim my wife.

Fannie held the letter in her lap. Why had Joseph used the analogy to the Odyssey? Did he know about her infidelity? Was Joseph coming home to murder her lover? Thank God she had not heard from the poet again. Nathan must have given him a lot of money. But what if Joseph's reference to Odysseus was really to inform her that he knew? But Joseph didn't behave in that fashion. Dear Joseph, he would never use guile with her. Oh God! she thought. Dear Joseph. Lost forever.

Fannie had stopped berating herself for stupidity. But she had done what she had done and that was that. It was by no means all her fault. Joseph was as much to blame as she.

In spite of his loving letters, she knew that if he were present, he would still treat her as if she were a possession. He would still place horses, business, and now the army before her. Poor Joseph. He was so much a part of the mundane world. It wasn't his fault that he could never fully enter hers. She did love him, but she could never again make love with him. She had soiled his honor.

She read his letter once again. Now he was in love with that *poseur* McClellan. Poor, sweet Joseph. He was in many ways so innocent. She didn't agree with his assessment of the war. Bull Run had proven more than the ineptness of General McDowell. It had shown to those that could see—her father for one, and she for another—that the war would continue for a very long time. She prayed for Joseph's safety and wondered if the best thing she could do for him, for her family, for her dear children, was to take her own life.

Joseph now trained the men ten hours a day. Then, with the other officers, he put in another four hours of studies in tactics. But no matter how long his hours, how tired he was, every night before retiring, Joseph wrote to Fannie. In the act of writing these letters he had come to a kind of one-sided reconciliation. No matter that she answered infrequently, and only with impersonal letters filled with news of the children, he was grateful for every stroke of her pen. His letters contained detailed descriptions of the men and horses, the minutia of cavalry training, his admiration for his men and how fast they learned, and how he respected their dedication. He often wrote in adoration of McClellan who was serenely training his mighty army, patiently enduring the wait for this army to be ready so he might lead it to Richmond and victory.

Every letter ended with passages overflowing with his love for Fannie and their babies.

Occasionally he wrote about God:

> ...However hard we work the men, they always have time for prayer. No matter how tired the boys are, there are impromptu prayer groups each evening after training. On Sundays they have a regular preacher to lead their services, but still the boys take turns standing and speaking about the Union and how God has sent them to save it. Sometimes I feel odd in observing how truly and how simply they believe in their Christian God. Can it be so easy? And what about the God the rebels pray to? Are there now two Christian Gods, one North and one South, contending with each other? And what about our Jewish Gods? Surely the Jewish-American God will throw His weight on the scale of the Union. It is inconceivable to me that He would allow the great work begun in Philadelphia to go the way of the Second Temple.
>
> Perhaps the Red Sea will not part for us until we ourselves wade into it up to our chins. But as hard as my men pray to their Christian Gods, as stalwart and as brave

they are in their God's service to preserve the Union, I know the task is not theirs alone. It is not just a Christian responsibility. However few we may be, we Jewish-Americans must be in this fight for the Union, must put all at hazard for the preservation of the great dream of America.

I think now, here in the encampment, I am experiencing the greater part of America. These men are the America I have not known till now. No matter how mean, or rough, how spiteful or petty, or how noble and kind; they have in common their love of the Union, of freedom, and of their God. They are fit denizens of the New Jerusalem. They are my brothers.

And they are funny. In addition to their sacrifice of whiskey to their God, they try not to swear or to play cards, and laughingly fail miserably at refraining from these last two "sins" and, do not blush, they even have certain women in the camp. I don't think them hypocrites. I know them to love and fear their Christian God. They believe their God will lead them to victory over the rebel sinners, and yet they knowingly sin. Why? Because they are Americans! And Americans know that it's they who determine their lives, not any king, not any God. We Americans are a new race upon this earth. All may indeed be foreseen, but we are the first race of men to take the full measure of the Free Will that has been given.

On November 20, 1861, Joseph's joy could hardly be contained: the Army of the Potomac was ready for war. To prove it, General McClellan ordered a grand review of sixty thousand troops to be held in Washington. As a mark of special distinction to honor their splendid achievements, the great man placed the Albany Invincibles at the head of the cavalry.

"War!" Joseph said to Loeb, who had come down for the grand review. "At last! We're going to war! Look at these men. Are they not magnificent? By next Passover we shall have freed the slaves."

The grand review was a triumph. As Joseph trotted his smart battalion past Loeb, he saluted him with an "Eyes right!" Secretary of War Cameron, mistakenly flattered, thought the salute was for him.

That night Joseph was to dine with Loeb. However, at the conclusion of the grand review a captain of McClellan's staff presented himself to Joseph and asked him to report immediately to the commander-in-chief of the Army of the Potomac.

Joseph saluted. "Major von Ritter reporting, sir." As before, McClellan strode around his desk and extended his hand. "At ease, major," he said. "It seems, Major von Ritter, that I am in your debt. Your work with the Albany Invincibles has been exemplary. I wish I had a thousand of you."

"Thank you, sir."

"And now, major, I am afraid I must call upon you for yet another service for which you are uniquely suited." He turned to an officer who stepped from the shadows. "May I present Major Allen."

Joseph instinctively disliked the officer whose eyes were evasive and whose manner was artificial, but he returned the off-hand salute.

"What follows," McClellan continued, "is between you and Major Allen. I cannot order you to do as he will ask. I can and shall implore you to do it. I do want you to know that however you choose you shall retain my full confidence and continued respect. Good day, sir." McClellan strode from the room and closed the door.

Major Allen was the *nom de guerre* of detective Allan Pinkerton, head of McClellan's private secret service. He crossed to the door and locked it. He then turned and stared past Joseph's shoulder. "Major von Ritter," he said, "General McClellan has an urgent need for information concerning rebel troop strength, rebel strategies, rebel troop movements."

"That is a proper role of the cavalry, Major Allen," Joseph answered. "We move in advance of the army to ascertain the enemy's position and strength. If we can take prisoners, we can also determine his intentions."

Pinkerton nodded impatiently. "Yes, yes, major. But the knowledge we seek now can only be had by penetrating the highest levels of the rebel aristocracy. We need someone to freely travel about the South and observe their armies, encampments, forts, their railroads and supply depots. We need a man who can insinuate himself into rebel army confidence and steal plans, battle orders. You take my meaning?"

Joseph felt a chill numbness at the back of his neck. "I do, sir," he said. "And if you're suggesting that I am such a person, a person to sneak about in people's homes, to lie to them and to steal from them, you are mistaken. I'm a cavalry officer. I shall meet my enemy on the field of honor. I bid you good-day, sir." He started for the door.

"General McClellan told me he didn't think you were a coward," Pinkerton said.

Joseph turned. "Coward? Are you inferring..."

"No, baron, I am not. What I'm saying is that most men have the easy courage to serve their country on the battlefield with flags and drums and the like. Damn few have the spirit it takes to do the real work. The dirty, secret—no flags and drums here—work that makes the victories possible. I'm talking about the stuff that will win the war. When General McClellan takes his army into battle, you think he doesn't need exact knowledge of how many men and guns the rebels have and where they are? You want him to go blind like McDowell at Bull Run? And how about the Reb spies? You want them to keep giving our secrets to Jeff Davis without we catch them and shoot them before they give us another Bull Run?"

"But why me?"

"You're our only German baron who happens to be some kind of genius horseman. You know how the Rebs love foreign titles? You know how nuts they are about horses?"

"But I'm well-known," Joseph said. "They'll know I'm a Union man."

"You'll grow a beard to cover that well-known scar, and pick another title, and don't speak such good English—you know, talk with a Dutch accent. You'll fool them." And if he didn't, Pinkerton thought, there were plenty more fools where Joseph came from.

§37

JOSEPH RODE TOWARD WILLARD'S HOTEL, REHEARSING HIS WORDS. He would tell Fannie how much he loved her. He would tell her they could fix whatever was wrong. He would ask her to list her grievances, and he would change his behavior. Would he give up the horse business for her? Yes! But he couldn't give up the war—that was a question of honor. She would understand that. She loved the

Union as much as he. She was right about the farm and the horses. They had caused him to neglect his duty to her. He had spent too much time away from her and the children. He'd sell the farm and move back to New York City. The hotel was just up ahead. How thrilled he'd been when he received Loeb's telegram saying Fannie was accompanying him to Washington.

Joseph checked in and the clerk directed him to the bar where Mr. Loeb was waiting.

The two shook hands. "I don't know what's happened between you and Fannie," Loeb said. "It took all my powers of persuasion and command to get her to come here. She won't discuss it with me. I say only this. Marriage is not always easy. There are times when it seems impossible. Those are the times when you must remember how you love your wife. Fannie is headstrong, spoiled and occasionally foolish. Go upstairs Joseph and repair whatever it is that's gone wrong. Just remember your love for her."

When Joseph entered the hotel suite, Fannie was seated on a divan in the parlor. They said nothing to each other until the bellboy left.

"I didn't want to come," Fannie said.

"It's all my fault," he replied.

"No," she said. "There is no fault." She spoke just above a whisper. "You are who you are. I am what I am. There's nothing to be done." She changed the subject. "And your battalion? Are they ready to ride to Richmond?"

"Soon. Fannie, I'll change. I promise. We can sell the farm."

"That would be foolish. Tell me about your battalion. Please." And then, changing her tone, she added, "It'll help to talk of other things."

"The children?"

"Yes. That would be good."

She told him about the family and when she was done, about the farm. Again she asked him about his work, and he told her about his new assignment.

"But why? Why you? It's the most horrendously stupid thing I ever heard of!" She'd read reports about Committees of Safety in the South lynching and shooting suspected spies. "I cannot believe General McClellan would permit such a waste of his best cavalry officer. He's the fool Poppa says he is!"

"Poppa thinks General McClellan is a fool?" Joseph was stunned.

"Yes. The man is a *poseur*. We cannot allow him to send you on this lunacy."

"I have accepted."

"Then you must now decline."

Joseph shook his head. "Fannie, your father is wise in many things. He's a great man. But he's not a general. Your father the banker is as wrong as the fools in the Congress who criticize General McClellan. They understand nothing of the science of war. That gorilla in the White House…"

"Joseph!"

Joseph continued, calm and cold. "In spite of the interference of the profiteers and the politicians, General McClellan will march this great army to Richmond when he's ready. He'll take that city and end the war. General McClellan has asked me to aid him in this enterprise. It's an honor to be so trusted."

"My God, Joseph, how can you be so stupid?"

"General McClellan is not a fool. The fool is in the White House! That country bumpkin has not only lost control over the government, but he now proposes to ruin the grandest army the world has ever seen. General McClellan won't let him do that. The army will be saved and when it's ready, and not a day sooner, we'll sweep across Virginia and save the Union."

"You dare say those things about President Lincoln?"

"Did you know that your father's good friend, Secretary of War Cameron, is a crook? Did you know Cameron and his crooked friends are plundering the army?"

"No, but I'll tell Poppa that he's doing so and Poppa will do something about it." She paused, "Oh. You don't think Poppa…"

"Good God! Fannie how could you think such a thing?"

"Why not, liar? You lied when you said you would love me forever!"

"I meant it then and I mean it now."

She laughed mirthlessly. "Liar! Look at your face. You're black with anger at me. Love me? You hate me, Joseph."

Joseph stared at her for a while and then, too angry to speak, he snatched his bag from the bed and stormed out of the suite.

A few moments later Loeb knocked at the door. Fannie let him in and then fell into his arms, weeping. He held her gently for a moment and then led her to a chair by the fire. Pulling up another, he sat next to her.

Fannie stared into the flames. "Poppa," she said. "If he dies, so will I."

"Shhh. Joseph isn't dying just yet."

"Poppa. He hates me."

"No, he doesn't, in spite of what you may have said to him."

"But I don't love him anymore."

"Yes, you do, but right now you don't know it."

"Can such a thing be?"

"With everybody."

"Then why don't I feel it?"

"Because other things are happening now. This is all part of a marriage. You'll have to struggle through it. I pray to God you make the right decisions."

"Has he left the hotel?"

"Yes."

"Poppa, send for him. Please send someone for him. Now!"

Loeb shook his head. "He's gone. You know what they have asked him to do?"

"Yes."

"He has gone to do it."

Joseph was ordered on six weeks' secret leave, the time required for a courier to cross the ocean to the ailing Count von Falkenbrecht, for the count to arrange a false identity with his cousin, General Baron von Ischel of the Imperial Austrian Horse Guards, and for the courier to return. He used this time to grow a full beard to cover his scar.

Except for Loeb, who agreed with his daughter about the foolishness and danger of such a mission, no one in the family had been told.

Nathan and the Albany Invincibles were informed that the army required Joseph's presence in the West. With Major Allen's guidance Joseph wrote a series of letters to Nathan which, from time to time, were eventually to be mailed from various distant cities.

When at last all was ready Joseph, with Stumpf traveling as his servant, took the train to Baltimore.

Shortly after his arrival the *Baltimore American* reported:

Our City was Honored this week with the arrival of gallant Austrian Nobleman Count von Chernowitz, Colonel of the Imperial Austrian Horse Guards.

The Count, who is stopping at Barnum's Hotel, said that he has come as an Unofficial Observer of the conflict that now engages our two great Nations. Although besieged with Invitations to dinners, teas and other Social Occasions, especially those where the most eligible of our City's fair Maidens might be present, the Count has with many a regret declined all but one. The Chivalrous Soldier will dine tomorrow night with Dr. Avery Sloan and Gentlemen of this City. Alas Dr. Sloan has no Daughters.

The *Baltimore American* was a crypto-pro-secessionist paper, and the announcement of Joseph's dinner with Dr. Sloan was a formal proclamation that Count von Chernowitz was a southern sympathizer. Insiders knew that Dr. Avery Sloan was the Most Noble Chief of the Knights of Liberty, a secret organization dedicated to the victory of the Confederacy.

Although Joseph was traveling in a French-style civilian wardrobe, he arrived at Dr. Sloan's house dressed in the white and gold uniform of the Austrian Imperial Horse Guards. Aside from the monocle and beard, Joseph had altered his appearance by trimming his mustache and then cutting his hair so short that a glimpse of his scalp showed through at the sides of his head. Calibrating the degree of southern snobbery and pretension, Joseph had selected the accent of an Austrian gentleman educated in English at Oxford.

Accompanying him was Stumpf in the uniform of a sergeant of the Imperial Horse Guards. After they were greeted by a black servant at the door, he took Joseph's cloak and stood waiting orders. At the dinner table he kept Joseph's wine and water glasses filled, and personally served Joseph his meal. Joseph never introduced him or explained his presence.

During dinner one of the assembled knights said he could help Joseph and his man cross the Potomac into Virginia. Others asked him to carry letters to friends and to certain members of the government in Richmond and Joseph assented. He wondered if the rest of this trip would be this easy.

The rain had been coming down since just before sunset. Although it was dry inside the closed carriage, the wet chill crept through Joseph's gum coat to the marrow of his bones. Stumpf rode with the driver, exposed to the elements. Joseph was worried about him, for he didn't seem well. He was as solid as ever and yet something was wrong. Stumpf should be in the dry coach with him, not up on the box. That would be too unusual in the South—a servant inside with the master. But perhaps a sergeant? It was worth a try.

Joseph called out for the driver to stop. "I require my sergeant's presence," he said in English. Then in German he added, "Sergeant Stumpf! You will bring the small black box and come here immediately." When Stumpf had complied with his orders, Joseph stuck his head out of the window. "Drive on."

The carriage lurched forward. Joseph opened the box which contained a bottle of schnapps, bread and Bavarian sausage. They spoke in German in case the driver could overhear.

"Eat," Joseph said. "Drink the schnapps and get warm. You will stay in here with me till we get to the boat."

Stumpf started to object. "The driver will suspect..."

Joseph cut him off. "This is an order. The driver will suspect nothing."

Stumpf nodded, "Herr Baron..."

Joseph interrupted, "Herr *Count*. You must be careful to call me Count von Chernowitz."

"Yes, Herr Count. Does the Count von Chernowitz desire another sip of schnapps?"

"One more. Then we must both sleep until we reach the boat."

"But I must watch."

"Sleep. That is an order, sergeant."

Joseph slept. Stumpf closed his eyes until Joseph's breathing became regular, and then opened them. With one hand on the pistol under his cloak, he kept watch for the next four hours until they reached a farm on the Potomac just southeast of the small town of Port Tobacco. The rain had let up but clouds covered the stars. As the carriage came to a halt, Stumpf shook Joseph awake. "I think we're here, Herr Count," he whispered.

Outside the carriage they heard a suspicious voice. "State your business," it said.

The driver responded with, "Are you white?"

The voice answered, "Down with blacks."

"I have two men and their baggage. They are bound for Richmond. League business. Can you go tonight?"

"Maybe. Let's have a look."

Stumpf got out and held the door for Joseph, who nodded to the dark shape standing next to the driver. "I am Count von Chernowitz. This is Sergeant Stumpf. I have business with the government of the Confederacy. Can you get us across the river into Virginia?"

"Maybe," the shape said. "You got the price?"

"How much?"

"Ten dollars, silver or gold."

"I am told that before the war a ferry crossing was five cents."

"You was told right. Ten dollars, gold or silver."

"Agreed." Joseph put a gold coin in the man's hand. The man slipped it into his pocket without looking at it.

"Follow me," the man said. He turned and was almost lost in the blackness of the night. Joseph trailed him down a barely discernible path to a clump of trees. Stumpf and the driver walked behind with the luggage.

A narrow finger of the river curled into the small copse where Joseph could make out a sailboat. As he stepped aboard he was surprised to find a flat bottom.

"Sorta like a skipjack," the dark shape said. He scurried about, preparing the small boat for the crossing. Stumpf and the coachman put the luggage aboard. As soon as it was stowed the coachman disappeared in the night.

"Once we push off, not a sound out of you," the dark shape said, getting out of the boat into the water. As the boat began to drift, the shape climbed in and raised a sail that seemed even blacker than the night. To the north Joseph could see some lights which he assumed was Port Tobacco. He also noticed lights moving on the river. Union blockaders, he guessed. He turned back toward the direction they were heading when something to the south of them entered his peripheral vision. A moving light. It was coming toward them.

Joseph whispered to the man at the tiller. "A light to the south."

"I seen 'em."

But the Yankee steamer thrashed by them without stopping.

Twenty minutes later the centerboard squeaked and the boat bumped into an embankment.

The dark shape helped them ashore with their luggage. "There's a house straight ahead, just over the hill," he said. "Keeps a light burning all night. He has some beds and will feed you something hot. He can get you to Hampstead in the morning, and there you can hire some horses to Fredericksburg. From there you can catch the train straight on to Richmond. 'Course you'll need a pass. You got a pass?"

"No. How do I get one?"

"From Captain Dinwoodie in Hampstead."

A cold, wet mile and a half away over soggy terrain, Joseph and Stumpf were greeted with less than the traditional southern hospitality. The house was filthy and there was nothing hot to drink. For another ten dollars in gold they were given two straw pallets on the floor. Both slept in their clothes.

In the middle of the night horses rode up to the door which was then flung open by a soldier in gray. From the overcast dawn behind him an officer and two more soldiers strode through, and three muskets were leveled at Joseph and Stumpf.

"Who the devil are you?" the officer asked. He was a narrow, mean-looking man.

In German, Joseph said to Stumpf, "We shall rise very slowly, our hands always in sight. You will stand at attention."

"What's that you're saying?" The officer was ready to fire.

Joseph told him the truth. He then added, "Permit me to introduce myself. I am Colonel Count von Chernowitz of the Imperial Austrian Horse Guards. This is Sergeant Stumpf. My country has sent me to be an observer of the Confederate victory, and without violating our neutrality to offer what assistance I may be privileged to tender."

"Well, I'll be damned. You can prove that, colonel?"

"Yes of course. May I open this case?"

"Sure." But the captain's pistol stayed on him.

Joseph pulled out a leather document case. "Here are my orders from General Baron von Ischel, commander of the Imperial Horse. There is also a letter from His Imperial Majesty's Minister of Foreign Affairs." Joseph looked up. "You do read German, captain?"

The captain shook his head.

Joseph was gratified to see the muzzle of the pistol drop. He was also amused to see that the captain and his men had grown friendlier with each mention of a title. Here was a readily apparent difference between the rebels and his own men, who had hooted at titles.

"Ah yes, I understand," Joseph said. "How foolish we Imperial Austrians are. We think the whole world speaks German. Had the emperor known, I am sure His Majesty would have had these translated. I am, however, also journeying with certain introductions from friends of the Confederacy in Baltimore to their good friends in Richmond.

He handed the papers to the captain, who studied the documents, even those written in German. When finished he looked up from the correspondence and holstered his pistol. He then saluted Joseph.

"Well colonel, how about we have us a hot breakfast? Then if you'd like, we'll ride with you to Fredericksburg."

"That would be excellent, captain. Thank you."

"Say, did Jenkins charge you ten dollars for the night?"

"He did."

"Hell, that's his Yankee price," the captain said. "He gets the money then lights out after me to come and arrest the spy." He turned to the landlord standing in the doorway of the other room. "Give'm back his money, Daniel. Man's come to help the cause.

"Colonel," the captain then asked. "You and the sergeant traveling with your uniforms?"

"We are."

"Well, sir, I suggest you wear them as much as you can. I'll issue you a pass to Richmond, but a uniform'll keep a lot of people from asking a lot of unnecessary questions. We got Safety Committees out there that arrest civilian strangers on sight. Sometimes they hang them before we get to question them. Best you wear your uniforms. People in the South respect a uniform."

Joseph and Stumpf changed into their green and gold field uniforms and breakfasted on ham, eggs, grits and coffee.

The thirty mile ride over muddy roads to Fredericksburg took seven hours. Joseph noted glumly that the captain and his six troopers were superb horsemen—every one of them rode better than any of the Albany Invincibles ever would. If this were true for all southern cavalry, the Union was in for a difficult time.

Joseph thought Fredericksburg a dreary little town, all red brick and white clapboard with muddy streets and thousands of soldiers. A train was leaving for Richmond in two hours, so he and Stumpf joined Captain Dinwoodie and several other officers for a mid-day meal. There Joseph learned that thirty thousand soldiers were waiting in and around Fredericksburg. The rumor was they were going to take Washington in the spring. Joseph was fascinated by the ease with which he gathered information.

Stumpf, who ate with the non-commissioned officers, was impressed with the rebels' toughness. In the Union camp he had seen boys playing at war. Here among the enemy the old soldier's nostrils detected the familiar odor of death.

§38

JOSEPH AND STUMPF ARRIVED IN RICHMOND AT NEARLY SIX THAT evening. They were surprised by the station's intense activity. The platform was crowded with troops waiting for trains, troops boarding trains, troops disembarking and civilians engaging in much the same activities. In the background a band was playing Dixie.

After they had descended from the car, a smartly turned-out young cavalry officer stepped up and saluted. "Colonel von Cherno-witz?"

Joseph and Stumpf returned the salute. "I am," Joseph said.

"Welcome to Richmond, sir. I'm Lieutenant Leander Cole, on the staff of General John H. Winder, provost marshal and com-mander of the military in this city. Captain Dinwoodie telegraphed of your arrival. General Winder sends his regrets at not being able to greet you personally, but hopes you will call on him in the morning. I have taken the liberty of booking you into the Monu-mental Hotel." He smiled. "It's not our best, and by no means the worst Richmond has to offer. The city is overcrowded. The new government and all the merchants come here to arm and feed and clothe the army and, as you can see, soldiers. The South is on the march, sir."

Joseph guessed Lieutenant Cole was about seventeen years old. Lithe and blond, he talked incessantly in a familiar accent.

"We are grateful for your hospitality," Joseph replied. "Please convey our appreciation to your general."

"I shall, sir. May I have the honor of escorting you to your hotel?"

"Much obliged, lieutenant."

Cole signaled and two slaves retrieved their baggage. Joseph could see that the lieutenant, although he tried not to let it show, was intimidated by Stumpf. As the slaves led Stumpf to the waiting carriage, Cole, staring after him in awe, said to Joseph, "Now that man's a soldier!"

Joseph nodded gravely. "Sergeant-Major Stumpf has fought in every European war in the last forty years." Then he smiled. "Lieutenant, perhaps you will dine with us?"

"I should be honored, count." He had been carefully rehearsing the words ever since he had been assigned to be the reception officer. Cole was already fascinated by Joseph. For a moment Joseph forgot the boy was his enemy. He was touched by his innocence.

The hotel was adequate. Though the management had provided a suite for the distinguished foreigner—Joseph was the first European nobleman ever to visit—they had no space for Stumpf but in the suite's parlor. Joseph was relieved to keep Stumpf so close. Downstairs the air was thick with cigar smoke and the floor slippery with mud and tobacco spit.

That night Cole met them at the foot of the narrow stairs. Joseph and Stumpf had changed into their white uniforms. As they walked through the crowded lobby to the restaurant, the roar of conversation ceased as they approached and continued even louder in their wake.

They were shown to a table in the center of the room. Stumpf as usual took his place behind Joseph's chair to serve him. The effect was as Joseph expected. Any man with enough money could have a black slave standing behind his chair. But it took genuine royalty to own a white man.

General Winder greeted Joseph cordially. He was most particularly interested in Joseph's account of his visits to the Army of the Potomac.

"Large, yes," Joseph said, "But soldiers? Never."

"Are the reports of the size of the Army of the Potomac accurate? A half a million men?"

"An exaggeration, I should say. I have personally visited every encampment around Washington. It's my estimate that there are not 150,000 men there, and they are of poor quality. But what is most important, they have no heart for battle."

They chatted for over an hour. "Colonel," Winder said, "I shall issue you a pass allowing you the freedom of this city and the Department of Henrico, which includes the county. Should you intend to travel in the Confederacy, I'll issue you a similar passport for the nation." He shook his head. "Can you imagine, sir? Passports to travel in America!" Then, pulling himself back from his anger, he looked into Joseph's eyes. "A warning of the utmost gravity, Count. You'll be hearing from a Miss Elizabeth Van Lew. She's a spinster, and considered to be eccentric. In fact there are some that call her Crazy Bet. However, she and her family are socially prominent, and to snub an invitation from her might be considered by Richmond society an insult to all of them. She's an eccentric but she's our eccentric, if you take my meaning."

Joseph returned the smile. "I do, sir."

"I'm sure her spies have already reported your presence in our city and I've no doubt that, as surely as we sit here, an invitation is being scratched out this very moment."

Joseph smiled. "But naturally I shall accept."

Returning to the hotel, Joseph found the dreaded invitation from Miss Elizabeth Van Lew.

The Van Lew mansion on Church Hill was directly across the street from the church where Patrick Henry had delivered his famous speech. A white-haired black servant greeted Joseph at the door, while Stumpf remained outside with the horses. He was then led into a parlor where a motley group was waiting to receive him.

Miss Van Lew, a tiny woman with tangled hair and mismatched clothing, stepped forward. "I trust all is well with Uncle George."

This was the watchword he had been told he would hear from Major Allen's Richmond agent. My God, Joseph thought, this socialite was a Union spy! Joseph answered with the countersign, "Uncle George is recovering from the bilious fever." At that, Miss Van Lew and the others in the room relaxed. He automatically bent and kissed Miss Van Lew's hand in the European manner.

"La, sir," she sighed. "You make a girl swoon. No one has kissed me like that since my first cotillion, which was long before you were born." She gestured toward the other guests. "Colonel von Chernowitz, may I present my fellow patriots. We are all that is left of the United States of America here in Richmond. My brother, John Van Lew, Miss Mary Bowser…"

Joseph had assumed the black lady was a servant or slave. Miss Van Lew anticipated his question. "Miss Bowser is an educated free black woman who once was a slave and now works as a paid servant in the home of Mr. Jefferson Davis." Miss Van Lew turned to a large man in a rough suit. "This is Mr. Samuel Ruth, who is superintendent of the Richmond, Fredericksburg & Potomac Railroad, and who sees to it that trains run late, break down, or the wrong freight goes to the wrong place." She next turned to a man who appeared to be a farmer. "Mr. Walter S. Rowley, whose farm is the first link in our line of communication to the North."

Next to him was a portly man in a well-cut dark suit. "Mr. Frederick W.E. Lohman owns the best eating establishment in Richmond. All of the rebel bigwigs eat and drink there—and my, my, how men in their cups do talk! And this bizarre-looking creature is Mr. Martin M. Lipscomb. Why people hereabouts think him as crazy as Crazy Bet."

The man did seem a bit odd to Joseph.

Miss Van Lew continued, "Mr. Lipscomb is an official contractor of food to the rebel hordes."

After Joseph had shaken everyone's hand, they sat down again. The servant who had opened the door for Joseph brought in tea. "And this is Uncle Tiberius," Miss Van Lew said. "He is a free man and a paid servant in this house. He's also a leader of the Loyal League. Uncle Tiberius, would you please tell Colonel von Chernowitz about the Loyal League?"

The old man put his serving tray on the table and turned to Joseph. He spoke in the soft accent of the house slave. "We're just about everywhere in the South. We colored folk want Uncle Abe to win the war and come down here and free all the slaves. There's lots of us. We're everywhere, and the white folks they don't never see us. Just like they don't never see the ground they walk on. But we're everywhere."

"And that," added Miss Van Lew, "means they are truly invisible. Armed with a letter from a white master sending them on an errand, they can go anywhere. The Loyal League helps with communications, and when someone must disappear they're invaluable. The Union that let them languish in slavery all these years doesn't deserve them, but there are no more loyal Americans than those of the Loyal League. Uncle Tiberius, Colonel von Chernowitz may need the help of the Loyal League one day. Would you tell him the passwords?"

"I surely would." He turned to Joseph. "You want to know if you have one of us in front of you, you say, 'I suppose you're a friend to Uncle Abe, ain't you now?' Then they say, 'And if I am, what do you want?' And you say, 'Light and Liberty.'"

Joseph, who spent the afternoon with his co-conspirators, was an integral part of their plans by the time he left. His reports on the rebel armies were to be sent to Major Allen via the lines of communication established by Miss Van Lew.

That night Joseph caroused with army officers he had met through Lieutenant Cole. He pretended to drink very much more than he did because Stumpf was in charge of filling his glass. He told outrageous tales of combat in Europe, but listened closely to the rebels' descriptions of their troop strength and strategies.

In the days that followed, Joseph consolidated his friendship with Lieutenant Cole and the other officers. Few southerners could resist the charm of a great horseman and Joseph used his talent to full advantage. He hunted, raced, played cavalry games and conversed at length about breeding and training. He was disheartened to confirm his first impression of southern horsemen. They all seemed to ride as if they had been born to the saddle, and they all had superb mounts. Except for the disbanded First American Hussars, the Union cavalry was no match for these traitor knights.

One day Joseph was invited by General Winder to witness an event that caused him to use Miss Van Lew's line of communication for the first time. He sent the following message to Major Allen:

THIS IS MOST URGENT. Yesterday, January 17, I witnessed a hellish device. It is a submersible torpedo. I am including my drawing of this machine. This little boat, cylindrical in shape with conical ends, is hand-propelled by the crew who work a screw. I actually was invited to inspect this boat. Please see my drawings. I witnessed it enter the water a half a mile upstream from a barge. One can follow its underwater progress by observing a large float on the surface of the water which carries the ventilation hose through which the crew breathe. The float is painted the same color as the water to render it partially invisible. Once under the victim ship, one of the three man crew dons diving armor and fastens the torpedo to the ship to be destroyed. The submarine boat then removes to a safe distance and lights its fuse. The result is deadly. I saw the barge blast into smithereens. But there is a defense against it. If our ships look out for the large green float, perhaps they can snag it and shut off the air to the fiends below.

News of this must be gotten to the fleet immediately as the blockade runners Thomas Jefferson and Patrick Henry are loaded with cotton for England and only wait for the destruction of the ships at the mouth of the James.

Over the next sixteen days Joseph busied himself with his social contacts in the government. On the seventeenth day Richmond was saddened when a Yankee ship observed the submersible's float and sent a cutter to snag it, thus drowning the crew.

Back in their suite, Joseph and Stumpf toasted their victory. As Joseph raised his glass of celebratory schnapps, a thought came to him. Or actually a voice—the same voice that had told him to go to America. Now it said, "My children have drowned and you celebrate?"

That night he had the cloud dream.

"It's time," Joseph told Cole a few days later, "that I do my duty to my government and tour the defenses of this city."

"You and they shall be impressed, colonel."

Joseph's next report from Richmond, transmitted to Major Allen via Miss Van Lew, included details and maps of the Richmond defenses. It ended with:

My work in Richmond is completed and I have accepted an invitation from Lt. Leander Cole to journey with him to his family plantation in Georgia.

In the company of Cole, his body servant, his three other slaves and six horses, Joseph and Stumpf journeyed from Richmond to Savannah. They changed railroads four times, traveling on the Richmond, Petersburg & Weldon Railroad, the Weldon & Wilmington Railroad, the Wilmington & Manchester Railroad, the Northeastern Railroad, and finally the Charleston & Savannah Railroad. They used the occasion of each new train to spend at least one night in the terminus city of the local line. This offered an opportunity to exercise the horses and meet Cole's kin, all of whom offered accommodations for men and animals.

Joseph recorded that only two of the five railroads were of the same gauge, and those two didn't connect. And he noted the military activity. Weldon, North Carolina and Florence, South Carolina consisted mostly of militia bands and recruiting officers. However, the fortifications in the important port of Wilmington, North Carolina were formidable. Joseph was pleased to find three blockade runners in the harbor unprepared for sea, which he confirmed in conversation.

At night he sketched from memory the Wilmington fortifications on very thin paper which he then folded and placed in a secret compartment in his dress busby.

The gray skies cleared as Joseph arrived in Charleston where he spent three days. Here at last was the gracious southern city Joseph had expected: lovely mansions overlooking a magnificent harbor, a two hundred year old theater, an exquisite church a la Christopher Wren, and in the harbor, with the Palmetto flag flying at its masthead, Fort Sumter.

Joseph and Stumpf were taken on an excursion to view the battered brick fort. From it they could see the stone-laden ships the Yankees had sunk in the channel leading to the open sea, and on the horizon they made out the smoke from the northern ships on patrol. Back in the city, Joseph observed the effectiveness of the blockade, as certain luxuries and numerous necessities were in short supply and prices for all goods were climbing.

He sketched the placement and caliber of the cannons at Sumter and the other forts in the harbor. Charleston, the report suggested, could best be taken by land, a fair amount of which he had covered in five days of fox hunting with Cole's local cousins.

Next Joseph took the Charleston & Savannah Railroad to Savannah. The countryside was low and dark, depressing Joseph and sending him morbid fantasies of capture, imprisonment and death. Savannah turned out to be as beautiful as Charleston and his spirits lifted somewhat.

On a tour of the city he asked, "And Fort Pulaski? Shall we see it? I understand it defends the mouth of the river?"

"We better see it tomorrow," Cole said, "because the very next day our plantation boat arrives to take us upriver to Rotherwood."

That night they stayed at the home of another Cole cousin. After dinner Joseph excused himself, saying he wasn't yet ready for bed, and that he wished to stroll by himself for a while.

Stumpf, who had been waiting up for him, joined him at the front gate. "I have to find a way of communicating with Major Allen," Joseph said. "Not far from here is a livery stable. At this hour only slaves should be there."

The stable Joseph had seen was a ten-minute walk. When they arrived Joseph found one slave, a groom. He scrambled to his feet as the two military men entered.

"In the morning I shall require a brougham and a matched set of trotting horses," Joseph said.

The slave looked at him as if Joseph were mad.

"Yes, massa." He spoke in a nearly incomprehensible dialect, part Gullah and part slave English. "But we don't got 'em."

"Let me speak to the owner."

"Ain't here."

"You mean to say you're here all alone?"

"Yes, massa."

Quietly Joseph spoke the words given him by Miss Van Lew's servant, Uncle Tiberius. "I suppose you are a friend to Uncle Abe, aren't you now?"

The slave carefully examined Joseph and Stumpf. Then he straightened up from his slight stoop. "And if I am, what do you want?"

Stumpf was watching the man's right hand, which had slipped into a rent in his trouser leg. He was sure it was now gripping a knife, but he decided against using his pistol, for the report could bring an unwelcome crowd. Instead he prepared himself to spring if that hidden hand moved again.

"Light and liberty," Joseph answered.

The hand relaxed. "The army took all the best horses. Maybe we got one back here you might like." He moved into the barn and

Joseph and Stumpf followed. In a dark empty stall the slave turned back to them.

"How come you know about the Loyal League?"

"From a friend. I need to get some urgent messages to a man in Washington. Can you do it?"

"The place Uncle Abe lives?"

"It is. Can you help get a message to a man in that city?"

"I can't but I know one as can. Leastways he can start it up the line. Will it help Uncle Abe win the war and set the slaves free?"

"It will."

"Then we do it."

"Will you be here tomorrow night at this time?"

"Yes."

"This man will bring you a packet. Will you take it to the man who can start it up the line?"

"I surely will."

Fort Pulaski was only a few miles downriver. There Joseph and Stumpf were met by the fort commander and treated to a band concert and lunch, served under a canopy on the battlement overlooking distant Tybee Island and the Atlantic Ocean beyond.

Joseph's report to Major Allen included his usual sketches and maps and pointed out that the lightly defended Tybee Island would be an excellent place from which to bombard the masonry fort. Like Sumter, it would probably crumble under the force of big guns.

The following morning Joseph and Stumpf accompanied Cole and his slaves, horses, and some of his cousins for the upriver trip to Rotherwood, the Cole plantation. The Rowena, the family's sternwheel plantation boat, was their principle means of travel to and from Savannah, a four-hour trip. The boat, which could transfer 200 bales of cotton at a time, consisted mostly of deck space covered by a canvas roof. It now held pens for the horses toward the stern, cargo mid-ship, and on the forward deck, sofas, tables and chairs.

After Joseph and Stumpf had accompanied Cole aboard, liveried house-slaves began preparations for a mid-morning meal. Joseph pulled his fur-lined cloak around his shoulders and was glad he had brought what had once seemed an inappropriate garment to the sunny South. As he came forward from the horses, Stumph was seized by a sudden fit of coughing.

Soon the Rowena started her journey upriver, and Joseph settled into a chair next to Cole; a slave placed a delicate porcelain cup of hot coffee laced with brandy in his hand.

"I couldn't help but notice your cargo," Joseph said. "Don't you grow vegetables and fruit on your plantation?"

Cole shook his head. "Land's too valuable to waste on food," he said. "We grow cotton on every inch. It's even cheaper to buy food for the slaves than let them grow their own the way granddaddy did. Lincoln's blockade has caused the price of cotton to quadruple on the London markets just since Sumter, and it's still going up." He raised his cup and said, "To the price of cotton, may she always rise."

"If I may be so rude to point out," Joseph said, "the South has no navy. How do you plan to break the blockade?"

"We won't. The English will, and the French. Even if we could ship cotton now, we don't want to. We'll make the Europeans so hungry for it they will declare for the Confederacy. Bet on it. Cotton is king."

Then the conversation turned to horses and war. Joseph encouraged Stumpf to tell stories of his campaigns, and Stumpf spoke in German while Joseph translated. Stumpf told of his adventures in Turkey, Egypt and the Crimea, of sieges and burning cities. Joseph noticed that Stumpf, although he tried to cover it up, was coughing regularly. Joseph made up his mind that before continuing their journey they would rest for as long as it took for him to recover. He wondered if he'd made a mistake in bringing Stumpf along.

The Rowena occasionally passed plantations and Cole related their histories. For the most part Joseph was disappointed in the houses. They were smaller than he had imagined. Here and there he spotted an attempt at Greek Revival which he usually found poorly executed. But as the southern slaveocracy didn't understand democracy, he thought, how could they understand its classic architecture?

By late morning the Rowena approached a bend in the river and gave off three long blasts of its steam whistle. Cole excitedly rose to his feet, as did the other guests.

"We're home!" Cole shouted.

Joseph looked up to see a gracious Greek Revival mansion, larger than Liberty Hall, and more beautiful. White and colonnaded, it stood at the top of a gentle rise from the river, shimmering amid the tan fields surrounding it. A road surfaced with crushed pink stone curved up to the main door. Three carriages, one occupied, and a pony cart filled with little girls had started down from the house followed by several wagons and preceded by a number of riders on horseback.

Senator Cole galloped up on a chestnut thoroughbred as magnificent as the six traveling with his son. Like Cole he was tall, thin and athletic. His hair was the same color as his horses, and it was long and free. Byronesque, Joseph thought.

The senator leaped from his horse and strode forward to grasp his son's hand, and Joseph found himself admiring the man. There, laughing and greeting his son and guests, was the romantic figure he had always wished he could be. Joseph observed that the other members of Cole's immediate family shared the same poetic beauty. Mrs. Cole was blonde, pretty, and nearly as enthusiastic as the senator. Of the three children, the eldest had her father's coloring, while the other two shared the pale blonde looks of their mother. Cole placed special emphasis on "Count" as he introduced Joseph.

After the horses were unloaded and saddled, the procession started for the house. On the way Joseph and the senator talked. "Count," the senator said. "My son has written of his admiration of your horsemanship, and I also understand from my son's letters you and your sergeant are experts in the techniques of European cavalry."

Joseph made a small, self-deprecating gesture.

The senator continued. "I'm colonel of the Cole Light Horse," he said. "We're not quite up to battalion strength, as so many of our best and bravest have gone off to defend other parts of the South. But those of us left remained here to protect our country from Yankee incursions."

"Fascinating," Joseph said.

"We'd be honored if you would demonstrate for us some of the techniques of the European cavalry."

"The honor would be mine," Joseph said. He felt ignoble. These were charming people whom he would have treasured before the war. His actions were still honorable, but he couldn't prevent vague self-loathing from oppressing his spirit.

In the house, Joseph and Stumpf were assigned adjoining rooms on the upper floor, along with a personal slave-valet. It seemed that with their entry into the house, Stumpf's cough had grown worse. Joseph ordered the slave to fill a hot bath for Stumpf and made him soak in it after downing several whiskeys. He then put him to bed.

Joseph returned to his own room to find the slave had refilled the tub and was waiting to help him bathe.

"What's your name?" Joseph asked as the slave helped him remove his damp uniform.

"I'm Cedric, massa."

"Have you always been a slave?"

Joseph didn't see the look Cedric gave him. "Yes, massa. I was born here on this plantation, about same time as Massa Senator. His daddy gave me to him right then. Me and him were raised up side by side."

"I suppose you are a friend of Uncle Abe, aren't you now?"

"No, sir. I don't know no Uncle Abe. Is he a slave around here?"

Joseph was only slightly disappointed. After all, he couldn't expect every slave in the South to be a member of the Loyal League. He had met many slaves who seemed to be loyal to the South. This one had been born on this plantation. He and the senator probably had an unbreakable, lifelong bond. Well, Joseph would just go on trying the pass word. He pulled away from his introspection to realize that the slave, whom he could see in the full-length mirror, was looking at him in wonder. Cedric had just removed Joseph's shirt and was staring at his back. Then Joseph remembered.

"Yes," he said, "those are scars from a whip."

"Yes, massa. I know," Cedric said quietly.

"I was a slave once, Cedric."

"No, massa. No white man ever be a slave."

"I was."

Joseph stepped out of his underpants and into the hot tub. Cedric tenderly sponged his back.

"Massa?"

"Yes?"

"It not be good if you take your shirt off around them."

"Them? Who?"

"White folks."

§39

After a fitful night, Joseph woke as tired as he had been when he went to bed. He was surprised by Stumpf's absence, for Stumpf considered it his duty to wake Joseph. From the sun streaming in the window, Joseph calculated that he had overslept by at least two hours. A chill premonition swept over him. He leaped out of bed and without bothering to pull a robe over his nightshirt, raced into Stumpf's room. There he found Stumpf lying on the floor. Blood stained his face. Joseph rolled him onto his back. The old man's breathing was irregular and came in tortured gasps. Gently Joseph lifted him to the bed and poured some whiskey in his hand and patted Stumpf's face with it.

"Hans!" he said softly. There was no response. "Hans!" he said louder. "Hans!"

"Lordy, lordy, lordy." Cedric had entered at the sound of Joseph's voice.

Joseph turned to him. "Is there a doctor?"

"I'll fetch Senator Cole." He left the room.

Joseph continued his attempts to revive Stumpf. At last, in desperation, he said, "Sergeant–Major Stumpf, I order you to open your eyes immediately!"

"Ja, Herr Baron." The words were hardly more than a breath. Stumpf opened his eyes, but they were cloudy and dim.

A few moments later the senator strode in, followed by Cole and Cedric. After a quick look at Stumpf, the senator instructed Cole to fetch the doctor and Cedric to bring warm water.

"Have you seen this before?" he asked Joseph.

"No. What it is?"

"Looks like consumption. The doctor is fifteen miles away. If he's home, he should be here in an hour. In the meantime let's do what we can for the poor devil."

Cedric arrived with a basin of water and towels, and Joseph and the senator carefully bathed Stumpf's face and upper body. Cedric removed the bloody bedclothes and brought in fresh linen.

Stumpf's eyes regained a degree of comprehension. He whispered, *"Ich bitte sie vergeben mir, Herr Baron."*

In German, Joseph replied, "There's nothing to forgive, my old friend. You're sick and soon the doctor will be here and you'll get better."

Stumpf feebly shook his head and spoke haltingly. "I do not think so. My God! To die in bed! Joseph, my boy, I thought I would die in battle. At least on a horse…"

"You will not die. Not now. Not in bed. You cannot die in bed. Stumpf, you are a soldier. You will not die in bed." He felt tears coming and fought them off. Stumpf would never forgive him tears. "Sip some whisky." He held the tumbler to Stumpf's lips, and the soldier managed a small swallow, then a larger one, and then a bit more.

"Yes," he said in German. "That's better." His voice was stronger. "With the Herr Baron's permission, I will now sleep." He closed his eyes, and his breathing eased.

The senator went to the door and softly called for Cedric, who entered and, at a motion from his master took a chair and sat by Stumpf. The senator led Joseph back to his room. "Mind if I join you while you dress?"

"No, I'm glad for the company." Joseph, shaken, carefully played the cool aristocrat. "Do you think he is dying?" Keeping his whip-scarred back away from the senator, Joseph discreetly replaced his night shirt with a crisp white shirt for the morning.

"Hard to say," the Senator said. "Your sergeant is old, but he seems to have a strong will. Who knows? What was it he was saying to you?"

"He said he would not die in bed. He comes from generations of soldiers. He said he can only die on horseback in battle. I ordered him to live. The man never disobeys an order."

"I don't understand German, but did I hear your sergeant refer to you as baron?"

Joseph lied easily. "Before my father's death," he said, "it was baron. I was born with the titles to several small holdings. From the time that I was ten, Sergeant Stumpf was assigned to me by my father as my teacher in arms. I was Herr Baron until I succeeded to my father's title."

The senator nodded appreciatively. "I was given Cedric when I was born. Until we were ten we were inseparable friends."

"Until I became his commanding officer, Sergeant Stumpf was my teacher and my best friend. The day I was commissioned, he stopped calling me Joseph…."

"I was under the impression your Christian name was Friederich."

"It is," Joseph said. "It is the first of seven names before von Chernowitz. In the family I will always be 'Little Joseph.' Even Stumpf, for all his training, sometimes slips and calls me Joseph."

"Count, let us look in on him and then I suggest you join us for breakfast."

"Thank you, but I should sit with Sergeant Stumpf."

"Cedric is with him. And count, if you will forgive so personal a comment, you could use some strong coffee and hot food. With luck, the doctor will be here by the time we've finished our meal. You may then need all your strength."

The doctor did arrive while Joseph was eating. And, after examining Stumpf, he invited Joseph and the senator to join him by Stumpf's bed.

"Will he live?" Joseph asked.

"Can't say," the doctor said. "Won't give odds either. But I promise you this. If he doesn't do as I tell him he'll die, and soon. I don't speak German, and his English is minimal. Before I leave I'd be comforted if you'd translate my instructions for him."

"Of course."

The doctor then took a large brown bottle from his bag. "This bottle contains a particularly noxious medicine with which I have had some success. Sergeant Stumpf is to take two tablespoons of it every four hours, except if he is sleeping. Sleep is better than any medicine I have." He produced another bottle, this one blue. "Here's some tincture of laudanum. If he has trouble sleeping give him this. And keep the windows shut in this room, especially at night. Night air is the worst thing for him. And for heaven's sake, sir, no more baths."

The doctor took his leave. The Cole family returned to their morning routine and Joseph, his mind on Stumpf, found himself unable to fulfill the simplest of social obligations.

"Perhaps," the senator said, "you'd care to see the plantation?"

Joseph welcomed the distraction.

The senator and Cole first took Joseph to the riding stables, paddocks and barns. Then, as they surveyed the fields, the senator explained how the plantation's work was done: how mud was dredged from the river and spread on the fields, forty oxcart loads to the acre, and how the white cotton was separated from yellow or stained cotton, and twigs and leaves picked out. Each slave was expected to sort sixty pounds of cotton a day.

In the building containing the cotton gin, Joseph learned how seed was separated from the cotton, and how it took nineteen hundred pounds of field cotton to make a single five hundred pound bale. Beyond the gin were three new warehouses.

"They hold all of our last crop and those of my neighbors," the senator said. "One thousand bales of the best cotton in the world."

Cole jumped in. "Once the English navy smashes the Yankee blockade they'll be worth a king's ransom."

Joseph touched the side of a bale and found it to be as ungiving as an oak plank.

He toured the workshops where machinery was repaired by slaves and, most importantly, the seed house where over the years the senator had selected the seeds from each crop, constantly trying to improve the quality of his cotton.

"Here is the future of the South," the senator said, displaying the seed sacks. "Seeds worth more than gold. Perhaps more powerful than the mightiest cannon. These seeds will give us our independence from the Yankee tyrants."

Joseph was taken to see two gigantic ice cellars sunk into the earth and filled with ice brought from the northern winters and packed in sawdust to last a year. Root cellars with fruit and vegetables were dug between the ice cellars, along with other cellars for preserves and canned goods.

The slave quarters startled Joseph. Each slave cottage, about fourteen by sixteen feet, was freshly whitewashed and neatly trimmed. Joseph thought many Yankee working men or slum dwellers would have been happy to live in such pretty little houses. There were so many they constituted a village.

The cotton fields ran right up to the slave doors, just as they did to the plantation house. The only places where land wasn't used to grow cotton were a few fields cultivated in the best grass for the thoroughbreds—the only green patches in fifteen hundred acres of mucked fields.

That evening after they had ridden back to the house, Joseph found Stumpf looking somewhat better. He was sitting up in bed while Cedric was serving him some hot soup.

"When do we see the herr senator's cavalry?" Stumpf asked.

"Tomorrow," Joseph said. "They've already been summoned. But you're going to stay in bed. I need you, Hans. You're of no value to our work if you remain sick. It is the obligation of the soldier to take care of himself so that he can perform his duty. Is that clear?"

"But to ruin the herr senator's cavalry..."

"I shall tend to that. Any suggestions?"

Stumpf shook his head. "First I must see them."

"I'll see them and tell you about them."

After dinner, as the cigars were lit and the port handed around, the talk was of the war. Union victories in the Cumberland and at Port Royal were considered anomalies. Lincoln and McClellan were ridiculed over Lincoln's General War Order Number One ordering an invasion of the South.

"Please, dear God, let them come," Cole said. He turned to Joseph. "Count, you've seen the Yankee cavalry. Tell the others what you've so often told me."

Joseph, wearing his white dress uniform, removed his monocle and looked about the room. "There's no comparison," he said. "The Yankees don't possess a match for the horses I have seen here. Their men cannot ride. They're farmers used to walking behind horses, not sitting on them. I predict that in any clash between the two cavalries, the Yankees shall be slaughtered."

"Count," the senator asked, "what do the European cavalry prefer in close fighting: the pistol or the saber?"

"The pistol," Joseph lied. "After all gentlemen, we live in modern times. The revolver with its six shots makes the saber a decorative relic of a time past. The Yankees, having no really experienced cavalry officers, still cling to the saber. This is a disastrous error." He smiled genially. "I am given to understand from Lieutenant Cole that all southerners are born on a horse and with a gun in hand."

"Well, sir," the senator said. "You'll be the judge of that tomorrow. The Cole Light Horse will be here promptly at ten and we'll show you our stuff."

The talk then turned to the future. As soon as the Yankees were whipped, the South would seize Cuba and then Mexico, and on down the isthmus to the continent of South America until the Confederacy, a vast slave empire, would be larger and more powerful than the old Union.

Before retiring Joseph looked in on Stumpf who slept while Cedric sat in a chair beside him. Joseph wondered if the slave ever slept.

In the morning Stumpf was bringing up less blood than the day before. He ate a better breakfast and seemed significantly stronger. Joseph told him his plans. "Have you ever seen a man who could get off accurate pistol shots on a charge in close fighting?"

"You. Perhaps a few, with luck."

"Why? You know I am an excellent shot, even at a gallop."

"Because, Herr Baron," Stumpf spoke with difficulty. "Until you know what it is to charge over uneven ground with the enemy shooting at you...a thousand horses coming to kill you, the noise, my God, the noise! Men screaming. Horses screaming. Even you will not shoot with accuracy. The saber is the only way for close fighting." It was the most he had spoken since his collapse and it exhausted him. Stumpf fell back on his pillow and closed his eyes.

One hundred and sixty-eight riders were barely enough to be called a battalion, but the Cole Light Horse were indeed handsome. They trotted up the drive in three squadrons, each of two companies, which meant that there were only twenty-eight men to a company. This wasn't even platoon size. But there were plenty of flags: the Georgia state flag, the Stars and Bars, a battalion battle-flag, three squadron guidons, and six company guidons.

Joseph liked the Cole Light Horse uniform: gray hussar-style jackets with black braiding and brass buttons, white cross belts over the left shoulders, powder blue trousers tucked into above-the-knee cavalier boots, and light gray hats with large white plumes on the broad right brim.

Joseph was pleased to see that while the men's horsemanship was superb, they knew little or nothing about formal drill. When they had completed their demonstration, Joseph delivered a lecture on the saber's obsolescence and the power of the pistol.

Earlier at Joseph's direction the senator had his slaves set up a pistol course. Hay bales with paper targets affixed to them had been arranged at varying heights and distances, along with jumps of fence rails ranging from two to five feet.

Joseph demonstrated the art of cavalry marksmanship, shooting at his targets from a dead run, from the apex of jumps, while initiating a jump, and while landing after a jump. He rode and fired using the traditional Hungarian hussar tactic of crouching on one stirrup, his horse between him and the target. His finale consisted of riding the whole course in reverse order, reins in his teeth, and accurately firing pistols from each hand.

The Cole Light Horse cheered and threw their hats in the air.

That evening Mrs. Cole went down to the dock in her grand brougham to meet a guest arriving by steamboat. Joseph watched from the verandah as the guest entered the carriage. She seemed familiar. He couldn't see her face, but something about the way she moved reminded him of the past.

"Mother's favorite cousin," Cole said to Joseph. "The most charming woman in the South. We are always grateful when Cousin Amalee comes visiting...."

Amalee! Joseph thought. The lady coming toward them was Amalee Fitzhugh-Reid! Would she recognize him? It had been six years. But now he was posing as an Austrian count, with a slight German accent.

The carriage pulled up to the verandah and the gentlemen all rose to their feet. Amalee Fitzhugh-Reid seemed absolutely unchanged. She had the same strong face, deep dark eyes and the warm laughter. Joseph instinctively put his monocle in his eye. No, he thought. He had affected the monocle on the ship. He let it drop into his hand and hid it in his pocket.

When presented to Joseph, Amalee curtsied and smiled without a sign of recognition. She passed on to the other guests, renewing old acquaintances and making small talk until she was shown to her room to freshen up.

Joseph also went upstairs to talk with Stumpf. "It can only be a matter of time," he said. "She'll recognize me. I can say von Ritter is my dear cousin, but the suspicion will be there. These people shoot strangers on suspicion."

"In this I cannot help," Stumpf said. "This is thinking. You must think. I will follow orders."

"Tomorrow I'll tell Cole that I am worried about you. It's too cold and wet here. In my country when one has the consumption, one goes to the high mountains. I'll say I have to take you to the Alps! We are leaving America."

At dinner Amalee seemed particularly attracted to him, even though he was careful not to wear a uniform, or pay attention to her. What was that look in her eyes? Did she recognize him? But Amalee talked only of her husband Major Ambrose Fitzhugh-Reid, her friends and her home.

Then as he was preparing for bed, Joseph realized that she never once asked him questions about his castle in Austria, or even if he were married or free to court a suitable southern belle—all the questions that every other woman he met in the South had asked. Why? Once, when he had turned to hold her in his peripheral vision, he saw her staring at him. She sensed his slight movement and quickly averted her eyes. Before retiring Joseph checked both pistols and unsheathed his saber, putting it by his bed. He slept fitfully.

Sometime after midnight he heard a noise. His door was silently opening. He put his hands on his pistols.

"Massa Count?" Cedric whispered softly.

"Is it Stumpf? I'll come immediately."

"No. It ain't. They are coming for you." The door was shut but he still whispered. "I heard them. Miz Amalee, she said you're a Yankee spy. She say she knew you on some boat. And she told how she saves Yankee newspapers what write about you, about how you are a Jew man and you're married to a rich Jew lady, about how you are famous and when the war come how you made a Yankee army up there. But young Massa, he said he don't believe you are a spy and she was mistaken. But she said she knows she's right and they best shoot you right away. And Massa Senator, he said in the morning young Massa is to ride and get the sheriff and when the sheriff come, they're going to ask you are you a spy."

"Why are you telling me this?"

"Because I know how come your back's been whipped."

"What do you know?"

"Day told it in the church. The Jews been slaves in Egyptland."

§40

JOSEPH SAT FOR A MINUTE, CONSIDERING HIS OPTIONS. HE COULD steal two horses and ride away. But where would he go? Horses were easily tracked. Besides, Stumpf was in no condition to sit a horse, let alone ride. They must get to Savannah and the livery stable where the groom would help. But how to get Stumpf to Savannah? If he left him behind the Coles would kill him.

Joseph turned to Cedric. "Is there a small boat?"

"Yes. In the boathouse next to the landing."

Joseph nodded. "Come with me."

They slipped out of his room and quietly moved to Stumpf's. Stumpf woke with Joseph's touch. Quickly the situation was explained.

"Go now," Stumpf said. "You cannot escape with me along."

"Cedric will help you shave off your mustache," Joseph said. "He'll help you dress. We'll wear civilian clothes. I'll shave my beard and join you in ten minutes."

When Joseph reappeared he was clean-shaven, in civilian clothes and armed with a revolver in a holster, the derringer in his waistband, and his nine-inch knife in his boot. Stumpf too had shaved and dressed, and was now lying on the bed with his eyes closed. Joseph touched him, and Stumpf struggled to his feet. Cedric went to the door, checked the hall and signaled that it was clear.

Once outside the room, Cedric led them to the end of the hall and the service stairs to the back door. As they descended the narrow staircase Joseph knew Stumpf was using the last of his strength. Joseph wasn't sure he could carry him to the boat landing.

Think! Joseph ordered himself. Cedric couldn't help carry Stumpf, for the slave was small and frightened. But Cedric could steady Stumpf while Joseph moved him to an over-the-shoulder carry. He would just have to have the strength to make it down to the boat landing.

Cedric opened the back door. Joseph was dragging Stumpf through it when four hands reached out of the dark and grabbed Stumpf. Two field slaves silently lifted Stumpf between them.

A third materialized next to Joseph. "Where we going, boss?"

"The boathouse," Joseph said. He turned to Cedric who was backing through the door. "God bless you, Cedric," he whispered.

Cedric's whisper came through the dark doorway. "And the Lord said, 'I will deliver you from slavery.' Day don't say that in church, but it's in the book." And he was gone.

The boathouse seemed darker than the night. The leader of the field hands lit a stub of a candle, whereupon Joseph saw four boats: a small red sailboat, an elegantly varnished lapstrake rowboat with a canopy, and two flat-bottomed work boats. The field hands carefully laid Stumpf in the bottom of one of the work boats.

The slave next to Joseph whispered, "This the best one. It slip in the shallows. Come dawn, you got to hide in the weeds. Go just by night. Current do most of the work."

"Thank you." Joseph stepped into the boat.

Just as they pushed him off, one of the slaves asked. "When Mars' Lincoln come free the slaves?"

"Soon," Joseph answered.

"We waiting."

The new moon gave no light but the stars were bright enough to define the river from its banks. Joseph felt the current take hold and experimented with rowing, exerting himself only to keep the boat as much in the center of the channel as possible.

From the sound of Stumpf's breathing Joseph could tell he was asleep. Good, he thought, let him gather strength.

They had been traveling for three hours when the first dim glow of dawn appeared above the trees. Joseph had no idea what that meant in miles or distance from Rotherwood. During the night he thought they had passed two plantations, but he wasn't sure. With luck their absence wouldn't be discovered for another two or three hours. When there was enough light to make out the foliage along the river bank, Joseph looked for a place to hide.

As the boat pulled toward the shore the current lessened, and while it was drifting Joseph found ample time to study the landscape. The sun began to make a pale, shrouded appearance. Joseph spotted a low hummock covered with dry brambles and eased the boat behind it. A small stream emerged into the river from the weed-choked embankment. Beyond the tall weeds was a tangle of untended forest. The stream, barely wider than the boat, shallowed quickly. Joseph pulled off his boots and stockings and eased himself over the side. Now the boat floated in the stream, its keel leaving a faint line in the mud below. The chill water shocked Joseph from his fatigue. His feet sank to his ankles in mud and he dragged the boat away from the river and into the woods. Joseph tied the rope to a tree and, being a good soldier, closed his eyes to get what sleep he could.

After having seen Joseph off, the field slaves left the boathouse and went directly to the stables. Quietly saddling two of the senator's best horses, they then led them upriver for a few miles. Next, putting raw pepper under their tails, they sent the horses running along a road leading away from the river.

In the morning Cedric reported to his master that their two guests had disappeared during the night. At about the same time the head slave-groom came running in from the stable to report that two horses and saddles were missing.

It took a while for the uproar to be organized into action. Then the stolen horses' tracks were found moving across the mucked fields and heading up the river road. The senator and Cole led a force in pursuit, and others were dispatched to alert neighbors and summon the Cole Light Horse.

By the time the riderless horses were captured, the slaves had bought Joseph and Stumpf the entire day.

Overcast weather and occasional rain kept them wet and cold. Stumpf shivered in his sleep. Joseph tried to warm him with his own body, but even in his half-sleep Stumpf fought him off. When Stumpf did wake, he spit more blood.

In the late afternoon, as the gray day began to lose its light, Joseph heard the beating of a paddle wheel. He soon heard voices too. He crouched and made his way to a spot from where he could see the river. The *Rowena* passed close to the embankment. The senator's voice rose above the rest. "A Company, disembark at Johnson's landing. B Company, the opposite side of the river. Captains Maclean and Duncan, you work your way back toward Rotherwood till you join up with the First Squadron."

The senator was doing what Joseph realized he too would have done. Once the missing rowboat had been discovered, the rebels would figure out that he and Stumpf would have to hole up during the daylight hours. With six companies of men scouring both shores, he and Stumpf would either be discovered or forced onto the river where the *Rowena* would intercept them.

The men were lighting torches on the boat. Then four big iron baskets blazing with pitch pine and hanging from long outriggers were swung fore and aft, illuminating the river from bank to bank.

Joseph worked his way back to the rowboat. Stumpf, awake, had his pistol in hand. "They know we're on the river," Joseph said, "so we must leave. If there's a Johnson's landing it must mean there's also a Johnson plantation. If I can, I'll steal a buggy or a wagon and we'll get to Savannah by road. If I can't, I'll set fire to the barns and the house. They'll have to come to the aid of the Johnsons and we'll try the river again. Perhaps there are Johnson slaves who can help us."

"Leave me," Stumpf said. Joseph ignored him and started across the stream, then he paused and turned back to look at Stumpf. The sergeant-major looked old and frail.

"I'll be back before dawn," Joseph said.

Less than twenty-five feet away the brush thinned and Joseph saw a narrow country road and, beyond that, open fields. In the distance were the lights of the plantation house and the torches of the Cole Light Horse. There was no cover between him and the plantation buildings.

The torches formed into a line of twos and started toward him. About fifty yards away they approached a brushy area. Ten men from the first rank dismounted, five used their sabers, methodically slashing their way through the brush, while behind them five more men kept their pistols at the ready. The remaining ten held their horses and, lining the road at intervals, leveled carbines at the brush.

Joseph remained still for as long as he could. The first brushy area was now cleared and the rebels headed in Joseph's direction. He could hear them talking, calling to him and Stumpf.

"Hey Yankees, come on out. We're gonna get you. We're real good at huntin' runaways. Y'all are just white niggers. Come on out, Yankees." Then, above the other voices, Joseph heard a familiar voice.

"Von Ritter, listen to me." It was Cole. "Surrender and you'll be safe. You'll go to prison but you won't be harmed. If you fire on us, you'll die."

They were getting closer to Joseph's cover. He changed plans. He couldn't cross the open fields to the plantation without being spotted, so Joseph made his way back to Stumpf.

The old man's breathing was worse. Bloody foam bubbled at the corners of his mouth. "You cannot save me. You must get back to the army." Joseph knew Stumpf was right. But the knowledge was unbearable. "This is war," Stumpf said. "War is no mercy. Go."

"No!" Joseph could hear the voices of the trackers getting closer. He had to make a decision. Stumpf was too weak to climb out of the boat. Joseph untied the rope and pulled the boat into the stream. There he towed it out into deep water and, when his feet began to float off the bottom, he attempted to swim out into the current. He didn't know how to swim but kept himself afloat by holding the rope.

Clumsily, he tried kicking his feet and moving his free arm like an oar. With a huge effort he managed to move the boat toward the center of the channel. The current caught it and the boat surged past him with such force that Joseph lost hold of the rope and tumbled under the surface of the river. With his first inhalation of water, Joseph coughed. He held his breath and, willing his body to relax, floated to the surface. He sucked in a lung full of air and held his breath again. This time when he started to sink he tried moving his hands up and down with force on the downward movement. Next he changed the forceful push of his hands to work like oars again. Slowly and erratically they propelled him through the water.

He heard voices. "Something's out there! You hear that splashing?"

He looked around and saw torches ten yards upstream. The current had carried him downstream from the searchers. He filled his lungs, sank until his feet touched bottom, and then propelled himself in the direction of the bank. This time, when he rose to the surface, it was inches from his eyes. He stood breathing carefully until he was rested. The torches were further upstream now, and the voices fainter.

Joseph worked his way along the shore, crouching as the river shallowed to keep just his nose above the surface. He pulled himself among the water plants and raised his eyes above the bank. He saw at least twenty torches a half a mile above him. He hauled himself out and lay quietly for a long time.

Downriver the sky suddenly exploded in red. It was a rocket. What did it mean? He waited. He heard hoofbeats from upriver. Twenty cavalrymen came pounding down the road past him. Joseph watched as they arrived at the plantation and rode to the boat landing. Then the *Rowena* arrived. Joseph could just make out the smokestack and patches of its illuminated superstructure through the trees around the landing.

The night was now dark enough for him to get to his feet. He moved toward his enemies as fast as his exhausted body would allow. By Johnson's landing a manicured copse of trees gave him ample cover. Joseph worked his way from tree to tree until, close to the steamer, he climbed one. On board the *Rowena* the men were taking a break. Slaves served food and hot drinks. The outriggers holding the flaming iron baskets had been swung inboard, the baskets extinguished and removed to be refilled with pitch. But something was hanging from one of the outriggers—Joseph couldn't quite make out what it was. Then the current shifted the boat slightly and the object hanging from the outrigger swung into view. It was Stumpf.

Joseph's mind froze his emotions before they could erupt and incapacitate him. How could the senator permit his men to hang Stumpf? Everyone knew that Stumpf was dying. Surely the honor these southerners spoke of so fervently should have prevented this.

What had Stumpf said to him? "This is war. No mercy." Joseph wondered where had he heard that before? Oh yes, Brannagan.

"Amalek." He spoke the word aloud. He looked up to see if the revelers on the boat had heard it too. They hadn't. Amalek? Why, he wondered, had he said that? Then he thought of words he hadn't read in many years. The words were spoken by the Jewish God to Samuel, who told them to Saul. "Now go attack Amalek, and proscribe all that belongs to him. Spare no one, but kill alike men and women, infants and sucklings, oxen and sheep, camels and asses."

He heard a blast from the steamboat whistle. Joseph looked up. He didn't know how much time had passed. The traitor cavalry, torches lit, were mounted and starting downriver. The steamboat separated from the dock and came toward Joseph, and Stumpf's body swung in the wind. Joseph stared at the gyrating figure until the boat passed the apex of its turn and blocked it from view.

After a long time had passed he could no longer hear the boat or the soldiers. The lights at the plantation house had been extinguished.

Joseph climbed down from his tree and walked toward the plantation outbuildings. He didn't crouch or try to conceal himself. The fields were dark with river muck. The night was pitch black. Joseph found his way to the barn by smell. The tack room was where he thought it might be. He took a bridle and saddle. A horse nickered and Joseph quietly calmed it. In the dark he went from stall to stall, examining the animals by touch. There were five. Joseph saddled the horse that felt best and quietly led him out of the barn and across the fields to the river road. There he mounted and headed upriver. The distance traversed in three hours on the river was retraced by one fast horse in less than an hour.

Only a few lights shone in the Coles' plantation house. Joseph silently opened doors at both ends of the big warehouses. He climbed to the tops of the cotton bales and levered shingles out of the roofs of the buildings, then splashed lamp oil on the cotton nearest the open doors and set fire to all three warehouses.

Next he ran to the seed house. The senator had called his seed more valuable than gold. "The future of the South," he had said. Joseph carefully poured lamp oil on the sacks of dry seed, sloshed it over the dry wooden walls, and lit them.

He dashed for one of the root cellars and entered just as the alarm was raised. But only one white overseer was present to command the blacks, and one hated man could not marshal 135 reluctant slaves in such a catastrophic emergency.

Joseph opened the root cellar door slightly and looked out. Slaves were running everywhere. The women from the house, Mrs. Cole, her three young daughters, Amalee and the other female guests, tried to assist but they only added to the confusion.

Joseph left the cellar and moved from flickering shadow to shadow until he entered the great house. He carefully opened all of the ground floor doors, propping Louis Quinze chairs against them to keep them ajar. Then going upstairs he entered his former room. His clothes were still in the armoire. Joseph changed into dry, clean clothes. He rejected his sabers. Instead, he went to Stumpf's room where he found Stumpf's saber and hung it from a belt around his coat.

"What you doing here?" It was Cedric.

"What did God do to Pharaoh when Pharaoh would not let the people go?" Joseph asked.

"He give them the ten plagues."

"Leave this house. Leave it now!"

Cedric turned and ran.

Joseph opened the upstairs windows to guarantee a good draft. Then, taking lamps from tables and wall sconces, he poured whale oil everywhere. Such elegant furniture and such fine silk draperies, he thought. Forgive me Karl, but in Amalek's house your painting is ugly. Joseph set fire to each of the ends of the T-shaped house. In five minutes the heat-induced draft drew the flames to the great center hall. In ten minutes the entire lower floor of Rotherwood was engulfed.

The *Rowena* steamed back at full speed and the Cole Light Horse dashed from the boat to help save what could be saved.

Joseph spotted his target in the confusion. He stepped from the cellar and waited for his moment. Cole had gathered a party of slaves and ran to the flaming house. Joseph followed, pushed his way through the slaves, and grabbed Cole by the shoulder and spun him around. Cole, taken by surprise, didn't act quickly enough. Joseph slashed Cole's throat with one quick movement of his nine-inch blade.

"No mercy," he said. Cole fell to the ground and died. The slaves quietly drifted away.

Joseph ran to his saddled horse, mounted, and rode across the fields to the boat landing. There was no crew aboard the steamboat—they had all gone to battle the fires. Joseph gently lowered Stumpf's body into his arms.

Lifting the saber from his belt, Joseph placed it in his friend's dead hand. He then set fire to the steamboat. Stepping onto the dock, he cut the mooring lines and the boat drifted out into the current, floating downriver until it went aground on the opposite shore. There it burnt to the waterline.

§41

JOSEPH GALLOPED UP TO EACH NEW PLANTATION ON HIS ESCAPE route and introduced himself as Captain Wade McVickker of Charleston. He told of the slave insurrection at Rotherwood and summoned every able-bodied man to ride to the rescue at once. Changing horses, he then rode off in the opposite direction. With the *Rowena* destroyed, the fastest means of communication along the river was via horse.

After arriving in Savannah, Joseph hid until midnight, when he went to the livery stable, where he found the same groom. Of all the Savannah cousins staying at Rotherwood, Joseph calculated that a captain in the Savannah Volunteer Artillery was closest to his own size and shape. After resting for two hours in the livery stable hay loft, Joseph went to the artillery captain's house and stole two of the four uniforms hanging in the armoire. He also took shirts, underwear, stockings, handkerchiefs, a travel bag and a good deal of money. Before leaving he opened a few upper windows and once again poured lamp oil on the lower floor. He then set it afire.

The slave-groom took Joseph to an unoccupied shack behind a tannery where Joseph changed into his uniform and waited until the train for Charleston arrived. He asked the slave to fetch him paper, pen and ink. When they arrived Joseph wrote out orders calling him to duty with the Army of Northern Virginia. He signed them with the name of a colonel invented for the purpose. But at the train no one even asked for his orders. The trip was pleasant, and some of the passengers told him about the slave uprising at Rotherwood caused by Yankee instigators. One had been hanged. The other was still at large.

Joseph arrived in Charleston six hours before the train to Wilmington via Florence. During the wait he strolled about the city, contemplating how to burn it. The great houses along the harbor, the houses that were the very cradle of secession, were too far apart to be sure of one passing the fire to the others unless the wind were exactly right. He wondered if General Beauregard was still in command in Charleston. He might find him and kill him. Then, while arguing the pros and cons, a better idea came to him. He should go to Richmond and cut off the head of Amalek by killing Jefferson Davis.

Once in Richmond he hailed a cab and drove to Miss Van Lew's house. Uncle Tiberius answered the door. He didn't recognize Joseph until he said, "I suppose you are a friend to Uncle Abe, aren't you now."

Miss Van Lew was startled by Joseph's condition. With maternal gentleness, she gave Joseph sixteen drops of laudanum. He slept for eighteen hours.

The next morning Uncle Tiberius reported to Miss Van Lew that Joseph was awake and hungry. When she went in to see him, she saw the madness fading. Now Joseph's eyes seemed merely tired.

"Did I speak of assassinating Jeff Davis?"

"You did."

"Miss Van Lew, I have been in a waking nightmare."

"Would you tell me what can you remember?"

He looked away from her. The sun was streaming in the window. "Everything. It was a game. Handsome uniforms, glorious horses, gaiety. I really liked Cole. He was a wonderful young man. I thought of myself when I was that age. A boy in a uniform playing soldier."

His eyes filled with tears, "Do you know that Amalee Fitzhugh-Reid is my dear friend? She wanted them to hang me. They hanged Hans. They hanged him and I killed Cole. Once, years ago, I killed a man, a criminal who was about to murder my wife. It never bothered me. But Cole? A nice young man playing at war."

"It is war," she said.

"I didn't understand. I thought I did, but I didn't."

"Last night you spoke of Amalek," Miss Van Lew said. "When you retired, I went to the Bible and read First Samuel. I thought a great deal about God's instruction to Saul to destroy all of Amalek, even the women and babies and all the animals. Joseph, did you kill the women and the babies and all the animals?"

"No."

"Why?"

"I couldn't."

"Did you consider that you were disobeying a command given you by God?"

"No." He thought for a while. "I'm not a religious man. At least not in a way other people are."

She quietly waited.

He said, "I killed that man who was about to kill my wife and me. I've never regretted it. The memory of the moment my bullet entered his brain has always stayed with me. There was a look of surprise on his face. He was astonished he was being killed. So was Cole. Cole was amazed he was dying. What do you think that means? Do we all think we are immortal? The Bible says we're made in God's image. Do we really believe that, like God, we are immortal? Or is it that some part of us is immortal?

"You asked if I am a religious man. That means, do I believe in God? I am a Jew. I am supposed to believe in the One God. Do you believe in the One God?"

"I do." She was becoming uncomfortable.

"I don't. Not the way Jews do. Or Christians. Not the way you do. If there is the One God—you know, the God that sees the fall of the sparrow—then that God is also supposed to suffer with each human death. When I killed, the astonishment in the men's eyes, was that the immortal God in them? Us? The immortal God was amazed at His little death. Most likely not. If there were such a God, we wouldn't have so much killing." He again sat quietly looking at the sunny window.

"And Amalek?" Miss Van Lew asked.

Joseph turned to her. "Have you read Charles Darwin?"

"No. We are told that his theories are far from Christian. I'm not even sure what his theories are, beyond saying that instead of being descended from Adam and Eve, we are the children of monkeys."

"My wife and I subscribe to Mr. Darwin's theory of evolution." His voice gained some strength. "In substance that theory says nature has a process of natural selection. Natural selection means that species constantly breed the next generations from the strongest stock, passing along to the next generations those physical and mental attributes that provide the greatest chance for that species to thrive. Man is descended from creatures that may have been apelike, but over thousands of years, through natural selection, we have evolved into what we now are. And what are we? The only species that can think. The only species that can conceive of creation—of gods. That's no accident. Thousands of years from now we'll be quite different. More highly evolved."

"Oh, dear."

"None of this is incompatible with the Bible or the concept of God or gods. Why can't the theory of evolution be part of God's creation, just like the Ten Commandments? What if it's God who has placed all mankind on an evolutionary journey that will eventually unite us with whatever He is? What if that is it?"

Joseph rose from the bed, pulled a blanket around his body, and began to pace. Each time he passed the sun's rays pouring in the window, he paused for its warmth. "You asked me about Amalek. This is proof of what I'm telling you. In the time of Saul, God saw that the Amalekites were the wrong strain. Wrong for evolution. Amalek could not advance man up the evolutionary ladder. Amalek would, in fact, retard mankind. So He told Saul to destroy them all. Perhaps God could have done it Himself, like the flood, but He needed us to do it so we would know what was done to make our efforts part of our evolution. The specific commands to destroy their animals were to erase even their memory from mankind. If the Jews had taken the animals, they would have always had reminders of the former owners. Primitive thinking. But the whole world was primitive then. This war, too, has to do with evolution. Perhaps all wars. Perhaps war is a tool of evolution. That's why I thought of Amalek.

"Slavery is an antediluvian throwback. We know from Exodus that it's morally wrong. But look what it's done to the South. It has created a whole class of people so corrupted by indolence and infected with the evil, they would destroy America—the New Jerusalem—to continue the evil. The rebels must be defeated not to save the Union but to save the evolutionary step upward that the Union is. You are a Christian?"

"Yes."

"Well, you Christians believe in the coming of the Messiah—we'll leave out the debate as to whether or not He has come once already—do you not?"

"Of course we do."

"We Jews and you Christians have that in common. We believe in the coming of the Messiah. But how? How will the Messiah come? Will the Messiah be a man or a woman? Will the Messiah be white or black? A Chinese sage? What if the Messiah is us? What if the ultimate end of evolution is man evolving into Messiah?"

"I beg your pardon?" Her discomfort grew with each of his words.

"The Declaration of Independence and the Constitution say that all humans have a natural right to become better than they might have been in the old countries. The reason for the Union is to have the strength to protect our precious documents—not the papers but the ideas—from the kings and emperors of the old countries. You know they look at this civil war as proof of the failure of our Democracy. Proof that the common man cannot rule himself. If the rebels triumph and America is destroyed, the coming of the Messiah will be delayed for as long as it takes for some new America to evolve. It could be hundreds of years. So, you see, the Confederacy is Amalek. It and all its works, and all memory of it, must be wiped out."

"Mr. von Ritter, you frighten me. You would destroy the South to save the Union. I would preserve the Union to save the South."

"I think I was insane when I burned Rotherwood. But while I was doing it I understood that the South can't be saved until all the wealth, all the power and all the privilege earned by the sweat of three hundred years of slavery is wiped away."

"You would impoverish the South?"

"Yes, ma'am."

"Destroy its cities?"

"Yes, ma'am."

"You would burn all of the South?"

"All but the possessions of those who never owned slaves."

"Then you place me in an impossible position, sir. I agree that slavery must be abolished. But I love my South, and I won't have such destruction as you envision descend upon her. I cannot have you under my roof. After dark, someone will come here to conduct you back across the Potomac. I shall protect you till they come. However, I do not wish to see you again."

She got up. "I shall go across the street to my church," she said. "There I shall pray to God that you never have your way." She paused in the doorway. "I once heard a man speak," she said. "He frightened me. I have not been so frightened till now. You speak just like that man. His name was John Brown."

§42

THE TRAIN FROM PHILADELPHIA PULLED INTO THE FREEHOLD
Station just at noon. The only passenger, Joseph, descended from
the cars and stood still for a moment. All was as he had left it. Fuzzy
buds softened the trees, and yellow forsythia bloomed in the front
yards. The windows in the shingled church across the street were
open and he could hear the choir practice. An empty farm wagon
rattled up Main Street. Two little boys were being chased by a fat
puppy past Lopatin's Dry Goods store.

He was home. Now he would fix everything. He'd already
decided what he would say. Once he finished, Fannie would fall into
his arms and all would be as it once had been. The spring would
be a new beginning. They would all go on picnics. He would teach
his oldest son to ride, and make up stories for the younger children.
It would be as he and Fannie had once dreamed.

When he was rested he would go back to the war. Only this time
it would be a clean war. Man against man. Cavalry against cavalry.
General McClellan had ordered him to rest and so he would. He
closed his eyes and could feel Fannie's arms and smell her hair.

"Good to see you home, major. Hear you been out west."

Startled, Joseph turned to Mr. Ebberson, the stationmaster,
standing next to him. "Yes," Joseph said. "Did my telegram arrive?"

"Yup. Sam ran it out to your place two days ago."

Joseph walked down Main Street. People greeted him and he
returned their kindness. But for his uniform, he was in the town as
he always had been, as if he had not already committed arson and
murder.

Mrs. Conover, the housekeeper, was waiting on the porch of
Liberty Hall. "Welcome back, Major von Ritter."

"Thank you, Mrs. Conover. Where is Mrs. von Ritter?"

"I thought you knew. Mrs. von Ritter is not here. She and the
children and the nannies have been at Mr. Loeb's house in New
York City these past five weeks."

When Hanschen saw Joseph standing in her drawing room, she burst into tears. "She's gone," Hanschen said. "With the children she is gone."

Baron Otto von Exing roared with laughter. As one of the many foreign adventurers who had come to the latest war, he was now a captain in the Confederate cavalry. He waved a Richmond paper. "Von Ritter? Baron von Ritter? Gentlemen, he is neither a 'von' nor a baron, your Yankee spy." His laughter turned ugly.

"He is a filthy Jew. I know this little Jewpig. Gershomsohn. And this Jewpig posed as von Chernowitz and you believed him?" He laughed again. "You! Tavern keeper. More drinks for everyone. I pay. Now. *Schnell!*" He snapped his fingers.

Collie Buford, the bartender at the taproom of the Fredericksburg Inn, wasn't amused. He wouldn't take a command like that from Jeff Davis, let alone some loudmouth Dutchman.

"Baron," said a cavalry major who had placed himself between von Exing and Buford, now reaching for an ax handle. "We're all glad to have you join our regiment. Being a stranger to our country, I guess you might not be up on our customs. I do hope you'll forgive me if I point out to you that we never use that tone of voice to a white man."

The laughter left von Exing. "Zo?"

"You see, baron," said the major, "here in America, all white men are equal. And most don't take too kindly to being shouted at. You'll find that especially true with the enlisted men."

Von Exing was amazed. "*Ja?* Naturally this I have heard, but until this moment—I swear, gentlemen—until this moment, I could not believe this was actually true." He looked at Collie Buford. "This applies even to servants?"

"Who you callin' a servant?" Collie Buford had now been joined by two other employees.

The major smiled at them. "Foreigner, boys. Got his English all mixed up. Didn't you, baron?" His eyes were hard and direct. "Big mistake, baron, wasn't it? Got your English all mixed up? Why don't you just say 'beg pardon' to these boys?"

When the major's meaning finally penetrated, von Exing was flabbergasted. "*Aber unglaublich!* You wish *me*, to these..."

"Americans. Confederate citizens," the major interjected. "You are quite right, captain. It is my wish that you apologize immediately."

Von Exing, too much the soldier not to understand that a wish from a superior officer was indeed a command, was caught in one of the more difficult moments of his military career. Except in a moment of nightmare past—and for that the Jew would pay—he had never apologized to an inferior. A tense and long moment followed while he attempted to think of the right words.

Behind the bar three hands gripped two ax handles and a bung-starter. The other officers unostentatiously made room for what might follow.

"You! Tavern keepers!" von Exing bellowed. "In the custom of your country I apologize! Good? Good. Now, immediately you will serve for everybody whiskey. *Schnell!*" He snapped his fingers.

Three wiry Virginians jumped over the bar at the big baron. Von Exing caught the first two with each of his huge fists in mid-air. They were unconscious and bleeding before they hit the sawdust. The third momentarily landed on his feet. As he swung his ax handle von Exing stepped aside and then, gracefully as a circus performer, lifted him over his head. He was about to throw him over the bar when a group of officers interposed their bodies between the endangered bottles of the back bar and von Exing.

"The whiskey!" they shouted.

Von Exing looked, saw what he was about to do, and gently placed the trembling bartender on his feet. "Now," he said it benevolently. "You bring whiskey for everybody."

The man stood transfixed.

"*Schnell!*" von Exing snapped his fingers. The man scurried behind the bar to set up the drinks.

One Sunday after church services for the Confederate forces on the Rappahannock, von Exing was approached by another officer.

"Captain von Exing, I am Captain Hamilton Cole of Charleston, South Carolina." After they saluted, Captain Cole continued, "I was most interested to hear that you had some knowledge of this spy, Von Ritter. You knew him?"

"A filthy Jewpig. Never a hussar even—a groom. Why do you ask this?"

"I have had the occasion to hunt with him during his charade as Count von Chernowitz. He certainly is an excellent horseman."

"A groom's familiarity with horses. Jews cannot ride."

"It was my cousin's plantation that this spy put to the torch. My young cousin, Leander Cole, was murdered during that affair. Although there are those that consider spying an honorable endeavor in war, we Coles do not. If you will forgive me, I couldn't help but feel from the things you said that your quarrel with this von Ritter is somewhat personal?"

"And if it is?"

"Then sir, it may be that you and the Coles have a mutual interest in seeing to this Israelite."

"Zo?"

"If it meets with your approval, I shall write to my cousin Senator Cole and invite him to our encampment."

"I should be delighted to meet the Herr Senator," von Exing said.

New York
March 15, 1862

My dear husband,

I call you dear because you are and always shall be dear to me. In some gentler way I shall always love you. But Joseph, how it pains me to pen these words for I know they shall grievously wound you, but write them I must. When you have read them I know you shall hate me. So be it.

Surely you have known as have I that our life together has grown cold. Oh Joseph, I beg you, if you have ever truly loved me, if you still feel any love for me, have compassion for me now. Have compassion for what has become of my life. You are rich in your life. You have your horses, your horse business, your horse friends, now your cavalry and your war. When our ardor cooled, I found I had nothing, nothing but empty hours filled with meaningless activity. How barren these last years have been. I know what a wicked woman I am to say such a thing when I have the children to love and I do truly love them. But they are not enough. Wicked. Wicked. Wicked. Yet it is who I am. I cannot live without passion.

I told Poppa that I wished to divorce you. He forbade it. See? Even that you have taken from me, my dear dear Poppa's love. Can you imagine? Poppa, My Poppa, threatened to disinherit me if I attempted such a thing. My Poppa said if I divorced you I would be penniless. Was ever such a tragedy played? My Poppa said that by law the fortune I had when I married you is legally yours! Oh the evil that men work upon us women! I had to tell My Poppa that unless you and he left my fortune intact for me to use as I see fit, I would take my own life. He believed me, as should you. For if I am thwarted in this I shall die by my own hand. Even men cannot prevent me from that. My Poppa called in Mr. Schiff, his lawyer, who told me the law will not allow me to divorce you as you have given me no cause that the law, men's law, will recognize. I know that I cannot live without the means to do so, so in this one instance I shall submit to the will of men. But you, being a man, you have choices that I do not.

You have reason enough to divorce me. I have denied you my bed this last year. By men's law that alone is sufficient reason. But there is more. By men's law there is even a greater reason, a reason so strong that should you decide to shoot me there is no court in America that would convict you.

Joseph, dear sweet Joseph, do not hate me for this. What follows was your fault as much as mine.

While you were away, I had an *affaire d'amour.* Ah yes, I can see you reaching for that little pistol. I can see the hate in your eyes. Joseph, let it not be so. Find room in your heart to forgive me. I know by all that is decent you should hate me. But remember who we once were and how different our love was from that of the mundane world. Yes. You must hate me a little. You shall need that hate to divorce me. To that end I shall tell you, my lover was a poet. I say was for it truly was only one moment of madness. I do not love him. It was merely *un petit divertissement.* Our assignation took place in his studio near Charley Pfaff's. I told Nathan about it. He made me promise I would never see my poor poet again.

Now you know all, and now you hate me. It is best for you to hate me now. Joseph, I know your sense of your honor. Perhaps you will seek out my lover and kill him. If you do I shall mourn him forever and you shall never again as long as I live look upon me. I should be afraid that your honor, like Othello's, might require that you kill me, but I am comforted by the knowledge that in your regard for me, you lack Othello's passion for his Desdemona.

I beg one boon of you. If you ever truly loved me, honor that love Joseph by divorcing me and returning my fortune to me. Do not let my father disinherit me.

I have taken the children with me to Paris, there to seek my great passion. The children ask about you. I tell them you are well and at the great war to save the Union. They are well.

Adieu,
Fannie

Fannie was correct. As Joseph read the letter in his father-in-law's study, he was sure he felt nothing. Yet tears coursed down his cheeks.

Joseph walked calmly to one of the chairs by the fireplace and idly thought that it was here he had sat all those years ago when he had asked Loeb for Fannie's hand in marriage. He glanced up at the framed Declaration of Independence, and then collapsed into the chair, hiding his face from God with his hands.

Nathan, warned by a telegram from Loeb, was at the station in Washington. The day was clear and the ground hard. Although the road back to the encampment of the Albany Invincibles was well trafficked, they were able to ride easily.

"Joseph," Nathan said. "My father telegraphed me about Fannie. I want to help."

"Thank you, Nathan." Joseph's voice was flat. "There is nothing you can do."

"Don't be so sure. I know her better than anyone. I love both of you. I'll do anything to protect you two."

Joseph turned in his saddle. "Like keeping her poet lover a secret from me?"

"To save you from a foolish mistake. To prevent..."

But Joseph cued Thunder to a fast trot and moved up through traffic.

Nathan caught up with him. "I did what was best for the two of you."

"Good. I'm glad you have my interests so at heart. Although my wife graciously wrote me of the affair, she neglected to mention the name of her paramour. She said you would be happy to supply me with his name and whereabouts."

"Joseph, I think it better you don't know. If you have business with this creature, let me do it for you."

Joseph smiled at him. "Thank you, Nathan, but I do my own killing."

"If you kill him, there'll never be any hope of a reconciliation between you and Fannie."

"Reconciliation? You think I'll ever take her back? She has asked for a divorce. I'll oblige her. She's asked for her fortune. I'll not oblige her. She has my children with her in Paris. I'm at war and cannot go there to claim them. Therefore I'll see to it that she's supported in her usual custom. When this war ends, if I survive, I shall take my children away from her. Now it's my intention to only divorce her. Should she engage in a way of life that dishonors me, I'll kill each of her lovers and then I'll kill her." Again he moved Thunder to a fast trot.

Again Nathan caught up with him. "No, you shall not kill Fannie."

"Really? Who is to prevent me?"

"You. It's not in your nature to do so."

"Ah, my nature. You presume to know my nature. You think because we've debated the nature of God, you can know my nature any more than we can know His? Perhaps it's the nature of men to kill when mortally offended, just as it may well be in the nature of God to make wars when He's offended. I can't kill? Not more than three weeks ago I killed a boy because he assisted in the capture and hanging of Stumpf. Then I burned his ancestral home, his barns, his cotton and his cotton seeds. Had his mother been present I would have cut her throat as well."

Instead of traveling with McClellan on the grand expedition to seize Richmond, the Albany Invincibles were assigned to General

McDowell to defend Washington. A Confederate army was threatening the city from the Rappahannock and from the Shenandoah. Although he was displeased at being kept from the assault on the rebel capital, Joseph spent the time mercilessly training his men. Over and over again, he used the better riders against the lesser-skilled in mock combat until the balance changed and the battles evened. Joseph never let them forget who it was they were to battle and how their Sergeant-Major Stumpf had died. As he trained them, he constantly looked for that elusive thing that would give his Yankee yeomen, dirt farmers and small town artisans an edge in their upcoming ordeal against the southern chivalry.

He avoided all personal contact with Nathan, treating him with military formality.

In his spare hours Joseph devoted himself to the duel, practicing with pistol, saber, épée and knife. On occasion Colonel Soulé, breaking away from his duties in Washington, joined Joseph for the blade practice. Cued by Nathan, Colonel Soulé attempted to intervene in the matter of Fannie and was politely but firmly rebuffed.

One day a courier arrived with orders. The Albany Invincibles were being ordered to the James River. They were at long last going to the war.

§43

"WHO," ASKED THE EMPRESS EUGENIE, "IS THAT?"

"The Baroness von Breitenstein, Your Majesty. An American."

"Ah."

"And a Jewess."

"Ah?"

"One of the Loebs."

"Ah?"

"The banking Loebs."

"Is it true that they are as rich as the Rothchilds?"

"They certainly live that way, Majesty. Their mansion on Avenue Murat is one of the wonders of Paris."

"Then I certainly must see it."

"Majesty, they are Jews."

The empress smiled. "My husband's uncle, Napoleon the First, you may recall, freed the Jews. He found them to be no better nor worse than the rest of us. And if these American Jews are as rich as our Rothchilds, perhaps they might be as helpful. Besides, there is something engaging about that woman. Look at her. She isn't beautiful, yet see how when she laughs beauty shines out of her. She is married?"

"Yes, Majesty, to a Baron von Ritter."

"A lover?"

"Not yet, Majesty. She has just arrived."

"And her husband, the baron, he is in Paris?"

"No, Majesty. He is in America fighting in their Civil War."

"Ah, the war in America. Poor creature, she is all alone in Paris?"

"She stays with her brother and his family. The brother is an idiot, but with so much money to spend he has become fashionable. There, Majesty, at the card table. The foolish-looking one is the brother."

The empress looked and laughed. "He looks like my little Fouquet." Fouquet was her spaniel. From that moment on, Isador was known throughout Paris society as "the spaniel."

"And over there, Majesty, talking to the baroness, is the spaniel's wife."

"She is not beautiful, but what an interesting face," the empress remarked. "Would you call that an intelligent face?"

"They say she has wit without a sharp tongue. Madame Carnot has her regularly at her salon."

"Ah? And does Madame Loeb have a lover?"

"The Duke de Mornay, Majesty."

"That accounts for his sudden prosperity." She laughed merrily and so did the courtiers surrounding her.

"She is truly the empress?" It took all of Fannie's will not to stare at the other side of the ballroom.

"Yes. Don't look, for God's sake."

"You've met her?"

"Not yet, but Albert has promised." The second night Fannie was in Paris, Bella had told her about her aristocratic lover, a genuine duke of the old regime. And so Fannie told Bella about her poet. Bella was aghast that Fannie had written to Joseph about her *petit voltigement* and vowed to do everything in her power to prevent a divorce. In Paris, Bella said, people understood. Husbands didn't divorce wives over love affairs any more than wives divorced husbands over mistresses. The key was discretion. One simply maintained the fiction of chastity. Everyone did it marvelously. So would Fannie.

"Oh, look!" Bella discreetly indicated an elegantly attired, spare man with white hair and a lean, clean-shaven face. "That's him!"

"Your lover? The duke?"

"Yes! Isn't he handsome?"

"But Bella, he is so old."

Bella smiled. "You have so much to learn. It is the man of experience who truly knows *l'art érotique*."

"Bella!"

"Look." Bella was ecstatic. "The empress has called him. See? They are laughing. Oh, my God, they are looking at us!"

The duke left the empress and headed toward them. Bella could hardly contain her glee. "Oh, my God, she has sent him for us. Fannie, do you know how to curtsy to royalty?"

The duke stopped in front of them and with a slight bow, said, "Madame Loeb. Perhaps you remember me." He looked slightly amused. "I am the Duke de Mornay. I had the honor of meeting you at Madame Carnot's."

Bella smiled back. "Of course, Your Grace. How nice to see you again." She extended her hand, and as he bent to kiss it he spoke just loudly enough for her and Fannie to hear.

"Tomorrow?"

Eyes glistening, Bella nodded. The duke then straightened and turned expectantly to Fannie.

"May I present my sister-in-law, the Baroness von Breitenstein," Bella said.

"I am honored, baroness." He bent over her hand as well. "The empress has asked me if I would be good enough to present you."

At the conclusion of their introductions, the empress asked Fannie about the latest news from the American war and of her husband. But happily married women, she knew, did not travel to foreign lands while their husbands were at war.

"Baroness, may I present Dionysus," the empress said. "I warn you the man is a scamp. He has a real name and a very old title but has renounced them and is now an anarchist. Truly I should have him shot. But he is a beautiful boy and an exquisite painter. It would be a pity to shoot him. Don't you think he is beautiful?"

Fannie looked up and saw a handsome young man with dark, mesmerizing eyes and long black curls. "Yes, Your Majesty. I think he is quite beautiful."

The empress was surprised: this provincial American girl was staring at Dionysus with frank lust. Who knows, she thought, the girl might be an amusing addition to the court. "Then take him baroness," she said. "Take him onto the floor and dance with him. He is my welcoming gift to you."

Joseph sat his horse and contemplated the landscape. The afternoon sun had heated the thick air to intolerable temperatures. Below he could see the Chickahominy River, black and greasy, through the woods lining its bank. He kept his eye on the trees. If an attack was to come, it would come from the tree line. But nothing seemed to be happening. Maybe they were in the wrong place. Maybe McClellan was the fool Fannie said he was. Joseph caught himself. Self-pity is despicable, he thought.

He gazed with longing at the battle taking place a mile away, furious that he wasn't in it. He was guarding guns that wouldn't be needed. He watched the battle and ached for the only thing that mattered to him now.

Billowing clouds of blue and black smoke obscured most of what Joseph yearned for. Time after time the Union forces, entrenched at the top of the hill, poured tons of metal into the raggedly advancing lines of the Confederacy. The rebels, mowed down row by row, reeled, fell back, reformed and were joined by more men in gray. Joseph was mesmerized by the details of real war. Battle flags advancing, halting, falling, advancing again. Men running, firing, dying. The concussion of cannons, the rattle of musketry and the screams of the wounded.

A sudden wind, the first of the storm that had been threatening since dawn, carried away the clouds of smoke that had been obscuring his full view.

God in Heaven, Joseph thought, would you look at that! The Reb flank is exposed. What an opportunity! I could lead my men down there and smash them to pieces. And then nothing could stop us from moving right on to Richmond.

As Joseph turned to look at his weary men resting on the hillside just above him, he caught sight of a rider coming up from the rear echelon. The man, an officer, cantered his sorrel thoroughbred as if on a Sunday ride in the park. Yet Joseph could see that the fellow was rudely dressed and his horse was too refined and too high-strung. In his view neither the man nor animal looked like they belonged on a battlefield.

Joseph didn't bother to duck as a stray rebel shell flew overhead. Had the Rebs spotted the batteries on the hilltop just above him? With his binoculars he quickly scanned the tree line below. There was no movement. Joseph now turned his glass on the officer riding toward him. The man wore a non-regulation big straw hat. Fair enough, Joseph thought. Maybe he took it from a dead Rebel. Perhaps he needed the big hat for his pink skin. The officer wore long blond tresses and an unkempt blond mustache.

"Custer," the officer said when he arrived. He saluted with a hand in a filthy gauntlet. "On the personal staff of General McClellan." Joseph thought his uniform the dirtiest he had ever seen on an officer.

Joseph returned the salute. "Von Ritter," he said. "Major Joseph von Ritter Baron von Breitenstein." My God, he thought, I never use the title. To Custer he continued, "I have command of this tattered remnant. At your service, sir."

They stared at each other: two boys in a schoolyard, one light, one dark. Neither yet twenty-four years old.

"German?" Custer's tone was intentionally insulting. The whole army knew some of the German regiments had gained a reputation for an unwillingness to fight.

"American," Joseph snapped back. He regained his calm and added, "Formerly of the Royal Wittelsbach Hussars. And you? English, perhaps? Under that mud, do I recognize the jacket? Queen's own?"

"American." Color rose to Custer's cheeks. "West Point. I have come directly from General McClellan's headquarters."

"You have orders?" In the distance a group of grays detached themselves and maneuvered as if to head in their direction. "If you'll be so kind as to excuse me...." Joseph asked Thunder for a swift canter and moved to a better vantage point. The Rebel troops had disappeared back into the clouds of smoke. Joseph watched for a moment more and returned to his caller in an elegant gait. Custer held his temper at this arrogance and smiled at Joseph.

"May I ask what your orders are, sir?" Custer said.

Joseph nodded toward the guns on the hill above them. "Remain in position here and defend these guns if attacked."

"How many men have you got?"

Joseph indicated the men behind him. "This is what's left of the First Battalion, Albany Invincibles. We rode here with five hundred and fifty men. They and their horses are worn out by nine days in the saddle with little or no provisions. We are grateful for our orders. It's the first rest we've had."

Custer grew impatient. "Look," he said, pointing to the battle. "The Rebs' flank is exposed. It's a perfect cavalry opportunity. Let's take your men and hit them."

"My orders are to stay here and defend these guns."

"Defend them from what? Ambrose Hill's entire army is there. The Rebs don't even know these guns are here. And even if they did, they don't have the troops to attack them. Do you understand, man? War is improvisation. One charge and we shall have the greatest victory in the whole Peninsula Campaign. And we'll be the heroes."

Custer's words made sense; Joseph knew this opportunity would soon vanish forever. But he had orders. He looked again at the trees shielding the river. There was no movement. He made his decision. Turning back to Custer, Joseph said, "My orders are to stay here and defend these guns."

"Major, I'm a West Point graduate, a captain in the regular army. That outranks a volunteer major any day of the week. And I'm a staff officer who enjoys the complete personal confidence of General McClellan," Custer said. "I'll take full responsibility."

"Captain," Joseph said. "There's no question of who outranks who. My orders are directly from General Fitz-John Porter. If you wish to change them I suggest you ride over there." Joseph pointed to the smoke-covered hill against which the Rebs were smashing themselves to pulp. "Ask him yourself."

"No time," Custer shouted. "Listen to me, you damned coward...."

Joseph slapped Custer from his horse before he could finish the sentence. The thoroughbred attempted to bolt and Custer scrambled to hold him. Then, when he was in his saddle again, he spoke.

"At your service, sir. When this engagement is over, send your seconds to me, unless your cowardice is served by taking refuge behind military regulations against the duel."

"That's twice you've called me a coward," Joseph said. "Choose the weapon you wish to be killed by now. Saber, épée, pistol..."

"Sure, Captain *Baron* American citizen," Custer said. "It'd pleasure me to know you were thinking about my choice for a while. Bowie knives. I am sure a gentleman of your fine breeding must have studied the art of the Bowie knife with the royal-whatever-you-called-them-hussars."

Joseph started to accept when a rattle of musketry from the hill stopped him. He and Custer looked up. The infantry supporting the artillery were firing at the tree line directly below them. The gunners frantically struggled to reposition the big guns to point down the slope. A line of gray and butternut uniforms emerged from the trees.

"A regiment!" Custer shouted.

"More," Joseph yelled. He rode the few yards back to his men and saw them already scrambling for their saddles. "Mount! Prepare to advance! "

The troopers quickly moved into formation.

"By column of fours, at a walk, forward ho!"

The Fighting First moved out.

"By troop, left into line, ho!"

The columns of four spread into three battle lines.

Leading his men over the crest of the hill, Joseph rode directly toward the oncoming rebel lines in the most perfect formation Custer had ever seen a Union cavalry perform. The Albany Invincibles moved down toward the tree line at a walk. In measured cadences, Joseph commanded, "Draw sabers. Trot." He heard the company commanders behind him repeating his orders and the rattle of steel coming out of iron scabbards.

Eyes on the tree line, Joseph, aware of the changing rhythm of horses' hooves as his men advanced to the trot, rode into his long-awaited first battle. Ahead of him the gray line paused and a thicket of muskets appeared followed by a cloud of gray smoke. Behind him Joseph heard the screams of horses and men, and above it all were the commands of the sergeants: "Close it up. Close it up, dammit. Right dress!" He rode on.

They were halfway there. Joseph could now see faces behind the guns. "Steady," he called. "Gallop. Right dress." Something tore at his sleeve. He heard the whine of bullets speeding past. Then, pointing his saber he shouted, "For Sergeant Stumpf! Charge!"

He was flying. They smashed into the rebel line, scattering the gray men. Weapons were thrown away as soldiers ran. Joseph slashed at terrified faces. All disappeared in splatters of blood. He sensed more than saw the shock of his troops in collision with the lines of Confederate foot soldiers. The rebel advance faltered and then turned. Something tapped his head. For a moment Joseph was blinded. He wiped hot liquid from his eyes and plunged on, continually slashing to his right and left. A Confederate officer on a white stallion lunged at him. Joseph parried the man's saber thrust and, with a powerful riposte, took the officer's arm off below the shoulder. The officer fell away, replaced by another who fired his pistol at point-blank range. Joseph felt the blow but couldn't tell where he was hit. Before the man could fire again Joseph drove his saber's point directly into the man's throat.

Custer, never more than a second behind Joseph, saw it all. Fresh rebel troops came screaming into the fight and Custer, seeing Joseph staggered by another wound and clinging to the neck of his horse, slashed his way to him. Taking Thunder's reins he shouted, "It's over. We're getting the hell out of here."

Under the cover of the six batteries firing from the hill above, Custer, with Joseph's blood-spattered stallion in tow, led the survivors of the Albany Invincibles back up the hill.

The headline in *The New York Herald* read:

"Captain Custer's gallant Cavalry Charge saves the Day."

§44

WHENEVER JOSEPH WAS CONSCIOUS, HE HEARD MOANING. ONCE he opened his eyes and saw the sun shining through a tattered white canvas just above his face. The canvas was supported by three muskets with their bayonets stuck into the soaking ground and a sword. Once he heard Custer shouting, "You damn well will find an ambulance! Damn you! Put him in a carriage, a wagon, a caisson.

But you get him back to the hospital or by God, sir, I'll blow your brains out!"

Later Joseph heard more voices next to him and above him. One weary voice said. "I believe Major von Ritter will die during the night. If he doesn't, perhaps then, we'll have time to amputate."

Again Joseph slipped into darkness, but this time it was night and he was awake. The moaning had abated. He was on a cot in a hospital.

"You've been wounded," Nathan said.

Joseph turned to the other side of his cot. Nathan stood in the shadows in his dress uniform.

"Nathan! Thank God! What happened? Did we win?"

"We stopped them with our charge," Nathan said. "It gave the artillery time to train on them and hit them with canister. Then the infantry drove them off."

"So we won."

"That engagement, yes. But each side is claiming victory. We killed thousands of them, but we didn't advance. How can it be a victory without an advance?"

"Why am I in the hospital?"

"You've been wounded," Nathan repeated.

"Bad?"

"Three times."

"Will I live?"

"Yes."

"Fannie?"

She was standing by him. He couldn't make out her face. "Fannie?"

It was another woman. She said, "When the sea covered the Egyptians, the host of ministering angels started to sing praises and God said, 'My creatures that I have made are dying, and you sing?' Do you know that Midrash?"

"I do."

"Why did God say that?"

"If God said it, it was to remind them—us—that all people are created in God's image. Unless, of course, it is He who is created in ours."

"This is serious," she said.

"He created us in His image. Satisfied?"

She laughed softly. "You think you are so clever. But you have sinned, you know."

"Which particular sin did you have in mind?"

"When you watched the battle, you longed for it."

"So?"

"When you rode into battle, you exulted in it."

"It was the most thrilling thing I have ever done."

"You loved killing."

"So?"

"So? So Numbers 31."

He fell back into the darkness.

All of Fannie's fantasies were coming true. While the court and *haute monde* were dazzling, the real world once inhabited by Ada Clare was unveiled to her by Dionysus.

"He's dangerous," Bella said.

"Ha! He thinks he's dangerous," Fannie smiled condescendingly. "He's a boy, barely twenty."

"He told you that?"

"And much, much more. His real name, for instance."

"I thought only the empress knew that."

"Now I know too. You see, I am his special confidant."

"Fannie, have you slept with him?"

"Not yet," she said. "God knows, I tried. I know he wants to as well, but the occasion just never seems to occur."

"Is he toying with you?"

Fannie laughed. "Oh no, dear sister. It's quite the other way round. The game is mine to play."

"Fannie. Be careful. This is Paris, not Charley Pfaff's. These people are..."

Fannie interrupted. "I know. I know. They're so *chic*, yes, and they know more about many of the things I want to learn. But this boy, in spite of all his outward sophistication, is just a boy. He is dear and beautiful and I mean to have him. But it will be on my terms and, I promise you, it shall not be the God Dionysus who will do all the teaching."

"Tell me about him," Bella said. "Who is he really? What's his real name?"

"I swore I'd never reveal it. But I can tell you he's of royal blood."

"Truly?"

Fannie nodded. "Of the *ancien régime*. And, it's so sad, he is dying."

"Fannie, no." How exquisitely beautiful, she thought.

"Yes. It's a rare disease. He doesn't expect to see his twenty-fifth birthday. I suppose it's why he lives so recklessly."

"Have you seen his paintings?"

"Not yet. Have you?"

"Good heavens no! Very few have. They say they are *trés charnel*. Only a very few people are permitted to purchase them, let alone view them. You know what else they say?"

"What?"

"That no woman has ever seen them without becoming his lover."

"But the empress…"

"Yes. At least that's what they say."

"The empress?"

"The empress."

For a while they sat in silence. Fannie stared out of the window at the Paris traffic. What could be more perfect? A dying artist. The lover of the empress of France. He knew everybody who counted: poets, painters, composers, and theater people. On his arm she had attended private performances of the most astonishing plays, and had been to a seance where the gypsy spiritualist had summoned the spirit of Lord Byron. At a street fair an Italian palm reader foretold a long life and many lovers. Dionysus, looking soulfully into her eyes, had said, "The Italian is a fraud. Your next lover shall be your last."

But Fannie was puzzled. Dionysus, in spite of his seductive talk, never even attempted to take her to bed. Fannie decided it was time for her to make the move.

Dionysus called for Fannie at eight o'clock on a warm, wet night. Although ready, she kept him waiting for a half an hour. At last she descended and entered his coach.

"Where are the others?" Fannie asked. The coach was empty.

"Tonight I thought we should be alone."

Fannie caught her breath.

"Would you like to see my paintings?" he asked.

She laughed. "I thought you were hiding them from me."

"Not hiding. Waiting."

"For what?"

"Now."

His studio was in a dark working-class section of Paris. The building's facade was dilapidated, as were those surrounding it. The street-level windows were bricked up, the windows above hidden by heavy wooden shutters.

The coachman climbed down and, opening two heavily timbered doors, led the horses into a cobbled courtyard. He then closed the doors and helped his passengers from the coach. Only a small oil lamp over an iron door lit the yard.

"It was from this stable," Dionysus whispered, "that the tumbrels were taken to carry the aristocrats to Madame La Guillotine each day of the Terror."

Fannie shivered. She hadn't expected any of this. She felt afraid.

Dionysus escorted her through a door into a dimly lit hall. Then he let go of her arm and stepped into the darkness at the end of the hall. He pulled aside a heavy damask curtain, and they were bathed in soft, rose-tinted golden light.

Fannie gasped. The room before her was an Arabian fantasy: a scarlet and gold silk tent hung from the room's center, its sides falling to the floor to cover all the walls. Illumination emanated from gold-filigreed Moorish lanterns hanging at irregular heights from peaks in the tent roof. The air was thick with incense. Oriental carpets covered the floor, making it nearly as soft as a bed. Embroidered silk cushions were strewn in piles about the room. At the center of the room near a silk-draped, raised platform stood an easel.

Suddenly a woman, veiled and naked beneath diaphanous scarlet silks, was kneeling at Dionysus' feet. He lifted a foot and allowed her to remove his shoes and then his stockings. When she finished she turned to Fannie.

"Your shoes," Dionysus said.

Fannie allowed the woman to remove her shoes.

"And the stockings," he whispered.

Fannie didn't want to appear unsophisticated, but her stockings were fastened high on her thighs. He looked at her, a half-smile on his lips. "It's the custom."

Fannie nodded. She felt the woman's hands reach up under her petticoats, touching and caressing her thighs as they found the fastenings. For the briefest moment the hands lingered. Then slowly, sensually, they rolled down her silk stockings.

Fannie, blushing, was humiliated.

Dionysus laughed. "Oh Fannie, my beautiful little provincial. You have so much to learn. Now I shall show you my paintings." He nodded to the woman who moved about the room, pulling black silk cords, raising curtains, revealing the paintings. Fannie was embarrassed to discover that her eyes wanted to look at the woman's body, her perfect breasts, the mass of dark hair below her belly.

"The paintings?" Dionysus whispered.

They were openly erotic: gods and goddesses coupling, copulating, and engaging in every imaginable sexual act. Fannie wanted to be naked like the women in the paintings.

She turned to Dionysus, now sitting at a low table by his easel, lighting an odd-looking pipe. "Hashish," he said. "You have smoked hashish before?"

"Of course," she lied. She watched as he inhaled. The woman helped her settle on a cushion next to him. Fannie noticed for the first time that she smelled of jasmine. The woman handed Fannie the pipe. She drew in the smoke and repressed a cough. This was easier than the cigars Ada taught her to smoke.

The woman took the pipe and, to Fannie's surprise, inhaled from it herself. Fannie's head felt airy and the light in the tent turned a deeper rose and a softer gold. The weightlessness in her head spread through her body and she felt her nipples become erect.

On the platform the woman was dancing in slow sensual movements that Fannie had never seen before. Fannie found it the most erotic dance she had ever seen. "Fatima is Egyptian, descended from the Pharaohs. She is my model." Dionysus spoke without taking his eyes from Fatima.

As she moved, Fatima's costume slipped slowly from her body until she was naked. Then she seemed to float toward Fannie. Taking her hands, she helped Fannie to her feet and led her to the stage.

Without words Fatima showed Fannie how to dance. Fannie, her body following the languorous movements, felt Fatima's hands caressing her. Fannie realized Fatima was unfastening her buttons. A moment later Fannie's dress slid from her body. Then came her undergarments. Fatima danced in front of her. Fannie matched her movements. Fatima moved closer and closer until she touched Fannie so lightly it was barely a touch. Nipple stroked nipple. Belly stroked belly. Fatima's tongue brushed Fannie's lips. Fannie opened her mouth, but the tongue slid away to the base of her neck, her breasts, her stomach, and lower.

Fannie, captured between dream and reality, rolled in the cushions—kissing, licking, tasting. Time after time she flew to unimaginable heights of ecstasy. Always she wanted more.

Her arms were drawn above her head. How delicious, she thought. Black silk cords were wrapped about her wrists and tied to something solid. Fannie turned her head to Dionysus. He was naked. He was indeed a God, she thought. Only a god would have an erection that size. He grinned. He looked a satyr. Suddenly nothing was beautiful anymore. The satyr's phallus terrifying. A hand covered her mouth and a black silk gag was pulled over it.

Fannie heard a whisper. "Roll the cow over," Dionysus rasped.

For three days Joseph had been in and out of a near-coma induced by shock and inexpert doses of laudanum. His right leg had been amputated just above the knee. When he finally opened his eyes he found Loeb and Moses Cohen sitting by his bed. Loeb reached out for his hand. Moses Cohen quietly chanted a blessing to the Ruler of the Universe.

"My boy," Loeb said. "My poor boy."

"They took my leg."

"It is God's will," Moses Cohen said.

"God's will," Joseph said. He fell back into unconsciousness.

The two men were still there the following morning.

"What has happened?" he asked.

"You have lost your leg," Moses Cohen said.

"No. It's more. Fannie! Has something happened to Fannie?"

Loeb shook his head. "No. Fannie and the children are safe in Paris." He took a breath. "Nathan is dead."

"He was killed in your battle," Moses Cohen said.

"But I saw him after the battle, that night, in the hospital. We talked. Nathan can't be dead. I spoke to him."

"A dream," Moses Cohen said.

"My son Nathan is dead," Loeb said. Tears ran down his face.

§45

"My god! my leg!" joseph woke up screaming.

Then the laudanum took effect and Joseph's pain eased into recurrent waves, then soft ripples, and then became unimportant.

He thought of Thunder. Will I never ride again? Of course I shall. Men have ridden with one leg. I'll learn how to do it. Then he thought of Nathan. Nathan was dead. He drifted back to sleep.

It was not Custer's habit to merely enter rooms. He assaulted them. The arrival jolted Joseph awake. His hand automatically reached for the laudanum.

"By Jinks, Major von Ritter," Custer said, "I do believe you're gonna live. You don't look it, but they say you are. Don't remember me, do you?"

"Custer."

"Right, Custer." He handed Joseph the nine-inch blade he had carried in his boot. "Found this in your boot just before they threw your leg away, so I guess you know how to use it as well as the saber. Right?"

"Yes."

"Knife-fighter? Am I correct?"

"Yes."

"The duel's off. I apologize. Where'd a New York society type learn knife-fighting?"

"I wasn't always such a swell."

"Good. Me neither. Can't keep callin' you Major von Ritter either. You got a friendly name? "

"Joseph."

"Anybody call you Joe?"

"Not any of my friends."

"Then Joseph will have to do. You call me Autie. People call me a lot of things, and I let them. Hell, I answer to most anything. But there's a few I permit to call me Autie. Now ain't you proud?"

"Thank you, Autie."

"Wasn't that an uncommonly interesting charge! A perfect blizzard of bullets and you rode into them like you meant harm to them Southron boys. And danged if you didn't give it to them. Joseph, next to me, you're the bravest man I ever saw. I told General McClellan about you too. Oh damnation! I forgot to tell you the best part. You got mentioned in dispatches. My recommendation, of course. Hell, you might just get a medal."

"Thank you, Autie." Joseph wondered why Custer was talking about it as if it were a game. "My brother-in-law was killed."

"Yeah, you lose people in battle."

"I still don't know how many men of the Fighting First we lost."

"Most all of them. Three hundred and twenty-six dead, 116 wounded, and half of them will buy the rabbit. Your battalion's gone. But don't you worry about it. You'll get another command." He sniffed. "You know, the way it stinks, your leg could be rotting." He started down the aisle of beds. "Doc!" he yelled. "Sawbones! Ho! Need a doc in here!"

When the doctor redressed the bandage, Joseph saw his amputated leg for the first time. The skin had been stitched into a neatish flap, and the stump was raw red, purple and yellow. A string hung from it. When the doctor gently tugged on the string Joseph felt an electric shock.

"Not yet, son," the doctor said. "When we can draw it out..."

"He means when it rots away," Custer said.

"We're looking for a good kind of infection in there," the doctor said. "When this string comes out, we'll check the pus. If it's the right kind, what we call laudable pus, you'll make it."

He rebandaged the stump, rose, and taking Custer with him, left.

In the silence that followed Joseph thought about the men of the Fighting First. He knew them all: their names, the names of their wives and children, how they talked and laughed, who was good with their horses, who was afraid. He cried for each one.

Soon he obtained lists of those who died. Those who lived came to see him. He organized them into shifts of letter writers and dictated letters home to the families of his beloved dead. In between letters he fell into deep, untroubled sleep.

Other times during the day different faces came to him, men he didn't know personally but whom he could see clearly. They were the rebels he had killed. In each face he saw the shock of the recognition of their life's end.

Loeb, busy with the finances of the war, came once more. Moses Cohen made the difficult journey on several occasions, including a trip to escort Joseph to a new hospital in Washington. The string hanging from Joseph's stump eventually rotted out. The pus was pronounced laudable.

Moses Cohen and Custer were present.

"Look out, Johnny Reb!" Custer said. "Joseph, you and me are gonna mow rebels like wheat at harvest time."

Moses Cohen stared in fascination.

"Excuse me, Captain Custer."

"Yes, reverend?"

"Am I to understand that you like war?"

Custer laughed. "Like it? Why reverend, I love it as much as I love my girl. Gotta go." He left.

"Never," Moses Cohen said to Joseph, "have I ever seen so much vitality in a man. He is as if God made him just for this war."

"And me?" Joseph asked. "For what did God make me?"

Moses Cohen didn't comment on Joseph's mention of the deity in the singular. "That, of course, is *the* question. Isn't it?"

"*The* question?"

"The only question. What does God want of us?"

Because they believed infection occurred more in stale air than fresh, the army doctors decided the ideal hospital was a well-ventilated tent. But since tents were impractical for the winter, two wooden hospitals were built in Washington with windows every eight feet and open-ridge ventilation to keep the air moving.

Joseph was assigned a bed in a room 130 feet long, twenty-five feet wide, and fourteen feet high. Although the room was built to circulate air, July in Washington was hot, muggy and still.

Joseph, like many other patients, was self-administering tincture of laudanum for his pain. Although the doctors prescribed precise dosages, anyone could purchase as much as he wanted from the hospital staff. As a result Joseph's ward was unusually peaceful and the officers in the beds around him, all amputees, established a woozy fellowship.

During his previous two weeks in the tent hospital he had decided that his night visitor, the shadowed face, was the Shechinah, the female emanation of the Unknown through whom God speaks to man. Her voice—the voice of the Shechinah—had told him to go to America. Her voice had quoted him passages from the Torah and from the Sayings of the Fathers, passages that had been so helpful in moments of crisis. He had seen the Shechinah before, too: in the Dittelheim synagogue when he had desecrated the Torah, in the knife fight with Brannagan, and when he killed the assassin. He had seen her but could never recall her face. But her voice? That he remembered, for it was the voice of the Shechinah. He knew of no place in the Jewish Tradition where the Shechinah made such appearances. Yet there she was. What did God want of him?

That first night in the Washington hospital he woke once and the Shechinah was there. But this time she was different. This time he could make out her face in the dim light. She smiled at him and her cool hand stroked his hair. When he tried to speak, she gently quieted him and whispered, "There now, close your eyes and sleep." Her voice was different too. He did what she requested, and felt her soothing hand caressing his face. He returned to oblivion.

Soon these visitations became a nightly event. Then she disappeared. He yearned for her. There was so much he needed to know. Then she returned. He could just make out her face. It was beautiful. So much so that he paid no attention to the fact that her voice was not the same.

Then she stopped coming again and his longing for her became unbearable. He increased his daily dosage of the opiate, passing from his dream-filled nights to semi-conscious days. Then on a bright August day, emerging from his torpid half-life, he reached for the bottle of laudanum. It wasn't on the nightstand. Panic chilled him. He felt around the floor. Nothing. Then a gentle hand touched his. He looked up and saw a beautiful woman with auburn hair and lucid blue eyes.

"I took it away," the woman said.

"He breaks my heart, Mother," Kate Woolsey said. She was sipping iced lemonade, sitting on her bed in the house she shared with her mother and a servant at the unfashionable end of E Street.

"Is this young major a gentleman?"

"Mother, he's rich and famous."

"Good family?"

"Remember the New York newspapers used to write about a German baron..."

"A baron! And written about in the newspapers! How lovely! Is he married?"

"His wife has run off and left him."

"Oh, well," Henrietta Woolsey said. "Beggars can't be choosers."

It took Kate two weeks to lower Joseph's dosage of laudanum to where he could sleep through the nights but remain conscious during the day. Kate extended her workday from ten to twelve hours so that she could tend to her other patients before spending her time with Joseph.

In their hours together she told him about herself. She told him how she loved her mother, whose people came to America on the Mayflower, and about her father, a good man who had built a prosperous horse furnishings business from nothing. She spoke of her childhood which had scandalized polite society because she insisted on becoming a horse trainer and how, over her mother's objections, her father had encouraged her. Joseph loved the sound of her voice which was deep and husky.

"Horses are in my blood," she said. "But if I have to work at something else, this is what I'm most suited for. When the war is over I'm going to do something impossible for a woman to even think of."

"That being?"

"Horses. Joseph, you can't imagine how I love horses. I shall make my way in this wicked man's world training racehorses. Well, to be perfectly truthful, I intend to ride them in the races too. But you men would never put up with a woman who could beat you in a fair race."

"Impossible. I've heard some women ride well. I have no doubt that you're one of them. But to beat a man in a fair race, both horses being equal?" He shook his head.

"How can you come to a conclusion like that?"

"Experience. I say it as a statement of fact. And there are those who say that I have something of a genius for horses."

"Do tell."

"I'll tell you more. In the near five years I've been married, I've been unable to get my wife even mounted in a sidesaddle."

"I've never met anyone who knows so much about horses," Kate told her mother. "You know, he doesn't believe in punishment. I've thought about that, but I've never seen it work. Can you imagine teaching horses just by touching them—no tarred knotted rope, no whips—just touch?"

"Does Major von Ritter ever speak of his family, dear?"

"I forget to ask him. We get started on horses and suddenly the time is gone."

"And his wife. Do you know any more of her?"

"It makes him very angry to speak about her. I think she has betrayed him."

"Ahh...," Mrs. Woolsey used the sigh to mask her thoughts of the major divorcing his wife. Divorce would ruin the wretched woman, but for the major it would add color as well as the patina of tragedy.

Fannie woke one afternoon with two important thoughts. The first was that she was at long last about to begin her grand tour of exotic Europe and Asia. Dionysus and Fatima were her companions and guides. Her second thought was that she had to save her children. Their best haven was with Joseph's parents in Dittelheim, where, two weeks later, she left them. She then traveled to Ascona in the Ticino region of Switzerland. At a lakeside villa she had rented for the summer, she met Dionysus and Fatima and some new friends from England, Lord and Lady Elphanstone, who looked and dressed so much alike it was difficult to tell which was which. The Elphanstones appeared to be rich but, like Dionysus, they expected Fannie to cover all the costs of their extravagant holiday.

The piper was dear, Fannie thought, but the dance was divine.

§46

ONE MORNING KATE SHOWED UP EARLIER THAN USUAL. WITH HER was a man with a sun-burnished face, deep-set dark eyes and long gray hair. "This is Mr. Wittcomb," she said. "My father thinks he's the best saddle maker in America. I told him your ideas."

Joseph extended his hand. "Joseph von Ritter."

"Lost your leg, did you?"

Joseph threw back the sheet to reveal the stump. "It won't stop me from riding."

"Don't suppose it would. Kate says you got an idea for a special saddle."

"I need a saddle I can mount and fix myself in without help. One I can fight from. It can't be regulation cavalry. I want something designed like an old Spanish war saddle, high cantle but with a slight curve around the hip on the right side to give me a little purchase there."

"Makes sense."

"And a kind of a stump stirrup, padded at the bottom and the leather only going around the front three quarters of the stump so I can pull out of it in a hurry, and yet stiff enough so that I can lean into it for saber slashes to the front, right and left. Can you make such a saddle for me?"

Wittcomb nodded. "Run a strap from the bottom of the cup, maybe to the off-side cinch ring."

"Good idea, but that will restrict my ability to move. You've made me think of something else. Can you attach the cup to the saddle on a slide and a pivot?"

"Six-inch slide do it?"

"Perfect. One other thing, I'll need a scabbard for my wooden leg. I plan to be able to walk up to my horse, mount with the leg on, and once in the saddle pull it off and put it in the scabbard."

"When do you get your leg?"

"About a month."

"It'll be ready."

Wittcomb left and Joseph turned to Kate. "Thank you," he said. "That was so good of you." He lay back on his pillow and, closing his eyes, smiled.

"Joseph?" Kate said.

"Yes?"

"Tell me about your wife."

"He just went black, Mother. He was like a horse the split second before it rears. I'm sure the stories are true. The woman has betrayed him."

Mrs. Woolsey sighed. Kate had never been easy. "Kate dear, you must give it up. The man is and will forever be socially unacceptable."

"Mother, he is a baron and a millionaire."

"Kate, I've found out about him. He's a Hebrew. Neither I nor your father, and certainly not polite society, will accept an Israelite."

"He's the greatest horseman in America. And he's a millionaire. And I mean to have him."

Loeb traveled to Washington each week to help finance the war. After his painful first visit at the hospital, he thought it better for Joseph to concentrate on how to live with his one leg than to cope with Fannie. Loeb therefore limited his visits to once every other week. Even then he kept the conversation to the war.

Despite his bitterness, Loeb loved Fannie and hoped to reclaim her. Isador and Bella, fearing for their own extravagant life-style, thought they were keeping him content with false reports of Fannie's well-being and good behavior. Because Isador was a fool, it didn't occur to him that other people were not.

Moses Cohen sat very close to the bed. What they discussed was private and so they spoke softly, and because it was holy they spoke in Hebrew.

"Could it have been the Shechinah?" Moses Cohen asked and answered. "Truly I have heard of such manifestations. But they are so rare and shrouded in such mystery that I can't be sure they've really happened. We are an old people with an ancient and powerful mystical tradition. In the distant past, men have married the Shechinah. There are records of those events. Perhaps she was present on those occasions, perhaps only in spirit. For many in the past centuries the Shechinah was as real as we are to each other. Perhaps they, like you, actually saw her. I can't deny your vision."

"It was her," Joseph said. "I have no doubt. She has been with me from the moment I challenged God."

"Like a Guardian Angel?"

"No, a messenger. Reb Moses, am I insane to think that God sent her? That God wants something from me?"

"God wants something from all of us. We pass our lives, if we are wise, trying to discover what that is. Perhaps you are luckier than most. Perhaps God has sent the Shechinah to tell you what He wants. Tell me again. When you first heard her voice, she said what?"

"She told me to come to America."

"And then?"

"From time to time she would tell me things from the Torah or the Talmud. They always helped me."

"How?"

"To question God. Does God send a messenger to make us question His existence?"

"To some. Perhaps from you God wants something special. Perhaps God loves you specially."

Joseph laughed sardonically. "God loves me? God loves me so much I was enslaved by Brannagan. God's love sent an assassin so I could I shoot away his head. God's love handed me a fine young man so I might burn his home and slash his throat. God in his special love for me has taken from me my wife and children, and my leg. If that's God's love, give me God's hate."

"When the Shechinah spoke to you," Moses Cohen said, "this last time on the night that Nathan of blessed memory, may he rest in peace, came to you, tell me again what she said."

Joseph closed his eyes and saw the shadowy female figure, and heard the familiar voice. "She said, 'When the sea covered the Egyptians, the host of ministering angels started to sing praises and God said, "My creatures that I have made are dying, and you sing?" Do you know that Midrash?' I thought I knew it. Do you?"

"I have read it as, 'My children are dying and you sing?' But it is the same. God is pained by every human death. Your parents are living. Perhaps you have never said *kaddish*."

"What does the prayer for the dead have to do with this?"

"It's unique in prayers for the dead in that it never mentions death. It's a special prayer in praise of God. There are many traditions concerning *kaddish*. The one that I've always loved is that the prayer is to comfort God on the loss of the precious life. Did you say Kaddish for the assassin you shot?"

"No."

"For the boy in the South?"

"No."

"And the soldiers you killed in the battle?"

"All of them were trying to kill me. All of them."

"So what else did the Shechinah say to you?"

"She said that I sinned because I loved the killing."

"Did you?"

"Yes. Is that why God took Nathan and all the others? Because I sinned? Is that why God took my leg? Because I loved war?"

"Perhaps. Who knows? You want me to speak for God? What man can? Moses. Only Moses for sure. The rest of us? We must study and pray and hope for understanding. And then she said more?"

"She said Numbers 31, and then she was gone or I fell asleep, I don't know."

"Why do you think she said Numbers 31?"

"It's about war."

"But what about war?"

"God tells Moses to avenge the Israelite people on the Midianites. So here God is starting a war."

"Yes, God makes it clear that war is sometimes necessary. It doesn't mean that the killing pains Him less. But look at the conditions God imposes."

"Conditions?"

"How do the Jews go to war on the Midianites?"

"Moses raises an army and goes to war."

"That is it? You think it was that simple? Reb Joseph, must I take out my book and make you read?"

"No. I know it."

"So tell me."

"A thousand men from each tribe took to the field."

"With...?"

"With what?"

"Come, Reb Joseph. Who went with the soldiers? And with what did they go?"

"You mean the priests, with the sacred objects?"

"I do. So now we have two of the conditions for war."

"One is the cause must be just."

"More. The cause must be compelling. Here it's so compelling that God, who loves all his creatures, even the Midianites, must inflict suffering on Himself to order this war. And the second condition?"

"The priests and the sacred objects and the holy trumpets?"

"Yes."

"You think that means we can only go to war with ritual?"

"I do. Why do I think that is what it means?"

"The ritual is to make us think about what we are about to do— remind ourselves of the awesome thing war is. Slaughter in the name of righteousness. But Reb Moses, there is where this whole argument comes apart. For centuries men have been slaughtering each other in God's name."

"For centuries men have been wrong."

"Every time?"

"Not every time. We know from the Holy Scriptures that there are times when we must fight. Also we know there are times when it is wrong to fight. To make war then is against God's will."

"Then how do we know which is which?"

"Sometimes we do and sometimes we don't. It's our life's work to study what it is that God wants of us."

"And this war?"

"What do you think?"

"I think the cause is just and compelling. We fight not only to end slavery but to preserve the New Jerusalem."

"You believe that?"

"With all my heart."

"America is the way to Messiah?"

"With all that I am."

"Even though the loss of your leg allows you to leave the army honorably, you choose to stay and fight?"

"It's not a choice. It's all there is. If I don't fight for my country, then I have lost more than my leg."

"Perhaps that's your answer. Perhaps all that has happened to you has been to bring you to this decision. Perhaps you know what God wants of you—some of it. Perhaps that is why the Shechinah comes to you."

"It has to be more important than just one soldier fighting. If I fight or don't fight, it will make no difference to the outcome of the war."

"That we cannot know. Numbers 31. What happened when the Israelite soldiers came back to the camp?"

Joseph was astonished to hear himself say, "Verse 15." He knew his Torah well enough to know what Numbers 31 was, but not well enough to quote every verse. "Moses said to them, 'You have spared every female! Yet they are the very ones who, at the bidding of Balaam, induced the Israelites to trespass against the Lord in the matter of Peor, so that the Lord's community was struck by the plague. Now therefore slay every male among the children and slay also every woman who has known a man carnally; but spare every young woman who has not had carnal relations with a man.'"

Moses Cohen nodded. "Reb Joseph, you surprise me. You know the whole Torah by heart?"

Joseph whispered his reply. "I didn't think I did."

They sat in silence for a moment until Moses Cohen asked, "So what do you think this passage means?"

Joseph answered without hesitation. "War isn't a game to be played between men of 'honor' replete with acts of chivalry. It's a thing of horror that must be concluded in horror."

"Why?"

"The more horrible it is, the quicker it will end and the more men will think carefully before they engage in it again."

"You have thought of this before? Perhaps before today you took out your Torah and studied Numbers 31 and have come to these conclusions?"

"I don't have the Holy Scriptures with me."

"When did you study Numbers 31 last?"

"I can't remember."

Moses Cohen took out his well-worn Torah, opened it, found what he was looking for and asked, "Can you tell me what is verse 19?"

Joseph answered almost immediately: "It's Moses speaking to the soldiers. He says, 'You shall stay outside the camp for seven days; everyone among you or among your captives who has slain a person or touched a corpse shall cleanse himself on the third and seventh days. You shall also cleanse every cloth, every article of skin, everything made of goats' hair, and every object of wood.' " Joseph's eyes came back into focus. He looked at Moses Cohen. "This is why she came to me. The killing is essential. But it's unclean."

"That's why God forbade David the warrior-king to build the Temple. Why his son Solomon had to be the one to do it."

"She's telling me that when the war is over I can be clean again—at least clean enough to go home. But how shall I clean myself when the killing is done?"

"We shall see when the time comes."

One morning Kate arrived to find Joseph sitting on the side of his bed. The effort had left him soaked in a clammy sweat.

Kate reached out to support him. "Joseph, what are you doing?"

"Kate, help me up."

"It's too early. You'll open your wound."

"I'm going to ride again. But I won't be able to if I don't start getting my leg strong. I've thought more about my saddle. What if I lose my wooden leg in battle? I have to learn to hop. Hop to my horse. I may even have to fight on foot. Hopping is essential. Be a good girl and help me. I promise if I feel anything bad I'll get right back in bed."

"Joseph..."

"Please, Kate?"

She shook her head.

"I'll make a deal with you," he said. "You help me now and every day from now on. When I'm fit, I'll put you on any horse you choose and race you around any course in the country. What do you say?"

"Okay, I'll help you up. Not because of a silly horse race promise, which I shall hold you to anyway, but because I can see that left to your own devices you'll do yourself harm."

"Good."

"But on one condition."

"What?"

"I'm in charge of how much you do and how often. Do we have a deal?"

"Deal. Now get me up."

A few days later on a bright, cool afternoon Kate arrived pushing a wheelchair made of bent oak and rattan. "Do you remember fresh air and blue sky?"

Just before she rolled the chair around the corner of the hospital a horse whinnied. Joseph knew the sound. It was for him. He reached down and, taking the wheel-tops, propelled the chair around the corner. There was Custer holding Thunder. Seeing Joseph, Thunder cast Custer aside and trotted across the green lawn. In a moment the horse stood before his master and, lowering his head, sniffed Joseph, nibbled his hand and sighed.

Joseph was unable to speak. He caressed his old friend. Thunder lowered his head until his nose was in Joseph's lap. He closed his eyes and Joseph gently pulled his ears. After a while Thunder lifted his head slightly and put it down, repeating the motion until Joseph understood.

"He wants me out of this contraption," he told Kate and Custer. Then he put an arm about the stallion's neck, allowing Thunder to assist him to a standing position. Once upright Joseph, oblivious to the others, stood against his horse, touching him.

"Soon," Joseph whispered to Thunder. "Soon."

When Kate decided Joseph had exerted himself as much he could bear she nodded to Custer, who signaled an orderly.

"I've got him a barn right close by," Custer said. He handed Thunder's lead to the orderly and helped Joseph back into the chair.

"Autie. Thank you. Have you met Miss Kate Woolsey? She's my nanny."

Custer bowed as elegantly as any cavalier. "I have had the honor. It was she who told me I couldn't see you without first bringing Thunder."

Kate settled Joseph into his bed and left to attend her other patients. Custer stared after her. "Now that, sir, is a fine woman. You married?"

"No," Joseph answered quickly. "What are you doing in Washington?"

"That damned ape in the White House and the lunatic he's got running the War Department have ordered the Army off the peninsula. Damn them! We could have taken Richmond!"

Joseph now knew Custer was mistaken about McClellan's ability to take anything, let alone a well-defended city. Again he changed the subject. "Autie, there's something I have been thinking about, and I need to know your opinion."

"At your service, sir."

"I've thought a great deal about the charge. I gave the wrong command."

"Rot! You did exactly the right thing."

"I lost a man who was dear to me and dearer to those that I love. And I lost almost the entire battalion. All those dead men..."

"Luck of the draw."

"I think not."

"Then to what do you ascribe it?"

"The rifled Springfield. The rifled Enfield," said Joseph.

"What's your point?"

"Those rifled muskets have an accurate range of eight hundred yards."

"Yes?"

"The old smooth-bore muskets have a range of two hundred yards, and then in the hands of an ordinary man they're not accurate. At two hundred yards against such weapons, a charge has a fair chance of being effective. At eight hundred yards against men trained with rifled muskets it's suicide."

"Are you saying the cavalry charge is no longer a suitable tactic?"

"I'm saying that had I been thinking of war instead of glory..."

"Good war is glory."

"What I mean is, my men were armed with Spencer repeating rifles, seven shots to a magazine. At my command they each carried two extra cartridge tubes loaded with seven shots each. That was twenty-one rapid-fire shots per man. I had, may God forgive me, 550 men, and thus the ability to fire 11,550 bullets at the enemy advancing up a slope against a defended position. Autie, do you understand? If I had left my men dismounted and placed them behind the earthworks alongside the infantry, we could have stopped the rebels with little or even no losses on our side. They may have had rifled Enfields, but it still takes one minute to load and fire any single-shot muzzle loader. My men were armed with Spencers that fire seven shots in twelve seconds. And I ordered a charge?"

"There's not an officer in the cavalry who would have done otherwise."

"Then we shall kill all our cavalry."

Custer grew grave.

"If I'd heard this talk from any other man I might consider him a touch disinclined to face the enemy. But I know you to be brave. Perhaps your wound has addled your brain. The cavalry charge is and always will be the most glorious form of war."

§47

At the end of August the Union once again suffered a defeat at Bull Run. A week later Lee panicked Washington and Pennsylvania by invading the Union through Maryland. Two weeks after that twenty-five thousand men were killed or maimed in the battles of Antietam—forty-eight hundred slain on both sides on the bloodiest day of the war. Lee's exhausted army retreated back across the Potomac and McClellan, who might have ended the war with a swift attack to prevent that crossing, once again sacrificed his country to his extreme reluctance to fight.

The population of Joseph's ward doubled to accommodate the wounded of Second Bull Run, and then increased again for the maimed of Antietam. Joseph gave up his bed and moved into a suite maintained by Loeb in the Willard Hotel; Kate still came by to help. Recovering his strength so that he might once more fight in battle became Joseph's main focus. He was convinced this was what God wanted of him.

Custer arrived with details of Antietam. Elated over the triumph, he was also furious with McClellan's staff for depriving him of the complete victory over Lee.

"Autie," Joseph said. "It wasn't his staff. It was him. McClellan isn't capable of victory. Your Young Napoleon would rather pose than be."

Custer was astonished enough to hold his temper, and then puzzled. He took Joseph very seriously. Although he didn't exactly understand what Joseph was saying, he was sure it was important. Yet McClellan was Custer's patron and his friend, and he felt he must defend him.

"What about General McClellan's recall from the peninsula?" Custer asked. "You think it was right for that ape in the White House to humiliate General McClellan?"

"Yes. The man in the White House is not an ape. I know. I know. For a while I thought like you, but I was wrong. It's odd how passion for the army can distort a man's thinking. President Lincoln is a man with an impossible job. He's bravely put some of the most capable men in America in his cabinet. To have them there he must endure knowing the most powerful of them covet his job and will run against him. Can he trust all of their advice and views? I for one can't imagine what I would do in the same position. He's commander-in-chief and has no military knowledge and has to trust the likes of McClellan. And when he's wrong tens of thousands of men die or are maimed. Could you do that?"

"Sure I could."

"My father-in-law, Mr. Loeb, visits with the president...."

"By Jinks, so you are married. You sly dog, leading the fair Kate on."

Joseph ignored him. "Mr. Lincoln doesn't have the money to fight this war. On both sides we're suffering catastrophic losses of life and he must accept it, order more battles and at the same time keep up the spirits of a stunned electorate. No one knows the dimensions of this war and yet with both Bull Runs and Antietam, no reasonable man can expect that it will be less than years of blood—rivers of it that will flow through President Lincoln's soul. He'll wade in blood wherever he goes. Can any man do this job?"

"McClellan."

"No. General McClellan can organize an army, equip it, train it and cause it to love him. But he's unable to move that army into battle. Your Young Napoleon lacks the very essence of a war commander. Forgive me, Autie, but your patron is a coward."

Custer started to show his anger. Joseph waved him off.

"I know he's your friend, and it's hard to hear a friend called coward. But I'm your friend too. Hear me out. If McClellan had pressed his advantage we could have taken Richmond in a matter of weeks. We outnumbered the rebels and outgunned them by significant margins. We controlled both the James and York rivers. Had McClellan not dithered before Yorktown we could have swept by Yorktown and Williamsburg, taken Richmond and ended the war. My God man, if it's true that McClellan actually had a copy of Lee's orders, Lee's troop dispositions, three days before Antietam..."

"It is true," Custer interrupted sadly. "I saw them."

"And he didn't immediately attack? He knew where Lee was. He knew that Lee had divided his army: Jackson, his hammer, with half the army at Harpers Ferry, and Lee with the other half of the army marching toward him right into a trap, utterly vulnerable. And still, with this overwhelming advantage, your hero didn't immediately take his vastly superior force, fall on Lee and destroy him. Would you have?"

"Well, yes. Of course."

"Do you understand what this...," he almost said coward again but spared his friend, "...overly cautious general has done? He has prolonged the war for years! Because of him oceans of blood shall wash across the land. Bloody, bloody McClellan!" Joseph was unable to say more. Custer, stunned by Joseph's passion, remained silent as well.

When he regained his balance, Joseph continued: "How odd that the soldiers love McClellan so, when he spends their blood in such a profligate way and for no gain. Gain? Hardly. Because he has spent it in the way he has, so much more and more now must be spent. And they love him. You love him."

Custer, confused by two loyalties, did the only thing possible. He changed the subject.

Near the end of the month Lincoln announced his Emancipation Proclamation. While tens of thousands of Union soldiers were angry at the proclamation—they weren't fighting to free the black man— Joseph was elated. Ending slavery would cleanse the Declaration of Independence and the Constitution. He now had his holy rationale for the war.

In October the doctor came and fitted Joseph with a wooden leg. Though it was padded with fleece it was painful, and he was told to wear it only for a few minutes at a time to build up his tolerance. Joseph ignored the pain and wore the device much longer. At first he needed two crutches to maneuver, but in less than a month he was using one.

Six weeks after the first fitting of his wooden leg, Joseph asked for, and was granted, medical leave. The army wanted to give him a medical discharge, but Loeb's intervention with Stanton prevented it. As a reward for his bravery Joseph was promoted to the rank of lieutenant colonel.

Kate had packed for Joseph and they walked to the coach together. Joseph saw Kate's bags lashed to the boot.

"I'm going with you to Thunder Farm," she said. She looked straight into his eyes. "I too have taken a well-earned leave of absence. When you return to the war, so shall I to the hospital. In the meantime, it's my duty to see to it that you are properly looked after while you complete your recovery."

"Thank you," he said. "A nurse and a horse trainer—how could I be more fortunate in my company?"

Thunder Farm and Liberty Hall were far grander than Kate expected. While she appreciated the mansion for its opulence, and was sure her mother would swoon over it, the horse operation thrilled her most. Touring it, she resolved to possess it.

The housekeeper, Mrs. Conover, had been informed that a nurse was coming with her maimed master and she was pleased. She knew he would have to return to Thunder Farm at some point, and she didn't feel comfortable with the idea of caring for a wounded man.

But after one look at Kate she was unhappy. Instead of a plain middle-aged woman, Mrs. Conover saw a girl far too young and pretty.

Mrs. Conover had prepared a guest room for the nurse so that she could be near her patient. Now she changed her mind and gave Kate a small room in the servants' wing, next to her own little suite.

Kate, unsure of Mrs. Conover's power and of her own relationship with Joseph, allowed the housekeeper to have her way in the matter of accommodations and all else pertaining to the house.

In his own home Joseph discovered that in spite of all the time he had spent in bed in the hospital and at the Willard Hotel, he was profoundly tired. His last thought before he fell asleep was a bitter one. It was of Fannie. He slept for eighteen hours.

Joseph was eating his breakfast when Kate came into the dining room. He was astonished to see her dressed as a man in trousers and boots.

She smiled. "It's one of the reasons I was never popular with the womenfolk back home. But you can't work horses in a dress and I refuse to ride sidesaddle. I'm afraid I've scandalized your domestic staff."

"Kate, you look quite beautiful."

She helped herself to porridge, maple syrup, and coffee and then strode back to the table. "While you've been sleeping I went to see the horses. Joseph, they are the most splendid beasts. I was surprised to see that you have held only so few back from the war."

He nodded. "Just the best brood mares, the mares in foal and those still nursing. Did you see the colts and the yearlings?"

"The most beautiful I ever saw."

"The two-year-olds?"

"No one is working them."

"The men are in the cavalry."

"I can work them."

He smiled. "Got to see you ride first."

"But I told you…"

"Yes, you did. And before you get on any of my horses, I have to see you ride."

"That's what your barn manager said."

"He's too old for the war, and too old to do much riding. Good with the ground work though. I'm lucky to have him." He smiled. "Wouldn't let you ride, huh?"

"Did you know that Mr. Wittcomb has sent your special saddle?"

"I was hoping." He pushed his chair back, raised himself, and hopped across the room to his crutch. "The damn wooden leg is no good. Perhaps if I had a knee, I could use one. But the damned thing hurts and gets in the way. The hell with it. Let's see my saddle."

It was on a saddle stand in the center of the elegant tack room. The stand was several feet lower than a horse's back, so it was relatively easy for Joseph to experiment with mounting and dismounting. Leather-covered iron grips had been built onto the top of the pommel and the right side of the cantle. By grasping them firmly, Joseph was able to take enough weight off his foot so that a light hop, coordinated with his arms pulling up his body, brought his foot into the stirrup. In the same movement he swung his stump over the saddle and placed it in the cup. After only a few tries he was pale and sweating.

"Bravo, Joseph. Well done," Kate said. "But I think that's enough for today. We'll work some more tomorrow."

Joseph shook his head. "Not just yet." He turned to Moon, the stable boy, "Get Thunder. Bring him to the arena."

"Moon, stop." Kate ordered.

Moon glanced at her with amazement and then trotted out of the tack room.

"Joseph, I'm your nurse." Kate wasn't smiling. "And nurse outranks lieutenant colonel."

"Thank you, Kate. I appreciate your concern. But now I'm going to ride my horse." He picked up his crutches and propelled himself to the enclosed arena.

Moon walked Thunder to the arena's center and tied him to the post. Then he ran back to the tack room and returned with the new saddle and a blanket. Joseph took an armchair on the low observation platform and, closing his eyes, desperately tried to relax.

Kate settled next to him. "Joseph, I've been nursing people long enough to know it takes a man many months to regain his strength after the kind of injuries you've suffered."

"I know what I must do."

"Ready," Moon called.

Joseph, carefully balancing on his crutches on the soft arena floor, made his way to Thunder. He touched his horse in the old familiar way and spoke softly. When he felt Thunder was completely relaxed, Joseph took hold of the two saddle handles and attempted to repeat what he had done earlier on the saddle stand. But the stirrup was now too high. His foot missed. He held onto the handles and tried again. Again he missed.

Moon stepped forward to assist but Joseph waved him away. Again and again he tried to make the hop into the stirrup until on the sixth time he was successful, although so exhausted he could barely swing his body into the saddle. When he was in the saddle and on his horse he felt whole once again.

Thunder knew something was wrong. Where was the comfort on his off-side? And who was that on his back? He began to snort and paw the ground. His master had gotten up on him, but was it his master on him?

Joseph felt the change in his horse. He leaned forward and spoke gently. Next he settled in the saddle and then with a slight shift of weight and a nearly imperceptible movement in his fingers, he asked Thunder to walk forward. Thunder did. Joseph asked for no more than a short walk. He was not sure he could circle the arena even once, nor if he had the strength to dismount. He brought Thunder to a halt in front of Kate at the observation platform. Then he dismounted and would have fallen but for Kate who quickly slipped her shoulder under his arm and helped him to the chair.

Joseph, his face white and wet, looked at her. "Now let me see you ride."

She started to object but he cut her off. "Now or never." To Moon he said, "Change saddles. Get her the little one I had made for Fannie." He didn't notice that he had said his wife's name.

"No," Kate said. "Just pull this one off. I'll ride bareback."

Moon looked at Joseph, who nodded his assent.

Kate quietly stepped to Thunder and touched him as she had seen Joseph do. In moments the great black stallion dipped his head to allow her to pull his ears. Then, without changing the mood, Kate grasped his mane and the reins and in one fluid movement vaulted to his back.

Thunder liked her. She was safe. She gave him comfort on both sides. When she asked for a walk he moved forward with a light happy step. Kate took him into a trot, then into a gathered canter. Kate adored the horse. Taking him through the classic dressage forms she lost herself in that adoration.

It was true, Joseph thought. The woman rode better than almost every man he knew. It was extraordinary, and now he knew he loved her.

Kate listened to Mrs. Conover's snoring through their adjoining wall before she crept from her room to Joseph's. He woke to her kiss. Months of longing and rage overtook him. He seized her and devoured her until he collapsed: exhausted, spent, fulfilled.

So that is fornication, Kate thought. Boring. No wonder married woman are so unhappy. Disgusting.

§48

WINTER HAD DESCENDED ON ASCONA WITH AN UNACCUSTOMED ferocity. The Villa Dolce, which had been pleasantly drafty in the fall, became impossible to heat and the revels ended. But the termination of Fannie's Swiss saturnalia had an official stamp as well. Ascona's police chief, backed by the mayor, had visited the day before to warn Dionysus and Fannie that their scandalous conduct had placed them in jeopardy with angry citizens. Their safety couldn't be guaranteed. The officials asked them to leave within the week.

Dionysus, Lord and Lady Elphanstone, and the Russian princess with her pale consort who had recently joined them broke out into uproarious laughter. How ridiculous the Swiss peasants were! Of course they would leave. Ascona was too cold. Morocco was the only place to winter. The Russians knew of a splendid palace that could be rented with servants, all of whom, male and female, had been in the owner's private harem. It was expensive. Dionysus said Fannie would pay. But Fannie's money was running out. There had been no response from her banks in New York or Paris, nor had Isador and Bella answered her urgent telegrams. She didn't tell Dionysus.

After Loeb received a letter from Joseph's parents telling of the children's arrival and their concern for Fannie, he wrote to Joseph to inform him of his children's whereabouts. He also said that he was stopping all but a small amount of Fannie's income from her bank accounts. He asked Joseph to authorize him to withhold the money he had his bank set aside for Fannie, explaining that he would arrange for Fannie to have just enough to live modestly. He would inform her that until she returned home the money would be continually reduced. Joseph agreed and asked Loeb to continue handling his daughter's finances without informing him.

Fannie promised Dionysus she would catch up with him in Rome and, while the others traveled to the south, she headed north to Bavaria and her children.

No matter what else, Fannie was their son's wife and the mother of their grandchildren. When she left the children with them more than a month before, Jakob had said to Rebecca, "There is trouble."

"So what kind of trouble can it be? He has another woman?"

"Who knows?"

"You think she was unfaithful?"

"Details are unimportant," he said. "What is important is they are *beshert* and they love each other and they have lost their way."

When Fannie arrived they saw that she was too thin, and exhausted. Rebecca and Jakob tried to help. They failed. Von Falkenbrecht, ill and confined to his bed, was told of Fannie's presence and sent for her. Although she liked the count, Fannie had no desire to see him. But Jakob wouldn't accept her objection so he drove her to the castle himself.

Fannie was appalled by the count's transformation. The shock nearly destroyed the wall she had built around her emotions. However, she resisted it.

Von Falkenbrecht was too close to his own death to see Fannie clearly. He insisted she sit by him and, holding her hand, reminisced about Joseph. Before she left he signaled to a servant who brought his battle sword to the bedside.

"This," von Falkenbrecht whispered, "is for Joseph, my own Baron von Breitenstein. I have carried it in every battle." A servant handed a thick envelope to Fannie. "And this is very important. From my king. Very important. You will put it into his hands. You will do this?"

"Yes," Fannie said, lying. She knew she would never see Joseph again.

Two days later Count von Falkenbrecht died and was buried in the family vault. The morning after the funeral Fannie handed over the sword and letter to Jakob for his son. In the afternoon Jakob drove her to the Dittelheim station. Fannie took the train for Munich, from where she could travel to Rome. Jakob waited for her to say anything to give him an opportunity to intervene, but he waited in vain. As the train pulled in, Jakob held her by her shoulders and then looked into her eyes.

"You are my daughter," he said. "Rebecca and I love you. We know our son. No matter what is happening, he loves you. You take the knowledge and you keep it. You keep it in your heart. One day the time will come when you will know it and trust it."

He led Fannie to the car and then turned back to his horse.

The detective, Herr Wunderlicht, once again employed by Klostermann & Co. arrived in Paris and went directly from the train station to the préfecture of police for the Fifth Arrondissement. The chief inspector, having received his telegram, was waiting with details of the life led by the lady in question.

"But one thing I shall tell you, this just between us," the chief inspector said. "What they have been doing has been so public that it is a scandal of monumental proportions. Before the scandal this Dionysus had certain very high—the highest, if you take my meaning—patronage. It has been withdrawn. We have our orders. Neither one may return to France."

The next morning Herr Wunderlicht took the train for Switzerland.

In Rome, Fannie tracked down the address Dionysus had telegraphed to her. It was a run-down sixteenth century palace just behind the Piazza Navona. The porter showed her to a once-grand apartment. A party was in progress. Besides Fatima, Lady Elphanstone, and the Russian princess, she was the only woman. The room was crowded with fashionable, dissolute, drunken men.

Dionysus glided up to her. "Did you get more money?"

"No."

"Then you will have to earn it." He turned from her and shouted something to the crowd. Suddenly they were all pulling out sheaves of liras.

Dionysus grinned. "And now the auction." Fannie loved that grin, for it promised pain and oblivion.

"Now what?" she asked. "What are you auctioning?"

"You."

"Me?"

"First your clothes. Stand on the table."

Fannie moved to the center of the room, where she stepped up on an ottoman, and then to a tabletop. When the bidding started, she was told what they had paid for and removed that article of clothing. Fatima and the Russian princess, to the intense gratification of the crowd, came to her, stopped her hands and proceeded to strip her. When Fannie was naked, Dionysus held aloft the cash he had collected and again addressed the assembly.

Fannie didn't know what he was saying and didn't care. Her body was on fire. She adored and hated the hungry eyes staring at her. The satyr, amused, turned to her.

"I have bet everything at ten to one in my favor that you can fuck every man in this room before dawn."

Senator Cole was raised in the southern Evangelical tradition. He did not gamble or swear. He believed in a God that rewarded the good and punished the evil. He read his Bible every day and attended church on Sundays. He was just and kind to his slaves. He was a man of honor and had fought more than one duel defending that honor. He believed the Civil War was about state rights, not slavery. While he knew slavery was the only humanitarian place for the black man in society, and often quoted the appropriate Old Testament passages to prove it, sometimes he wondered.

After the destruction of his plantation and the death of his son, the senator found solace in the war. He believed it was just, honorable and forced on an unwilling South. His unit, the Cole Legion of the Georgia Volunteer Light Horse, was mustered into the Army of Northern Virginia and attached to Jeb Stuart. Although Senator Cole held the rank of colonel, those who knew him continued to call him senator. He had two goals in life. One was to defeat the Union, and the other was to personally kill Joseph von Ritter. Yet after meeting with Baron von Exing, who shared his passion for the latter, the senator found the man distasteful. Thus it was with surprise and repugnance that the senator received the announcement that Baron von Exing was waiting outside the tent.

Lee's armies were celebrating. The day before at Fredericksburg the Union had suffered its worst defeat yet. Lee trounced Burnside, and Union losses stood at nearly thirteen thousand while the South had lost five.

The baron was, as usual, drunk.

Von Exing saluted in an offhand manner. He had already sensed the senator's distaste and considered it provincial snobbism, the southern aristocrats' foolish aping of European nobility. "Senator Cole. I bring interesting news."

The senator resented von Exing's use of the familiar "senator" rather than the more formal "colonel," but let it go.

"The little Jew," von Exing said, "is back with their army. I would have found him and killed him if he had been in the battle. But for him to die in battle is too good."

The senator understood, although the baron didn't, that in the matter of von Ritter they weren't allies. They were competitors. And he felt he had the greater right to kill Joseph.

"Where is he?" the senator asked.

"He commands these Albany Invincibles." Von Exing shook his head and smiled. "But not for long. I have a plot."

"Oh?"

"We know where he is. We have Yankee prisoners. I have found two who will shoot him in the next battle from behind. A coward's death for the little Jew."

"Under no circumstances. You hear me, sir? If the Lord sees fit to take him in battle, so be it. Otherwise, it is my intention to avenge my son by my own hand."

"But you are a gentleman. You cannot duel with a Jew. You destroy them like vermin."

"Baron, this is America. The man is an officer and therefore a gentleman. If I can, I shall challenge him. If a meeting cannot be arranged then I'll seek him out in battle. I know his face and now thanks to you, his regiment. I'll find him. As for this conversation, I shall report it to General Stuart. I'm sure he'll agree with me that if Colonel von Ritter is found after a battle with bullet holes in his back, you shall personally be held responsible. I shall call you to account for it. Good day to you, sir."

Von Exing was afraid of Joseph and he was afraid of the senator. Therefore, he agreed.

The Albany Invincibles were down to only a third of their strength. They had fought in every major engagement and the survivors, now battle-wise veterans, were pleased with the appointment of Joseph as their new colonel.

Joseph saw his first duty as the necessary replenishment of the regiment. Taking several officers from the Albany area, he went North and in a matter of weeks recruited the necessary men.

Next he supplied the entire regiment with the Spencer repeating rifles and concentrated on teaching them rapid-fire marksmanship. He allowed no time for himself. He worked every waking hour, building his own strength seven days a week.

Late in December, Loeb and Moses Cohen arrived in Washington. In response to Loeb's telegram, Joseph met them in the suite at the Willard Hotel. Joseph saw at once that both men were grave. Loeb handed Joseph a copy of a military document.

Headquarters Thirteenth Army Corps
Department of the Tennessee; Oxford, Mississippi
December 17, 1862

The Jews as a class, violating every regulation of trade established by the Treasury Department, also department orders, are hereby expelled from the department within twenty-four hours from the receipt of this order by post commanders.

They will see that all this class of people are furnished with passes and required to leave; and any one returning after such notification will be arrested and held in confinement until an opportunity occurs of sending them out as prisoners, unless furnished with permits from these headquarters [sic].

No passes will be given these people to visit headquarters for the purpose of making personal application for trade permits.

By order of Major General Grant,
JOHN A. RAWLINS, A.A.G.

Joseph collapsed into a chair.

"Impossible," he said. "This is America."

"It is possible, because it was done," Moses Cohen said. "It will be impossible to stand because it is America."

"The difference between America and Europe," Loeb said, "is here we can and we shall fight this General Grant and his General Order Number Eleven."

"Here," Moses Cohen joined in, "we are not only able to fight such things, but we are obligated to do so if we're to be good Americans."

"How?" Joseph asked. "He's a general."

"And the president is commander-in-chief," Loeb said. "The army exists at the will of Congress." He picked up a sheaf of papers. "This afternoon, if you will, you'll accompany us to visit with the president."

"Of course I shall. Can the man who wrote the Proclamation of Emancipation tolerate this?"

"He is a politician. He has a war. Grant is one of his few fighting generals. Unless we act, he may."

"No," Moses Cohen said. "Joseph is right. The man who signed the Emancipation will not accept this from even the most winning of generals."

"In any event, we must fight for our proper place in America." Loeb tapped the papers in his hand. "In a few weeks' time, Mr. Lincoln will receive a document containing certain powerful resolutions from the board of delegates of the American Israelites— the formal protest of our community. In the meantime I'll hand him this evidence. It will appear next week in the *Cincinnati Enquirer* and also other papers. Joseph, do you know about the quasi-legal cotton trade between the Union and the South?"

"No. How can there be such a thing?"

"The house of Loeb doesn't engage in it, but many bankers do. In Memphis, and in other points of contact between the two sides, the South is selling cotton to the North at vastly inflated prices. This trade can only be carried on with the issuance of permits by our high army officers. Certain officers have made fortunes in partnership with traders. A few of these traders are Jews. The majority are not. One trader, Jesse R. Grant, the father and partner of Major General Ulysses S. Grant, made a contract to purchase rebel cotton and ship it to New York, but lacking capital formed an agreement with the Mack brothers. They're Jews I know. They are disreputable men. General Grant's responsibility in the partnership was to supply the necessary permissions for the cotton to be passed through the Union lines. Three hundred bales were purchased and shipped. They realized a profit of 400,000 dollars. But the Macks cheated the Grants out of all of it. Hence, General Order Number Eleven."

"A Union general buys from the South so they can purchase arms to use against us?" Joseph asked. "My God! Shiloh. Twenty-five thousand dead on both sides, and Grant gives the rebels money for arms? It's impossible."

"It's possible, it's legal, and it happened."

"We must tell the president!"

"He knows. For the moment, the cotton trade can't be stopped. Political considerations. But General Order Number Eleven can be revoked and apologized for. That I promise you."

As Lincoln offered his condolences to Loeb on the loss of Nathan, Joseph saw in his eyes the same knowledge he had seen in the eyes of the Shechinah when she told him of God's sadness at the death of any mortal. If God could have a face, Joseph thought, Lincoln's was it.

Before the president read the material Loeb handed him, he apologized for Grant's general order. He promised he had already planned to order its revocation. He also offered an apology from Grant and the government, but asked Loeb to leave the timing to him. It was a delicate and complex matter, for the nation could hardly afford to alienate Grant now.

Tucking the papers in a pocket, Lincoln turned his attention to Joseph. He asked about his wounds and congratulated him on his bravery in continuing in his command. Lincoln was particularly interested in Joseph's comments on the proper use of cavalry. Had not Lincoln's secretary, Nicolay, announced his next appointment, they might have talked another hour. Before leaving, Joseph told Lincoln about his friend Captain George Armstrong Custer, an officer of great fighting ability who could be the North's answer to Jeb Stuart. The president nodded to Nicolay who wrote down the name.

Once outside the White House, Moses Cohen paused and said the Hebrew prayer thanking God for His creation of miracles. When finished he turned to his companions, tears in his eyes and said,

"Can there be doubt that America is a way to the age of Messiah? Not when God gives us such a leader as this holy man. Perhaps it is not by chance he is named Abraham."

After supper Moses Cohen retired early, leaving Loeb alone with his son-in-law. They lit their cigars and Loeb rose and paced the suite's sitting room. Joseph waited, fearing the subject about to be broached.

Loeb turned from studying the fire. "Now we must speak of Fannie."

Joseph said nothing.

"On Monday," Loeb continued, "I sail for Paris. I'll go to Bavaria and see your parents and the children. I've had reports of Fannie. They're bad. If they are true you will have to divorce her."

Joseph nodded. "When the war is over," he said. "Now there can only be the war."

At the end of January, Loeb arrived at the Gershomsohn farm in Bavaria. Although he discussed Joseph and Fannie with Jakob and Rebecca, he couldn't bring himself to reveal what he had learned from the Klostermann & Co. detective. He agreed with Joseph and his parents that, until the war ended, it was best to leave the children there.

Dionysus and Fannie, her money reduced to a trickle, were unwelcome in Rome. Their sexual escapades shocked all but the most decadent of the fashionable world, and when the money ran out, so did they. The Elphanstones left for Morocco with wealthy friends from England. The Russian princess and her pale consort moved to the French Riviera. Even Fatima had left, taking up with a Levantine dealer of rare essences.

Fannie's Roman creditors were threatening jail. Though she and Dionysus were living in a squalid little house just outside of Rome, Dionysus had great hopes of a fortune coming in on the evening train from Florence.

Loeb descended from the car and was met by his bankers. He was taken directly to a suite in the Grand Hotel. After he had bathed and eaten, he received Herr Wunderlicht who summed up his report.

"But Herr Wunderlicht, this is all gossip."

"Forgive me, Herr Loeb. I have proof."

"What proof?"

"First, I have certain gentlemen who have said they have participated in these debaucheries."

"Said is no proof."

Herr Wunderlicht opened his leather dispatch case and removed a package wrapped in red silk. "Then I have these. They are vile, but they are what you have hired me to find." Loeb did not reach for the scarlet packet.

"What are they?"

"I was approached by this Dionysus who showed me these photographs. They are from his paintings of the Baroness von Ritter engaged in unspeakable acts. He is prepared to deliver to you the paintings and the glass plates from which the photographs have been made for the sum of 200,000 dollars. His price was originally one million, but I pointed out to him that it was an impossible sum. After considerable negotiating, in the course of which I found it necessary to mention certain highly placed persons in the police, we arrived at an acceptable amount. I must warn you, sir. Even with the threat of prison, the man and your daughter are desperate. If you don't pay him he will put the paintings up for sale in New York City."

Loeb motioned for Herr Wunderlicht to open the packet. One by one he examined the paintings. When he was done, he looked up at Herr Wunderlicht. "You bring this Dionysus to me tomorrow at noon," he said. "I shall have the money."

Herr Wunderlicht shook his head. "I'm sorry, sir. These things don't work that way. He'll only make the exchange in a public place. I am instructed to say that, if you agree, you are to bring the money to the Cafe Borgia in the Campo di Fiori at four o'clock tomorrow. I am to escort you there, identify you to him and depart."

Loeb nodded.

The following day Loeb sat across a cafe table from Fannie's lover in a room filled with working class Romans. He studied Dionysus, whom he found overly handsome and dissolute. The thought occurred to him that the man was dying of consumption.

Dionysus tried his most engaging smile. "I bring you regards from your daughter."

Loeb didn't answer.

Dionysus tried to wait the old man out. He was unable to do so. "You brought the cash?"

Loeb nodded.

"Then I suppose you would like to see my paintings? You know, the emperor of France would pay me much more than this for them. Much more."

Loeb said nothing.

Dionysus began to sweat. His hands shook as he placed his roll of paintings on the table next to the case containing the glass plates.

Loeb waited.

Dionysus untied the ribbons holding the roll closed. He turned the loose edges to Loeb.

Loeb carefully leafed though the edges so that no one else could see. They were the paintings of his daughter. Then he checked the case to confirm that the glass plates were also there. He retied the roll and closed the case. On top of it he placed his own package. He saw how Dionysus stared at it. Yes, Loeb thought. The man is desperate to feed his habit.

"I pay the money this time," Loeb said. "But never again. If you have kept any photographs, or make more paintings, I won't buy them again."

Dionysus attempted a gentlemanly protest but was cut short.

"When I leave Europe," Loeb continued, "I leave behind instructions with certain people. If any of this filth ever surfaces, anywhere in the world, you shall land in prison. No one, not even the empress of France, will lift a finger to help you. Have I made myself clear?"

Dionysus nodded.

"Answer me. Have you understood?"

"I have."

Loeb stood, took the roll of paintings and the case, and left.

Dionysus, fingers shaking, reached for the money. When his hands were on it, he called to the departing Loeb, "Any words for your dear daughter?"

Loeb paused, turned, and held Dionysus in his gaze.

"I have no daughter."

In his hotel room, Loeb systematically cut the paintings into strips and fed them into the fireplace. Then he carefully smashed each photographic plate into powdered glass, throwing the residue into the fire. When the job was completed he pulled some of the white ash from the fireplace with the poker and rubbed it onto his face. Then he ripped his coat and tore his shirt. Loeb turned to face east and recited the *kaddish,* the Hebrew prayer for the dead. His beloved Fannie was no more.

§49

Dionysus never returned to Fannie. He took Loeb's money and left for Morocco. Loeb was correct. The man was a drug addict and he was sick with consumption. So was Fannie.

Joseph missed Custer. After McClellan's dismissal from the Army of the Potomac, Custer had taken a long leave of absence to go home to Michigan where he wooed his true love, Elizabeth Clift Bacon. His letters to Joseph were filled with passion for his Libby, despair that her father didn't approve, and rage at Lincoln and Stanton for dismissing McClellan.

Joseph's letters to Custer contained the details of his growing ability in the saddle and the restoration of his regiment. He longed to share with Custer his excitement over the Emancipation Proclamation, but he suspected that it was of far less interest to his friend than the war.

Joseph didn't write to Custer about Kate. In fact, when he was apart from Kate, Joseph hardly thought of her. On those few occasions when he did, his reflections were angrily erotic. And, although he forced himself to not think of his wife, Fannie came unbidden like the Shechinah in the night.

Soulé, now a brigadier general and still, in spite of his protests and requests for transfer to the cavalry, provost-marshal of Washington, had heard of Joseph's return. He quickly reestablished contact.

He visited Joseph's encampment often and the two men resumed their dueling practice—saber on horseback. When Joseph suggested they attempt to duel on foot, General Soulé objected. He was quite sure it would be impossible for a one-legged man to engage in a duel. But Joseph insisted they try. In the beginning, General Soulé was correct, as Joseph was unable to find a constant balance.

One Sunday afternoon, as they were sitting on the wet ground in near despair, they were approached by a squat, brutal-looking sergeant.

He saluted. "Excuse me," he said. "But if you don't mind my butting in, sirs, I'd like to say something."

"Yes, sergeant?"

"I'm from the New York Second. Name's Conkling. I heard about what's been going on here. You don't remember me, but I know you, colonel. I mean from Brannagan's."

Joseph stiffened, and with a hand from General Soulé rose to his foot. "Yes?"

"I'm from Five Points, was a Dead Rabbit. Seen you cut up Slobbery Grimes. Seen you a lot. You was the best knife man I ever seen. I been watching this. The predicament you got, colonel, is that saber's too heavy. You ain't never gonna hop and be balanced. But if you get knocked off your horse, I bet you could hop and knife fight. Betcha."

As the man said it, Joseph knew he was right.

"But it is impossible. A knife against a saber?" General Soulé said. "Impossible."

"Sergeant Conkling," Joseph said, his face full of purpose. "Do you have a knife on you?"

"Yes, sir. Just happens I do. Took the edge and point off it too. You know, just in case." He handed Joseph a knife with a nine-inch blade, very much like the one Joseph once carried in his boot.

Joseph hefted it, made a few practice passes and turned to General Soulé. "General, *en garde!*"

General Soulé smiled, took the offensive stance and carefully advanced on Joseph. His first lunge was with the caution of a friend who would not hurt another. Joseph parried the lunge, hopped inside the blade and put the blunted point of the knife on Soulé's chest. "Now, my friend," Joseph said. "Come at me for real."

General Soulé nodded and attacked in force. Joseph was knocked down. But thereafter Joseph practiced knife against saber whenever General Soulé could join him, and knife against knife with Sergeant Conkling on a near-daily basis.

Upon his return from Europe, Loeb sent a telegram summoning Joseph to New York. When Joseph arrived at the Loeb mansion, he found it in mourning. Hanschen saw him in the hall and embraced him. She was wearing black and her eyes were red from weeping.

Joseph, who had seen so much death, thought he was inured to it. But now its chill filled him with apprehension.

Hanschen stepped back, tears streaming down her face. "My daughter," she said. "My daughter." She could hardly say the words.

"My God. Oh God in Heaven. Fannie. My Fanschen is gone. Go to him, Joseph. Go to him."

Numbed by fear, Joseph held Hanschen. "My God, is she dead?"

"Go to him." Hanschen pulled away and ran down the hall.

Shaking, Joseph opened the sitting room doors and entered. It was only civility that caused Loeb to rise from his seat. Joseph noticed ash on Loeb's forehead. His jacket lapel was slashed and he was in his stocking feet.

"Is Fannie dead?" Joseph asked.

The old man nodded. "To me she is," he said. "To me, my daughter is no more. And now to you it must also be so." He turned and lifted the stack of photographs of the infamous paintings from the table beside his chair. "I have destroyed everything but these. Look at them. We shall put them in the fire and we shall mourn together." He handed the photographs to Joseph.

When he had dueled with von Exing Joseph felt killing rage. Then when he fought Brannagan he felt it again. And when he burned Rotherwood and slashed Cole's throat, the anger had returned with greater intensity. But the rage in those incidents couldn't match what Joseph now felt looking at these pictures. His anger so overwhelmed him that his mind involuntarily shut down, shielding Joseph with an inert, cold shroud. Joseph studied each picture. He looked at every obscene detail, burning it into his mind forever. He studied his wife's face, so distorted with evil indulgence she seemed hideous. He strode to the fireplace and threw the photographs into the flames. The fire blistered Fannie's image, turned it black and then to ash.

Without looking at Loeb, he asked, "Is she dead?"

"To me."

"Then she is alive?"

"Not to me. My daughter is dead."

He's right, Joseph thought. She is dead.

"Will you say *kaddish* with me?"

Joseph stared at Loeb. "No, I won't. I've said *kaddish* for Nathan and for all those brave men who have died in this war. I won't profane it. I must go now."

Joseph started for the door. "I was in Bavaria," Loeb said.

Joseph turned. "My children?"

"Well and happy."

"My parents?"

"In excellent health. Your father is teaching your son Washington to ride. Your parents are wonderful with the children. Your mother says they make her young again."

Joseph nodded. "I'll go to them when the war is over," he said. "If I die I want them to come back here to you. I want them to be Americans. You and Hanschen will raise them?"

"Of course."

"They are to never know about their mother. Tell them about how wonderful their mother was when she was young. Tell them she died loving them. Will you do that?"

"Yes."

The men stood staring at each other. Then Loeb remembered. "You know about von Falkenbrecht?"

"Yes. I had a letter from my father."

Loeb turned and picked up von Falkenbrecht's war saber, and the letter. "These he sent to you."

Joseph mused for a moment over the saber. "He carried this into every battle in his life. I won't dishonor this one." Then he opened the letter and wept.

Schloss Falkenbrecht
November, 1862

My Dear Baron von Breitenstein, my dear Joseph who has been my only son:

I am dying. It is no great thing to die in bed. I would have preferred to die in battle. Neither poor Stumpf nor I have been lucky to have that last honor. At least I die of an old wound. An amusing consolation.

I am precluded by blood, by family and by the inflexible rules of my class from leaving you my title or my Bavarian estates. But I do leave to you the estate of Breitenstein, a good place for the wild boar and for roebuck shooting, so at least you have the land to go with your title. The title, democrat that you are, (what a pity, you are such a good aristocrat) will be important for you at least one more time.

I am enclosing a letter from His Majesty, confirming your title, confirming that you are noble, confirming that von Exing (the king dislikes the von Exings almost as much as I) may not refuse to fight you on the basis of rank. If he refuses your challenge now, he will be publicly known for what we know him to be privately—a coward. He is there in America on the wrong side. Leave it to a von Exing to fight for slavery. Find him. Challenge him. Kill him. It is a question of your honor and of mine. It is my dying request of you.

I send you my sword to carry into battle. It shall bring you the same success I have had. I die knowing this much I have done to protect your life. So, having safeguarded your life and your honor, I am not such a fool as to burden you with the departing ravings of an old man.

Hail and farewell!
Von Falkenbrecht

Enclosed was the crested and sealed letter from the king of Bavaria, signed by the monarch himself.

On January 26, 1863, Major General Joseph Hooker was named commander of the Army of the Potomac, replacing the unfortunate Ambrose Burnside. Hooker, unknown to even those who appointed him, had one genuine talent for the military. The man could organize and train an army. The army's morale was at an extreme low ebb: it distrusted its commanders, the men were deserting at an enormous rate, and the senior officers were spending more time fighting each other than the enemy. Worst of all was the cavalry which was misused, badly equipped and dispersed under the command of various infantry units.

Hooker fed his army with fresh food and clothed them with badly needed new uniforms and boots; he gave them unit identity with badges and began to instill an *esprit de corps*. He improved the hospitals, replenished the depleted ranks of the old regiments; but most of all he emancipated the cavalry, creating an independent cavalry corps under the command of Brigadier General Stoneman. It was with this act that Joseph's true calvary war commenced.

The Albany Invincibles were assigned to the Second Cavalry Division, under the command of Brigadier General W. W. Rainsford. They were to be one of seven regiments.

The men were delighted to be joining "Fighting Joe" Hooker. They knew nothing of Rainsford but they were sure Fighting Joe would lead them into battle soon.

Joseph flung himself into the logistics of moving his regiment to the new division camp. The Albany Invincibles were the last to arrive. Joseph paraded his regiment into camp, formed them in perfect order before the headquarters, and presented himself and his officers to General Rainsford. For the occasion Joseph wore his artificial leg.

Joseph was unimpressed with Rainsford. He seemed undefined and soft.

After the formalities, Joseph and his staff were shown the area for their camp. As soon as windbreaks, dry footing and sheltered feeding stations were established for the horses, the men put up their own tents and the daily routine was reestablished.

Joseph drilled his regiment three to four times the hours spent by the other six regiments. When not at regimental duties, he continued to work with Thunder and on his saber, pistol and knife practice. In the dark hours he studied von Clausewitz's volumes *On War,* and Jomini's *The Art of War.* In the interest of knowing his enemy, Joseph read everything he could about the South, including the latest Richmond newspapers. His Torah was never taken from his book trunk. The Shechinah didn't come to him and he all but forgot her.

Kate, sensing that she too might be forgotten, came to see him. After her first visit she told her mother that it wasn't that Joseph had lost interest in her, but that he was obsessed by the war. She would bide her time.

When he could, Custer came visiting and instantly began to chafe at his own inaction. He wanted command of one of Joseph's squadrons, which Joseph would have gladly given him, but Custer couldn't leave McClellan until the monumental "Report on the Organization of the Army of the Potomac and its Campaigns in Virginia and Maryland" was completed.

Early in April, Hooker ordered Rainsford to cross the Rappahannock River at Scamon's Ford. The spring campaigns had begun.

§50

AT LAST—WAR!

Joseph stood with his fellow regimental commanders as General Rainsford explained the plan of action. "Gentlemen," he said, "we have word that Fitzhugh Lee with his entire brigade is encamped at Culpepper. I'm ordered to proceed at once. We shall cross the Rappahannock at Scamon's Ford and engage this rebel cavalry. We shall rout it, destroy it or capture it. General Hooker's orders are that we are not to return until we have done so or find it impossible to do so. I do not foresee that impossibility."

Rainsford did foresee what he considered most important—an implied promise of promotion to major general with the success of this engagement. Joseph foresaw a battle of cavalry against cavalry and he was sure his men were up to it, even if it meant head-on, saber-to-saber engagements.

Rainsford enjoyed issuing his orders. "We shall move swiftly." Those were exactly the words the president and the cabinet liked to hear. No McClellan he. Rainsford looked over at the two reporters from the New York papers. The public would like those words too. "In two hours we'll ride for Titusville, approximately six miles from Scamon's Ford. Once assembled there, we'll proceed on the following morning to cross the ford and engage the enemy."

The Albany Invincibles were assigned first position on the march to Titusville. The twenty-one hundred men and horses, proceeding in a column of twos down the narrow country road, stretched out for six miles. The horses had been well-fed, watered, and were rested so that none fell out of the line of march. But due to confusion in command and supply, the six-gun battery of horse artillery didn't start out for Titusville until six hours after the departure of the main body of the Second Division.

On his own, Joseph sent a squad of his fastest horses and best scouts ahead. When his column arrived in Titusville, they were waiting for him. A lieutenant reported that the river crossing was unguarded. He and his men had explored as far as a woods a mile and a half from the other side.

"Well done, lieutenant," Joseph said. "See to your men and horses. General Rainsford will be here shortly and I expect we'll directly be engaged."

The lieutenant saluted and left. Joseph called for Sergeant Conkling.

"Sir?"

"I want prisoners. After the battle bring them all to me."

"Yes, sir. Do you want I should first get 'em talkative? You know, Dead Rabbit style?"

"No, sergeant. Prisoners will never be mistreated in this regiment. Am I clear on that subject?"

At the meeting of regimental commanders in Rainsford's tent Joseph was astonished by the order to detach two regiments, thirteen hundred men, to guard the fords north of Scamon's and to watch for a surprise attempt at a flanking movement.

"Sir, if I may?" Joseph asked.

Rainsford nodded. "Colonel von Ritter."

"Fitzhugh Lee is reported to have about eight hundred men. Not enough to divide his force and flank us."

"We can't be sure of that."

"General, in any event, no matter how many men he has, let me take my regiment. We can be at the ford an hour before dark, where we'll cross and make a fortified position—rifle pits, logs. I can hold the south bank until your arrival with the main body. Surely by now Fitzhugh Lee knows of our presence here. He must attempt to prevent our crossing Scamon's Ford. If I move now we can hold all five of his brigades till you arrive. Sir, we would then be in a position to move out before dawn and overwhelm them with our entire force."

"Thank you, Colonel." Rainsford was careful with Joseph, who was a hero and had serious political connections—all reasons why Rainsford had requested that the Albany Invincibles join his division. "We only assume it's Fitzhugh Lee by himself. It could be Stuart's whole force. There could also be infantry. There is a railroad at Culpepper. The infantry could be arriving this very moment. Caution, sir, will win the day. Gentlemen, the advance to Scamon's Ford shall commence at four in the morning."

It took the Second Division four hours to cover the six miles from Titusville to Scamon's Ford. When they arrived they found that the rebels had felled trees in the ford and had fortified the opposite bank with sharpshooters in the rifle pits Joseph had wanted to dig.

Rainsford ordered the First Rhode Island to dismount one hundred men and attack. They were beaten back on three successive attempts. Before the fourth, Joseph approached the general. "Sir," he said, "if the Rhode Islanders keep the enemy busy, my men have scouted a place just to the north where I can swim twelve of them across. There are only about sixty of the Reb rifles. We can flank them with our Spencers."

"Go to it, colonel."

Joseph selected twelve of his best and they followed him as he worked his way through the woods to a position a half a mile north of the ford and around a shallow bend. Another attack by the Rhode Islanders occupied the rebels while Joseph led his men into the freezing river. Once across they remounted and rapidly, in single file, followed a path in the direction of the gunfire. Fifty yards from the rebel sharpshooters they dismounted, left the horses with two men, and made their way to a small rise above the river. Below them the rebels were spread out in rifle pits too hastily dug to have provided any protection to the rear.

Joseph signaled a line. The ten troopers lay on their bellies, aimed, and on a signal from Joseph commenced firing. With each volley ten rebels fell. By the time half of them were killed, the others threw down their weapons and surrendered. Several died in the process. Joseph saw Sergeant Conkling deliberately shoot one man who had both hands in the air.

"Sergeant Conkling! Put your rifle on the ground."

Conkling stared at him, his face in mocking complicity.

"I order you to put your rifle on the ground. Now!"

Conkling dropped his Spencer. Joseph turned to another officer. "Lieutenant Cranston, place this man under arrest. If he shows any sign of resistance, shoot him." Joseph turned and walked back for his horse.

Thunder waited for his master, excited by the battle. Joseph mounted, caressed the great black horse, and headed him toward the ford which was now being cleared of the trees. He was surprised to find Thunder so calm, and also surprised to find a similar emotion in himself. This was nothing like his first battle—no jubilance, no rage, no lust to kill—it was just war. Then why was he going to court-martial Sergeant Conkling?

"Well done, colonel." General Rainsford shook Joseph's hand. "Now, sir, when we have watered the horses, your regiment is to take the right. I shall be in the center and McFee the left."

As they finished watering, Joseph looked at his watch. It was nearly one o'clock. Half the day was gone and they had not yet encountered Fitzhugh Lee's main force. General Rainsford had some of the cautious dawdling aura of McClellan. Joseph wondered if the man was afraid to fight.

Skirmishers returned from the forest across the road ahead to report it thinly wooded, swampy and about half a mile deep. No enemy were in sight. On the other side of the woods were unfenced fields about four miles across and from one to two miles in breadth: perfect ground for a cavalry-to-cavalry engagement. Would they have it? If reconnaissance was correct, Fitzhugh Lee had under a thousand men. Rainsford made another error—still fearing a flanking attack, he separated the right and the left of his line by too great a distance. Their numerical superiority was being uselessly discarded.

Joseph rode with his command. Three miles from the center, Joseph emerged from the woods to see three brigades of Fitzhugh Lee's command waiting for him six hundred yards away. They sat their horses with the insolence of champions waiting for a mismatched contender. Joseph brought his command to a halt.

"Draw sabers!"

A clatter of steel was followed by quiet. The air seemed very still. The Albany Invincibles waited. Then, with a warbling shrill, the southerners charged.

Joseph held his men in position until the enemy was a hundred yards away. The call sounded: "Charge!" Thunder exploded forward. Over the noise Joseph thrilled at the sound of his own buglers. Ahead of him he could see that the southerners were armed with pistols. It was to be sabers against pistols! He felt an odd sense of joy and then he was among them.

Horses plunged and reared, spun and fell. The rebel pistols were nearly useless in this whirling madness. Joseph exulted. This was the kind of fighting that the saber was intended for! He slashed to the right and left; arms, faces and heads burst into blood; horses slammed against horses, trampling men and parts of men.

"Draw your pistols, you Yankees, and fight like gentlemen!" shouted a rebel trooper. Joseph killed him.

The rebels, like a helter-skelter mob, broke and ran. "After them!" Joseph shouted. His men followed, screaming in victory. But their horses were as tired as the rebels' and didn't have the goad of fear driving them. The rebels gained some ground, and then artillery shells began to burst in the air above the Invincibles. Joseph called a halt and raced his command to safer ground. The battlefield was littered with many rebel bodies, but only six of his command were dead, and only twice that number wounded.

A courier rode up and saluted. "Sir, General Rainsford wishes you to immediately form up on him. We shall advance in a line."

Joseph gave his orders and his regiment formed up with the center, right and left advancing together.

Fitzhugh Lee attacked again, this time with his whole force. Once again the rebel pistols were no match for the Yankee sabers. Joseph on the right and McFee on the left began to force back both of Lee's flanks. The southern general ordered a retreat to the cover of his big guns, and Rainsford called a halt to his advance and sent for his regimental commanders.

"Gentlemen, I congratulate you," he said. "The enemy has retired from the field. The victory is ours. It is now half past five."

Joseph was astounded. How could that be? It had just been one o'clock.

Rainsford was positive his second star was assured. He didn't wish to spoil it. "There are only a few hours of sunlight left. I have had reports of the sounds of cars moving at Culpepper. That can only mean the rebels are bringing up their infantry. We shall recross the Rappahannock and celebrate our victory."

"Sir," Joseph said. He wondered why the others didn't speak. "We've won on the field, but if we move swiftly while Lee is in confusion we could take his whole encampment."

Rainsford, who saw agreement with Joseph on the faces of his other officers, was annoyed. "Hazardous. It would be a desperate attack," he said carefully. "Even to withdraw now with these exhausted animals and enemy infantry arriving any moment is hazardous. I salute your valor, sir. Gentlemen, we shall withdraw to the safety of the north bank. Colonel von Ritter, you and your gallant Invincibles have the honor of being our rear guard."

That night Joseph reviewed the list of prisoners—one hundred and seventeen were taken. He invited the senior officer, a captain, to dine with him. The southerner, his gray uniform dirty and bloody, was Joseph's age. His demeanor was correct, polite, and wary.

"Captain Ruffin, sir. First Virginia Cavalry." He saluted.

"Colonel von Ritter. Albany Invincibles." Joseph returned the salute. "Please, Captain Ruffin, won't you sit?" Joseph offered him a camp chair.

Captain Ruffin nodded and sat.

"Wine?" Joseph started to pour.

The man nodded. "Thank you, sir."

"You will do me the honor of dining with me?"

"My men?"

"They will be served before my men. It's our custom."

"Then I will dine with you, sir. I thank you for your hospitality."

Joseph raised his glass, "To life."

Captain Ruffin nodded. "I can drink to that," he said. "To life, sir."

When they had sipped their wine, Joseph's orderly began serving the meal of canned vegetables and fresh beef.

"Your men fought bravely," Joseph said.

"You astonished us, sir. It was the first time we ever saw Yankee cavalry fight. Your sabers were an amazement. We won't be so taken again."

"I don't doubt it. Captain Ruffin, I'll be plain with you. I am, with all of my might, trying to understand why it is you are at war with us."

"Is this to be a discussion of the peculiar institution, sir?"

"If you fight for slavery, I suppose then it shall be. Do you fight for slavery?"

"If you are an abolitionist, not as you imagine it."

"I am, but I believe I have an open mind. I've seen too many precious to me die already not to try with all my might to understand you. We're enemies and yet both Americans. We share the same history and heroes. You have Washington, Jefferson and Jackson on your stamps. You've chosen to duplicate our constitution with the additions about slavery and the right to secede."

"That's the tragedy, sir. We are in so many ways the same. But it's you who have forgotten the Declaration of Independence. It's you who choose to forge a central government that is no less than despotism. We fight for the right of each state to rule itself, the right of each man to live his own life, enjoy his own property without the pervasive interference of an all-powerful central government."

"It's not slavery then?"

"Only as it's a symbol of property. But of the peculiar institution itself? It was dying, sir. Had you but patience you would have seen the South of its own bring to an end this unhappy institution, and without blood. Have you read Charles Darwin, sir?"

"Of course."

"And you subscribe to his theories?"

"I do."

"As to whether or not we are descended from apes, I have my reservations, but in this work is an application to the institution of slavery. It was becoming burdensome to us. I know of plantations where the cost of the slaves has regularly exceeded their ability to earn. And this I also say to you: Many southerners, myself included, have long harbored ambivalence as to its morality."

Joseph was touched. "I've never heard a southerner say that before."

"Nor might never again. But I've said it in public. I've said it in my classroom."

"You're a teacher?"

"Rhetoric and philosophy. The University of Virginia."

"Are you a religious man?"

"I am."

"Do you believe God is on your side?"

"I do. God is on our side."

"How can you be sure?"

"Colonel, if you learn nothing else of us, understand this. You northerners are a complex set of Christians: Catholic, Presbyterian, Anglican, et cetera...."

Joseph chose not to mention his own religion.

Ruffin continued. "It's to your northern cities the great unwashed migrations have come: the Germans, Irish, and the Italians. You're a diverse lot. But we in the South are from the same stock. We're mostly Evangelical Christians with a sprinkling of Anglicans, and even they are touched with our Evangelical beliefs. Our God is compassionate and wrathful. If we do good, He rewards us. If we are bad, He punishes us. Is God on our side? Are we not winning the war? Have we not won every major engagement?"

"And today? What have you done that your God let you lose this battle?"

Ruffin smiled. "We didn't lose. It was you who retreated back across the Rappahannock. Fitzhugh Lee is still in his camp at Culpepper. You came to dislodge him and you failed."

"And you? You are our prisoner. Has your God failed you?"

"It is I who have failed Him. I have sinned, and now I must pay for it."

That night Joseph woke to find the Shechinah by his bed.

§51

As always, he couldn't quite make out her face.

"What does God want from me?" Joseph asked.

She didn't reply.

"Did you hear Captain Ruffin? He says God is on their side. He's a good and religious man. A good Christian. He believes God is on his side. But God is on our side, isn't He?"

The Shechinah smiled.

"If there really is only one God, He can't be on both sides, can He?"

She remained silent.

"Is He on any side?"

She stared at him with amusement.

"Answer me, damn you! This is serious."

She didn't answer.

"You know what I think? I think that when I believed in many Gods I was right. The South has its God. The North its too. Both Christian. Our Jewish Gods have no power in this. The strongest Christian God will win. Isn't that right? What do you think of that?"

The Shechinah was silent.

"But if there really is only one God, and that God is really the Unknown, then It could be for neither side or for both sides. The war is part of an impossible-to-know plan. The Unknown has an unknowable plan. Am I right?"

Slowly, almost imperceptibly, the Shechinah nodded.

"The war was necessary?"

She nodded again.

"Why? Why was it necessary for Nathan to die? And all those good men on both sides of the battle to die? Why would the Unknown want that? How could the Unknown want this war? Any war?"

The Shechinah said, "All is foreseen and yet free will is given." Then she left.

Joseph woke an hour before reveille. Was it a dream? She had quoted Rabbi Akiba: "All is foreseen, yet free will is given."

What did God want from us? Was this bloody war foreseen? If it was, and the Unknown was all-powerful, what did free will have to do with it? How could all be foreseen and yet free will be given? Joseph squeezed his brain. All is foreseen....

And then he understood. What did God want from him? *To help the Union win the war.* How? It was not something he could do by himself. How? Why him? Did God want more? Probably, but what he knew for now was enough.

"All" was the key word. That was it! All. All the possibilities— and it was by free will that one possibility became reality while another did not. It was an act of free will that brought the first slaves to the Americas. Perhaps there were other turning points in the progression of slavery in America where free will caused the institution to grow and harden so that by the time Jefferson wrote the Declaration of Independence, he and the founding fathers no longer possessed the free will to end slavery. Trapped by the momentum of slavery, they created the greatest democracy the world had ever known, yet with the disease of the Civil War festering in its guts. Free will changes the direction of history's tide, and then is carried along by that tide until swept aside by another act.

So the current of history had carried the Union toward the Civil War. It was all but inevitable. But still the current could have been diverted into another channel and the war avoided. The North could have let the South go in peace. It was an act of free will on Lincoln's part that he chose to defend the Union. There had to be a divine reason for the war, a reason beyond the freeing of the slaves, beyond the preservation of the Union.

Over and over again Joseph worked the paradox of Akiba: All is foreseen yet free will is given. Answers that had eluded him for so long now coursed through his mind. All is *foreseen*, not all is *ordained.* By free will man changes his destiny. The Messiah can only come by acts of free will. Man must choose to evolve toward Messiah.

All is foreseen. All was a key. All meant every possibility was foreseen. It was free will that selected the possibility that became reality. The outcome of the war was by no means preordained. Either side could win and it would still be foreseen. Free will and free will alone would determine the victor.

If free will was stronger in the South than in the North, the South would win the war. The logical result of that catastrophic end would be the Union and the Confederacy breaking up into ever-smaller, squabbling states and those two guarantors of free will, the Declaration of Independence and the Constitution, disappearing into anarchic chaos. The violent side of America would triumph. It would be an end to the New Jerusalem. Ruffin was fighting on the wrong side. Would he ever come to know it?

The task was to make sure he did—he and all the decent people of the South. The southern will to resist had to be broken. Southern will flowed from moral certainty. Joseph vowed to study and understand it until he knew how to remove that moral certainty from the South.

General Rainsford was not promoted after Scamon's Ford. Instead, Hooker rebuked him for his withdrawal from the field. Convinced that Joseph was a factor in his rebuke, Rainsford arranged for General Pleasanton to request the Albany Invincibles to be a detached brigade of the First Division.

During the first week of April, Joseph noted in the southern press that the women of Richmond had instigated a bread riot. He was compassionate for their suffering but also grimly satisfied that his theory of the will to fight was being demonstrated. The southern will was cracking. Yet at the same time an anti-war movement was building in the North. Joseph thought the war could become a question of which civilian population would crack first.

Rumors that Hooker was preparing to end the war with one battle were circulating among the men. Then on April 12 the orders came. General Stoneman was commanded to leave Pleasanton in camp with just three small brigades of cavalry, to proceed with ten thousand men and horses up the Rappahannock, and to immediately cross the river west of the Orange & Alexandria Railroad. The

Albany Invincibles went with Stoneman. Joseph was elated. This was what cavalry was made for. They were to ride around Lee's flank, destroying all railroads and bridges and, when Hooker fell on the rebels with the full weight of the Army of the Potomac, Lee was to find the cavalry astride his only direct communication with his base at Richmond. But Stoneman wasted the only two days of good weather. In the night of April 14, the night before the delayed crossing, it began to rain heavily. By morning the Rappahannock had risen eight feet and was flowing so swiftly as to be completely impassable.

Abraham Lincoln telegraphed Hooker.

> Executive Mansion
> Washington, April 15, 1863
> Major General Hooker
>
> It is now 10:15 P.M. An hour ago I received your letter of this morning, and a few minutes later your dispatch of this evening. The latter gives me considerable uneasiness. The rain and mud, of course, were to be calculated upon. Gen. S. is not moving rapidly enough to make the expedition come to anything. He has now been out three days, two of which were unusually fine weather, and all three without hindrance from the enemy, and yet he is not twenty-five miles from where he started. To reach his point, he still has sixty to go; another river, the Rapidan, to cross, and will be hindered by the enemy. By arithmetic how many days will it take him to do it? I do not know that any better can be done, but I greatly fear it is another failure already. Write me more often. I am very anxious.
>
> > Yours truly,
> > A. Lincoln

At last, two weeks late, Stoneman took his forces across the river. Then for ten days his cavalry destroyed everything in its path: rail depots, trains, miles of tracks, trestles, canal locks, canal boats, and storehouses. They captured hundreds of horses and mules, but were scrupulous not to harm the civilian population, for their orders were specific: "Do not violate the...recognized rules of civilized warfare."

In light of his new discoveries, Joseph began to find this an odd state of affairs. How could war be civilized? The more brutal it was, the sooner it would end. Therefore brutality saved lives. He was sure civilians had to suffer. It was not just the armies of the South that chose war. It was the South itself. The southern women in particular were known to be almost rabid in their passion for the war—bloodthirsty Amalee Fitzhugh-Reid being but an example. The whole population was growing food for the rebel armies, making their guns and powder, sewing their uniforms, running their trains, and paying hard cash to support the carnage. However, true to his orders, Joseph kept his men in check. There were no "foraging" parties among the Virginia farmers. If food or animals were requisitioned, they were paid for with Yankee dollars worth more than Confederate paper.

Ten days later, after the men had made their way back across the Rappahannock, they heard of Hooker's defeat at Chancellorsville. Here was more proof for the southerners that God was indeed on their side.

And to Joseph's dismay, in a season when the weather was improving, the Army of the Potomac once again went into its camps.

On May 20, Stoneman, suffering from Hooker's ire, took a leave of absence and Pleasanton assumed command of the cavalry. Then on June 8, Joseph was startled and pleased by the arrival of his friend Custer.

Custer saluted. "Captain Custer reporting, sir. Voluntary aide to General Pleasanton," he said. "Colonel, you now have a friend in a high place. Good thing, too. Nothing worse than a detached brigade."

"It's about time you showed up. I thought I was going to have to win this war without you."

"You? The whole outfit is moving out in the morning, and you they were going to send off on some goose chase to the north. But I convinced General Pleasanton that you were almost as brave as me, and that the Invincibles should be in the vanguard."

"Where are we going?"

"The entire reb cavalry is at Culpepper: Stuart, both Lees, Jones, Jenkins, Robertson. All of them. Buford scouted them out. And it looks like Poppa Lee's got his army moving north. He's going to invade Maryland again. All that cavalry in one place can only mean

one thing—a screen for Bobby Lee's infantry. We, sir, are going to
go bust up that cavalry."

He handed Joseph a sheet of paper. "Your orders, sir."

Joseph studied them. Custer was right. The Invincibles were to
lead off the march, crossing at Scamon's, Beverly and Kelly's Fords,
and then head straight for Culpepper.

"And we're taking three thousand infantry with us," Custer said.
"They'll be a moving *point d'appui*—that's West Point for a moving
point of support. We cut the rebs up and run them into the infantry.
Good-bye, Jeb Stuart. Good-bye rebel cavalry. This will be truly
splendid."

Eight days later the Union cavalry crossed the Rappahannock
and surprised Jeb Stuart, who had been occupying his time with two
grand reviews and a ball. Mistakes in command were made and
recovered on both sides. And on both sides men fought bravely.
Once again the rebel cavalry learned respect for the Yankee
horsemen. Both sides claimed victory. Both sides were wrong.

Joseph and the Invincibles fought hard and well. Seven officers
and nineteen men were lost. Half the horses were killed. Joseph and
Thunder emerged exhausted, unhurt and triumphant.

Custer at last had the glorious battle he had lusted for. In sight
of his commanders he appropriated two squadrons of the Invincibles
whose own officers had been killed and, with Joseph's permission,
charged across a cornfield exposed to artillery, dashed up a steep
slope, jumped a stone wall and carried the guns.

Upon returning from the battle Joseph telegraphed Loeb. He
used the company code.

> I am convinced that Captain George Armstrong Custer
> of General Pleasanton's staff is a powerful asset for the
> Union. I should be grateful for any effort you make for his
> advancement.
>
> Joseph

On June 16, 1863, General Robert E. Lee took the Army of
Northern Virginia across the Potomac once again into Maryland.
This time Harrisburg, Pennsylvania, was the apparent objective, but
the true strategy was to draw the Army of the Potomac out into the
open on a battleground of Lee's choice and to destroy it. The Davis
government in Richmond had prepared a peace offering to Lincoln.

The letter was to be placed in the American president's hands upon the announcement of Lee's victory.

On June 27, Lincoln had his fill of Hooker and replaced him with Major General George Meade. A cautious conservative, Meade's first act was surprising. He telegraphed Commanding General Halleck, requesting that Captain George Armstrong Custer be jumped to brigadier general.

§52

SEEKING TO DESTROY THE ARMY OF NORTHERN VIRGINIA BEFORE it advanced to Harrisburg, Major General George Meade cautiously set the great blue tide in motion. Rivulets trickled out of the camps around Washington, flowing into others, merging in ever-thickening streams until a gigantic flood swelled inexorably northward.

Meade sent the cavalry in every direction searching for the enemy. On July 1, General Buford's cavalry rode through Gettysburg and ran into Ewell's rebel troops. Buford dismounted his men and defended his forward position until General Hancock arrived with the infantry. (Buford's decision preserved the high ground for the Union. Ewell, who commanded sufficient force to seize the advantageous positions of Cemetery Ridge and Cemetery Hill from the Yankees, blundered in not doing so.) Meade, in spite of his caution, brought the whole Army of the Potomac to Gettysburg. Now if Lee chose to fight, it wouldn't be on ground of his choosing. The high water mark of the Confederacy had been reached and, in a crimson tide, began to ebb.

The following day General Kilpatrick's division was sent up the York Turnpike to prevent rebel cavalry from turning the Union flank east of Culp's Hill. Kilpatrick ordered Custer to range ahead of the division to find Stuart.

The Albany Invincibles, down to ninety-three men and officers, were attached to Brigadier General Custer's Michigan brigade. Joseph rode with Custer at the head of the column as they advanced up a narrow road toward the hamlet of Wasserburg. He studied his friend. The scruffy captain with his filthy uniform was gone. Now Joseph saw a sixteenth-century cavalier, dressed in velvet and gold braid. Custer wore a specially tailored navy shirt with an open, soft collar displaying his star of command on each point. An extravagant yellow silk scarf fluttered at his neck and his golden hair was combed, brushed and glistening. He had chosen his costume, Custer thought, to inspire his men. He didn't know it also mocked the southern gentry. Joseph was pleased with his part in selecting the ensemble. He thought the more brilliant Custer's victories were, the more humiliated would be the rebel cavaliers.

As they approached Wasserburg an artillery shell tore into the ground close by them. The road ahead was barricaded. "Three guns, and it looks like about thirty dismounted cavalry," Joseph said.

"Thirty, huh? Then that's how many I'll take with me," Custer said. "I shall have those guns."

Joseph looked at him with disbelief. "Beg pardon, general, but would you ride this way with me?"

Custer followed Joseph away from his suite of officers.

Joseph spoke only loud enough for Custer to hear. "Autie," he said. "You're a general now. You're too important to risk yourself leading a squadron action. Besides, this is the wrong situation for a charge. Make a demonstration here at the front. Send four squadrons, two around each flank. This has to be a dismounted action."

Custer considered Joseph's suggestion. While Joseph was the smartest man he knew, Joseph didn't always have to be right. "No glory in it," Custer said.

Thirty men charged head-on into the guns, and the rebels were waiting with canister shot. Sixteen of the Yankees never reached the barricade. The remainder followed their leader as he jumped it. Five more died as they sailed across. Custer and the survivors did as much damage as they could, and jumped back across the barricade. The young general returned to his column with one sergeant and two enlisted men.

Joseph was angry and Custer saw it. Having satisfied his honor, Custer then ordered Joseph's plan. The guns were captured and the surviving rebels taken prisoner.

Joseph questioned them carefully. Stuart was coming down the road east of Gettysburg. If Kilpatrick's whole division moved rapidly toward Hunterstown they would intercept the rebel cavalry.

The two cavalries confronted each other toward the end of that hot July day, the second day of the great battle being fought at Gettysburg three miles to the east, the day of the bloody struggles for the hills known as Big and Little Round Top. In a mostly dismounted engagement, Kilpatrick and Stuart's men warred with each other for two hours. At the end of the day both sides remained where they had been at the commencement of the fighting. Both sides claimed victory. Stuart was convinced that he had kept the Yankees from attacking the rear of the rebel army. Kilpatrick reported that he had "driven the enemy from this point at great loss."

In this battle Joseph, deploying his carbineers effectively, continually drove back superior numbers of rebels. It was further proof that a dismounted cavalryman with a repeating rifle was far more effective than on his horse swinging a saber. The rebels also dismounted and fought, but with far less effect. Their single shot Enfields had a greater accurate range than the repeating Spencers, but the rebels seemed to have less stomach for the dismounted fighting. It's always a question of will, Joseph thought. Deprived of their horses, the southern cavalrymen fought hard and fought bravely, but without their customary spirit. Their will to win had been eroded and they weren't aware of it. Joseph confirmed this observation with prisoner interviews that night.

As usual, before retiring, Joseph went to Custer's tent for coffee and talk. The two men sat in the dark outside of Custer's tent smoking Cuban cigars. Custer spoke quietly. "Truth is, there's no love lost between me and George Meade," he said. "Give him this though. He knew I should be leading the brigade and he went and got me my star. And he got the army to Gettysburg and he ain't retreating. Bobby Lee's getting whipped and that's a fact."

"Lee puzzles me," Joseph said. "He should not have fought here. After today he should be retreating to safer ground, but he isn't."

"Man's a fighter."

"Maybe too much a fighter."

"What do you mean by that?" Custer asked. "How can a soldier be too much a fighter?"

"I'm not sure yet. He shouldn't have fought us here at Gettysburg, and especially not once we had the high ground. If he's here tomorrow and he attacks again he'll lose. He has to know that. Yet I believe he will attack. Why?"

" 'Cause he's brave."

"Brave is not always enough. A general has to think beyond brave. It's his job to think carefully so that so many brave men do not die every time he chooses to fight. Which reminds me..."

Custer raised a hand. "Now don't start lecturing me."

Joseph ignored him. "That was a foolish thing you did this morning," he said. "Brave but foolish. The men you took with you died unnecessarily. You unnecessarily risked your life."

"They died with their boots on which is what they wanted. And the risk I took was important. The men expect a brave leader. I do things like that and they'll follow me to hell. That is part of being a general too. What'd you tell me the other day? Symbolic? It's just like Thunder being unkillable."

"What?"

"You didn't know that? The men believe Thunder's immortal. They think he can't be killed in a battle. The whole corps believes he's their luck. As long as you keep taking him into battle and coming back with him, we'll keep winning."

"This is disastrous. I'll send Thunder back to the farm immediately."

"Now why would you do a thing like that?"

"If he should be brought down," Joseph could not bring himself to use the word killed, "it'll play havoc with the men's will to fight."

"He ain't gonna get killed. Thunder and me are the same. Ain't our time to die. Damn! I forgot." He reached into his pocket and extracted a pair of shoulder boards on which silver eagles had been embroidered. "You've been brevetted a colonel of volunteers. And, I tell you, before this war is over, they'll be begging you to accept the same commission in the regular army."

Joseph was pleased with the advance in rank, and touched because he knew his friend had arranged for it. But the news concerning Thunder disturbed him. Why hadn't Thunder been shot? Why hadn't he thought about it? Were the men right? Was Thunder a living sign from the Shechinah, from God? If that were the case, perhaps Custer was right about himself too. Perhaps his foolhardy behavior was also protected. If it was divine intervention, it didn't occur to Joseph to wonder for how long.

On the third and final day of the battle of Gettysburg, Lee ordered Stuart to place his entire force on the eastern battle flank where he could protect the army's rear and, if the opportunity presented itself, sweep around behind the Union forces at the same moment as Longstreet's frontal attack on the Union center was to take place. If such a thing were achieved, the nearly suicidal charge might succeed in pushing the Yankee defenders off their ridge and once again bring victory to Lee.

Lee was fighting in the wrong terrain, but Stuart wasn't. Three miles east of Lee's left flank was a wooded ridge overlooking a wide plain of cultivated fields, from which Stuart could get at the Yankee rear and create such havoc that Lee could destroy the Army of the Potomac. With four brigades hidden by the woods, Stuart had the advantage in numbers and surprise.

In a confusion of orders the Yankee cavalry had been divided with only Gregg's division, of which Custer's brigade was part, on the east and unaware of what was hidden by the woods. Conflicting orders caused Gregg to become overly extended.

Stuart sent a line of skirmishers out of the woods. In the distance, the great cannonade preceding Pickett's charge had commenced.

Joseph and Custer watched as the Third Pennsylvania, the First Maryland and the First New Jersey engaged the rebels, were driven back, and in turn drove the skirmishers back.

"Stuart has all his brigades in those woods," Joseph said. He couldn't see them but he was sure.

Custer, his glasses to his eyes, saw nothing but the skirmishers. "How do you know?"

"Logic. This is the route to Meade's rear. They have to make a try. Can't do it with less than everything. Besides, it's his nature."

"I can't see them. Seems I should see something. Nope. The skirmishers are a feint. He's going to attack somewhere else."

A messenger galloped up and saluted. "Sir," he said. "General Kilpatrick orders you to join generals Farnsworth and Merritt south of the Round Tops. From there you are to swing around the rebel right to attack his rear."

Joseph thought the order was one of the stupidest he'd ever heard.

Custer saluted. "Thank you, lieutenant. Please inform General Kilpatrick we shall be there directly."

The officer galloped away. Custer turned to Joseph. "I guess we better move on," he said.

"Autie," Joseph said. "It's a stupid order."

"It's an order from my superior. It has to be obeyed."

"Stuart's in those woods. If we move now, we'll endanger the army."

Custer was becoming annoyed. "That was a direct order from a superior officer."

"Autie…"

"General."

"General Custer, sir. May I respectfully point out that when we first met, you demanded I disobey my orders. We had words over that."

"Yes, and you were going to knife-fight me over it. Well, I was wrong then, and you are wrong now. I shall, as you did, obey my orders."

A group of officers were riding toward them. "Here's General Gregg," Joseph said. "You ask him to countermand Kilpatrick's orders. You'll be in the clear and you may have all the glory of saving the day."

General Gregg and his suite rode up. "What do you make of it, Custer?"

"Stuart's in those woods, sir."

"You think so?"

"I'm sure of it, sir. Logic. This is the route to Meade's rear."

At that moment a flaw in Stuart's planning caused both Hampton's and Fitzhugh Lee's brigades to emerge from the woods two miles earlier than intended.

"By God," Gregg exclaimed. "You're right!"

"Sir," Joseph interjected. "We've just had orders to join Generals Farnsworth and Merritt."

Gregg looked at Joseph and knew exactly what the colonel was saying. He faced Custer. "General, you didn't receive written orders did you?"

"No, sir."

"Then I can only assume they were badly transmitted or misunderstood. You shall send for clarification directly we are finished this engagement."

"Yes sir," Custer said.

Dispositions were made. Union horse artillery came into action, enfilading the rebel skirmishers. They were driven back. The First Virginia attacked and almost smashed through. Hand-to-hand fighting broke out everywhere.

Jeb Stuart sent *aides de camp* to all of his commanders, constantly issuing new orders, constantly maneuvering to break the Yankee lines. He was failing and he knew it, but he couldn't acknowledge it. Again and again he flung his men at the blue guns.

"Major von Exing. That gap to the right? You see it?"

Von Exing nodded. "*Ja*, Herr General."

"Take the Fifth. Go through it and get at those guns from the rear."

The Virginians charged down one slope and up another toward the gap in the Yankee line. The dismounted Albany Invincibles raced to meet them. They beat the rebels to the crest of the hill and with perfect discipline assumed prone, kneeling and standing positions. As the Virginians advanced, Joseph, astride Thunder, gave the order to fire—six volleys in the space of time the rebels took to fire one. The wall of lead stopped the charge. Continuous rapid-fire volleys shattered the survivors who broke and raced for the safety of their own lines.

Von Exing, his face wild with rage, raced up to a group of sharpshooters. "One thousand dollars in gold to the man that brings down that black horse!"

A dozen rifles swung up, and then paused. A sergeant looked up from his long sight. "What black horse?"

Von Exing looked back across the corpse-strewn battlefield. The black horse was gone. But he had seen Joseph and that was enough.

Von Exing turned back to the sergeant. "Still, you spread the word," he said. "One thousand in gold I pay to the man who shoots down this black horse and kills the rider. One thousand I pay."

The sergeant squinted at him. "Major, you talking 'bout Thunder?"

"*Ja*, Thunder."

"No, sir. Shoot that horse on purpose, sir, and the man that does it, his whole outfit got bad luck. That horse dies in battle, that's one thing, but on purpose? Hell major, everybody knows that. Plain bad luck."

§53

DESPITE LINCOLN'S URGINGS, GENERAL MEADE, LIKE McCLELLAN after his victory at Antietam, hesitated. Meade thought the rebels too strong, although he possessed accurate intelligence from his own cavalry to the contrary. Lee's retreating army was vulnerably extended along the line of march, low on ammunition and exhausted. A swift pursuit of the weakened army of Northern Virginia and the war might have ended. It didn't.

What few engagements did take place were the result of Union cavalry probes running into the screen thrown up by the Confederate cavalry.

"Sir."

Joseph looked up from his book. A lieutenant stood at the tent flap. "Lieutenant?"

"A prisoner, sir. A colonel. Says he would like you to come see him."

"Well, bring him here."

"He's pretty badly wounded, sir. Says he knows you."

"Name?"

"Sorry, sir. He said it, but what with all the noise, I just didn't get it."

Joseph got up, put the book on his bench and looked at it. When, he wondered, had he started reading the Torah again?

Joseph did not want to recognize him. He had long ago buried those memories of his madness. Senator Cole was lying on a cot, dying. His face had been washed but blood foamed at his mouth as he spoke, and blood soaked the bandages about his chest and stomach.

Joseph stood mute, waiting.

"I am dying," the senator rasped. "I saw you in the battle. Wanted to kill you with my own hand."

"Had I seen you, I would have done the same."

"My slave Cedric said you killed Leander."

"I did."

"I forgive you, Joseph von Ritter. In the name of my Savior Jesus Christ, I forgive you for my home that you burned, for my son. I forgive you and beg you to do the same for me, for Sergeant Stumpf."

Joseph dropped to his knee, his crutch falling to the floor, scorching tears coursing down his face. "What are you saying?"

"The carnage. For what? God has forsaken us. We are in the wrong. We must forgive each other. Do you forgive me?"

"With God as my witness, I do," Joseph said, and took his hand.

The senator smiled and closed his eyes. With the last breath in him he whispered, "Von Exing. With Stuart." Then he died.

"Of course you'll have to fight him," Custer said. "Oh, this is gonna be grand!" He strode to the tent flap. "Major, I want a big white flag, four men with torches, and a bugler that knows how to sound the parlay. Get my horse and Colonel von Ritter's." He turned to Joseph. "You want Thunder or one of the others?"

"Thunder." Joseph felt an old excitement grow within him. An offering, he thought, to God. "Autie," he said quietly. "Get a wagon and an honor guard. I would like to take the senator to be buried by his own people."

Jeb Stuart, accompanied by his suite of officers including von Exing, rode out to meet the Custer party. The rain had stopped and a slight breeze fluttered the two torch-lit white flags.

Custer and Stuart greeted each other formally. Stuart expressed the gratitude of his officers and men for the return of Senator Cole's body. Von Exing was dumbfounded to see Joseph beside Custer. What was the damned Jew doing there?

After the military formalities were completed Custer said, "General Stuart, allow me to present Colonel von Ritter, whose business may be of some moment to you and your staff."

Von Exing shivered. He touched his saber. It was loose in its scabbard. Quietly he loosened the flap on his holster.

Jeb Stuart studied Joseph and Thunder. He saluted. "Baron," he said. "Your reputation precedes you."

Joseph returned the salute. "I thank you, sir. The matter I wish to present is one of honor."

"Indeed."

"It is not one touched by the causes or issues of this war, but stems from events in the old country."

"Please continue, sir."

"Baron von Exing, of your staff, and I have unfinished business. With your permission, sir?"

"Baron von Ritter, curiosity overwhelms me. Granted."

Joseph saluted, and walked Thunder over to confront von Exing, who wanted to shoot the Jew but could find no way to do it and retain the respect of his fellow officers. Flecks of foam gathered at the corners of his mouth.

"Baron von Exing," Joseph said. "I shall not offend these honorable officers with a recounting of your behavior and that of your family. You are a coward. With the permission of our commanders, I invite you to meet me tomorrow an hour after sunup."

"Jew, you cannot challenge me. I am Baron Otto Karl Gotthold Justus von Exing. I do not duel with commoners. It is forbidden."

Joseph extracted the letter from his tunic. "This is a letter from the king of Bavaria. It confirms my title, Baron von Breitenstein, and specifically orders Baron von Exing to accept my challenge." He rode closer to von Exing, holding the letter so that torch light reflected from it. "Von Exing, I am sure you will recognize the seals, perhaps even the signature. Now, coward, you must fight me."

"Major von Exing," Jeb Stuart said. "As this is a European matter, I release you from my order concerning the duel."

"*Ja*, I will fight you. You are the challenger. I have the right to choose the weapons. Épée."

The soldiers, North and South, were shocked.

"Major, the man has but one leg," Stuart said.

Von Exing missed the menacing tone of Stuart's voice. "*Ja*," he said. "To choose the weapon is my right."

"Major, you have only two choices," Stuart said. "Pistol or mounted saber. Please state your preference."

Von Exing understood he was cornered. But mounted it would not be like last time. This time he would not be taken by surprise. This time he was an experienced warrior, not a foolish drunk young hussar. "Mounted saber," he said.

Joseph couldn't sleep. How was it possible for Senator Cole to forgive him? And why had he forgiven Cole? He hated the South even more for their civilized pretensions performed during the very acts of their barbarous crime.

Von Exing stayed up for hours, drinking and thinking of the morning's encounter. The trick, he thought, was to get the Jew off his horse. Get him on the ground and cut him in half before it looked bad. Yes. He must not look bad. But he had to be sure. He went to his trunk, and at the bottom found something he'd picked up on his Sicilian campaign. The Sicilian bandits, he thought, knew how to win. The device was too complicated for battle, but it had worked excellently on card cheaters. He removed his shirt and fitted the apparatus along his forearm, testing the spring several times. Then, from its case, he lifted the double-barreled, derringer copy made by the Italian gunsmith Vittarosa. It was five inches long, exquisitely tooled, and inlayed with gold. It was only a .32-caliber, but that was enough. Von Exing fitted the little pistol to the spring-catch and tested it. If he used it correctly, at the right moment, no one would see it and the report of the pistol would be covered by the cheering of thousands of men.

Custer slept well. He knew Joseph was the best duelist in the army. He was pleased with the arrangements he had made with Jeb Stuart, too. Both cavalries, gray and blue, would witness the event. They would arrive at their respective sides unarmed and under flags of truce. A coin toss settled the matter of which band played first. Custer didn't mind that the rebels had won, for he was sure that they would be amazed and charmed when they heard his band. It had been agreed that neither *Dixie* nor the *Battle Hymn of the Republic* would be played.

Jeb Stuart was equally pleased. His band was playing first. No Yankee band could be its equal. It might hearten von Exing. Odd, he thought, how a man could be born an aristocrat from a very old family and still not be a gentleman. But seeing a Confederate officer defeat in single combat the best the Union had to offer would go some way to cheering up the men after Gettysburg.

The rain had stopped in the night. Trees still dripped moisture, the ground was soft but manageable. Seconds from both the North and the South walked the terrain of the impending duel, removing any rocks and agreeing on the exact spot where the encounter would take place. An hour later with the cloud cover nearly touching the tops of the low green hills on opposite sides of the field, the dismounted, unarmed cavalrymen made their way to the slopes and faced each other. At first they didn't speak across the divide, more out of social unease than enmity, but then a boy from New Jersey shouted, "Hey Johnny Reb, why does a chicken cross the road?"

A Virginian shouted back, "I dunno Yankee-boy. How come the chicken crossed the road?" When New Jersey shouted back the answer, both sides fell about laughing.

The seconds preceded the two duelists onto the field. Both Joseph and von Exing wore white shirts, one with blue trousers, the other in gray.

Silence overcame the men.

The seconds showed the duelists the selected ground. They then examined the sabers of the combatants, placed the men twenty yards apart and retired from the field. The marshal, chosen by lot, placed his horse equidistant from the duelists.

Joseph kept the marshal in his peripheral vision while never taking his eyes off von Exing. The German was riding a chestnut Irish hunter, about the same size as Thunder but less cared for. He wouldn't have Thunder's quickness or stamina, especially carrying von Exing's great weight.

Von Exing carefully studied Joseph's odd saddle, judging the weakness of a man with only one leg. He concluded Joseph's cut would be weakest on the missing leg side. Good, he thought, the Jewpig doesn't know I can fight with either arm.

The marshal said, "Gentlemen, draw sabers." He drew his own and saluted both. They returned the salute, and then saluted each other. As they did, von Exing thought of how to kill Joseph instantly.

Joseph stared at his lifelong enemy. His saber felt heavy in his hand, and his arms were tired. He didn't want to fight so much as sleep. The marshall backed his horse ten paces, and then dropped the point of his saber.

Thunder saw it before Joseph and lunged forward. Joseph was momentarily startled. Why hadn't he seen it first? He raised his saber, pointing it directly at the oncoming German, whose weapon was raised in the same classic charge position, right arm extended, saber pointed directly at the enemy's eyes.

They were separated by only sixty feet, yet with both horses running full force that first moment of contact seemed to take forever. Von Exing was passing to Joseph's left to take advantage the greatest power of a right arm slash. Joseph balanced for it, but then a odd thing happened. At the last moment, in a display of excellent horsemanship, von Exing took his horse to the right instead of the left and at the same time shifted his saber to his left hand. When the blow came, Joseph wasn't ready. Von Exing pushed aside Joseph's riposte and, if Thunder hadn't instantly pirouetted, von Exing would have taken off Joseph's head. But there was a slash on Joseph's face.

The gray cheered, the blue groaned, and von Exing exulted. He would win. He wheeled his horse to finish the job. But where was Joseph? He was coming up behind him. Von Exing turned to face him but he was too late.

Joseph, now awake, his face stinging from the wound, his killing rage coursing through him, didn't slash at von Exing as the German had expected. Instead he lunged, driving the point of his saber into von Exing's left arm. Von Exing's howl of rage and pain was drowned by the crowd's roar. Joseph backed Thunder away and pointed to von Exing's saber on the ground.

"Pick it up," he said in German.

Von Exing dismounted, grabbed his saber and remounted, charging Joseph before he was completely in the saddle and taking him by surprise—a trick he had learned from the Berbers. Joseph parried the blow and slashed back, forcing von Exing into a disadvantageous move to his left. Thunder was around and upon him before von Exing could recover. Joseph feinted with a high cut and attempted to drive the point of his saber below von Exing's parry. But von Exing parried both strokes and came back with a heavy blow, aimed not at Joseph but at Thunder's leg.

Thunder saw it coming and spun away. Joseph's back was now toward von Exing who tore at his horse's mouth but could not get the animal around fast enough to take advantage of it. Joseph turned again and with a furious series of blows drove von Exing away in a panicked flight. The crowd went wild! Here was the kill. But Joseph, instead of pursuing von Exing and killing him with a thrust to his retreating spine, reined Thunder in and waited. Now both sides cheered Joseph's gallantry.

Von Exing gathered his wits. He yanked his hunter into a tight turn and shifted his saber to his wounded left arm. He wasn't sure he could swing the arm, but it didn't matter. It just had to look as though he could. He charged directly at Joseph. As he had anticipated, his side screamed the rebel yell. When he came within six feet of Joseph he crouched in the saddle, stretching his right arm along side his horse's neck to gain as much concealment as he could, pointed his hand at Thunder's advancing head, and pressed the mechanism against his side. The derringer popped into his hand, all but a half-inch of its barrel concealed by his fingers. Von Exing squeezed the trigger. He could hardly hear the report of the pistol. As quickly as it fired, the derringer jerked back into his sleeve.

To most of the crowd, it looked as though Thunder had stumbled. In the same instant Joseph allowed the forward-falling movement of the horse to catapult him from the saddle. He tucked his head under and rolled as he hit the soft, wet ground.

The great black horse lay inert in the mud. The crowd fell silent.

Stunned, gasping for breath, Joseph lay on the ground for a moment then pushed himself to a sitting position. Von Exing turned his horse and shifted his saber back to his good right hand. He then walked the horse deliberately toward the fallen man.

The assembled soldiers on both sides remained silent. Some held their breaths.

Joseph looked up to see the German coming toward him. He looked around for his saber. It was too far away. Von Exing was grinning. In German he said, "I will do it slowly, like the Turks, one piece at a time." He put the hunter into a slow canter.

Joseph reached into his boot and extracted his nine-inch blade, and in the same motion rose on his one leg. As von Exing came closer Joseph began hopping in movements calculated to confuse the German's horse. He moved with a power and grace that surprised von Exing.

"Hop, hop, little rabbit," von Exing said. "You will not escape. Hop, hop."

The crowd remained silent.

Von Exing turned his horse in a circle around Joseph, enclosing him in a way that prevented him from escaping. He kept von Exing's saber in his peripheral vision where he could monitor it, but his attention focused on the horse. When the circle was small enough so that von Exing's saber could reach him, Joseph feinted to the right and propelled himself down and into the animal. In the same moment he inserted his knife between the third and fourth ribs of von Exing's horse, where it cut through flesh and muscle and into the left ventricle of the horse's heart. It died instantly.

Von Exing was pinned under the horse's body, his right arm unable to move. Joseph hopped over to the German's fallen saber and picked it up. Then he hopped back to von Exing and put the saber's point against his enemy's neck.

Joseph fully intended to kill him.

Von Exing stared up at him in blind terror.

Joseph paused.

The crowd waited.

To his own astonishment Joseph said, "I forgive you. Baron Otto Karl Gotthold Justus von Exing, I forgive you. Go and leave me in peace." Then flinging the saber away, Joseph pulled von Exing from under the horse and hopped away.

Von Exing rose and turned toward Joseph, "You dare to forgive me?" He raised his hand and pressed the lever under his arm. The deadly little pistol snapped in his hand and he fired.

Joseph crashed to the ground.

§54

Because joseph was hopping, because von exing was in a wild rage, at the distance fired with the low muzzle velocity of such a short barrel the shot went high. At the same moment Joseph suddenly began to turn. The .32-caliber slug, making a small wound, entered Joseph's head just behind his eyes and, as the lead shot deformed, it exited at an angle which destroyed Joseph's left eye.

When Joseph fell to the ground, von Exing shouted in wild triumph. He looked to the Confederate cavalry to receive his just homage. But every man there turned from him and walked silently away.

Custer, two Union doctors and four stretcher bearers rushed Joseph to a small hospital tent at the edge of the dueling field.

"I don't think it extends beyond the posterior wall of the orbit," the doctor said.

"What's that mean, major?" Custer asked.

"The wound is confined to the eye socket. I don't think it has extended into the cranial vault or has damaged the brain."

"Why is he out cold?"

"Concussion. A kind of twilight state, general. Ahhh..." He gently removed a small fragment of bone. "Piece of the sphenoid. Back of the eye socket bone. Ah, ha...here's another splinter."

"Is he going to live?" Custer asked.

"Don't know, general. What I do know is I better stop this exploration for fear of damaging the brain. He's losing too much blood. Nasty bleeders, these head wounds."

The doctor carefully packed the wound with lint and then covered it with colloidian and a pressure dressing. Joseph's good eye was left unbandaged.

"His pulse is strong and steady," the doctor said to Custer. "Fast under these circumstances is normal."

"Why is he moaning? Is he waking up?" As if Joseph's condition was the doctor's fault, Custer was becoming hostile to him.

"General, I'm not going to hurt this boy," the doctor said. "If I can I'm going to save him. Right now he's in a state of shock. He should be coming around."

The doctor then examined Joseph's nose. "He doesn't seem to be leaking any cerebrospinal fluid through his nose." He looked up at Custer. "Another good sign. Well, I've done all I can for the moment. The rest is up to him. Next few hours will tell."

A lieutenant entered the tent and saluted. "A reb officer, General Custer, under a flag of truce."

"Send him in, lieutenant."

A Confederate captain entered and saluted. "General Stuart's respects, sir," he said. "He offers you and your men his apology for Major von Exing's unbecoming conduct. General Stuart wished me to inquire as to the condition of Colonel von Ritter."

Custer was mollified by the apology and answered as politely. "Thank General Stuart for me," he said. "Colonel von Ritter's lost an eye. Don't know if he's going to live yet." Then he had a thought. "Doc, can he be moved?"

"We'll know better in about twenty-four hours. I wouldn't move him till then."

Custer turned back to the rebel officer. "My compliments to General Stuart. If he would oblige us, I'd like the truce to remain in effect for another twenty-four hours."

"Sir," the rebel officer replied, "General Stuart has authorized me to inform you that he is prepared to hold the truce for such a time period. However, since in this matter we are in the wrong, General Stuart suggests that we are obligated to give up the field. We shall withdraw some miles distant. Tomorrow he'll send word of our location and we may resume our business with each other."

"Agreed. Thank you, captain," Custer said.

They exchanged salutes and the captain left.

As he walked back into the camp all ranks avoided speaking to von Exing. His elation withered. Then as he moved through the men they formed a silent gauntlet, down which von Exing strode with less and less confidence.

Jeb Stuart stepped into place at the end of the alley. "Major von Exing," he said, his voice soft with distaste. "Your behavior, sir, has brought disgrace upon us all. You are forthwith relieved of duty. I shall expect your letter of resignation from the Army of the Confederate States of America by sundown. I also expect you to be gone from this encampment by that time, sir." He turned and walked away.

Joseph emerged from his semi-conscious state into excruciating pain. The doctors administered morphine. Joseph felt the pain subside like a wave withdrawing from a beach. "Thank you," he whispered. He fell back into a deep sleep.

At the end of the twenty-four hour truce, scouts reported to Custer that the rebel cavalry was ten miles distant.

Custer had to pursue them. He ordered an ambulance and an escort to take Joseph to Washington. He couldn't spare a doctor.

Joseph heard the voices first.
"Is there any evidence of infection?"
"No."
"Meningeal infection?"
"No. But we may have missed that. There's considerable damage to his posterial orbital area." .
"I suggest a careful watch for infection in his remaining eye."
Joseph slowly became aware of the room. It was the hospital in Washington. He had been there before. The same sounds, smells, doctors, nurses and orderlies; the men in beds, all talking softly or moaning. He was awake but he had an odd disconnected state of mind. Perhaps it was laudanum.
Two doctors were standing by his bed. Behind them was Kate. Dear Kate, he thought. She had come to take care of him.
One of the doctors saw his unbandaged eye open.
"You're awake, colonel. Good. We'll have a look at that wound if we may."
Joseph nodded.
The doctors removed the bandage over Joseph's eye. He saw Kate turn from his wound.
"Colonel," the doctor said, "a most extraordinary wound. You are very lucky the bullet missed the brain. And unless I am mistaken, you're also lucky to have no infection of the membrane that covers the brain." He turned to the other doctor. "You may repack the wound as before."

As the army surgeon began to rebandage him, Joseph realized the doctor who had examined him wasn't in the army. He said, "Civilian...?"

"Sent here by your father-in-law," he said.

He woke once in the night and Kate was there. She kissed him and bathed his face with a cool cloth.

He woke again and Kate was gone.

Later, just before dawn, the Shechinah came to him.

"Will I live?" he asked.

"If you choose."

"I want to live."

"The choice is yours."

"I will live."

"Good."

"Why did Senator Cole forgive me?"

"Rabbi Gamalial said: 'Let this be a sign to you that whenever you are compassionate, the Compassionate One will have compassion upon you.' "

"Is that why I forgave von Exing? I didn't plan to do that. I wanted to kill him. I hated him."

She looked at him with sadness in her eyes. "Rabbi Johanan said, 'So learn that hate of man for his fellow man is a sore sin before God.' Do you hate von Exing now?"

"No. Now he is nothing in my life."

"And the rebels? The southern chivalry? The slave-owning aristocrats? Surely you must still hate them?"

"No." He was curious about his answer. How odd. Where had his hate gone? Joseph slept.

In the morning he woke to Kate's cool hand on his cheek.

"Good morning, colonel, my darling," she said. Love illuminated her face as she went about the business of caring for him.

When the pain began to reappear, she uncorked a bottle. "For the pain," she said.

"No more laudanum."

"We have something better, Joseph. Morphine." She filled a syringe from the bottle. "This is how we administer it now."

Joseph shrank from the needle. "Will it hurt?"

She smiled, "Yes, but only for a moment. The relief is immediate. I've been giving them to you ever since you arrived."

Then it became as it had been before in the same hospital. Weeks went by, marked only by days and nights that blended into one another. Also as before Kate put in extraordinary hours. She read to Joseph, spoke to him of their happy future at Thunder Farm, and told him about all the good news of the war. But none of it made sense. It was the sound of her voice that he liked: caring, warm, strong, safe.

The Shechinah came to him almost every night, but for the most part he couldn't remember what they said to each other. But he knew it was important.

As Joseph's physical strength returned, Kate began reducing the drug's dosage. Over a two-week period Joseph's mind cleared and the pain lessened until it had become only an ache, and he was free of the drug. One night he noticed that his right eye was hurting, but he ignored it.

In the morning Kate brought him his breakfast. While he ate she brought him up to date on the war. The Union was doing well. Joseph seemed so strong she decided to take a chance. "Joseph," she said, "I've been thinking about Thunder Farm."

"Oh?"

"I thought that if the doctors say it's all right, we could go there for the rest of your recovery. I could care for you, and you could be outside much of the time which I think would be good for you. You could watch me work the horses and tell me what to do. It would be so good for you."

"I'd like that. It'll be strange without Thunder."

"You know what they say. Love your horses but don't get sentimental about them. And look what beautiful colts he threw. We'll have more Thunders."

He shook his head to say no, and as he did so he noticed an increase of pain in his right eye. When he looked back at Kate his vision was slightly blurred. He thought perhaps it was a tear for Thunder.

Kate, completely occupied with her plans to become mistress of Thunder Farm, saw none of his pain. She talked of training schedules, of feeding techniques, of a plan by which she might race the local gentry over the cross-country course. She never noticed exactly when Joseph fell asleep.

When he awoke she was gone, but his vision was still blurred. His good eye was hurting more than when he had fallen asleep.

His eye was worse the following day. He felt as if he were looking through a rippled glass. That morning when the doctor made his rounds, Joseph asked him to examine him.

The doctor bent to stare into his eye. "Strain," he lied. "You only have one eye now. You must learn to take care of it. I suggest you keep it closed as much as you can. Give it some rest."

The next day Joseph's pain was the same, but his vision worse. The doctor returned with another doctor. Kate accompanied them. The doctor said, "This is Dr. Leigh. He's the eye expert around here."

Dr. Leigh sat on the edge of the bed and examined Joseph's eye. When he was done, he said, "You have sympathetic ophthalmia."

"What's that, doctor?" Kate asked.

He ignored her and put his hand on Joseph's shoulder. "Colonel, it's something we have a name for but know nothing about. Except that it happens."

"What happens?" Joseph asked.

"The uninjured eye takes on the trauma of the injured. It's a kind of infection. You are losing the sight of this eye too."

"But then I would be totally blind!" Joseph was unable to suppress a sob. "Blind." His anger replaced his sob. "You can't! Blind! You can't! I've given a leg and an eye! You can't take the other eye!"

Dr. Leigh patted his shoulder. "You must be brave. It's not I, nor anyone else here who takes your eye. It's the will of God."

"God? God! What does He want of me?"

"I wish I could help you, but I can't. Perhaps if you consulted with your pastor..."

Joseph struggled for control. "How much time do I have to see?"

"A few days."

"Now, Kate," Henrietta told her daughter. "You must really give it up. It was never right, even with the horse farm and all, never right. A Jew, dear? A leg gone, and now his eyes? No, no, no. My daughter must not spend the rest of her life nursing a blind cripple. A Jew. It's against God. I always thought so."

Kate had known from the moment she burst into her mother's boudoir what her mother would say. Kate agreed with her. She couldn't, even for a fortune and a beautiful horse farm, become the permanent nurse to a blind cripple.

On the seventh day, Joseph awoke to darkness. The pain had gone. He thought he should be angry or in despair, but he wasn't. The world was forever shut from his sight, and yet he found his most dominant emotion was curiosity. He felt as though he had been cast ashore in a strange land, a place of sounds and smells, of air currents moving against his face. Kate didn't come that day so he asked another nurse to send two telegrams for him. One was addressed to Emmanuel Loeb, the other to General Custer. They both said: "I am blind. Joseph." He didn't send them to evoke pity. It was merely a statement of fact.

The Shechinah came to him, but now he didn't know if it was day or night. At last he could see her clearly. She was beautiful.

"Why am I blind?" he asked her.

She answered, "Who is so blind as the chosen one, so blind as the servant of the Lord?"

"What does that mean?"

"You must decide for yourself."

Custer was startled when he saw Joseph so gaunt and pale. "By Jinks, you look fine!" he said.

Joseph smiled. "You, sir, are a damned liar."

Custer laughed. "Well then, I've seen wet kittens looked more fit for battle."

"No, Autie. No more battles."

"Are you truly blind?"

"Truly."

"The nation has lost a fine soldier. The best I've ever known."

"Thank you, Autie. I'm astonished that I'm alive and unable to fight. I was sure it was what God wanted of me, to win the war. I was sure that somehow I was destined to win the battle that would save the Union." He laughed. "And I was put out of the war in a personal matter, von Exing no less."

"He's gone."

"Von Exing?"

"Yes. They cashiered him. And you know what? He put that little derringer of his in his mouth and pulled the trigger. Too bad, I'd like to have done it. And I'll tell you something else. We've had a skirmish or two with Jeb Stuart's boys since that day. They don't fight as well. I personally questioned some of the prisoners we took. What I get is, these rebs really believe that the big Dutchman shooting Thunder like that was bad luck for them. Big bad luck. They're sure acting like it."

"Thunder was a magical steed. Lying here thinking about him, I know I was privileged to have him so long. I have four of his colts. Now of course I won't sell them...."

Custer interrupted, "Except for the one you are saving for me."

"Except for the one I am saving for you. Tell me about what has been happening."

"Well, they got this guerrilla, Mosby. Him and his raiders have been playing pure hell behind our lines. I've been chasing them."

Joseph became excited. "There. That's the danger."

"Nuisance more than real danger."

"No. That is the great danger. It's the only way they can win— if this Mosby is successful and they get it into their heads to fight the whole war that way. Remember what von Clausewitz wrote about Napoleon in Spain?"

"Sort of. I wasn't a great student, Joseph."

"If the South gets it into its head to fight the whole war as a guerrilla action, she'll win her independence. The Confederate states are too huge to conquer. The best we could do is capture and hold cities or fortified areas, but the countryside would belong to them. The night would belong to them. They'd bleed us until northern public opinion would force us to let them go."

Custer was once again amazed by his friend's astonishing ability to think. "You believe that could really happen?"

"If, God forbid, Lee should ever die or be replaced, say, by Longstreet—it might."

"How come all of a sudden you're praying for Bobby Lee?"

"Because I've had time to think. Lee will destroy the South. He may think he is saving them. But he's not. Each of his victories costs them more than the men they can never replace. While the soldiers cheer their victories, the families of the dead and maimed are questioning them. They're asking why their God has smitten them. They're wondering if God is really on their side. If we can get them to believe that God has forsaken them, they'll lose. It's now a race to see which of the populations, South or North, will tire first. Autie, you must destroy this Mosby. Punish him. Humiliate him. Don't let him become the stuff of legend."

"I'll get him."

"And I'll tell you something else. You won't like this."

"Try me."

"The key is the southern people. You get behind Lee's lines and do to the civilian population what Mosby is trying against us. Burn their homes and barns and crops..."

Custer was offended. "Whoa there. Whoa. We don't make war on civilians."

"You prove to them that not Lee nor any other Confederate Army can protect them in their homes, that their government can't protect them and that all they treasure is vulnerable, and they'll come to believe God is against them. Autie, make cruel war now and you will save thousands and thousands of lives on both sides."

Custer shook his head and tried to smile. "I'm going to put that talk down to the stuff they're giving you. We don't war on civilians."

Two days later Loeb sent his train for Joseph. Kate hadn't visited the hospital from the day he was blinded and she didn't respond to his note telling her he was going to New York City. He understood, and he tried not to blame her. But he did.

§55

HANSCHEN HAD DONE HER CRYING WEEKS AGO. FROM THE TIME they had invited Joseph to stay with them for his recovery, she had prepared herself to be brave. But the sight of the frail man being helped from the carriage was more than she could bear. Loeb envied his wife's tears. The perpetual pain in his soul grew by the dimensions of Joseph's ruin. How did so much good—his children, his America—turn to so much bad? He hugged Joseph and said, "Welcome, son." Joseph tried to comfort Hanschen. She held him and wept until Loeb gently disengaged her and, with the assistance of a male nurse, led Joseph inside.

"We have turned the small sitting room into a bedroom for you, so you won't have to climb stairs."

"Thank you, Poppa."

As the days and weeks passed, Joseph gained strength. He learned his way around the house. Loeb and Hanschen avoided any mention of Fannie. Joseph was relieved. He wasn't ready himself for such an effort.

Moses Cohen came every day. Sometimes he and Joseph spoke of the Shechinah, sometimes they engaged in talmudic debate, and they too avoided the subject of Fannie.

Karl Albert showed up. He had been drawing war sketches for various European newspapers and had seen almost as much action as Joseph. After talking of the war, of battles and politics, they became silent.

"Karl, what is it?"

"Joseph, I've been afraid to ask. Have you heard from Soulé?"

"Not for a while."

"Then you don't know."

"He's dead?"

"Yes."

"How?"

"At last his pleadings for action were heard and he was posted to the Army of the Cumberland. He was to have his own brigade of cavalry. I saw him just before he left. He was so happy. Then he arrived in Chattanooga and he fell ill on his third day there. He was dead in the morning."

They sat silently for a long time. At last Karl Albert said, "I am leaving America."

"Why?"

"I can no longer bear the carnage. Leave the picture making to the photographers. Reality is the art of this war. I am a romantic painter. There is no romance in the slaughter. I don't think I shall ever forgive the Americans for what I've seen. Now I need to heal my eyes. I need to paint hope."

"You return to Germany?"

"No. Remember at your Passover seder when you told the story of how the Jews were afraid to step into the sea of reeds? And how the Egyptian armies were in sight and still the Jews were afraid, until one old man went into the water and then the others followed? Only then could they risk their lives for their belief, and when their faith became an act of will, God parted the sea."

"Nachshon Ben Amminadav was that man."

"I want to paint that."

Several days later a letter arrived from Bavaria, from Joseph's father. Loeb read it to Joseph.

> Dittelheim
> September 14, 1863
> My beloved son:
> Your mother and I pray every day—yes I pray now to your Unknown and Unknowable. I even accept that "I will be what I will be." I pray to "I will be what I will be." You have brought me to that. Your mother and I pray for you, that you may find happiness in this life in spite of your afflictions. I know you Joseph. I know what you are made of. I know you can and will make a decent and full life for yourself. Horses? They were a wonderful part of your life and you were the very best that I have ever seen. So now you will become the very best at something else. What? When you are stronger you shall find out. You shall make a choice and then succeed.
> But for now I ask a thing of you that I know will be very hard for you to give. You must come here immediately. Your wife, our daughter, Fannie is here. She is dying. She has the consumption. The doctor says it will not be long before she begins to spit up blood, and once she does she will die quickly. If you come immediately you may arrive before her end.
> I know how you and Loeb feel. I know what she has done. She has told me. No matter. The children, if for no other reason, are reason enough for you to come. I cannot tell you to forgive your wife. That is between you and her. But I will not have my grandchildren see their mother die in agony and without the forgiveness of their father.
> Joseph, my son, come. Come now before it is too late. Come now before you lose something more precious to you than your sight.
>
> Poppa

Loeb had kept his voice neutral during the reading. Joseph was enraged. How dare his father? Loeb refused to discuss the matter. He had no daughter. And so it fell to Moses Cohen.

"It is with a heavy heart, Joseph, that I remind you of what you already know," he said. "In our tradition there are three crimes for which the Jew is expected to accept death rather than commit: murder, idolatry and infidelity. But you are not a traditional Jew."

"I'm a traditional man," Joseph said. "I'm a man of honor. She's dishonored me, my name, my children and my family."

"I have always admired you, my friend, for your willingness to look beyond conventional wisdom. So why did you at the last moment spare von Exing? Why did you forgive him?"

"I don't know. I think it was because Senator Cole had forgiven me."

"Joseph, it's not like you to say 'I don't know.' Surely you've thought about it. Had you not forgiven him, you would not now be blind."

"I haven't been able to think about that."

"That too isn't the kind of reply I expect from you. God has given you a gift. *Sagi-nahor*. It's a word from the Talmud for blind. It means 'Full of Light.' Your life now is to use that light."

Joseph laughed derisively. "Really? You think I see better now?"

"Perhaps if you give to your blindness what you have given to your quest for God, you may."

"And my wife who has dishonored me? Is there a word in the Talmud that turns whoredom into virtue and honor?"

"No, but there is an interesting story in the Torah. Genesis 38."

"Are you now going to tell me of Judah and Tamar? I know the tale."

"Good. Tell it to me."

"We both know it. This is foolish."

"Foolish? Have our discussions ever been foolish, my friend? I'm saddened. This is the first time you have closed your mind to me."

"What do you want me to do?"

"Tell me of Judah and Tamar."

Joseph sighed and started the tale in a petulant voice. "Tamar married Judah's first son, Er. Er died. He displeased God and God killed him."

"Tell me or don't tell me. But Joseph, do me the honor of taking me seriously." Joseph accepted the rebuke.

"I forgive you. Go on."

"It was the tradition for the widow to marry the next oldest brother. This was Onan, who didn't want to have his child bear his brother's name, and so spilled his seed on the ground. God killed him for that. The next son, Shelah, was too young to marry, so Judah told Tamar to live as a widow in her father's house till the boy was old enough to marry."

"And?"

"And he forgot about her. The boy Shelah grew to the right age and still Judah forgot about her. Tamar heard Judah was coming near her father's place to inspect some sheep, and set herself on the road dressed as a harlot. He saw her and asked how much. He didn't have the payment and so she told him to leave his staff and his seal as security for the promised payment. He had her, left, and forgot about her. Later when he heard his daughter-in-law was pregnant, he gave orders to burn her. So she sent his seal and staff to him and said that the owner was the father of her child. He then ordered her to not be burned and forgave her, saying that the fault was his, as he had not kept his promise to marry her to the youngest son when he came of age. Is that what you want?"

"Almost. Judah's exact words were, 'She is more innocent than I.' She had twins, the first to come out was not the first but the second, and his name was Peretz. In the Tradition, Peretz is the ancestor of the Messiah. So this is not an insignificant Bible story. This is serious."

Joseph was silent for a while. When he spoke again, he spoke quietly. "It is really a question of honor. What is honor? Where does real, true honor occur? Perhaps I didn't kill von Exing because to do so would have been dishonor, an act of vanity, a vainglorious display of *noblesse oblige* from a Jew to a born aristocrat. The night I got my father's letter, the Shechinah came to me. She reminded me of the trial by ordeal, Numbers 5, how a woman accused of adultery was given a bitter cup to drink. They made it with all kinds of foul stuff. If she got sick she was guilty. One of the ingredients— the most important—was a parchment on which had been written the name of God. The ink washed off into the brew. The Shechinah then quoted the Talmud to me. 'For the sake of peace between a man and a woman, even God's name may be erased.' "

Joseph turned away from Moses Cohen and whispered, "Oh, my God."

§56

At BREMEN, JOSEPH AND MOSES COHEN DISEMBARKED AT THE VERY same dock from which Joseph had begun his journey nearly a decade before. Joseph felt a momentary pang of discomfort for the innocent boy who had stumbled through these streets many years in the past.

When he and Moses Cohen were seated in the carriage taking them to Klostermann & Co., he said, "Reb Moses, what a fool I was when I was last in this city."

"You were a boy. Boys are fools."

"I was arrogant and ignorant."

"Also the natural province of boys."

"Yet I acted from free will, and look what it brought me. Mrs. Bussey. Brannagan."

"So, Reb Joseph, you think it was free will? Free will can only come after education. You did not run away from Dittelheim as an act of free will. Desecrating the Torah, that was your act of free will. From it flowed everything else. From it you fought and humiliated von Exing, so you were compelled to run. You didn't choose America. God sent you there. Any decisions you made on the way were as a water bug being carried downriver on a torrent deciding to feed on this or that mite. But downriver it goes."

"So when in my life did I begin to exercise my free will?"

"You tell me."

Joseph thought for a while, then said, "Hercules."

"Who?"

"Hercules, the old Percheron at Brannagan's, the horse who found me in the gutter and saved me. When Brannagan was going to sell him to die in agony, I killed him to save him. Did I ever tell you about the nightmare I used to have?"

"No."

Joseph told him about the clouds.

"Do you still have this dream?"

"Not for a long time."

"So what did it mean?"

"I've thought about it. Many times. But now that I am blind I have found a few answers."

"And?"

"You won't laugh?"

"Reb Joseph, really!"

"Forgive me. It was easier to talk about God when I believed there were many gods. In the Binding, when Abraham and Isaac start up to the place where the altar will be made, they see a cloud. The holy teachings say the cloud represents the Shechinah."

"Yes."

"It isn't the first time the cloud is used as an emanation or symbol of God. I just never made the association when I was young."

Moses Cohen nodded, "When Moses went up the Sinai he was enveloped in a cloud for six days, and God appeared on the seventh. You stood on a mountain naked and terrified in the sight of God. First the one God whom you would deny, and then the many who came together to be one. So why did the dream stop coming to you?"

"She came to me instead. The Shechinah."

"And? Joseph I have waited years for this moment. Do not be coy with me."

"I have come to believe in the One God, the God with no name, the Unknown and Unknowable."

Moses Cohen laughed. "Jew at last!"

"Blind one-legged Jew. Why did God do that?

"Did He?"

"You know, I saw the cloud once in real life. But I didn't recognize it till I lost my sight."

"So?"

"It was my first battle. One cannon fired and there was a puff of smoke like the little cloud. Then they all began to fire and the smoke filled the universe. It was the battle in which I ordered the charge that killed Nathan. Free will."

"You think free will means not making mistakes?"

"No. I don't know. Am I better off a one-legged blind man? Did I do that? Did God do that?"

"Maybe both of you."

"What does God want of me?"

"Do we ever know?"

"I don't know."

Fannie lay in the feather bed that had been Joseph's. She knew Joseph was coming and was as powerless to stop him as she was powerless to stop the disease that was choking her to death. The doctor said she would die when she started coughing blood, but where was it? Where was death? She longed to die. Then she heard the sound of the coach, and of Rebecca crying out at the sight of her son. And then Joseph's voice mixed with the children's. Poor babies to be born to such bad parents. There was another voice. Moses Cohen. She was wracked by a spasm of coughing. Gasping, Fannie looked to her handkerchief. No blood.

Later she woke. Joseph was seated in a chair by her bed. Blue glasses covered his eyes. He had only one leg.

Another spasm of coughing seized her. Joseph remained seated. His father or his mother would have tried to comfort her. Joseph sat.

When the coughing ceased he said, "Then you are awake."

"Yes," she said, and suddenly Joseph saw her as she was that first night when she had come to him in his room above the stable. He felt for his crutch, stood and made his way to the door. He then closed the door behind him and descended the stairs. His parents and Moses Cohen were waiting in the kitchen. He turned in the opposite direction, went through the front door and fell down the steps. His father helped him to his feet.

"New steps," Jakob said. "Come, let me show you around the place. There have been changes." His voice was flat with restrained anger.

As they explored his former home, Joseph knew that some of the changes weren't good. There were very few horses.

"Poppa, why don't I hear horses being worked?"

"When von Falkenbrecht died his idiot nephew inherited all. He knows nothing of horses, and he hates Jews. What horses I sell now I sell for commercial purposes. The Trakehners, the thoroughbreds are long gone. But your mother and I won't starve. I've saved my money. We own our land and have no debts. We're all right. And you? Are you all right?"

"I am rich…"

"I didn't mean money."

"No, Poppa, I'm not all right. I'm a blind one-legged horseman."

"I didn't mean that either. You've just seen your wife. Are you all right?"

"She is not my wife."

"You have a divorce? Civil? Religious? A divorce?"

"No."

"Then she's your wife."

"Poppa, I don't wish to discuss it."

"I think you do. You didn't travel halfway across the world to not discuss it."

"I came for my children."

"I can't imagine why. When did you care about them more than your horses and your fame and your money?"

"Poppa!"

"I too have been a bad Poppa. I raised my son not to know how to be a Poppa himself. So now that you can't be a famous horseman, you might learn to be a good father. Blind and crippled doesn't keep you from being a good father."

"I won't hear this!"

"Why? You still have ears. You have a soul. You're my son."

Joseph wheeled on his crutch, started in the direction of the house and slammed into a newly built fence. This time his father didn't help him to his feet.

As Joseph felt about the ground for his crutch, his father said, "A good father sometimes does not help his blind and crippled son get to his feet. That's what your children are like—like you now. They need a father to lift them up, to guide them into manhood." Jakob turned and headed for the house. "I'll be in the kitchen. Come if you can find it."

Ten minutes later Joseph came back into the house, sweating and dirty. Both Moses Cohen and Rebecca started to help him to a chair. Jakob stopped them.

Jakob said, "Come, son. Your mother has made hot chocolate. Come and sit."

Joseph understood the challenge. He found his way to an empty chair. When he was seated and soothing his scraped hands with the heat from the cup his mother defiantly placed in them, he said, "You're right, Poppa. I've been a bad father. I'll learn to be better."

"Good."

"You saw Fannie…," Moses Cohen said.

"I didn't *see* her."

"Joseph, there's no time for this. Your wife is dying," Moses Cohen said.

Joseph hated himself for his childish behavior. "She coughed. I said, 'so you are awake,' and when she said 'yes,' the sound of her voice drove me from the room."

Rebecca put her arms around her son, and her face to his. He felt her tears. She asked, "Why Joseph? Why did her voice drive you away from her?"

"Momma, I love her so. I have always loved her. So much death, Momma, so much, and now she too…"

Rebecca held her son for a long time. The others remained silent. After a while, Joseph let go of her and rose. "I think I can find my way to the stairs. But if someone will make sure I don't fall over a chair I would appreciate it."

Fannie heard him coming. She saw the door swing open. He stood there for a moment and carefully made his way to her bedside. When he touched the bed with his crutch, he put both hands on it and lowered himself to his knee. Once secure, his hands searched for hers. Then holding them, he said, "I beg you, Fannie. Forgive me."

"Forgive *you*? Joseph, I'm the whore…."

"What you did was terrible. I wanted to kill you for it."

"You should have."

"Fannie. You think I didn't see when you were beginning to be lonely? You think I didn't know you were unhappy in our marriage? I knew and I pushed the knowledge away from me. The horses were more important than your happiness. My career was more important than your happiness. I betrayed you, Fannie, long before you did me."

She wept to hear the words. "Joseph, I betrayed you from the beginning. Ada Clare. I wanted *la vie passionelle*. God forgive me! In the beginning I was using you…."

"I know. But then we were in love."

"I loved you so. But you went away from me."

"God forgive me. I never shall again."

"No, not God. Me, Joseph. I forgive you." She reached out and with a feeble hand caressed his cheek. "Joseph, I was so lost. I had all I needed to make me happy. So lost. I became angry. I hated you. The affair with the poet…"

"No," he said. "We can talk later."

"Now!" She raised her voice and then coughed. "I'm dying. I've lain here thinking about this moment. I must say it all."

"Fannie, please don't die. Please. Dear God, we can begin again. Please don't die."

Her hand rested on his bowed head, her fingers gently stroking his hair. "You saw the pictures. I wanted you to suffer. I thought I hated you. I was lost. Joseph?"

He was weeping. "Yes, my beloved?"

"Will you, when I die, hold me? Let me die in your arms?"

Joseph stayed in her room for the next weeks. By day he held her hand, caressed her face, bathed it with cool cloths. By night he slept on the floor beside her bed. When they could they spoke of their lives. She made him promise to be a good father and she vowed that, if God let her live, she would be a perfect mother.

The doctor was examining Fannie. "You cough less?"

Joseph answered for her. "Yes. She coughs less and the sound is less deep."

"How much less?"

"By half."

The doctor smiled. "I make no promises. But by now there should have been blood in the sputum. You have never coughed blood. I believe, baroness, that you will recover."

"I won't die?"

"You will recover."

When Fannie took her first steps Moses Cohen, hoping that all would now be well, returned to New York.

Each passing week Fannie grew stronger. She and Joseph spent hours with the children, and more hours walking in the Bavarian snows. Nothing was left unsaid. They peeled off layers of poisonous wrappings until at last they returned to the place where they once loved each other with purity. In touching that purity they found renewal. The winter snow began to melt and Fannie and Joseph began to talk of home, of Thunder Farm and Liberty Hall. One afternoon at dinner the whole family sat about the kitchen table. "Poppa, Momma," Joseph said. "Fannie is well enough to travel. It's time she and the children and I return to our home. But, Poppa, we have a business proposition for you."

"Business?"

"We both know I can no longer train horses. But you can. Come back with us. Be my partner."

"Please, Poppa. Please, Momma." Fannie said. "We need you. How good it will be for the children to grow up with both sets of grandparents. Please come."

"Of course we will come," Rebecca said.

"To live?" Joseph asked. "To be Americans?"

"Yes," Jakob answered.

On March 9, 1864, Ulysses S. Grant, the first lieutenant general since George Washington, took command of the Union forces. On April 4, he appointed his friend Philip Sheridan as commander of the cavalry. Shortly after that General Grant and his friend General Sherman met for cards and serious talk with General Sheridan and his friend General Custer. During that meeting Custer repeated the things Joseph had taught him about the need to bring the war to the general population of the South, to break their will. The three older generals listened carefully.

In New York City, Moses Cohen had done his work well. He told the Loebs of his visit with their daughter. When he was done, Hanschen said, "If Joseph forgives his wife, how can we not forgive our daughter?" Loeb was relieved.

The horseman rode the big gray at the jump. To even the most experienced eye, jump twenty-six looked lethal: a pole fence placed on the crest of a short rise at the end of a steep downhill grade. The grade was just long enough so that if a horse gained too much speed before it jumped, it would touch down too far on the other side of the fence and wouldn't be able to recover quickly enough to avoid crashing into the opposite embankment.

An older man rode near the horseman.

"Twenty yards!" Joseph's father shouted.

Joseph eased the gray down to a slower gait while carefully counting the hoof beats.

Just before Jakob called the next cue Joseph shouted, "Don't tell me!" Then to himself he said, "Five. Four. Three. Two—Now!" and then on the word "Spinoza!" urged his horse into the jump.

Jakob watched his son clear the first barrier, land perfectly on the opposite embankment, scamper to the top and clear the next jump in perfect form.

"The last four with no cues!" Joseph shouted.

From the seat of her buggy parked on a hill, Fannie watched her husband take the last jumps. She always watched, and always trembled in fear. Once she knew it was over, she composed herself and drove the buggy toward the two men.

Joseph was strapping on his leg. "Fannie," he said, "I can do it without cues. I can do the whole course without cues. I count. I judge the speed and count the hoofbeats."

"But Joseph…"

He interrupted her. "I designed the course, Fannie. I know the exact distance between the jumps. I can do it. I just did the five hardest on my own—counting. It's simple. You count the hoofbeats."

Fannie looked at Jakob, who shrugged.

"We'll discuss it later," she said to Joseph. "Now the children are waiting for their Poppa to have tea with them."

Joseph climbed into the buggy. His father had picked the horse for Fannie to drive, a twenty-four-year-old gelding who refused to move faster than a shuffle. It took them fifteen minutes to cover the ground a healthy man could walk in five.

Under Jakob's care, Thunder Farm prospered. Joseph not only learned to ride the course at Thunder Farm, but enjoyed a modicum of new fame as, on behalf of various charities, he demonstrated his skills at horse shows and county fairs. Liberty, a colt of Thunder's, grew to be an even greater stallion than his sire. And Fannie, her health recovered, lived a placid life at Liberty Hall. She carefully raised her children, loved her husband, ran her house and in her quiet moments wrote poetry which she showed to no one, not even Joseph.

Joseph, who could see nothing, lived out his days with a vision of his wife as she had been when he first met her. They and their five children enjoyed full lives well into the next century.

THE END

EPILOGUE

§ *From the New York Jewish Chronicle: April 12, 1865:*

COLONEL JOSEPH RITTER'S SPEECH ON THE OCCASION OF THE Community Passover seder presented by Temple Emanu-El, at the Grand Ball Room of the St. Nicholas Hotel, New York City, on April 11, 1865. In attendance were the Congregation and Guests.

Before the Commencement of the traditional Pesach Ceremony, Mr. Emerich Hessman, the President of the Congregation, welcomed the Congregants, Guests, and then Hazzan Moses Cohen introduced the Guest of Honor.

Colonel Joseph von Ritter, a Hero of the Civil War, celebrated Horseman, and well-known figure of New York Jewish Society, though Blinded and suffering a loss of a leg during the War, made his way from his place at the head Table to the Lectern with a Grace and Dignity that belied his Infirmities. He was welcomed with enthusiasm.

The Text of Colonel von Ritter's Speech:

Members of Temple Emanu-El, I thank you for this opportunity. Two days ago General Lee surrendered the Army of Northern Virginia to General Grant. Tomorrow the formal surrender will take place. It is reasonable to assume that this is the "de facto" end of the war. Shortly the army of General Johnston will surrender to General Sherman, with the remnants of the rebel armies in the West to quickly follow. The war is over. The war is won.

I have come home from the war crippled and blind, and you honor me by asking me to speak to you. When I was a boy I discovered a quotation of Baruch Spinoza. It was too long to say in moments of stress, and so I shortened it to a personal battle cry, "Spinoza!" The exact quote is: "He who would distinguish the true from the false must have an adequate idea of what is true and what is false." I have spent my life in pursuit of that knowledge, some small sum of which I offer you now. Spinoza!

Tonight we have not only a traditional Passover seder but a glorious victory celebration.

It is especially significant that this, our ceremony of remembering how we were slaves and how God reached out his hand to free us, comes on the eve of our participating in the freeing of the black people of the South. This is truly an historic moment of great rejoicing.

Forgive me if while celebrating the freedom of the black people, about which I shall have more words later, I do not speak with the traditional catch phrases of the triumph of the righteous North over the evil southern slave masters, those rebels, those evil men who would destroy the Union.

Rabbi Hananiah, one of our ancient sages, a man who spoke with revelation said: "Before his beating the criminal is called 'the Wicked Man,' but after his beating he is called 'Thy Brother.' "

When I went to war against the South I hated them. During the war I fought them with all my might. I have killed them with these hands. I have been grievously wounded by them both in body and spirit. But now it is over. We have won. The South fought with valor and honor but they were defeated. There is no dishonor for them in that defeat. Two days ago when General Lee surrendered to General Grant, it was not just the beginning of the end of the Confederacy. It was also the beginning of the healing of America.

The southern people believe their defeat is the will of God. We of the North must not be so proud as to assume our victory anything other than the will of God.

I cannot hate southerners anymore. I forgive them for the hurt they have done me, and I pray they will forgive me the harm I have done them.

My fellow Jews, when you invited me to speak here I recalled a Passover seder in my home five years ago. At that seder I spoke for the first time of the "Jewish-

American." It was a conceit of my wife and me. Young and foolish as we were at the time it was, nevertheless, a good idea. Over the years of the war I have thought more about it and know now that, however naive we were in those days, Fannie and I were right. To be a Jewish-American makes me a better Jew than if I were an American-Jew.

Why are we Jews? Why did God choose us? Why has God led us to America? Why is our history, no matter what our suffering, entwined with the enduring study of Torah and Talmud—the study of our relationship to God?

To be a Jew is to remember. To be a Jew is to be at one with, to seek to know the one God, the Unknown. To be a Jew is to seek the Messiah. But for the Messiah to come we, humankind, all peoples must become perfect. Can we—you and I—become perfect? Not likely. But can each generation become better than the last? Hopefully. In our country, in this New Jerusalem, in the United States of America, each generation is able to provide for the betterment of the one to follow. A miracle of history. No permanent classes. We, all of us, can reach out to make ourselves what we will. It is the glory of America that we each have the right to decide our own way of being. It is the obligation of Americans to make the country stronger and freer for each succeeding generation. And for what? For more money? No, not just for money. Money is the smallest part of it. It is to be free to be better. To be free to grow to Messiah.

Have no doubt, America is the New Jerusalem. The Pilgrims believed it. The Founding Fathers believed it. I believe it.

As Jews we know where the Messiah will come. He will come to Jerusalem. But is Jerusalem a specific place? Is Jerusalem really a city of crumbling stones in the Turkish Empire? I think not. Perhaps it is the will of God that Jerusalem is a place not of stones but the place where humans strive most for the perfection of man. So tonight when we say, "Next year in Jerusalem," I think we mean that next year may we have brought this country closer to Messiah.

There is no doubt in my mind but that the American Declaration of Independence and the Constitution of the

United States of America are revelation past and ongoing, just as are the Torah and Talmud. The Declaration of Independence and the Constitution for which we have just fought so bloody a war are direct paths to Messiah. They are as worthy of study, protection and perpetuation as are Torah and Talmud. No country has ever existed like ours. In our whole history we Jews have never, not since the Roman conquest, been equal owners, equal rulers of the country in which we lived except here, in the United States of America.

We are not guests in the United States of America as we have been everywhere else for nearly two thousand years. We are not guests. We are owners. We are home. We are equal partners. But a partnership only exists because each partner brings something of value, a thing or quality unique to that partner, to advance the enterprise.

What do we Jewish-Americans bring? Five thousand six hundred and twenty-five years of history. The wisdom of Torah and Talmud. It is a rich and complex contribution. We owe it to our country as surely as we owe it to ourselves to be true to our heritage and open-handed in the sharing of it.

Tonight we commemorate a most important historic event of our history. Tonight we remind ourselves and the world that we were once slaves. This Passover, the first since the end of the war to free the slaves, we are to remind ourselves and offer to our fellow Americans the admonition found in the Haggadah. "In each generation, we must see ourselves as having personally gone out of Egypt." Perhaps if we do this well we shall believe it, each of us, and in so believing make it a gift to our partners the non-Jewish-Americans.

With the war over, we have two tasks in America. One, to welcome back our southern family. The other, to offer the black man the fruits of what God did for us when we were freed.

To welcome back our southern family we have only to remind ourselves of Teshuva, return and renewal. In a way our task is somewhat simpler than that of our Christian partners. We, by our Tradition, are not obligated to love our enemies. We are merely obliged to welcome them back, to give them a fair shake. Rabbi Hama said, "Even though your enemy has risen up early to kill you and he comes hungry and thirsty to your house, give him food and drink." Our southern partners in this American enterprise are hungry and thirsty. We must give them food and drink. My namesake forgave his brothers for plotting to kill him and for selling him into slavery. Can I do less? Can you?

As Jews we are obligated to join with President Lincoln to welcome back the South and to prevent the radicals in Congress from the punishing Reconstruction they plan. The South has paid a terrible price for their rebellion. Welcome them home.

Like the South, we have paid a terrible price for their rebellion, but as Judah took upon himself the responsibility for Tamar's adultery, so we must take on our share of the blame for the events that led to this war between the states. By all that is Jewish, we of the North may not hold ourselves blameless. Teshuva, which is central to who we are, means return, renewal. In the spirit of Teshuva we must offer our southern family a return to wholeness.

As for the black people, that is more complex. For three hundred years they have been denied education, stripped of the tools and skills needed to survive in a society such as ours. But who better to reach out to them with those needed tools and skills, with education, than us? God's Chosen People.

God's Chosen People.

Why did God choose us?

This is what I believe. We were chosen not, as we sometimes comfort ourselves with believing, because we were the very best, the purest, people on earth. Consider that the opposite may have been true. Perhaps God chose us because we were the most impossible, stiff-necked, stubborn, wild, ignorant, unteachable, savage people on the planet. If He could make us into a civilized nation, if He could turn us of all peoples into scholars and seekers after purity, longers for Messiah, then He could easily do it to all the others.

Now we have these Negroes, the very lowest in our society. We, all of America, owe them fair wages for three hundred years of servitude. We Jewish-Americans owe them our knowledge—the learning we acquired on our own rise from slaves to partners. Perhaps our experience of suffering over the past eighteen hundred years will help them avoid a similar fate.

My friend Moses Cohen, with citations from Torah and Talmud, insists that God blinded me so that I can see more clearly. Allow me then to humor him and to tell you what I see.

I see a newer, stronger America. I see an America that will become the most powerful nation on earth. I see an America so successful that American democracy will overwhelm all the kingdoms, dictatorships and empires of the world. I see an America that will inspire all people to seek their freedom and in so doing make the entire world the New Jerusalem. Perhaps it is only when the whole world is Jerusalem that the Messiah will come.

I see that the North, under the inspired and gentle leadership of Abraham Lincoln, will welcome back the South as equal partners. I see that North and South will work together to educate the freed people and raise them to equal partnership.

When we, North and South, have repaid our debt to the black people, when they are in all respects equal to the rest of us, they then will make contributions to our mutual enterprise that will raise this nation to heights as yet undreamed of. Allow me to conclude with this from Rabbi Akiba:

"Everything is foreseen, yet free will is given."

ACKNOWLEDGMENTS

Wᴵᴛʜᴏᴜᴛ ᴛʜᴇ ꜰʀɪᴇɴᴅsʜɪᴘ ᴀɴᴅ ᴡɪsᴅᴏᴍ ᴏꜰ ᴛᴡᴏ ʟᴀᴡʏᴇʀs and a judge, this book would never have been written. It is with a profound sense of gratitude that this author thanks Gerald W. Palmer and Gary Feess for their brilliant lawyering in defense of his rights, and their unswerving friendship in support of his life. Judge Richard Gadbois—then sitting on the Superior Court bench and a stranger, now a federal judge and a friend—with a Solomonaic judgment made this book and much, much more possible.

Susan Freedman headed up the research and, when she was unsure of where to find what, found the people who knew. My friend and teacher, Rabbi Chaim Seidler-Feller, was the first rabbi not to throw me out when I broached the subject of multiple Gods. David Gordis, Rabbi Philip Bentley, and my unendingly patient teacher, Yehudis Fishman, led me into and through the Tradition. Thanks too to the good people of the American Jewish Archives.

It was my father, Sidney K. Flicker, business man and horse trainer, who taught me to avoid business, love horses and live in honor. Horse-genius Linda Tellington-Jones brought me to a deeper understanding of my horses which fed into the pages of this book. Barbara Van Cleve, honored photographer of the modern West, introduced me to the quarter horse and the wild rides of "filly chasing" on her Montana ranch.

Two people were there for me in the long-gone days of my youthful striving and again at the end of their lives. Barna Ostertag, who in her ninth decade listened to chapters read over the phone and encouraged me to make the transition from the screen to the page; and Zev Putterman, who took time off from saving his junkies and ex-cons to hear a chapter each week and then struggle with me about Jews, God and America. Both are gone now, but part of them will live as long as the thoughts printed on these pages.

I owe a special thanks to Jane Gelfman, sometimes my agent, always my friend and true supporter.

Walter Beakel, acting teacher, director, neighbor and longtime friend from my earliest days in the theatre, never stopped urging me to complete this book with no view to anything but the truth.

Tom Rees M.D., not just a sculptor of faces but a modeler of souls, was there to help me with the medical detail and always lent a steady supply of courage.

My editors, Gene Stone and Bill Blitz; Gene guided me through the change from screen-writing to prose. Bill not only put up with my ignorance of grammar, but was patient with my dyslexia. Bill is also the publisher and designer of this book, for which I am ever-grateful. Jean Lamuniere was sent by the Unknown at the last minute to create the design for the cover.

And finally, I am grateful to the ever-calm Reverend Pat Moore; my secretary, librarian, and the first detector of misplaced commas and rotten spelling.

Ted Flicker